WORTH POCKET COMPANIONS

TRAVEL &
ADVENTURE

Short Stories by Great Writers

WORTH POCKET COMPANIONS

Other titles in the series

Travel & Adventure

Short Stories by Great Writers

Selected by
ROSEMARY GRAY

WORTH POCKET COMPANIONS

First published in 2012 by
Worth Press Limited, Cambridge, UK
www.worthpress.co.uk

The reset text, concept, design and production
specification copyright © Worth Press Limited 2012

A catalogue record for this book is available
from the British Library

ISBN   978 1 84931 071 0

Cover design Bradbury & Williams
Typeset in Great Britain by Antony Gray
Printed and bound in China by Imago

1

Contents

EDITH WHARTON

Edith Wharton was born in 1862 into a wealthy New York family. In 1885 she married a Boston socialite; the couple travelled widely and settled in France in 1907, but the marriage was unhappy and they divorced in 1913. Her first major novel was *The House of Mirth* (1905); many short stories, travel books, memoirs and novels followed, including *Ethan Frome* (1911), *The Reef* (1912) and *The Age of Innocence* (1920). Wharton was decorated for her humanitarian work during the First World War. She died in France in 1937.

A Journey

As she lay in her berth, staring at the shadows overhead, the rush of the wheels was in her brain, driving her deeper and deeper into circles of wakeful lucidity. The sleeping-car had sunk into its night-silence. Through the wet window-pane she watched the sudden lights, the long stretches of hurrying blackness. Now and then she turned her head and looked through the opening in the hangings at her husband's curtains across the aisle . . .

She wondered restlessly if he wanted anything and if she could hear him if he called. His voice had grown very weak within the last months and it irritated him when she did not hear. This irritability, this increasing childish petulance seemed to give expression to their imperceptible estrangement. Like two faces looking at one another through a sheet of glass they were close together, almost touching, but they could not hear or feel each other: the conductivity between them was broken. She, at least, had this sense of separation, and she fancied sometimes that she saw it reflected in the look with which he supplemented his failing words. Doubtless the fault was hers. She was too impenetrably healthy to be touched by the irrelevancies of disease. Her self-reproachful tenderness was tinged with the sense of his irrationality: she had a vague feeling that there was a purpose in his helpless tyrannies. The suddenness of the change had found her so unprepared. A year ago their pulses had beat to one robust measure; both had the same prodigal confidence in an exhaustless future. Now their energies no longer kept step: hers still bounded ahead of life, preëmpting unclaimed regions of hope and activity, while his lagged behind, vainly struggling to overtake her.

When they married, she had such arrears of living to make up; her days had been as bare as the whitewashed schoolroom where she forced innutritious facts upon reluctant children. His coming had broken in on the slumber of circumstance, widening the present till it became the encloser of remotest chances. But imperceptibly the horizon narrowed. Life had a grudge against her; she was never to be allowed to spread her wings.

At first the doctors had said that six weeks of mild air would set him right; but when he came back this assurance was explained as having of course included a winter in a dry climate. They gave up their pretty house, storing the wedding presents and new furniture, and went to Colorado. She had hated it there from the first. Nobody knew her or cared about her; there was no one to wonder at the good match she had made, or to envy her the new dresses and the visiting-cards which were still a surprise to her. And he kept growing worse. She felt herself beset with difficulties too evasive to be fought by so direct a temperament. She still loved him, of course; but he was gradually, undefinably ceasing to be himself. The man she had married had been strong, active, gently masterful: the male whose pleasure it is to clear a way through the material obstructions of life; but now it was she who was the protector, he who must be shielded from importunities and given his drops or his beef-juice though the skies were falling. The routine of the sick-room bewildered her; this punctual administering of medicine seemed as idle as some uncomprehended religious mummery.

There were moments, indeed, when warm gushes of pity swept away her instinctive resentment of his condition, when she still found his old self in his eyes as they groped for each other through the dense medium of his weakness. But these moments had grown rare. Sometimes he frightened her: his sunken expressionless face seemed that of a stranger; his voice was weak and hoarse; his thin-lipped smile a mere muscular contraction. Her hand avoided his damp soft skin, which had lost the familiar roughness of health; she caught herself furtively watching him as she might have watched a strange animal. It frightened her to feel that this was the man she loved; there were hours when to tell him what she suffered seemed the one escape from her fears. But in general she judged herself more leniently, reflecting that she had perhaps been too long alone with him, and that she would feel differently when they were at home again, surrounded by her robust and buoyant family. How she had rejoiced when the doctors at last gave their consent to his going home! She knew, of course, what the decision meant; they both knew. It meant that he was to die; but they dressed the truth in hopeful euphemisms, and at times, in the joy of preparation, she really forgot the purpose of their journey, and slipped into an eager allusion to next year's plans.

At last the day of leaving came. She had a dreadful fear that they would never get away; that somehow at the last moment he would fail her; that the doctors held one of their accustomed treacheries in reserve; but nothing happened. They drove to the station, he was installed in a seat with a rug over his knees and a cushion at his back, and she hung out of the window waving unregretful farewells to the acquaintances she had really never liked till then.

The first twenty-four hours had passed off well. He revived a little and it amused him to look out of the window and to observe the humours of the car. The second day he began to grow weary and to chafe under the dispassionate stare of the freckled child with the lump of chewing-gum. She had to explain to the child's mother that her husband was too ill to be disturbed, a statement received by that lady with a resentment visibly supported by the maternal sentiment of the whole car . . .

That night he slept badly and the next morning his temperature frightened her: she was sure he was growing worse. The day passed slowly, punctuated by the small irritations of travel. Watching his tired face, she traced in its contractions every rattle and jolt of the tram, till her own body vibrated with sympathetic fatigue. She felt the others observing him too, and hovered restlessly between him and the line of interrogative eyes. The freckled child hung about him like a fly; offers of candy and picture-books failed to dislodge her: she twisted one leg around the other and watched him imperturbably. The porter, as he passed, lingered with vague proffers of help, probably inspired by philanthropic passengers swelling with the sense that 'something ought to be done'; and one nervous man in a skullcap was audibly concerned as to the possible effect on his wife's health.

The hours dragged on in a dreary inoccupation. Towards dusk she sat down beside him and he laid his hand on hers. The touch startled her. He seemed to be calling her from far off. She looked at him helplessly and his smile went through her like a physical pang.

'Are you very tired?' she asked.

'No, not very.'

'We'll be there soon now.'

'Yes, very soon.'

'This time tomorrow – '

He nodded and they sat silent. When she had put him to bed

and crawled into her own berth she tried to cheer herself with the thought that in less than twenty-four hours they would be in New York. Her people would all be at the station to meet her – she pictured their round unanxious faces pressing through the crowd. She only hoped they would not tell him too loudly that he was looking splendidly and would be all right in no time; the subtler sympathies developed by long contact with suffering were making her aware of a certain coarseness of texture in the family sensibilities.

Suddenly she thought she heard him call. She parted the curtains and listened. No, it was only a man snoring at the other end of the car. His snores had a greasy sound, as though they passed through tallow. She lay down and tried to sleep . . . Had she not heard him move? She started up trembling . . . The silence frightened her more than any sound. He might not be able to make her hear – he might be calling her now . . . What made her think of such things? It was merely the familiar tendency of an over-tired mind to fasten itself on the most intolerable chance within the range of its forebodings . . . Putting her head out, she listened; but she could not distinguish his breathing from that of the other pairs of lungs about her. She longed to get up and look at him, but she knew the impulse was a mere vent for her restlessness, and the fear of disturbing him restrained her . . . The regular movement of his curtain reassured her, she knew not why; she remembered that he had wished her a cheerful good-night; and the sheer inability to endure her fears a moment longer made her put them from her with an effort of her whole sound tired body. She turned on her side and slept.

She sat up stiffly, staring out at the dawn. The train was rushing through a region of bare hillocks huddled against a lifeless sky. It looked like the first day of creation. The air of the car was close, and she pushed up her window to let in the keen wind. Then she looked at her watch: it was seven o'clock, and soon the people about her would be stirring. She slipped into her clothes, smoothed her dishevelled hair and crept to the dressing-room. When she had washed her face and adjusted her dress she felt more hopeful. It was always a struggle for her not to be cheerful in the morning. Her cheeks burned deliciously under the coarse towel and the wet hair about her temples broke into strong upward tendrils. Every inch of her was full of life and elasticity. And in ten hours they would be at home!

She stepped to her husband's berth: it was time for him to take his early glass of milk. The window-shade was down, and in the dusk of the curtained enclosure she could just see that he lay sideways, with his face away from her. She leaned over him and drew up the shade. As she did so she touched one of his hands. It felt cold . . .

She bent closer, laying her hand on his arm and calling him by name. He did not move. She spoke again more loudly; she grasped his shoulder and gently shook it. He lay motionless. She caught hold of his hand again: it slipped from her limply, like a dead thing. A dead thing? . . . Her breath caught. She must see his face. She leaned forward, and hurriedly, shrinkingly, with a sickening reluctance of the flesh, laid her hands on his shoulders and turned him over. His head fell back; his face looked small and smooth; he gazed at her with steady eyes.

She remained motionless for a long time, holding him thus; and they looked at each other. Suddenly she shrank back; the longing to scream, to call out, to fly from him, had almost overpowered her. But a strong hand arrested her. Good God! If it were known that he was dead they would be put off the train at the next station –

In a terrifying flash of remembrance there arose before her a scene she had once witnessed in travelling, when a husband and wife, whose child had died in the train, had been thrust out at some chance station. She saw them standing on the platform with the child's body between them; she had never forgotten the dazed look with which they followed the receding train. And this was what would happen to her. Within the next hour she might find herself on the platform of some strange station, alone with her husband's body . . . Anything but that! It was too horrible – She quivered like a creature at bay.

As she cowered there, she felt the train moving more slowly. It was coming then – they were approaching a station! She saw again the husband and wife standing on the lonely platform; and with a violent gesture she drew down the shade to hide her husband's face.

Feeling dizzy, she sank down on the edge of the berth, keeping away from his outstretched body, and pulling the curtains close, so that he and she were shut into a kind of sepulchral twilight. She tried to think. At all costs she must conceal the fact that he was dead. But how? Her mind refused to act: she could not plan, combine. She could think of no way but to sit there, clutching the curtains, all day long . . .

She heard the porter making up her bed; people were beginning to move about the car; the dressing-room door was being opened and shut. She tried to rouse herself. At length with a supreme effort she rose to her feet, stepping into the aisle of the car and drawing the curtains tight behind her. She noticed that they still parted slightly with the motion of the car, and finding a pin in her dress she fastened them together. Now she was safe. She looked round and saw the porter. She fancied he was watching her.

'Ain't he awake yet?' he enquired.

'No,' she faltered.

'I got his milk all ready when he wants it. You know you told me to have it for him by seven.'

She nodded silently and crept into her seat.

At half-past eight the train reached Buffalo. By this time the other passengers were dressed and the berths had been folded back for the day. The porter, moving to and fro under his burden of sheets and pillows, glanced at her as he passed. At length he said: 'Ain't he going to get up? You know we're ordered to make up the berths as early as we can.'

She turned cold with fear. They were just entering the station.

'Oh, not yet,' she stammered. 'Not till he's had his milk. Won't you get it, please?'

'All right. Soon as we start again.'

When the train moved on he reappeared with the milk. She took it from him and sat vaguely looking at it; her brain moved slowly from one idea to another, as though they were stepping-stones set far apart across a whirling flood. At length she became aware that the porter still hovered expectantly.

'Will I give it to him?' he suggested.

'Oh, no,' she cried, rising. 'He – he's asleep yet, I think – '

She waited till the porter had passed on; then she unpinned the curtains and slipped behind them. In the semi-obscurity her husband's face stared up at her like a marble mask with agate eyes. The eyes were dreadful. She put out her hand and drew down the lids. Then she remembered the glass of milk in her other hand: what was she to do with it? She thought of raising the window and throwing it out; but to do so she would have to lean across his body and bring her face close to his. She decided to drink the milk.

She returned to her seat with the empty glass and after a while the porter came back to get it.

'When'll I fold up his bed?' he asked.

'Oh, not now – not yet; he's ill – he's very ill. Can't you let him stay as he is? The doctor wants him to lie down as much as possible.'

He scratched his head. 'Well, if he's *really* sick – '

He took the empty glass and walked away, explaining to the passengers that the party behind the curtains was too sick to get up just yet.

She found herself the centre of sympathetic eyes.

A motherly woman with an intimate smile sat down beside her. 'I'm real sorry to hear your husband's sick. I've had a remarkable amount of sickness in my family and maybe I could assist you. Can I take a look at him?'

'Oh, no – no, please! He mustn't be disturbed.'

The lady accepted the rebuff indulgently.

'Well, it's just as you say, of course, but you don't look to me as if you'd had much experience in sickness and I'd have been glad to assist you. What do you generally do when your husband's taken this way?'

'I – I let him sleep.'

'Too much sleep ain't any too healthful either. Don't you give him any medicine?'

'Y–yes.'

'Don't you wake him to take it?'

'Yes.'

'When does he take the next dose?'

'Not for – two hours – '

The lady looked disappointed. 'Well, if I was you I'd try giving it oftener. That's what I do with my folks.'

After that many faces seemed to press upon her. The passengers were on their way to the dining-car, and she was conscious that as they passed down the aisle they glanced curiously at the closed curtains. One lantern-jawed man with prominent eyes stood still and tried to shoot his projecting glance through the division between the folds. The freckled child, returning from breakfast, waylaid the passers with a buttery clutch, saying in a loud whisper, 'He's sick;' and once the conductor came by, asking for tickets. She shrank into her corner and looked out of the window at the flying trees and houses, meaningless hieroglyphs of an endlessly unrolled papyrus.

Now and then the train stopped, and the newcomers on entering the car stared in turn at the closed curtains. More and more people seemed to pass – their faces began to blend fantastically with the images surging in her brain . . .

Later in the day a fat man detached himself from the mist of faces. He had a creased stomach and soft pale lips. As he pressed himself into the seat facing her she noticed that he was dressed in black broadcloth, with a soiled white tie.

'Husband's pretty bad this morning, is he?'

'Yes.'

'Dear, dear! Now that's terribly distressing, ain't it?' An apostolic smile revealed his gold-filled teeth.

'Of course you know there's no sech thing as sickness. Ain't that a lovely thought? Death itself is but a deloosion of our grosser senses. On'y lay yourself open to the influx of the sperrit, submit yourself passively to the action of the divine force, and disease and dissolution will cease to exist for you. If you could indooce your husband to read this little pamphlet – '

The faces about her again grew indistinct. She had a vague recollection of hearing the motherly lady and the parent of the freckled child ardently disputing the relative advantages of trying several medicines at once, or of taking each in turn; the motherly lady maintaining that the competitive system saved time; the other objecting that you couldn't tell which remedy had effected the cure; their voices went on and on, like bell-buoys droning through a fog . . . The porter came up now and then with questions that she did not understand, but that somehow she must have answered since he went away again without repeating them; every two hours the motherly lady reminded her that her husband ought to have his drops; people left the car and others replaced them . . .

Her head was spinning and she tried to steady herself by clutching at her thoughts as they swept by, but they slipped away from her like bushes on the side of a sheer precipice down which she seemed to be falling. Suddenly her mind grew clear again and she found herself vividly picturing what would happen when the train reached New York. She shuddered as it occurred to her that he would be quite cold and that someone might perceive he had been dead since morning.

She thought hurriedly: 'If they see I am not surprised they will suspect something. They will ask questions, and if I tell them the truth they won't believe me – no one would believe me! It will be terrible' – and she kept repeating to herself: 'I must pretend I don't know. I must pretend I don't know. When they open the curtains I must go up to him quite naturally – and then I must scream.' . . . She had an idea that the scream would be very hard to do.

Gradually new thoughts crowded upon her, vivid and urgent; she tried to separate and restrain them, but they beset her clamorously, like her schoolchildren at the end of a hot day, when she was too tired to silence them. Her head grew confused, and she felt a sick fear of forgetting her part, of betraying herself by some unguarded word or look.

'I must pretend I don't know,' she went on murmuring. The words had lost their significance, but she repeated them mechanically, as though they had been a magic formula, until suddenly she heard herself saying: 'I can't remember, I can't remember!'

Her voice sounded very loud, and she looked about her in terror; but no one seemed to notice that she had spoken.

As she glanced down the car her eye caught the curtains of her husband's berth, and she began to examine the monotonous arabesques woven through their heavy folds. The pattern was intricate and difficult to trace; she gazed fixedly at the curtains and as she did so the thick stuff grew transparent and through it she saw her husband's face – his dead face. She struggled to avert her look, but her eyes refused to move and her head seemed to be held in a vice. At last, with an effort that left her weak and shaking, she turned away; but it was of no use: close in front of her, small and smooth, was her husband's face. It seemed to be suspended in the air between her and the false braids of the woman who sat in front of her. With an uncontrollable gesture she stretched out her hand to push the face away, and suddenly she felt the touch of his smooth skin. She repressed a cry and half started from her seat. The woman with the false braids looked around, and feeling that she must justify her movement in some way she rose and lifted her travelling-bag from the opposite seat. She unlocked the bag and looked into it; but the first object her hand met was a small flask of her husband's, thrust there at the last moment, in the haste of departure. She locked the bag and closed her eyes . . . his face was there again, hanging between her eyeballs and lids like a waxen mask against a red curtain . . .

She roused herself with a shiver. Had she fainted or slept? Hours seemed to have elapsed; but it was still broad day, and the people about her were sitting in the same attitudes as before.

A sudden sense of hunger made her aware that she had eaten nothing since morning. The thought of food filled her with disgust, but she dreaded a return of faintness, and remembering that she had some biscuits in her bag she took one out and ate it. The dry crumbs choked her, and she hastily swallowed a little brandy from her husband's flask. The burning sensation in her throat acted as a counter-irritant, momentarily relieving the dull ache of her nerves. Then she felt a gently-stealing warmth, as though a soft air fanned her, and the swarming fears relaxed their clutch, receding through the stillness that enclosed her, a stillness soothing as the spacious quietude of a summer day. She slept.

Through her sleep she felt the impetuous rush of the train. It seemed to be life itself that was sweeping her on with headlong inexorable force – sweeping her into darkness and terror, and the awe of unknown days. Now all at once everything was still – not a sound, not a pulsation . . . She was dead in her turn, and lay beside him with smooth upstaring face. How quiet it was! –

and yet she heard feet coming, the feet of the men who were to carry them away . . . She could feel too – she felt a sudden prolonged vibration, a series of hard shocks, and then another plunge into darkness: the darkness of death this time – a black whirlwind on which they were both spinning like leaves, in wild uncoiling spirals, with millions and millions of the dead . . .

*   *   *

She sprang up in terror. Her sleep must have lasted a long time, for the winter day had paled and the lights had been lit. The car was in confusion, and as she regained her self-possession she saw that the passengers were gathering up their wraps and bags. The woman with the false braids had brought from the dressing-room a sickly ivy-plant in a bottle, and the Christian Scientist was reversing his cuffs. The porter passed down the aisle with his impartial brush. An impersonal figure with a gold-banded cap asked for her husband's ticket. A voice shouted, 'Baig-gage express!' and she heard the clicking of metal as the passengers handed over their checks.

Presently her window was blocked by an expanse of sooty wall, and the train passed into the Harlem tunnel. The journey was over; in a few minutes she would see her family pushing their joyous way through the throng at the station. Her heart dilated. The worst terror was past . . .

'We'd better get him up now, hadn't we?' asked the porter, touching her arm.

He had her husband's hat in his hand and was meditatively revolving it under his brush.

She looked at the hat and tried to speak; but suddenly the car grew dark. She flung up her arms, struggling to catch at something, and fell face downward, striking her head against the dead man's berth.

JOSEPH CONRAD

Joseph Conrad was born in the Ukraine to Polish parents in 1857 and orphaned as a child. He longed for a life at sea from an early age and in 1874 began a twenty-year career as a sailor. In 1886 he became a British subject and eight years later devoted himself to being a full-time writer. He married Jessie George – the mother of his two sons – in 1895. Publication of his first novel, *Almayer's Folly*, when he was thirty-eight, marked the beginning of a career as a novelist that was to produce such classics as *Lord Jim* (1900), *Nostromo* (1904) and *Under Western Eyes* (1911). Conrad died in 1924 at a point when his stature as a writer of considerable significance was firmly established.

An Outpost of Progress

1

There were two white men in charge of the trading station. Kayerts, the chief, was short and fat; Carlier, the assistant, was tall, with a large head and a very broad trunk perched upon a long pair of thin legs. The third man on the staff was a Sierra Leone negro, who maintained that his name was Henry Price. However, for some reason or other, the natives down the river had given him the name of Makola, and it stuck to him through all his wanderings about the country. He spoke English and French with a warbling accent, wrote a beautiful hand, understood bookkeeping, and cherished in his innermost heart the worship of evil spirits. His wife was a negress from Loanda, very large and very noisy. Three children rolled about in sunshine before the door of his low, shed-like dwelling. Makola, taciturn and impenetrable, despised the two white men. He had charge of a small clay storehouse with a dried-grass roof, and pretended to keep a correct account of beads, cotton cloth, red kerchiefs, brass wire and other trade goods it contained. Besides the storehouse and Makola's hut, there was only one large building in the cleared ground of the station. It was built neatly of reeds, with a verandah on all the four sides. There were three rooms in it. The one in the middle was the living-room, and had two rough tables and a few stools in it. The other two were the bedrooms for the white men. Each had a bedstead and a mosquito net for all furniture. The plank floor was littered with the belongings of the white men: open half-empty boxes, torn wearing apparel, old boots; all the things dirty, and all the things broken, that accumulate mysteriously round untidy men. There was also another dwelling-place some distance away from the buildings. In it, under a tall cross much out of the perpendicular, slept the man who had seen the beginning of all this; who had planned and had watched the construction of this outpost of progress. He had been, at home, an unsuccessful painter who, weary of pursuing fame on an empty stomach, had gone out there through high protections. He had been the first chief of that station. Makola had watched the energetic artist die of fever in the just finished house with his usual kind of 'I told you so' indifference. Then, for a time, he dwelt alone with his family, his account books, and the Evil Spirit that rules the lands under the equator. He got on very well with his god. Perhaps he had propitiated him by a promise of more white men to play with, by and by. At any rate the director of the Great Trading Company, coming up in a steamer that resembled an enormous sardine box with a flat-roofed shed erected on it, found the station in good order, and Makola as usual quietly diligent. The director had the cross put up over the first agent's grave, and appointed Kayerts to the post. Carlier was told off as second in charge. The director was a man ruthless and efficient, who at times, but very imperceptibly, indulged in grim humour. He made a speech to Kayerts and Carlier, pointing out to them the promising aspect of their station. The nearest trading-post was about three hundred miles away. It was an exceptional opportunity for them to distinguish themselves and to earn percentages on the trade. This appointment was a favour done to beginners. Kayerts was moved almost to tears by his director's kindness. He would, he said, by doing his best, try to justify the flattering confidence, etc., etc. Kayerts had been in the Administration of the Telegraphs, and knew how to express himself correctly. Carlier, an ex-non-commissioned officer of cavalry in an army guaranteed from harm by several European Powers, was less impressed. If there were commissions to get, so much the better; and, trailing a sulky glance over the river, the forests, the impenetrable bush that seemed to cut off the station from the rest of the world, he muttered between his teeth, 'We shall see, very soon.'

Next day, some bales of cotton goods and a few cases of provisions having been thrown on shore, the sardine-box steamer went off, not to return for another six months. On the deck the director touched his cap to the two agents, who stood on the bank waving their hats, and turning to an old servant of the company on his passage to headquarters, said, 'Look at those two imbeciles. They must be mad at home to send me such specimens. I told those fellows to plant a vegetable garden, build new storehouses and fences, and construct a landing-stage. I bet nothing will be done! They won't know how to begin. I always thought the station on this river useless, and they just fit the station!'

'They will form themselves there,' said the old stager with a quiet smile.

'At any rate, I am rid of them for six months,' retorted the director.

The two men watched the steamer round the bend, then,

ascending arm in arm the slope of the bank, returned to the station. They had been in this vast and dark country only a very short time, and as yet always in the midst of other white men, under the eye and guidance of their superiors. And now, dull as they were to the subtle influences of surroundings, they felt themselves very much alone when suddenly left unassisted to face the wilderness: a wilderness rendered more strange, more incomprehensible by the mysterious glimpses of the vigorous life it contained. They were two perfectly insignificant and incapable individuals, whose existence is only rendered possible through the high organisation of civilised crowds. Few men realise that their life, the very essence of their character, their capabilities and their audacities, are only the expression of their belief in the safety of their surroundings. The courage, the composure, the confidence; the emotions and principles; every great and every insignificant thought belongs not to the individual but to the crowd: to the crowd that believes blindly in the irresistible force of its institutions and of its morals, in the power of its police and of its opinion. But the contact with pure unmitigated savagery, with primitive nature and primitive man, brings sudden and profound trouble into the heart. To the sentiment of being alone of one's kind, to the clear perception of the loneliness of one's thoughts, of one's sensations – to the negation of the habitual, which is safe, there is added the affirmation of the unusual, which is dangerous; a suggestion of things vague, uncontrollable and repulsive, whose discomposing intrusion excites the imagination and tries the civilised nerves of the foolish and the wise alike.

Kayerts and Carlier walked arm in arm drawing close to one another as children do in the dark; and they had the same, not altogether unpleasant, sense of danger which one half suspects to be imaginary. They chatted persistently in familiar tones. 'Our station is prettily situated,' said one. The other assented with enthusiasm, enlarging volubly on the beauties of the situation. Then they passed near the grave. 'Poor devil!' said Kayerts. 'He died of fever, didn't he?' muttered Carlier, stopping short. 'Why,' retorted Kayerts, with indignation, 'I've been told that the fellow exposed himself recklessly to the sun. The climate here, everybody says, is not at all worse than at home, as long as you keep out of the sun. Do you hear that, Carlier? I am chief here, and my orders are that you should not expose yourself to the sun!' He assumed his superiority jocularly, but his meaning was serious. The idea that he would, perhaps, have to bury Carlier and remain alone, gave him an inward shiver. He felt suddenly that this Carlier was more precious to him here, in the centre of Africa, than a brother could be anywhere else. Carlier, entering into the spirit of the thing, made a military salute and answered in a brisk tone, 'Your orders shall be attended to, chief!' Then he burst out laughing, slapped Kayerts on the back, and shouted, 'We shall let life run easily here! Just sit still and gather in the ivory those savages will bring. This country has its good points, after all!' They both laughed loudly while Carlier thought: That poor Kayerts; he is so fat and unhealthy. It would be awful if I had to bury him here. He is a man I respect . . . Before they reached the verandah of their house they called one another 'my dear fellow'.

The first day they were very active, pottering about with hammers and nails and red calico, to put up curtains, make their house habitable and pretty; resolved to settle down comfortably to their new life. For them an impossible task. To grapple effectually with even purely material problems requires more serenity of mind and more lofty courage than people generally imagine. No two beings could have been more unfitted for such a struggle. Society, not from any tenderness, but because of its strange needs, had taken care of those two men, forbidding them all independent thought, all initiative, all departure from routine; and forbidding it under pain of death. They could only live on condition of being machines. And now, released from the fostering care of men with pens behind the ears, or of men with gold lace on the sleeves, they were like those lifelong prisoners who, liberated after many years, do not know what use to make of their freedom. They did not know what use to make of their faculties, being both, through want of practice, incapable of independent thought.

At the end of two months Kayerts often would say, 'If it was not for my Melie, you wouldn't catch me here.' Melie was his daughter. He had thrown up his post in the Administration of the Telegraphs, though he had been for seventeen years perfectly happy there, to earn a dowry for his girl. His wife was dead, and the child was being brought up by his sisters. He regretted the streets, the pavements, the cafés, his friends of many years; all the things he used to see, day after day; all the thoughts suggested by familiar things – the thoughts effortless, monotonous and soothing of a government clerk; he regretted all the gossip, the small enmities, the mild venom and the little jokes of government offices. 'If I had had a decent brother-in-law,' Carlier would remark, 'a fellow with a heart, I would not be here.' He had left the army and had made himself so obnoxious to his family by his laziness and impudence, that an exasperated brother-in-law had made superhuman efforts to procure him an appointment in the Company as a second-class agent. Having not a penny in the world, he was compelled to accept this means of livelihood as soon as it became quite clear to him that there was nothing more to squeeze out of his relations. He, like Kayerts, regretted his old life. He regretted the clink of sabre and spurs on a fine afternoon, the barrack-room witticisms, the girls of garrison towns; but, besides, he had also a sense of grievance. He was evidently a much ill-used man. This made him moody, at times.

But the two men got on well together in the fellowship of their stupidity and laziness. Together they did nothing, absolutely nothing, and enjoyed the sense of the idleness for which they were paid. And in time they came to feel something resembling affection for one another. They lived like blind men in a large room, aware only of what came in contact with them (and of that only imperfectly), but unable to see the general aspect of things. The river, the forest, all the great land throbbing with life, were like an immense emptiness. Even the brilliant sunshine disclosed nothing intelligible. Things appeared and disappeared before their eyes in an unconnected and aimless kind of way. The river seemed to come from nowhere and flow nowhither. It flowed through a void. Out of that void, at times, came canoes, and men with spears in their hands would suddenly crowd the yard of the station. They were naked, glossy black, ornamented with snowy shells and glistening brass wire, perfect of limb. They made an uncouth babbling noise when they spoke, moved in a stately manner, and sent quick, wild glances out of their startled, never-resting eyes. Those warriors would squat in long rows, four or more deep, before the verandah, while their chiefs bargained for hours with Makola over an elephant tusk. Kayerts sat on his chair and looked down on the proceedings, understanding nothing. He stared at them with his round blue eyes, called out to Carlier, 'Here, look! look at that fellow there – and that other one, to the left. Did you ever see such a face? Oh, the funny brute!'

Carlier, smoking native tobacco in a short wooden pipe, would swagger up twirling his moustaches, and, surveying the warriors with haughty indulgence, would say, 'Fine animals. Brought any bone? Yes? It's not any too soon. Look at the muscles of that fellow – third from the end. I wouldn't care to get a punch on the nose from him. Fine arms, but legs no good below the knee. Couldn't make cavalrymen of them.' And after glancing down complacently at his own shanks, he always concluded: 'Pah! Don't they stink! You, Makola! Take that herd over to the fetish' (the storehouse was in every station called the fetish, perhaps because of the spirit of civilisation it contained) 'and give them up some of the rubbish you keep there. I'd rather see it full of bone than full of rags.'

Kayerts approved.

'Yes, yes! Go and finish that palaver over there, Mr Makola. I will come round when you are ready, to weigh the tusk. We must be careful.' Then, turning to his companion: 'This is the tribe that lives down the river; they are rather aromatic. I remember, they have been once before here. D'ye hear that row? What a fellow has got to put up with in this dog of a country! My head is split.'

Such profitable visits were rare. For days the two pioneers of trade and progress would look on their empty courtyard in the vibrating brilliance of vertical sunshine. Below the high bank, the silent river flowed on, glittering and steady. On the sands in the middle of the stream, hippos and alligators sunned themselves side by side. And stretching away in all directions, surrounding the insignificant cleared spot of the trading post, immense forests, hiding fateful complications of fantastic life, lay in the eloquent silence of mute greatness. The two men understood nothing, cared for nothing but for the passage of days that separated them from the steamer's return. Their predecessor had left some torn books. They took up these wrecks of novels, and, as they had never read anything of the kind before, they were surprised and amused. Then during long days there were interminable and silly discussions about plots and personages. In the centre of Africa they made the acquaintance of Richelieu and of d'Artagnan, of Hawkeye and of Father Goriot, and of many other people. All these imaginary personages became subjects for gossip as if they had been living friends. They discounted their virtues, suspected their motives, decried their successes; were scandalised at their duplicity or were doubtful about their courage. The accounts of crimes filled them with indignation, while tender or pathetic passages moved them deeply. Carlier cleared his throat and said in a soldierly voice, 'What nonsense!' Kayerts, his round eyes suffused with tears, his fat cheeks quivering, rubbed his bald head, and declared, 'This is a splendid book. I had no idea there were such clever fellows in the world.' They also found some old copies of a home paper. That print discussed what it was pleased to call 'Our Colonial Expansion' in high-flown language. It spoke much of the rights and duties of civilisation, of the sacredness of the civilising work, and extolled the merits of those who went about bringing light, and faith, and commerce to the dark places of the earth. Carlier and Kayerts read, wondered, and began to think better of themselves. Carlier said one evening, waving his hand about, 'In a hundred years, there will be perhaps a town here. Quays, and warehouses, and barracks, and – and – billiard-rooms. Civilisation, my boy, and virtue – and all. And then, chaps will read that two good fellows, Kayerts and Carlier, were the first civilised men to live in this very spot!' Kayerts nodded, 'Yes, it is a consolation to think of that.' They seemed to forget their dead predecessor; but, early one day, Carlier went out and replanted the cross firmly. 'It used to make me squint whenever I walked that way,' he explained to Kayerts over the morning coffee. 'It made me squint, leaning over so much. So I just planted it upright. And solid, I promise you! I suspended myself with both hands to the cross-piece. Not a move. Oh, I did that properly.'

At times Gobila came to see them. Gobila was the chief of the neighbouring villages. He was a grey-headed savage, thin and black, with a white cloth round his loins and a mangy panther skin hanging over his back. He came up with long strides of his skeleton legs, swinging a staff as tall as himself, and, entering the common room of the station, would squat on his heels to the left of the door. There he sat, watching Kayerts, and now and then making a speech which the other did not understand. Kayerts, without interrupting his occupation, would from time to time say in a friendly manner: 'How goes it, you old image?' and they would smile at one another. The two whites had a liking for that old and incomprehensible creature, and called him Father Gobila. Gobila's manner was paternal, and he seemed really to love all white men. They all appeared to him very young, indistinguishably alike (except for stature), and he knew that they were all brothers, and also immortal. The death of the artist, who was the first white man whom he knew intimately, did not disturb this belief, because he was firmly convinced that the white stranger had pretended to die and got himself buried for some mysterious purpose of his own, into which it was useless to enquire. Perhaps it was his way of going home to his own country? At any rate, these were his brothers, and he transferred his absurd affection to them. They returned it in a way. Carlier slapped him on the back, and recklessly struck off matches for his amusement. Kayerts was always ready to let him have a sniff at the ammonia bottle. In short, they behaved just like that other white creature that had hidden itself in a hole in the ground. Gobila considered them attentively. Perhaps they were the same being with the other – or one of them was. He couldn't decide – clear up that mystery; but he remained always very friendly. In consequence of that friendship, the women of Gobila's village walked in single file through the reedy grass, bringing every morning to the station fowls, and sweet potatoes, and palm wine, and sometimes a goat. The Company never provisioned the stations fully, and the agents required those local supplies to live. They had them through the good-will of Gobila, and lived well. Now and then one of them had a bout of fever, and the other nursed him with gentle devotion. They did not think much of it. It left them weaker, and their appearance changed for the worse. Carlier was hollow-eyed and irritable. Kayerts showed a drawn, flabby face above the rotundity of his stomach, which gave him a weird aspect. But being constantly together, they did not notice the change that took place gradually in their appearance, and also in their dispositions.

Five months passed in that way.

Then, one morning, as Kayerts and Carlier, lounging in their chairs under the verandah, talked about the approaching visit of the steamer, a knot of armed men came out of the forest and advanced towards the station. They were strangers to that part of the country. They were tall, slight, draped classically from neck to heel in blue fringed cloths, and carried percussion muskets over their bare right shoulders. Makola showed signs of excitement, and ran out of the storehouse (where he spent all his days) to meet these visitors. They came into the courtyard and looked about them with steady, scornful glances. Their leader, a powerful and determined-looking negro with bloodshot eyes, stood in front of the verandah and made a long speech. He gesticulated much, and ceased very suddenly.

There was something in his intonation, in the sounds of the long sentences he used, that startled the two whites. It was like a reminiscence of something not exactly familiar, and yet resembling the speech of civilised men. It sounded like one of those impossible languages which sometimes we hear in our dreams.

'What lingo is that?' said the amazed Carlier. 'In the first moment I fancied the fellow was going to speak French. Anyway, it is a different kind of gibberish from what we ever heard.'

'Yes,' replied Kayerts. 'Hey, Makola, what does he say? Where do they come from? Who are they?'

But Makola, who seemed to be standing on hot bricks, answered hurriedly, 'I don't know. They come from very far. Perhaps Mrs Price will understand. They are perhaps bad men.'

The leader, after waiting for a while, said something sharply to Makola, who shook his head. Then the man, after looking round, noticed Makola's hut and walked over there. The next moment Mrs Makola was heard speaking with great volubility.

The other strangers – they were six in all – strolled about with an air of ease, put their heads through the door of the store-room, congregated round the grave, pointed understandingly at the cross, and generally made themselves at home.

'I don't like those chaps – and, I say, Kayerts, they must be from the coast; they've got firearms,' observed the sagacious Carlier.

Kayerts also did not like those chaps. They both, for the first time, became aware that they lived in conditions where the unusual may be dangerous, and that there was no power on earth outside of themselves to stand between them and the unusual. They became uneasy, went in and loaded their revolvers. Kayerts said, 'We must order Makola to tell them to go away before dark.'

The strangers left in the afternoon, after eating a meal prepared for them by Mrs Makola. The immense woman was excited, and talked much with the visitors. She rattled away shrilly, pointing here and pointing there at the forests and at the river. Makola sat apart and watched. At times he got up and whispered to his wife. He accompanied the strangers across the ravine at the back of the station-ground, and returned slowly looking very thoughtful. When questioned by the white men he was very strange, seemed not to understand, seemed to have forgotten French – seemed to have forgotten how to speak altogether. Kayerts and Carlier agreed that the nigger had had too much palm wine.

There was some talk about keeping a watch in turn, but in the evening everything seemed so quiet and peaceful that they retired as usual. All night they were disturbed by a lot of drumming in the villages. A deep, rapid roll near by would be followed by another far off – then all ceased. Soon short appeals would rattle out here and there, then all mingle together, increase, become vigorous and sustained, would spread out over the forest, roll through the night, unbroken and ceaseless, near and far, as if the whole land had been one immense drum booming out steadily an appeal to heaven. And through the deep and tremendous noise sudden yells that resembled snatches of songs from a madhouse darted shrill and high in discordant jets of sound which seemed to rush far above the earth and drive all peace from under the stars.

Carlier and Kayerts slept badly. They both thought they had heard shots fired during the night – but they could not agree as to the direction. In the morning Makola was gone somewhere. He returned about noon with one of yesterday's strangers, and eluded all Kayerts's attempts to close with him: had become deaf apparently. Kayerts wondered. Carlier, who had been fishing off the bank, came back and remarked while he showed his catch, 'The niggers seem to be in a deuce of a stir; I wonder what's up. I saw about fifteen canoes cross the river during the two hours I was there fishing.' Kayerts, worried, said, 'Isn't this Makola very queer today?' Carlier advised, 'Keep all our men together in case of some trouble.'

2

There were ten station men who had been left by the director. Those fellows, having engaged themselves to the Company for six months (without having any idea of a month in particular and only a very faint notion of time in general), had been serving the cause of progress for upwards of two years. Belonging to a tribe from a very distant part of this land of darkness and sorrow, they did not run away, naturally supposing that as wandering strangers they would be killed by the inhabitants of the country; in which they were right. They lived in straw huts on the slope of a ravine overgrown with reedy grass, just behind the station buildings. They were not happy, regretting the festive incantations, the sorceries, the human sacrifices of their own land; where they also had parents, brothers, sisters, admired chiefs, respected magicians, loved friends, and other ties supposed generally to be human. Besides, the rice rations served out by the Company did not agree with them, being a food unknown to their land, and to which they could not get used. Consequently they were unhealthy and miserable. Had they been of any other tribe they would have made up their minds to die – for nothing is easier to certain savages than suicide – and so have escaped from the puzzling difficulties of existence. But belonging, as they did, to a warlike tribe with filed teeth, they had more grit, and went on stupidly living through disease and sorrow. They did very little work, and had lost their splendid physique. Carlier and Kayerts doctored them assiduously without being able to bring them back into condition again. They were mustered every morning and told off to different tasks – grass-cutting, fence-building, tree-felling, etc., etc., which no power on earth could induce them to execute efficiently. The two whites had practically very little control over them.

In the afternoon Makola came over to the big house and found Kayerts watching three heavy columns of smoke rising above the forests. 'What is that?' asked Kayerts. 'Some villages burn,' answered Makola, who seemed to have regained his wits. Then he said abruptly: 'We have got very little ivory; bad six months' trading. Do you like get a little more ivory?'

'Yes,' said Kayerts eagerly. He thought of percentages which were low.

'Those men who came yesterday are traders from Loanda who have got more ivory than they can carry home. Shall I buy? I know their camp.'

'Certainly,' said Kayerts. 'What are those traders?'

'Bad fellows,' said Makola indifferently. 'They fight with people, and catch women and children. They are bad men, and got guns. There is a great disturbance in the country. Do you want ivory?'

'Yes,' said Kayerts. Makola said nothing for a while. Then:

'Those workmen of ours are no good at all,' he muttered, looking round. 'Station in very bad order, sir. Director will growl. Better get a fine lot of ivory, then he say nothing.'

'I can't help it; the men won't work,' said Kayerts. 'When will you get that ivory?'

'Very soon,' said Makola. 'Perhaps tonight. You leave it to me, and keep indoors, sir. I think you had better give some palm wine to our men to make a dance this evening. Enjoy themselves. Work better tomorrow. There's plenty palm wine – gone a little sour.'

Kayerts said yes, and Makola, with his own hands, carried the big calabashes to the door of his hut. They stood there till the evening, and Mrs Makola looked into every one. The men got them at sunset. When Kayerts and Carlier retired, a big bonfire was flaring before the men's huts. They could hear their shouts and drumming. Some men from Gobila's village had joined the station hands, and the entertainment was a great success.

In the middle of the night, Carlier, waking suddenly, heard a man shout loudly; then a shot was fired. Only one. Carlier ran out and met Kayerts on the verandah. They were both startled. As they went across the yard to call Makola, they saw shadows moving in the night. One of them cried, 'Don't shoot! It's me, Price.' Then Makola appeared close to them. 'Go back, go back, please,' he urged, 'you spoil all.'

'There are strange men about,' said Carlier.

'Never mind; I know,' said Makola. Then he whispered, 'All right. Bring ivory. Say nothing! I know my business.'

The two white men reluctantly went back to the house, but did not sleep. They heard footsteps, whispers, some groans. It seemed as if a lot of men came in, dumped heavy things on the ground, squabbled a long time, then went away. They lay on their hard beds and thought: 'This Makola is invaluable.' In the morning Carlier came out, very sleepy, and pulled at the cord of the big bell. The station hands mustered every morning to the sound of the bell. That morning nobody came. Kayerts turned out also, yawning. Across the yard they saw Makola come out of his hut, a tin basin of soapy water in his hand. Makola, a civilised nigger, was very neat in his person. He threw the soapsuds skilfully over a wretched little yellow cur he had, then turning his face to the agent's house, he shouted from the distance, 'All the men gone last night!'

They heard him plainly, but in their surprise they both yelled out together: 'What!' Then they stared at one another.

'We are in a proper fix now,' growled Carlier.

'It's incredible!' muttered Kayerts.

'I will go to the huts and see,' said Carlier, striding off.

Makola coming up found Kayerts standing alone.

'I can hardly believe it,' said Kayerts tearfully. 'We took care of them as if they had been our children.'

'They went with the coast people,' said Makola after a moment of hesitation.

'What do I care with whom they went – the ungrateful brutes!' exclaimed the other. Then with sudden suspicion, and looking hard at Makola, he added: 'What do you know about it?'

Makola moved his shoulders, looking down on the ground. 'What do I know? I think only. Will you come and look at the ivory I've got there? It is a fine lot. You never saw such.'

He moved towards the store. Kayerts followed him mechanically, thinking about the incredible desertion of the men. On the ground before the door of the fetish lay six splendid tusks.

'What did you give for it?' asked Kayerts, after surveying the lot with satisfaction.

'No regular trade,' said Makola. 'They brought the ivory and gave it to me. I told them to take what they most wanted in the station. It is a beautiful lot. No station can show such tusks. Those traders wanted carriers badly, and our men were no good here. No trade, no entry in books; all correct.'

Kayerts nearly burst with indignation. 'Why!' he shouted, 'I believe you have sold our men for these tusks!' Makola stood impassive and silent. 'I – I – will – I,' stuttered Kayerts. 'You fiend!' he yelled out.

'I did the best for you and the Company,' said Makola imperturbably. 'Why you shout so much? Look at this tusk.'

'I dismiss you! I will report you – I won't look at the tusk. I forbid you to touch them. I order you to throw them into the river. You – you – !'

'You very red, Mr Kayerts. If you are so irritable in the sun, you will get fever and die – like the first chief!' pronounced Makola impressively.

They stood still, contemplating one another with intense eyes, as if they had been looking with effort across immense distances. Kayerts shivered. Makola had meant no more than he said, but his words seemed to Kayerts full of ominous menace! He turned sharply and went away to the house. Makola retired into the bosom of his family; and the tusks, left lying before the store, looked very large and valuable in the sunshine.

Carlier came back on the verandah. 'They're all gone, hey?' asked Kayerts from the far end of the common room in a muffled voice. 'You did not find anybody?'

'Oh, yes,' said Carlier, 'I found one of Gobila's people lying dead before the huts – shot through the body. We heard that shot last night.'

Kayerts came out quickly. He found his companion staring grimly over the yard at the tusks, away by the store. They both sat in silence for a while. Then Kayerts related his conversation with Makola. Carlier said nothing. At the midday meal they ate very little. They hardly exchanged a word that day. A great silence seemed to lie heavily over the station and press on their lips. Makola did not open the store; he spent the day playing with his children. He lay full-length on a mat outside his door, and the youngsters sat on his chest and clambered all over him.

It was a touching picture. Mrs Makola was busy cooking all day as usual. The white men made a somewhat better meal in the evening. Afterwards, Carlier smoking his pipe strolled over to the store; he stood for a long time over the tusks, touched one or two with his foot, even tried to lift the largest one by its small end. He came back to his chief, who had not stirred from the verandah, threw himself in the chair and said, 'I can see it! They were pounced upon while they slept heavily after drinking all that palm wine you'd allowed Makola to give them. A put-up job! See? The worst is, some of Gobila's people were there, and got carried off too, no doubt. The least drunk woke up, and got shot for his sobriety. This is a funny country. What will you do now?'

'We can't touch it, of course,' said Kayerts.

'Of course not,' assented Carlier.

'Slavery is an awful thing,' stammered out Kayerts in an unsteady voice.

'Frightful – the sufferings,' grunted Carlier, with conviction.

They believed their words. Everybody shows a respectful deference to certain sounds that he and his fellows can make. But about feelings people really know nothing. We talk with indignation or enthusiasm; we talk about oppression, cruelty, crime, devotion, self-sacrifice, virtue, and we know nothing real beyond the words. Nobody knows what suffering or sacrifice means – except, perhaps, the victims of the mysterious purpose of these illusions.

Next morning they saw Makola very busy setting up in the yard the big scales used for weighing ivory. By and by Carlier said: 'What's that filthy scoundrel up to?' and lounged out into the yard. Kayerts followed. They stood by watching. Makola took no notice. When the balance was swung true, he tried to lift a tusk into the scale. It was too heavy. He looked up help-lessly without a word, and for a minute they stood round that balance as mute and still as three statues. Suddenly Carlier said:

'Catch hold of the other end, Makola – you beast!' and together they swung the tusk up. Kayerts trembled in every limb. He muttered, 'I say! Oh! I say!' and putting his hand in his pocket found there a dirty bit of paper and the stump of a pencil. He turned his back on the others, as if about to do something tricky, and noted stealthily the weights which Carlier shouted out to him with unnecessary loudness. When all was over, Makola whispered to himself: 'The sun's very strong here for the tusks.' Carlier said to Kayerts in a careless tone: 'I say, chief, I might just as well give him a lift with this lot into the store.'

As they were going back to the house Kayerts observed with a sigh: 'It had to be done.'

And Carlier said: 'It's deplorable, but, the men being Company's men, the ivory is Company's ivory. We must look after it.'

'I will report to the director, of course,' said Kayerts.

'Of course; let him decide,' approved Carlier.

At midday they made a hearty meal. Kayerts sighed from time to time. Whenever they mentioned Makola's name they always added to it an opprobrious epithet. It eased their conscience. Makola gave himself a half-holiday, and bathed his children in the river. No one from Gobila's villages came near the station that day. No one came the next day, and the next, nor for a whole week. Gobila's people might have all been dead and buried for any sign of life they gave. But they were only mourning for those they had lost by the witchcraft of white men, who had brought wicked people into their country. The wicked people were gone, but fear remained. Fear always remains. A man may destroy everything within himself, love and hate and belief, and even doubt; but as long as he clings to life he cannot destroy fear: the fear, subtle, indestructible, and terrible, that pervades his being; that tinges his thoughts; that lurks in his heart; that watches on his lips the struggle of his last breath. In his fear, the mild old Gobila offered extra human sacrifices to all the evil spirits that had taken possession of his white friends. His heart was heavy. Some warriors spoke about burning and killing, but the cautious old savage dissuaded them. Who could foresee the woe those mysterious creatures, if irritated, might bring? They should be left alone. Perhaps in time they would disappear into the earth as the first one had disappeared. His people must keep away from them, and hope for the best.

Kayerts and Carlier did not disappear, but remained above on this earth that, somehow, they fancied had become bigger and very empty. It was not the absolute and dumb solitude of the post that impressed them so much as an inarticulate feeling that something from within them was gone, something that worked for their safety, and had kept the wilderness from interfering with their hearts. The images of home; the memory of people like them, of men that thought and felt as they used to think and feel, receded into distances made indistinct by the glare of unclouded sunshine. And out of the great silence of the surrounding wilderness, its very hopelessness and savagery seemed to approach them nearer, to draw them gently, to look upon them, to envelop them with a solicitude irresistible, familiar and disgusting.

Days lengthened into weeks, then into months. Gobila's people drummed and yelled to every new moon, as of yore, but kept away from the station. Makola and Carlier tried once in a canoe to open communications, but were received with a shower of arrows and had to fly back to the station for dear life. That attempt set the country up and down the river into an uproar that could be very distinctly heard for days. The steamer was late. At first they spoke of delay jauntily, then anxiously, then gloomily. The matter was becoming serious. Stores were running short. Carlier cast his lines off the bank, but the river was low, and the fish kept out in the stream. They dared not stroll far away from the station to shoot. Moreover, there was no game in the impenetrable forest. Once Carlier shot a hippo in the river. They had no boat to secure it, and it sank. When it floated up it drifted away, and Gobila's people secured the carcase. It was the occasion for a national holiday, but Carlier had a fit of rage over it, and talked about the necessity of exterminating all the niggers before the country could be made habitable. Kayerts mooned about silently; spent hours looking at the portrait of his Melie. It represented a little girl with long bleached tresses and a rather sour face. His legs were much swollen, and he could hardly walk. Carlier, undermined by fever, could not swagger any more, but kept tottering about, still with a devil-may-care air, as became a man who remembered his crack regiment. He had become hoarse, sarcastic, and inclined to say unpleasant things. He called it 'being frank with you'. They had long ago reckoned their percentages on trade, including in them that last deal of 'this infamous Makola'. They had also concluded not to say anything about it. Kayerts hesitated at first – was afraid of the director.

'He has seen worse things done on the quiet,' maintained Carlier, with a hoarse laugh. 'Trust him! He won't thank you if you blab. He is no better than you or me. Who will talk if we hold our tongues? There is nobody here.'

That was the root of the trouble! There was nobody there; and being left there alone with their weakness, they became daily more like a pair of accomplices than like a couple of devoted friends. They had heard nothing from home for eight months. Every evening they said, 'Tomorrow we shall see the steamer.' But one of the Company's steamers had been wrecked, and the director was busy with the other, relieving very distant and important stations on the main river. He thought that the useless station, and the useless men, could wait. Meantime Kayerts and Carlier lived on rice boiled without salt, and cursed the Company, all Africa, and the day they were born. One must have lived on such a diet to discover what ghastly trouble the necessity of swallowing one's food may become. There was literally nothing else in the station but rice and coffee; they drank the coffee without sugar. The last fifteen lumps Kayerts had solemnly locked away in his box, together with a half-bottle of Cognac, 'in case of sickness', he explained. Carlier approved. 'When one is sick,' he said, 'any little extra like that is cheering.'

They waited. Rank grass began to sprout over the courtyard. The bell never rang now. Days passed, silent, exasperating and slow. When the two men spoke, they snarled; and their silences were bitter, as if tinged with the bitterness of their thoughts.

One day after a lunch of boiled rice, Carlier put down his cup untasted, and said: 'Hang it all! Let's have a decent cup of coffee for once. Bring out that sugar, Kayerts!'

'For the sick,' muttered Kayerts, without looking up.

'For the sick,' mocked Carlier. 'Bosh! . . . Well! I am sick.'

'You are no more sick than I am, and I go without,' said Kayerts in a peaceful tone.

'Come! out with that sugar, you stingy old slave-dealer.'

Kayerts looked up quickly. Carlier was smiling with marked insolence. And suddenly it seemed to Kayerts that he had never seen that man before. Who was he? He knew nothing about him. What was he capable of? There was a surprising flash of violent emotion within him, as if in the presence of something undreamt of, dangerous and final. But he managed to pronounce with composure, 'That joke is in very bad taste. Don't repeat it.'

'Joke!' said Carlier, hitching himself forward on his seat. 'I am hungry – I am sick – I don't joke! I hate hypocrites. You are a hypocrite. You are a slave-dealer. I am a slave-dealer. There's nothing but slave-dealers in this cursed country. I mean to have sugar in my coffee today, anyhow!'

'I forbid you to speak to me in that way,' said Kayerts with a fair show of resolution.

'You! – What?' shouted Carlier, jumping up.

Kayerts stood up also. 'I am your chief,' he began, trying to master the shakiness of his voice.

'What?' yelled the other. 'Who's chief? There's no chief here. There's nothing here: there's nothing but you and I. Fetch the sugar – you pot-bellied ass.'

'Hold your tongue. Go out of this room,' screamed Kayerts. 'I dismiss you – you scoundrel!'

Carlier swung a stool. All at once he looked dangerously in earnest. 'You flabby, good-for-nothing civilian – take that!' he howled.

Kayerts dropped under the table, and the stool struck the grass inner wall of the room. Then, as Carlier was trying to upset the table, Kayerts in desperation made a blind rush, head low, like a cornered pig would do, and overturning his friend, bolted along the verandah and into his room. He locked the door, snatched his revolver and stood panting. In less than a minute Carlier was kicking at the door furiously, howling, 'If you don't bring out that sugar, I will shoot you at sight, like a dog. Now then – one – two – three. You won't? I will show you who's the master.'

Kayerts thought the door would fall in, and scrambled through the square hole that served for a window in his room. There was then the whole breadth of the house between them. But the other was apparently not strong enough to break in the door, and Kayerts heard him running round. Then he also began to run laboriously on his swollen legs. He ran as quickly as he could, grasping the revolver, and unable yet to understand what was happening to him. He saw in succession Makola's house, the store, the river, the ravine and the low bushes; and he saw all those things again as he ran for the second time round the house. Then again they flashed past him. That morning he could not have walked a yard without a groan.

And now he ran. He ran fast enough to keep out of sight of the other man.

Then as, weak and desperate, he thought, 'Before I finish the next round I shall die,' he heard the other man stumble heavily, then stop. He stopped also. He had the back and Carlier the front of the house, as before. He heard him drop into a chair cursing, and suddenly his own legs gave way, and he slid down into a sitting posture with his back to the wall. His mouth was as dry as a cinder, and his face was wet with perspiration – and tears. What was it all about? He thought it must be a horrible illusion; he thought he was dreaming; he thought he was going mad! After a while he collected his senses. What did they quarrel about? That sugar! How absurd! He would give it to him – didn't want it himself. And he began scrambling to his feet with a sudden feeling of security. But before he had fairly stood upright, a common-sense reflection occurred to him and drove him back into despair. He thought: If I give way now to that brute of a soldier, he will begin this horror again tomorrow – and the day after – every day – raise other pretensions, trample on me, torture me, make me his slave – and I will be lost! Lost! The steamer may not come for days – may never come. He shook so that he had to sit down on the floor again. He shivered forlornly. He felt he could not, would not move any more. He was completely distracted by the sudden perception that the position was without issue – that death and life had in a moment become equally difficult and terrible.

All at once he heard the other push his chair back; and he leaped to his feet with extreme facility. He listened and got confused. Must run again! Right or left? He heard footsteps. He darted to the left, grasping his revolver, and at the very same instant, as it seemed to him, they came into violent collision. Both shouted with surprise. A loud explosion took place between them: a roar of red fire, thick smoke; and Kayerts, deafened and blinded, rushed back thinking: I am hit – it's all over. He expected the other to come round – to gloat over his agony. He caught hold of an upright of the roof – 'All over!' Then he heard a crashing fall on the other side of the house, as if somebody had tumbled headlong over a chair – then silence. Nothing more happened. He did not die. Only his shoulder felt as if it had been badly wrenched, and he had lost his revolver. He was disarmed and helpless! He waited for his fate. The other man made no sound. It was stratagem. He was stalking him now! Along what side? Perhaps he was taking aim this very minute!

After a few moments of an agony frightful and absurd, he decided to go and meet his doom. He was prepared for every surrender. He turned the corner, steadying himself with one hand on the wall, made a few paces, and nearly swooned. He had seen on the floor, protruding past the other corner, a pair of turned-up feet. A pair of white naked feet in red slippers. He felt deadly sick, and stood for a time in profound darkness. Then Makola appeared before him, saying quietly: 'Come along, Mr Kayerts. He is dead.' He burst into tears of gratitude: a loud, sobbing fit of crying. After a time he found himself sitting in a chair and looking at Carlier, who lay stretched on his back. Makola was kneeling over the body.

'Is this your revolver?' asked Makola, getting up.

'Yes,' said Kayerts; then he added very quickly. 'He ran after me to shoot me – you saw!'

'Yes, I saw,' said Makola. 'There is only one revolver; where's his?'

'Don't know,' whispered Kayerts in a voice that had become suddenly very faint.

'I will go and look for it,' said the other gently. He made the round along the verandah, while Kayerts sat still and looked at the corpse. Makola came back empty-handed, stood in deep thought, then stepped quietly into the dead man's room, and came out directly with a revolver, which he held up before Kayerts. Kayerts shut his eyes. Everything was going round. He found life more terrible and difficult than death. He had shot an unarmed man.

After meditating for a while, Makola said softly, pointing at the dead man who lay there with his right eye blown out, 'He died of fever.'

Kayerts looked at him with a stony stare.

'Yes,' repeated Makola thoughtfully, stepping over the corpse, 'I think he died of fever. Bury him tomorrow.'

And he went away slowly to his expectant wife, leaving the two white men alone on the verandah.

Night came, and Kayerts sat unmoving on his chair. He sat quiet as if he had taken a dose of opium. The violence of the emotions he had passed through produced a feeling of exhausted serenity. He had plumbed in one short afternoon the depths of horror and despair, and now found repose in the conviction that life had no more secrets for him; neither had death! He sat by the corpse thinking; thinking very actively, thinking very new thoughts. He seemed to have broken loose from himself altogether. His old thoughts, convictions, likes and dislikes, things he respected and things he abhorred, appeared in their true light at last! Appeared contemptible and childish, false and ridiculous. He revelled in his new wisdom while he sat by the man he had killed. He argued with himself about all things under heaven with that kind of wrong-headed lucidity which may be observed in some lunatics. Incidentally he reflected that the fellow dead there had been a noxious beast anyway; that men died every day in thousands; perhaps in hundreds of thousands – who could tell? – and that, in the number, that one death could not possibly make any difference; couldn't have any importance, at least to a thinking creature. He, Kayerts, was a thinking creature. He had been all his life, till that moment, a believer in a lot of nonsense like the rest of mankind – who are fools; but now he thought! He knew! He was at peace; he was familiar with the highest wisdom! Then he tried to imagine himself dead, and Carlier sitting in his chair watching him; and his attempt met with such unexpected success that in a very few moments he became not at all sure who was dead and who was alive. This extraordinary achievement of his fancy startled him, however, and by a clever and timely effort of mind he saved himself just in time from becoming Carlier. His heart thumped, and he felt hot all over at the thought of that danger. Carlier! What a beastly thing! To compose his now disturbed nerves – and no wonder! – he tried to whistle a little. Then, suddenly, he fell asleep, or thought he had slept; but at any rate there was a fog, and somebody had whistled in the fog.

He stood up. The day had come, and a heavy mist had descended upon the land: the mist penetrating, enveloping and silent; the morning mist of tropical lands; the mist that clings and kills; the mist white and deadly, immaculate and poisonous. He stood up, saw the body, and threw his arms above his head with a cry like that of a man who, waking from a trance, finds himself immured for ever in a tomb. '*Help!* . . . *My God!*'

A shriek, inhuman, vibrating and sudden, pierced like a sharp dart the white shroud of that land of sorrow. Three short, impatient screeches followed, and then, for a time, the fog-wreaths rolled on, undisturbed, through a formidable silence. Then many more shrieks, rapid and piercing, like the yells of some exasperated and ruthless creature, rent the air. Progress was calling to Kayerts from the river. Progress and civilisation and all the virtues. Society was calling to its accomplished child to come, to be taken care of, to be instructed, to be judged, to be condemned; it called him to return to that rubbish heap from which he had wandered away, so that justice could be done.

Kayerts heard and understood. He stumbled out of the verandah, leaving the other man quite alone for the first time since they had been thrown there together. He groped his way through the fog, calling in his ignorance upon the invisible heaven to undo its work.

Makola flitted by in the mist, shouting as he ran, 'Steamer!

Steamer! They can't see. They whistle for the station. I go ring the bell. Go down to the landing, sir. I ring.'

He disappeared. Kayerts stood still. He looked upwards; the fog rolled low over his head. He looked round like a man who has lost his way; and he saw a dark smudge, a cross-shaped stain, upon the shifting purity of the mist. As he began to stumble towards it, the station bell rang in a tumultuous peal its answer to the impatient clamour of the steamer.

The managing director of the Great Civilising Company (since we know that civilisation follows trade) landed first, and incontinently lost sight of the steamer. The fog down by the river was exceedingly dense; above, at the station, the bell rang unceasing and brazen.

The director shouted loudly to the steamer: 'There is nobody down to meet us; there may be something wrong, though they are ringing. You had better come, too!'

And he began to toil up the steep bank. The captain and the engine-driver of the boat followed behind. As they scrambled up the fog thinned, and they could see their director a good way ahead. Suddenly they saw him start forward, calling to them over his shoulder: 'Run! Run to the house! I've found one of them. Run, look for the other!'

He had found one of them! And even he, the man of varied and startling experience, was somewhat discomposed by the manner of this finding. He stood and fumbled in his pockets (for a knife) while he faced Kayerts, who was hanging by a leather strap from the cross. He had evidently climbed the grave, which was high and narrow, and after tying the end of the strap to the arm, had swung himself off. His toes were only a couple of inches above the ground; his arms hung stiffly down; he seemed to be standing rigidly at attention, but with one purple cheek playfully posed on the shoulder. And, irreverently, he was putting out a swollen tongue at his managing director.

MARK TWAIN

Samuel Langhorne Clemens was born in Missouri in 1835, the son of a lawyer. Early in his childhood, the family moved to Hannibal, Missouri – a town which would provide the inspiration for St Petersburg in *Tom Sawyer* and *Huckleberry Finn*. After a period spent as a travelling printer, Clemens became a river pilot on the Mississippi – a time he would look back upon as his happiest. When he turned to writing in his thirties, he adopted the pseudonym Mark Twain ('Mark Twain' is the cry of a Mississippi boatman taking depth measurements, and means 'two fathoms'), and a number of highly successful publications followed, including *The Prince and the Pauper* (1882), *Huckleberry Finn* (1884) and *A Connecticut Yankee* (1889). His later life, however, was marked by personal tragedy and sadness, as well as financial difficulty. In 1894, several businesses in which he had invested failed, and he was declared bankrupt. Over the next fifteen years – during which he managed to regain some measure of financial independence – he saw the deaths of two of his beloved daughters, and his wife. Increasingly bitter and depressed, Twain died in 1910, aged seventy-five.

The Belated Russian Passport

One Fly makes a Summer – *Pudd'nhead Wilson's Calendar*

1

A great beer-saloon in the Friedrichstrasse, Berlin, towards mid-afternoon. At a hundred round tables gentlemen sat smoking and drinking; flitting here and there and everywhere were white-aproned waiters bearing foaming mugs to the thirsty. At a table near the main entrance were grouped half a dozen lively young fellows – American students – drinking goodbye to a visiting Yale youth on his travels, who had been spending a few days in the German capital.

'But why do you cut your tour short in the middle, Parrish?' asked one of the students. 'I wish I had your chance. What do you want to go home for?'

'Yes,' said another, 'what is the idea? You want to explain, you know, because it looks like insanity. Homesick?'

A girlish blush rose in Parrish's fresh young face, and after a little hesitation he confessed that that was his trouble.

'I was never away from home before,' he said, 'and every day I get more and more lonesome. I have not seen a friend for weeks, and it's been horrible. I meant to stick the trip through, for pride's sake, but seeing you boys has finished me. It's been heaven to me, and I can't take up that companionless dreariness again. If I had company – but I haven't, you know, so it's no use. They used to call me Miss Nancy when I was a small chap, and I reckon I'm that yet – girlish and timorous and all that. I ought to have *been* a girl! I can't stand it; I'm going home.'

The boys rallied him good-naturedly, and said he was making the mistake of his life; and one of them added that he ought at least to see St Petersburg before turning back.

'Don't!' said Parrish, appealingly. 'It was my dearest dream, and I'm throwing it away. Don't say a word more on that head, for I'm made of water, and can't stand out against anybody's persuasion. I *can't* go alone; I think I should die.' He slapped his breast pocket, and added: 'Here is my protection against a change of mind; I've bought ticket and sleeper for Paris, and I leave tonight. Drink, now – this is on me – bumpers – this is for home!'

The goodbyes were said, and Alfred Parrish was left to his thoughts and his loneliness. But for a moment only. A sturdy middle-aged man with a brisk and businesslike bearing, and an air of decision and confidence suggestive of military training, came bustling from the next table, and seated himself at Parrish's side, and began to speak, with concentrated interest and earnestness. His eyes, his face, his person, his whole system, seemed to exude energy. He was full of steam – racing pressure – one could almost hear his gauge-cocks sing. He extended a frank hand, shook Parrish's cordially, and said, with a most convincing air of strenuous conviction, 'Ah, but you *mustn't*; really you mustn't; it would be the greatest mistake; you would always regret it. Be persuaded, I beg you; don't do it – don't!'

There was such a friendly note in it, and such a seeming of genuineness, that it brought a sort of uplift to the youth's despondent spirits, and a telltale moisture betrayed itself in his eyes, an unintentional confession that he was touched and grateful.

The alert stranger noted that sign, was quite content with that response, and followed up his advantage without waiting for a spoken one, 'No, don't do it; it would be a mistake. I have heard everything that was said – you will pardon that – I was so close by that I couldn't help it. And it troubled me to think that you would cut your travels short when you really *want* to see St Petersburg and are right here almost in sight of it! Reconsider

50

it – ah, you *must* reconsider it. It is such a short distance – it is very soon done and very soon over – and think what a memory it will be!'

Then he went on and made a picture of the Russian capital and its wonders which made Alfred Parrish's mouth water and his roused spirits cry out with longing. Then, 'Of course you must see St Petersburg – you *must*! Why, it will be a joy to you – a joy! I know, because I know the place as familiarly as I know my own birthplace in America. Ten years – I've known it ten years. Ask anybody there; they'll tell you; they all know me – Major Jackson. The very dogs know me. Do go; oh, you must go; you must, indeed.'

Alfred Parrish was quivering with eagerness now. He would go. His face said it as plainly as his tongue could have done it. Then – the old shadow fell, and he said, sorrowfully, 'Oh no – no, it's no use; I can't. I should die of the loneliness.'

The major said, with astonishment: 'The loneliness! Why, I'm going *with* you!'

It was startlingly unexpected. And not quite pleasant. Things were moving too rapidly. Was this a trap? Was this stranger a sharper? Whence all this gratuitous interest in a wandering and unknown lad? Then he glanced at the major's frank and winning and beaming face, and was ashamed; and wished he knew how to get out of this scrape without hurting the feelings of its contriver. But he was not handy in matters of diplomacy, and went at the difficulty with conscious awkwardness and small confidence. He said, with a quite overdone show of unselfishness, 'Oh no, no, you are too kind; I couldn't – I couldn't allow you to put yourself to such an inconvenience on my – '

'Inconvenience? None in the world, my boy; I was going tonight, anyway; I leave in the express at nine. Come! we'll go together. You shan't be lonely a single minute. Come along – say the word!'

So that excuse had failed. What to do now? Parrish was disheartened; it seemed to him that no subterfuge which his poor invention could contrive would ever rescue him from these toils. Still, he must make another effort, and he did; and before he had finished his new excuse he thought he recognised that it was unanswerable. 'Ah, but most unfortunately luck is against me, and it is impossible. Look at these' – and he took out his tickets and laid them on the table. 'I am booked through to Paris, and I couldn't get these tickets and baggage coupons changed for St Petersburg, of course, and would have to lose the money; and if I could afford to lose the money, I should be rather short after I bought the new tickets – for there is all the cash I've got about me' – and he laid a five-hundred-mark banknote on the table.

In a moment the major had the tickets and coupons and was on his feet, and saying, with enthusiasm, 'Good! It's all right, and everything safe. They'll change the tickets and baggage pasters for *me*; they all know me – everybody knows me. Sit right where you are; I'll be back right away.' Then he reached for the banknote, and added, 'I'll take this along, for there will be a little extra to pay on the new tickets, maybe' – and the next moment he was flying out at the door.

2

Alfred Parrish was paralysed. It was all so sudden. So sudden, so daring, so incredible, so impossible. His mouth was open, but his tongue wouldn't work; he tried to shout, 'Stop him,' but his lungs were empty; he wanted to pursue, but his legs refused to do anything but tremble; then they gave way under him and let him down into his chair. His throat was dry, he was gasping and swallowing with dismay, his head was in a whirl. What must he do? He did not know. One thing seemed plain, however – he must pull himself together, and try to overtake that man. Of course the man could not get back the ticket-money, but would he throw the tickets away on that account? No; he would certainly go to the station and sell them to someone at half-price; and today, too, for they would be worthless tomorrow, by German custom. These reflections gave him hope and strength, and he rose and started. But he took only a couple of steps, then he felt a sudden sickness and tottered back to his chair again, weak with a dread that his movement had been noticed – for the last round of beer was at his expense; it had not been paid for, and he hadn't a pfennig. He was a prisoner – Heaven only could know what might happen if he tried to leave the place. He was timid, scared, crushed; and he had not German enough to state his case and beg for help and indulgence.

Then his thoughts began to persecute him. How could he have been such a fool? What possessed him to listen to such a manifest adventurer? *And here comes the waiter!* He buried himself in the newspaper – trembling. The waiter passed by. It filled him with thankfulness. The hands of the clock seemed to stand still, yet he could not keep his eyes from them.

Ten minutes dragged by. The waiter again! Again he hid behind the paper. The waiter paused – apparently a week – then passed on.

Another ten minutes of misery – once more the waiter; this time he wiped off the table, and seemed to be a month at it; then paused two months, and went away.

Parrish felt that he could not endure another visit; he must take his chance and run the gauntlet; he must escape. But the waiter stayed around about the neighbourhood for five minutes – months and months seemingly, Parrish watching him with a despairing eye, and feeling the infirmities of age creeping upon him and his hair gradually turning grey.

At last the waiter wandered away – stopped at a table, collected a bill, wandered farther, collected another bill, wandered farther – Parrish's praying eye riveted on him all the time, his heart thumping, his breath coming and going in quick little gasps of anxiety mixed with hope.

The waiter stopped again to collect, and Parrish said to himself, it is now or never! and started for the door. One step – two steps – three – four – he was nearing the door – five – his legs shaking under him – was that a swift step behind him? – the thought shrivelled his heart – six steps – seven, and he was out! – eight – nine – ten – eleven – twelve – there *is* a pursuing step! – he turned the corner, and picked up his heels to fly – a heavy hand fell on his shoulder, and the strength went out of his body!

It was the major. He asked not a question, he showed no surprise. He said, in his breezy and exhilarating fashion, 'Confound those people, they delayed me; that's why I was gone so long. New man in the ticket-office, and he didn't know me, and wouldn't make the exchange because it was irregular; so I had to hunt up my old friend, the great mogul – the station-master, you know – hi, there, cab! cab! – jump in, Parrish! – Russian consulate, cabby, and let them fly! – so, as I say, that all cost time. But it's all right now, and everything straight; your luggage reweighed, rechecked, fare-ticket and sleeper changed, and I've got the documents for it in my pocket; also the change – I'll keep it for you. Whoop along, cabby, whoop along; don't let them go to sleep!'

Poor Parrish was trying his best to get a word in edgeways, as the cab flew farther and farther from the bilked beer-hall, and now at last he succeeded, and wanted to return at once and pay his little bill.

'Oh, never mind about that,' said the major, placidly; 'that's all right, they know me, everybody knows me – I'll square it next time I'm in Berlin – push along, cabby, push along – no great lot of time to spare, now.'

They arrived at the Russian consulate, a moment after-hours, and hurried in. No one there but a clerk. The major laid his card on the desk, and said, in the Russian tongue,

'Now, then, if you'll visa this young man's passport for Petersburg as quickly as – '

'But, dear sir, I'm not authorised, and the consul has just gone.'

'Gone where?'

'Out to the country, where he lives.'

'And he'll be back – '

'Not till morning.'

'Thunder! Oh, well, look here, I'm Major Jackson – he knows me, everybody knows me. You visa it yourself; tell him Major Jackson asked you; it'll be all right.'

But it would be desperately and fatally irregular; the clerk could not be persuaded; he almost fainted at the idea.

'Well, then, I'll tell you what you do,' said the major. 'Here's stamps and the fee – visa it in the morning, and start it along by mail.'

The clerk said, dubiously, 'He – well, he may perhaps do it, and so – '

'May? He *will!* He knows me – everybody knows me.'

'Very well,' said the clerk, 'I will tell him what you say.' He looked bewildered, and in a measure subjugated; and added, timidly: 'But – but – you know you will beat it to the frontier by twenty-four hours. There are no accommodations there for so long a wait.'

'Who's going to *wait*? Not I, if the court knows herself.'

The clerk was temporarily paralysed, and said, 'Surely, sir, you don't wish it sent to Petersburg!'

'And why not?'

'And the owner of it tarrying at the frontier, twenty-five miles away? It couldn't do him any good, in those circumstances.'

'Tarry – the mischief! Who said he was going to do any tarrying?'

'Why, you know, of course, they'll stop him at the frontier if he has no passport.'

'Indeed they won't! The chief inspector knows me – everybody does. I'll be responsible for the young man. You send it straight through to Petersburg – Hôtel de l'Europe, care of Major Jackson; tell the consul not to worry, I'm taking all the risks myself.'

The clerk hesitated, then chanced one more appeal. 'You must bear in mind, sir, that the risks are peculiarly serious, just now. The new edict is in force.'

'What is it?'

'Ten years in Siberia for being in Russia without a passport.'

'Mm – damnation!' He said it in English, for the Russian tongue is but a poor stand-by in spiritual emergencies. He mused a moment, then brisked up and resumed in Russian: 'Oh, it's all right – label her St Petersburg and let her sail! I'll fix it. They all know me there – all the authorities – everybody.'

3

The major turned out to be an adorable travelling companion, and young Parrish was charmed with him. His talk was sunshine and rainbows, and lit up the whole region around, and kept it gay and happy and cheerful; and he was full of accommodating ways, and knew all about how to do things, and when to do them, and the best way. So the long journey was a fairy dream for that young lad who had been so lonely and forlorn and friendless so many homesick weeks. At last, when the two travellers were approaching the frontier, Parrish said something about passports; then started, as if recollecting something, and added, 'Why, come to think, I don't remember your bringing my passport away from the consulate. But you did, didn't you?'

'No; it's coming by mail,' said the major, comfortably.

'C–coming – by – mail!' gasped the lad; and all the dreadful things he had heard about the terrors and disasters of passportless visitors to Russia rose in his frightened mind and turned him white to the lips. 'Oh, major – oh, my goodness, what will become of me! How *could* you do such a thing?'

The major laid a soothing hand upon the youth's shoulder and said, 'Now don't you worry, my boy, don't you worry a bit. I'm taking care of you, and I'm not going to let any harm come to you. The chief inspector knows me, and I'll explain to him, and it'll be all right – you'll see. Now don't you give yourself the least discomfort – I'll fix it all up, easy as nothing.'

Alfred trembled, and felt a great sinking inside, but he did what he could to conceal his misery, and to respond with some show of heart to the major's kindly pettings and reassurings.

At the frontier he got out and stood on the edge of the great crowd, and waited in deep anxiety while the major ploughed his way through the mass to 'explain to the chief inspector'. It seemed a cruelly long wait, but at last the major reappeared. He said, cheerfully, 'Damnation, it's a new inspector, and I don't know him!'

Alfred fell up against a pile of trunks, with a despairing, 'Oh, dear, dear, I might have known it!' and was slumping limp and helpless to the ground, but the major gathered him up and seated him on a box, and sat down by him, with a supporting arm around him, and whispered in his ear, 'Don't worry, laddie, don't – it's going to be all right; you just trust to me. The sub-inspector's as near-sighted as a shad. I watched him, and I know it's so. Now I'll tell you what to do. I'll go and get my passport chalked, then I'll stop right yonder inside the grille where you see those peasants with their packs. You be there, and I'll back up against the grille, and slip my passport to you through the bars, then you tag along after the crowd and hand it in, and trust to Providence and that shad. Mainly the shad. You'll pull through all right – now don't you be afraid.'

'But, oh dear, dear, *your* description and *mine* don't tally any more than – '

'Oh, that's all right – difference between fifty-one and

nineteen, just entirely imperceptible to that shad – don't you fret, it's going to come out as right as nails.'

Ten minutes later Alfred was tottering towards the train, pale and in a collapse, but he had played the shad successfully and was as grateful as an untaxed dog that has evaded the police.

'I told you so,' said the major, in splendid spirits. 'I knew it would come out all right if you trusted in Providence like a little trusting child and didn't try to improve on His ideas – it always does.'

Between the frontier and Petersburg the major laid himself out to restore his young comrade's life, and work up his circulation, and pull him out of his despondency, and make him feel again that life was a joy and worth living. And so, as a consequence, the young fellow entered the city in high feather and marched into the hotel in fine form, and registered his name. But instead of naming a room, the clerk glanced at him enquiringly, and waited. The major came promptly to the rescue, and said, cordially, 'It's all right – you know me – set him down, I'm responsible.' The clerk looked grave, and shook his head.

The major added, 'It's all right, it'll be here in twenty-four hours – it's coming by mail. Here's mine, and his is coming, right along.'

The clerk was full of politeness, full of deference, but he was firm. He said, in English, 'Indeed, I wish I could accommodate you, major, and certainly I would if I could; but I have no choice, I must ask him to go; I cannot allow him to remain in the house a moment.'

Parrish began to totter, and emitted a moan; the major caught him and stayed him with an arm, and said to the clerk, appealingly, 'Come, you know me – everybody does – just let him stay here the one night, and I give you my word –'

The clerk shook his head, and said, 'But, major, you are endangering me, you are endangering the house. I – I hate to do such a thing, but I – I *must* call the police.'

'Hold on, don't do that. Come along, my boy, and don't you fret – it's going to come out all right. Hi, there, cabby! Jump in, Parrish. Palace of the General of the Secret Police – turn them loose, cabby! Let them go! Make them whiz! Now we're off, and don't you give yourself any uneasiness. Prince Bossloffsky knows me, knows me like a book; he'll soon fix things all right for us.'

They tore through the gay streets and arrived at the palace, which was brilliantly lighted. But it was half-past eight; the prince was about to go in to dinner, the sentinel said, and couldn't receive anyone.

'But he'll receive *me*,' said the major, robustly, and handed his card. 'I'm Major Jackson. Send it in; it'll be all right.'

The card was sent in, under protest, and the major and his waif waited in a reception room for some time. At length they were sent for, and conducted to a sumptuous private office and confronted with the prince, who stood there gorgeously arrayed and frowning like a thundercloud. The major stated his case, and begged for a twenty-four-hour stay of proceedings until the passport should be forthcoming.

'Oh, impossible!' said the prince, in faultless English. 'I marvel that you should have done so insane a thing as to bring the lad into the country without a passport, major, I marvel at it; why, it's ten years in Siberia, and no help for it – catch him! support him!' for poor Parrish was making another trip to the floor. 'Here – quick, give him this. There – take another draught; brandy's the thing, don't you find it so, lad? Now you feel better, poor fellow. Lie down on the sofa. How stupid it was of you, major, to get him into such a horrible scrape.'

The major eased the boy down with his strong arms, put a cushion under his head, and whispered in his ear, 'Look as damned sick as you can! Play it for all it's worth; he's touched, you see; got a tender heart under there somewhere; fetch a groan, and say, "Oh, mamma, mamma"; it'll knock him out, sure as guns.'

Parrish was going to do these things anyway, from native impulse, so they came from him promptly, with great and moving sincerity, and the major whispered: 'Splendid! Do it again; Bernhardt couldn't beat it.'

What with the major's eloquence and the boy's misery, the point was gained at last; the prince struck his colours, and said, 'Have it your way; though you deserve a sharp lesson and you ought to get it. I give you exactly twenty-four hours. If the passport is not here then, don't come near me; it's Siberia without hope of pardon.'

While the major and the lad poured out their thanks, the prince rang in a couple of soldiers, and in their own language he ordered them to go with these two people and not lose sight of the younger one a moment for the next twenty-four hours; and if, at the end of that term, the boy could not show a passport, impound him in the dungeons of St Peter and St Paul, and report.

The unfortunates arrived at the hotel with their guards, dined under their eyes, remained in Parrish's room until the major went off to bed, after cheering up the said Parrish, then one of the soldiers locked himself and Parrish in, and the other one stretched himself across the door outside and soon went off to sleep.

So also did not Alfred Parrish. The moment he was alone with the solemn soldier and the voiceless silence his machine-made cheerfulness began to waste away, his medicated courage began to give off its supporting gases and shrink towards normal, and his poor little heart to shrivel like a raisin. Within thirty minutes he struck bottom; grief, misery, fright, despair, could go no lower. Bed? Bed was not for such as he; bed was not for the doomed, the lost! Sleep? He was not the Hebrew children, he could not sleep in the fire! He could only walk the floor. And not only could, but must. And did, by the hour. And mourned, and wept, and shuddered, and prayed.

Then all-sorrowfully he made his last dispositions, and prepared himself, as well as in him lay, to meet his fate. As a final act, he wrote a letter:

MY DARLING MOTHER – When these sad lines shall have reached you your poor Alfred will be no more. No; worse than that, far worse! Through my own fault and foolishness I have fallen into the hands of a sharper or a lunatic; I do not know which, but in either case I feel that I am lost. Sometimes I think he is a sharper, but most of the time I think he is only mad, for he has a kind, good heart, I know, and he certainly seems to try the hardest that ever a person tried to get me out of the fatal difficulties he has gotten me into.

In a few hours I shall be one of a nameless horde plodding the snowy solitudes of Russia, under the lash, and bound for that land of mystery and misery and termless oblivion, Siberia! I shall not live to see it; my heart is broken and I shall die. Give my picture to *her*, and ask her to keep it in memory of me, and to so live that in the appointed time she may join me in that better world where there is no marriage nor giving in marriage, and where there are no more separations, and troubles never come. Give my yellow dog to Archy Hale, and the other one to Henry Taylor; my blazer I give to brother Will, and my fishing things and Bible.

There is no hope for me. I cannot escape; the soldier stands there with his gun and never takes his eyes off me, just blinks; there is no other movement, any more than if he was dead. I cannot bribe him, the maniac has my money. My letter of credit is in my trunk, and may never come – *will* never come, I know. Oh, what is to become of me! Pray for me, darling mother, pray for your poor Alfred. But it will do no good.

4

In the morning Alfred came out looking scraggy and worn when the major summoned him to an early breakfast. They fed their guards, they lit cigars, the major loosened his tongue and set it going, and under its magic influence Alfred gradually and gratefully became hopeful, measurably cheerful, and almost happy once more.

But he would not leave the house. Siberia hung over him black and threatening, his appetite for sights was all gone, he could not have borne the shame of inspecting streets and galleries and churches with a soldier at each elbow and all the world stopping and staring and commenting – no, he would stay within and wait for the Berlin mail and his fate. So, all day long the major stood gallantly by him in his room, with one soldier standing stiff and motionless against the door with his musket at his shoulder, and the other one drowsing in a chair outside; and all day long the faithful veteran spun campaign yarns, described battles, reeled off explosive anecdotes, with unconquerable energy and sparkle and resolution, and kept the scared student alive and his pulses functioning. The long day wore to a close, and the pair, followed by their guards, went down to the great dining-room and took their seats.

'The suspense will be over before long, now,' sighed poor Alfred.

Just then a pair of Englishmen passed by, and one of them said, 'So we'll get no letters from Berlin tonight?'

Parrish's breath began to fail him. The Englishmen seated themselves at a nearby table, and the other one said, 'No, it isn't as bad as that.'

Parrish's breathing improved.

'There is later telegraphic news. The accident did detain the train formidably, but that is all. It will arrive here three hours late tonight.'

Parrish did not get to the floor this time, for the major jumped for him in time. He had been listening, and foresaw what would happen. He patted Parrish on the back, hoisted him out of his chair, and said, cheerfully, 'Come along, my boy, cheer up, there's absolutely nothing to worry about. I know a way out. Bother the passport; let it lag a week if it wants to, we can do without it.'

Parrish was too sick to hear him; hope was gone, Siberia present; he moved off on legs of lead, upheld by the major, who walked him to the American legation, heartening him on the way with assurances that on his recommendation the minister wouldn't hesitate a moment to grant him a new passport.

'I had that card up my sleeve all the time,' he said. 'The minister knows me – knows me familiarly – chummed together hours and hours under a pile of other wounded at Cold Harbour; been chummies ever since, in spirit, though we haven't met much in the body. Cheer up, laddie, everything's looking splendid! By gracious! I feel as cocky as a buck angel. Here we are, and our troubles are at an end! If we ever really had any.'

There, alongside the door, was the trademark of the richest and freest and mightiest republic of all the ages: the pine disk, with the planked eagle spread upon it, his head and shoulders among the stars, and his claws full of out-of-date war material; and at that sight the tears came into Alfred's eyes, the pride of country rose in his heart, Hail Columbia boomed up in his breast, and all his fears and sorrows vanished away; for here he was safe, safe! not all the powers of the earth would venture to cross that threshold to lay a hand upon him!

For economy's sake the mightiest republic's legations in Europe consist of a room and a half on the ninth floor, when the tenth is occupied, and the legation furniture consists of a minister or an ambassador with a brakeman's salary, a secretary of legation who sells matches and mends crockery for a living, a hired girl for interpreter and general utility, pictures of the

American liners, a chromo of the reigning President, a desk, three chairs, kerosene-lamp, a cat, a clock and a cuspidor with the motto 'In God We Trust.'

The party climbed up there, followed by the escort. A man sat at the desk writing official things on wrapping paper with a marker. He rose and faced about; the cat climbed down and got under the desk; the hired girl squeezed herself up into the corner by the vodka-jug to make room; the soldiers squeezed themselves up against the wall alongside of her, with muskets at shoulder arms. Alfred was radiant with happiness and the sense of rescue. The major cordially shook hands with the official, rattled off his case in easy and fluent style, and asked for the desired passport.

The official seated his guests, then said, 'Well, I am only the secretary of legation, you know, and I wouldn't like to grant a passport while the minister is on Russian soil. There is far too much responsibility.'

'All right, send for him.'

The secretary smiled, and said: 'That's easier said than done. He's away up in the wilds, somewhere, on his vacation.'

'Ger–reat Scott!' ejaculated the major.

Alfred groaned; the colour went out of his face, and he began slowly to collapse inside his clothes. The secretary said, wonderingly, 'Why, what are you Great-Scotting about, major? The prince gave you twenty-four hours. Look at the clock; you're all right; you've half an hour left; the train is just due; the passport will arrive in time.'

'Man, there's news! The train is three hours behind time! This boy's life and liberty are wasting away by minutes, and only thirty of them left! In half an hour he's the same as dead and damned to all eternity! By God, we *must* have the passport!'

'Oh, I am dying, I know it!' wailed the lad, and buried his face in his arms on the desk.

A quick change came over the secretary, his placidity vanished away, excitement flamed up in his face and eyes, and he exclaimed, 'I see the whole ghastliness of the situation, but, Lord help us, what can I do? What can you suggest?'

'Why, hang it, give him the passport!'

'Impossible! totally impossible! You know nothing about him; three days ago you had never heard of him; there's no way in the world to identify him. He is lost, lost – there's no possibility of saving him!'

The boy groaned again, and sobbed out, 'Lord, Lord, it's the last of earth for Alfred Parrish!'

Another change came over the secretary.

In the midst of a passionate outburst of pity, vexation and hopelessness, he stopped short, his manner calmed down, and he asked, in the indifferent voice which one uses in introducing the subject of the weather when there is nothing to talk about, 'Is that your name?'

The youth sobbed out a yes.

'Where are you from?'

'Bridgeport.'

The secretary shook his head – shook it again – and muttered to himself. After a moment, 'Born there?'

'No; New Haven.'

'Ah–h.' The secretary glanced at the major, who was listening intently, with blank and unenlightened face, and indicated rather than said, 'There is vodka there, in case the soldiers are thirsty.' The major sprang up, poured for them, and received their gratitude. The questioning went on.

'How long did you live in New Haven?'

'Till I was fourteen. Came back two years ago to enter Yale.'

'When you lived there, what street did you live on?'

'Parker Street.'

With a vague half-light of comprehension dawning in his eye, the major glanced an enquiry at the secretary. The secretary nodded, the major poured vodka again.

'What number?'

'It hadn't any.'

The boy sat up and gave the secretary a pathetic look which said, 'Why do you want to torture me with these foolish things, when I am miserable enough without it?'

The secretary went on, unheeding: 'What kind of a house was it?'

'Brick – two storey.'

'Flush with the sidewalk?'

'No, small yard in front.'

'Iron fence?'

'No, palings.'

The major poured vodka again – without instructions – poured brimmers this time; and his face had cleared and was alive now.

'What do you see when you enter the door?'

'A narrow hall; door at the end of it, and a door at your right.'

'Anything else?'

'Hat-rack.'

'Room at the right?'

'Parlour.'

'Carpet?'

'Yes.'

'Kind of carpet?'

'Old-fashioned Wilton.'

'Figures?'

'Yes – hawking-party, horseback.'

The major cast an eye at the clock – only six minutes left! He faced about with the jug, and as he poured he glanced at the secretary, then at the clock – enquiringly. The secretary nodded; the major covered the clock from view with his body a moment, and set the hands back half an hour; then he refreshed the men – double rations.

'Room beyond the hall and hat-rack?'

'Dining-room.'

'Stove?'

'Grate.'

'Did your people own the house?'

'Yes.'

'Do they own it yet?'

'No; sold it when we moved to Bridgeport.'

The secretary paused a little, then said, 'Did you have a nickname among your playmates?'

The colour slowly rose in the youth's pale cheeks, and he dropped his eyes. He seemed to struggle with himself a moment or two, then he said, plaintively, 'They called me Miss Nancy.'

The secretary mused awhile, then he dug up another question, 'Any ornaments in the dining-room?'

'Well, y – no.'

'*None?* None at *all*?'

'No.'

'The mischief! Isn't that a little odd? Think!'

The youth thought and thought; the secretary waited, slightly panting. At last the imperilled waif looked up sadly and shook his head.

'Think – *think*!' cried the major, in anxious solicitude; and poured again.

'Come!' said the secretary, 'not even a *picture*?'

'Oh, certainly! but you said ornament.'

'Ah! What did your father think of it?'

The colour rose again. The boy was silent.

'Speak,' said the secretary.

'Speak,' cried the major, and his trembling hand poured more vodka outside the glasses than inside.

'I – I can't tell you what he said,' murmured the boy.

'Quick! quick!' said the secretary; 'out with it; there's no time to lose – home and liberty or Siberia and death depend upon the answer.'

'Oh, have pity! he is a clergyman, and – '

'No matter; out with it, or – '

'He said it was the hellfiredest nightmare he ever struck!'

'Saved!' shouted the secretary, and seized his pen and a blank passport. '*I* identify you; I've lived in the house, and I painted the picture myself!'

'Oh, come to my arms, my poor rescued boy!' cried the major. 'We will always be grateful to God that He made this artist! – if He did.'

KATHERINE MANSFIELD

Kathleen Mansfield Beauchamp (1888–1923), who wrote short stories under the name Katherine Mansfield, was born in Wellington, New Zealand, daughter of a banker, who was later knighted. Her first story was published when she was nine, and later, when at Queen's College, London, she edited the college magazine, but her plans then were for a musical career. In 1909 she married George Bowden, but left him after a few days. In 1911 she met John Middleton Murry, whom she married in 1918 when she obtained a divorce from her first husband. Ill-health due to lung trouble made her move about seeking a congenial climate, and she lived at different times in France and in Germany. In 1920 *Bliss and Other Stories* made her famous. Other collections were *The Garden Party* (1922), *The Dove's Nest* (1923), *Something Childish* (1924) and *The Aloe* (1930). In 1922 she went to Paris for special treatment and died at Fontainebleau. Her *Poems* were published in 1923 and her autobiographical *Journal* (1927), *Letters* (1928) and *Scrapbook* (1940) were all edited by her husband after her death.

The Journey to Bruges

'You got three-quarters of an hour,' said the porter. 'You got an hour mostly. Put it in the cloakroom, lady.'

A German family, their luggage neatly buttoned into what appeared to be odd canvas trouser legs, filled the entire space before the counter, and a homoeopathic young clergyman, his black dicky flapping over his shirt, stood at my elbow. We waited and waited, for the cloakroom porter could not get rid of the German family, who appeared by their enthusiasm and gestures to be explaining to him the virtue of so many buttons. At last the wife of the party seized her particular packet and started to undo it. Shrugging his shoulders, the porter turned to me. 'Where for?' he asked.

'Ostend.'

'Wot are you putting it in here for?'

I said, 'Because I've a long time to wait.'

He shouted, 'Train's in 2.20. No good bringing it here. Hi, you there, lump it off!'

My porter lumped it. The young clergyman, who had listened and remarked, smiled at me radiantly. 'The train is in,' he said, 'really in. You've only a few moments, you know.' My sensitiveness glimpsed a symbol in his eye. I ran to the bookstall. When I returned I had lost my porter. In the teasing heat I ran up and down the platform. The whole travelling world seemed to possess a porter and glory in him except me. Savage and wretched I saw them watch me with that delighted relish of the hot in the very much hotter. 'One could have a fit running in weather like this,' said a stout lady, eating a farewell present of grapes. Then I was informed that the train was not yet in. I had been running up and down the Folkestone express. On a higher platform I found my porter sitting on the suitcase.

'I knew you'd be doin' that,' he said airily. 'I nearly come and stop you. I seen you from 'ere.'

I dropped into a smoking compartment with four young men, two of whom were saying goodbye to a pale youth with a cane. 'Well, goodbye, old chap. It's frightfully good of you to have come down. I knew you. I knew the same old slouch. Now, look here, when we come back we'll have a night of it. What? Ripping of you to have come, old man.' This from an enthusiast, who lit a cigar as the train swung out, turned to his companion and said, 'Frightfully nice chap, but – lord – what a bore!' His companion, who was dressed entirely in mole, even unto his socks and hair, smiled gently. I think his brain must have been the same colour: he proved so gentle and sympathetic a listener. In the opposite corner to me sat a beautiful young Frenchman with curly hair and a watch-chain from which dangled a silver fish, a ring, a silver shoe and a medal. He stared out of the window the whole time, faintly twitching his nose. Of the remaining member there was nothing to be seen from behind his luggage but a pair of tan shoes and a copy of *The Snark's Summer Annual*.

'Look here, old man,' said the Enthusiast, 'I want to change all our places. You know those arrangements you've made – I want to cut them out altogether. Do you mind?'

'No,' said the Mole faintly. 'But why?'

'Well, I was thinking it over in bed last night, and I'm hanged if I can see the good of us paying fifteen bob if we don't want to. You see what I mean?' The Mole took off his pince-nez and breathed on them. 'Now I don't want to unsettle you,' went on the Enthusiast, 'because, after all, it's your party – you asked me. I wouldn't upset it for anything, but – there you are – you see – what?'

Suggested the Mole: 'I'm afraid people will be down on me for taking you abroad.'

Straightway the other told him how sought after he had been. From far and near, people who were full up for the entire month of August had written and begged for him. He wrung the Mole's heart by enumerating those longing homes and vacant chairs dotted all over England, until the Mole deliberated between crying and going to sleep. He chose the latter.

They all went to sleep except the young Frenchman, who took a little pocket edition out of his coat and nursed it on his knee while he gazed at the warm, dusty country. At Shorncliffe the train stopped. Dead silence. There was nothing to be seen but a large white cemetery. Fantastic it looked in the late afternoon sun, its full-length marble angels appearing to preside over a cheerless picnic of the Shorncliffe departed on the brown field. One white butterfly flew over the railway lines. As we crept out of the station I saw a poster advertising the *Athenaeum*. The Enthusiast grunted and yawned, shook himself into existence by rattling the money in his trouser pockets. He jabbed the Mole in the ribs. 'I say, we're nearly there! Can you get down those beastly golf-clubs of mine from the rack?' My heart yearned over the Mole's immediate future, but he was cheerful and offered to find me a porter at Dover, and strapped my parasol in with my rugs. We saw the sea. 'It's going to be beastly rough,' said the Enthusiast. 'Gives you a head, doesn't it? Look here, I know a tip for sea-sickness, and it's this: You lie on your back – flat – you know, cover your face, and eat nothing but biscuits.'

'Dover!' shouted a guard.

In the act of crossing the gangway we renounced England. The most blatant British female produced her mite of French: we '*S'il vous plaît?*'d one another on the deck, '*Merci*'d one another on the stairs, and '*Pardon*'d to our heart's content in the saloon. The stewardess stood at the foot of the stairs, a stout, forbidding female, pock-marked, her hands hidden under a businesslike-looking apron. She replied to our salutations with studied indifference, mentally ticking off her prey. I descended to the cabin to remove my hat. One old lady was already established there.

She lay on a rose and white couch, a black shawl tucked round her, fanning herself with a black feather fan. Her grey hair was half covered with a lace cap and her face gleamed from the black drapings and rose pillows with charming old-world dignity. There was about her a faint rustling and the scents of camphor and lavender. As I watched her, thinking of Rembrandt and, for some reason, Anatole France, the stewardess bustled up, placed a canvas stool at her elbow, spread a newspaper upon it, and banged down a receptacle rather like a baking tin . . .

I went up on deck. The sea was bright green, with rolling waves. All the beauty and artificial flower of France had removed their hats and bound their heads in veils. A number of young German men, displaying their national bulk in light-coloured suits cut in the pattern of pyjamas, promenaded. French family parties – the female element in chairs, the male in graceful attitudes against the ship's side – talked already with that brilliance which denotes friction! I found a chair in a corner against a white partition, but unfortunately this partition had a window set in it for the purpose of providing endless amusement for the curious, who peered through it, watching those bold and brave spirits who walked 'for'ard' and were drenched and beaten by the waves. In the first half-hour the excitement of getting wet and being pleaded with, and rushing into dangerous places to return and be rubbed down, was all-absorbing. Then it palled – the parties drifted into silence. You would catch them staring intently at the ocean – and yawning. They grew cold and snappy.

Suddenly a young lady in a white woollen hood with cherry bows got up from her chair and swayed over to the railings. We watched her, vaguely sympathetic.

The young man with whom she had been sitting called to her. 'Are you better?'

Negative expressed.

He sat up in his chair. 'Would you like me to hold your head?'

'No,' said her shoulders.

'Would you care for a coat round you? . . . Is it over? . . . Are you going to remain there?' . . . He looked at her with infinite tenderness. I decided never again to call men unsympathetic, and to believe in the all-conquering power of love until I died – but never put it to the test. I went down to sleep.

I lay down opposite the old lady, and watched the shadows spinning over the ceilings and the wave-drops shining on the portholes.

In the shortest sea voyage there is no sense of time. You have been down in the cabin for hours or days or years. Nobody knows or cares. You know all the people to the point of indifference. You do not believe in dry land any more – you are caught in the pendulum itself, and left there, idly swinging. The light faded.

I fell asleep, to wake to find the stewardess shaking me. 'We are there in two minutes,' said she. Forlorn ladies, freed from the embrace of Neptune, knelt upon the floor and searched for their shoes and hairpins – only the old and dignified one lay passive, fanning herself. She looked at me and smiled.

'Grâce de Dieu, c'est fini,' she quavered in a voice so fine it seemed to quaver on a thread of lace.

I lifted up my eyes. 'Oui, c'est fini!'

'Vous allez à Strasbourg, madame?'

'No,' I said. 'Bruges.'

'That is a great pity,' said she, closing her fan and the conversation. I could not think why, but I had visions of myself perhaps travelling in the same railway carriage with her, wrapping her in the black shawl, of her falling in love with me and leaving me unlimited quantities of money and old lace . . . These sleepy thoughts pursued me until I arrived on deck.

The sky was indigo blue, and a great many stars were shining: our little ship stood black and sharp in the clear air. 'Have you the tickets? . . . Yes, they want the tickets . . . Produce your tickets!' . . . We were squeezed over the gangway, shepherded into the custom-house, where porters heaved our luggage on to long wooden slabs, and an old man wearing horn spectacles checked it without a word. 'Follow me!' shouted the villainous-looking creature whom I had endowed with my worldly goods. He leapt on to a railway line, and I leapt after him. He raced along a platform, dodging the passengers and fruit waggons, with the security of a cinematograph figure. I reserved a seat and went to buy fruit at a little stall displaying grapes and greengages. The old lady was there, leaning on the arm of a large blond man, in white, with a flowing tie. We nodded.

'Buy me,' she said in her delicate voice, 'three ham sandwiches, *mon cher*!'

'And some cakes,' said he.

'Yes, and perhaps a bottle of lemonade.'

'Romance is an imp!' thought I, climbing up into the carriage. The train swung out of the station; the air, blowing through the open windows, smelled of fresh leaves. There were sudden pools of light in the darkness; when I arrived at Bruges the bells were ringing, and white and mysterious shone the moon over the Grand Place.

ROBERT LOUIS STEVENSON

Robert Louis Stevenson (1850–94) was born in Edinburgh, son of Thomas Stevenson the lighthouse engineer. He studied at Edinburgh, became a lawyer (1875), then turned to writing travel sketches, essays and short stories for magazines. The archetypal adventure story *Treasure Island* (1883) brought him fame, and entered him on a course of romantic fiction which included *Kidnapped* (1886), *The Strange Case of Dr Jekyll and Mr Hyde* (1886), *The Master of Ballantrae* (1889), *Catriona* (1893) and the unfinished *Weir of Hermiston* (1896), considered his masterpiece. He suffered from a chronic bronchial condition and in 1888 he settled for health reasons at Vailima, Samoa, where he died of a cerebral haemorrhage six years later.

The Beach at Falesá

1

A South Sea Bridal

I saw that island first when it was neither night nor morning. The moon was to the west, setting, but still broad and bright. To the east, and right amidships of the dawn, which was all pink, the day-star sparkled like a diamond. The land breeze blew in our faces, and smelt strong of wild lime and vanilla; other things besides, but these were the most plain; and the chill of it set me sneezing. I should say I had been for years on a low island near the line, living for the most part solitary among natives. Here was a fresh experience: even the tongue would be quite strange to me; and the look of these woods and mountains, and the rare smell of them, renewed my blood.

The captain blew out the binnacle lamp.

'There!' said he, 'there goes a bit of smoke, Mr Wiltshire, behind the break of the reef. That's Falesá, where your station is, the last village to the east; nobody lives to windward – I don't know why. Take my glass, and you can make the houses out.'

I took the glass; and the shores leaped nearer, and I saw the tangle of the woods and the breach of the surf, and the brown roofs and the black insides of houses peeped among the trees.

'Do you catch a bit of white there to the east'ard?' the captain continued. 'That's your house. Coral built, stands high, verandah you could walk on three abreast; best station in the South Pacific. When old Adams saw it, he took and shook me by the hand. "I've dropped into a soft thing here," says he. "So you have," says I, "and time too!" Poor Johnny! I never saw him again but the once, and then he had changed his tune – couldn't get on with the natives, or the whites, or something; and the next time we came round there he was dead and buried. I took and put up a bit of a stick to him: "John Adams, *obit* eighteen sixty-eight. Go thou and do likewise." I missed that man. I never could see much harm in Johnny.'

'What did he die of?' I enquired.

'Some kind of sickness,' said the captain. 'It appears it took him sudden. Seems he got up in the night, and filled up on Pain-Killer and Kennedy's Discovery. No go: he was booked beyond Kennedy. Then he had tried to open a case of gin. No go again: not strong enough. Then he must have turned to and run out on the verandah, and capsized over the rail. When they found him, the next day, he was clean crazy – carried on all the time about somebody watering his copra. Poor John!'

'Was it thought to be the island?' I asked.

'Well, it was thought to be the island, or the trouble, or something,' he replied. 'I never could hear but what it was a healthy place. Our last man, Vigours, never turned a hair. He left because of the beach – said he was afraid of Black Jack and Case and

Whistling Jimmie, who was still alive at the time, but got drowned soon afterwards when drunk. As for old Captain Randall, he's been here any time since eighteen-forty, forty-five. I never could see much harm in Billy, nor much change. Seems as if he might live to be Old Kafoozleum. No, I guess it's healthy.'

'There's a boat coming now,' said I. 'She's right in the pass; looks to be a sixteen-foot whaler; two white men in the stern sheets.'

'That's the boat that drowned Whistling Jimmie!' cried the captain; 'let's see the glass. Yes, that's Case, sure enough, and the darkie. They've got a gallows bad reputation, but you know what a place the beach is for talking. My belief's that Whistling Jimmie was the worst of the trouble; and he's gone to glory, you see. What'll you bet they ain't after gin? Lay you five to two they take six cases.'

When these two traders came aboard I was pleased with the looks of them at once, or, rather, with the looks of both, and the speech of one. I was sick for white neighbours after my four years at the line, which I always counted years of prison; getting tabooed, and going down to the Speak House to get it taken off; buying gin and going on a break, and then repenting; sitting in the house at night with the lamp for company; or walking on the beach and wondering what kind of a fool to call myself for being where I was. There were no other whites upon my island, and when I sailed to the next, rough customers made the most of the society. Now to see these two when they came aboard was a pleasure. One was a negro, to be sure; but they were both rigged out smart in striped pyjamas and straw hats, and Case would have passed muster in a city. He was yellow and smallish, had a hawk's nose to his face, pale eyes, and his beard trimmed with scissors. No man knew his country, beyond he was of English speech; and it was clear he came of a good family and was splendidly educated. He was accomplished too; played the accordion first-rate; and give him a piece of string or a cork or a pack of cards, and he could show you tricks equal to any professional. He could speak, when he chose, fit for a drawing-room; and when he chose he could blaspheme worse than a Yankee boatswain, and talk smart to sicken a Kanaka. The way he thought would pay best at the moment, that was Case's way, and it always seemed to come natural, and like as if he was born to it. He had the courage of a lion and the cunning of a rat; and if he's not in hell today, there's no such place. I know but one good point to the man: that he was fond of his wife, and kind to her. She was a Samoa woman, and dyed her hair red, Samoa style; and when he came to die (as I have to tell of) they found one strange thing – that he had made a will, like a Christian, and the widow got the lot: all his, they said, and all Black Jack's, and the most of Billy Randall's in the bargain, for it was Case that kept the books. So she went off home in the schooner *Manu'a*, and does the lady to this day in her own place.

But of all this on that first morning I knew no more than a fly. Case used me like a gentleman and like a friend, made me welcome to Falesá, and put his services at my disposal, which was the more helpful from my ignorance of the native. All the better part of the day we sat drinking better acquaintance in the cabin, and I never heard a man talk more to the point. There was no smarter trader, and none dodgier, in the islands. I thought Falesá seemed to be the right kind of a place; and the more I drank the lighter my heart. Our last trader had fled the place at half an hour's notice, taking a chance passage in a labour ship from up west. The captain, when he came, had found the station closed, the keys left with the native pastor, and a letter from the runaway, confessing he was fairly frightened of his life. Since then the firm had not been represented, and of course there was no cargo. The wind, besides, was fair, the captain hoped he could make his next island by dawn, with a good tide, and the business of landing my trade was gone about lively. There was no call for me to fool with it, Case said; nobody would touch my things, everyone was honest in Falesá, only about chickens or an odd knife or an odd stick of tobacco; and the best I could do was to sit quiet till the vessel left, then come straight to his house, see old Captain Randall, the father of the beach, take pot-luck, and go home to sleep when it got dark. So it was high noon, and the schooner was under way before I set my foot on shore at Falesá.

I had a glass or two on board; I was just off a long cruise, and the ground heaved under me like a ship's deck. The world was like all new painted; my foot went along to music; Falesá might have been Fiddler's Green, if there is such a place, and more's the pity if there isn't! It was good to foot the grass, to look aloft at the green mountains, to see the men with their green wreaths and the women in their bright dresses, red and blue. On we went, in the strong sun and the cool shadow, liking both; and all the children in the town came trotting after with their shaven heads and their brown bodies, and raising a thin kind of a cheer in our wake, like crowing poultry.

'By the by,' says Case, 'we must get you a wife.'

'That's so,' said I; 'I had forgotten.'

There was a crowd of girls about us, and I pulled myself up and looked among them like a bashaw. They were all dressed out for the sake of the ship being in; and the women of Falesá are a handsome lot to see. If they have a fault, they are a trifle broad in the beam; and I was just thinking so when Case touched me.

'That's pretty,' says he.

I saw one coming on the other side alone. She had been fishing; all she wore was a chemise, and it was wetted through. She was young and very slender for an island maid, with a long face, a high forehead, and a shy, strange, blindish look, between a cat's and a baby's.

'Who's she?' said I. 'She'll do.'

'That's Uma,' said Case, and he called her up and spoke to

her in the native. I didn't know what he said; but when he was in the midst she looked up at me quick and timid, like a child dodging a blow, then down again, and presently smiled. She had a wide mouth, the lips and the chin cut like any statue's; and the smile came out for a moment and was gone. Then she stood with her head bent, and heard Case to an end, spoke back in the pretty Polynesian voice, looking him full in the face, heard him again in answer, and then with an obeisance started off. I had just a share of the bow, but never another shot of her eye, and there was no more word of smiling.

'I guess it's all right,' said Case. 'I guess you can have her. I'll make it square with the old lady. You can have your pick of the lot for a plug of tobacco,' he added, sneering.

I suppose it was the smile stuck in my memory, for I spoke back sharp. 'She doesn't look that sort,' I cried.

'I don't know that she is,' said Case. 'I believe she's as right as the mail. Keeps to herself, don't go round with the gang, and that. Oh no, don't you misunderstand me – Uma's on the square.' He spoke eager, I thought, and that surprised and pleased me. 'Indeed,' he went on, 'I shouldn't make so sure of getting her, only she cottoned to the cut of your jib. All you have to do is to keep dark and let me work the mother my own way; and I'll bring the girl round to the captain's for the marriage.'

I didn't care for the word marriage, and I said so.

'Oh, there's nothing to hurt in the marriage,' says he. 'Black Jack's the chaplain.'

By this time we had come in view of the house of these three white men; for a negro is counted a white man, and so is a Chinese! a strange idea, but common in the islands. It was a board house with a strip of rickety verandah. The store was to the front, with a counter, scales, and the poorest possible display of trade: a case or two of tinned meats; a barrel of hard bread; a few bolts of cotton stuff, not to be compared with mine; the only thing well represented being the contraband, firearms and liquor. If these are my only rivals, thinks I, I should do well in Falesá. Indeed, there was only the one way they could touch me, and that was with the guns and drink.

In the back room was old Captain Randall, squatting on the floor native fashion, fat and pale, naked to the waist, grey as a badger, and his eyes set with drink. His body was covered with grey hair and crawled over by flies; one was in the corner of his eye – he never heeded; and the mosquitoes hummed about the man like bees. Any clean-minded man would have had the creature out at once and buried him; and to see him, and think he was seventy, and remember he had once commanded a ship, and come ashore in his smart togs, and talked big in bars and consulates, and sat in club verandahs, turned me sick and sober.

He tried to get up when I came in, but that was hopeless; so he reached me a hand instead, and stumbled out some salutation.

'Papa's pretty full this morning,' observed Case. 'We've had an epidemic here; and Captain Randall takes gin for a prophylactic – don't you, papa?'

'Never took such a thing in my life!' cried the captain indignantly. 'Take gin for my health's sake, Mr Wha's-ever-your-name – 's a precautionary measure.'

'That's all right, papa,' said Case. 'But you'll have to brace up. There's going to be a marriage – Mr Wiltshire here is going to get spliced.'

The old man asked to whom.

'To Uma,' said Case.

'Uma!' cried the captain. 'Wha's he want Uma for? 's he come here for his health, anyway? Wha' 'n hell's he want Uma for?'

'Dry up, papa,' said Case. ' 'Tain't you that's to marry her. I guess you're not her godfather and godmother. I guess Mr Wiltshire's going to please himself.'

With that he made an excuse to me that he must move about the marriage, and left me alone with the poor wretch that was his partner and (to speak truth) his gull. Trade and station belonged both to Randall; Case and the negro were parasites; they crawled and fed upon him like the flies, he none the wiser. Indeed, I have no harm to say of Billy Randall beyond the fact that my gorge rose at him, and the time I now passed in his company was like a nightmare.

The room was stifling hot and full of flies; for the house was dirty and low and small, and stood in a bad place, behind the village, in the borders of the bush and sheltered from the trade. The three men's beds were on the floor, and a litter of pans and dishes. There was no standing furniture; Randall, when he was violent, tearing it to laths. There I sat and had a meal which was served us by Case's wife; and there I was entertained all day by that remains of a man, his tongue stumbling among low old jokes and long old stories, and his own wheezy laughter always ready, so that he had no sense of my depression. He was nipping gin all the while. Sometimes he fell asleep, and awoke again, whimpering and shivering, and every now and again he would ask me why I wanted to marry Uma. 'My friend,' I was telling myself all day, 'you must not come to be an old gentleman like this.'

It might be four in the afternoon, perhaps, when the back door was thrust slowly open and a strange old native woman crawled into the house almost on her belly. She was swathed in black stuff to her heels; her hair was grey in swatches; her face was tattooed, which was not the practice in that island; her eyes big and bright and crazy. These she fixed upon me with a rapt expression that I saw to be part acting. She said no plain word, but smacked and mumbled with her lips, and hummed aloud, like a child over its Christmas pudding. She came straight across the house, heading for me, and, as soon as she was alongside, caught up my hand and purred and crooned over it like a great cat. From this she slipped into a kind of song.

'Who the devil's this?' cried I, for the thing startled me.

'It's Fa'avao,' says Randall; and I saw he had hitched along the floor into the farthest corner.

'You ain't afraid of her?' I cried.

'Me 'fraid!' cried the captain. 'My dear friend, I defy her! I don't let her put her foot in here, only I suppose 's different today, for the marriage. 's Uma's mother.'

'Well, suppose it is; what's she carrying on about?' I asked, more irritated, perhaps more frightened, than I cared to show; and the captain told me she was making up a quantity of poetry in my praise because I was to marry Uma. 'All right, old lady,' says I, with rather a failure of a laugh, 'anything to oblige. But when you're done with my hand, you might let me know.'

She did as though she understood; the song rose into a cry, and stopped; the woman crouched out of the house the same way that she came in, and must have plunged straight into the bush, for when I followed her to the door she had already vanished.

'These are rum manners,' said I.

''s a rum crowd,' said the captain, and, to my surprise, he made the sign of the cross on his bare bosom.

'Hillo!' says I, 'are you a Papist?'

He repudiated the idea with contempt. 'Hard-shell Baptis',' said he. 'But, my dear friend, the Papists got some good ideas too; and tha' 's one of 'em. You take my advice, and whenever you come across Uma or Fa'avao or Vigours, or any of that crowd, you take a leaf out o' the priests, and do what I do. Savvy?' says he, repeating the sign, and winked his dim eye at me. 'No, *sir*!' he broke out again, 'no Papists here!' and for a long time entertained me with his religious opinions.

I must have been taken with Uma from the first, or I should certainly have fled from that house, and got into the clean air, and the clean sea, or some convenient river – though, it's true, I was committed to Case; and, besides, I could never have held my head up in that island if I had run from a girl upon my wedding-night.

The sun was down, the sky all on fire, and the lamp had been some time lighted, when Case came back with Uma and the negro. She was dressed and scented; her kilt was of fine tapa, looking richer in the folds than any silk; her bust, which was of the colour of dark honey, she wore bare only for some half a dozen necklaces of seeds and flowers; and behind her ears and in her hair she had the scarlet flowers of the hibiscus. She showed the best bearing for a bride conceivable, serious and still; and I thought shame to stand up with her in that mean house and before that grinning negro. I thought shame, I say; for the mountebank was dressed with a big paper collar, the book he made believe to read from was an odd volume of a novel, and the words of his service not fit to be set down. My conscience smote me when we joined hands; and when she got her certificate I was tempted to throw up the bargain and confess. Here is the document. It was Case that wrote it, signatures and all, in a leaf out of the ledger:

> This is to certify that Uma, daughter of Fa'avao of Falesá, island of —, is illegally married to Mr John Wiltshire for one week, and Mr John Wiltshire is at liberty to send her to hell when he pleases.
>
> John Blackamoar
> Chaplain to the Hulks
>
> *Extracted from the Register by William T. Randall,*
> *Master Mariner*

A nice paper to put in a girl's hand and see her hide away like gold. A man might easily feel cheap for less. But it was the practice in these parts, and (as I told myself) not the least fault of us white men, but of the missionaries. If they had let the natives be, I had never needed this deception, but taken all the wives I wished, and left them when I pleased, with a clear conscience.

The more ashamed I was, the more hurry I was in to be gone; and our desires thus jumping together, I made the less remark of a change in the traders. Case had been all eagerness to keep me; now, as though he had attained a purpose, he seemed all eagerness to have me go. Uma, he said, could show me to my house, and the three bade us farewell indoors.

The night was nearly come; the village smelt of trees and flowers and the sea and bread-fruit cooking; there came a fine roll of sea from the reef, and from a distance, among the woods and houses, many pretty sounds of men and children. It did me good to breathe free air; it did me good to be done with the captain and see, instead, the creature at my side. I felt for all the world as though she were some girl at home in the Old Country, and, forgetting myself for the minute, took her hand to walk with. Her fingers nestled into mine, I heard her breathe deep and quick, and all at once she caught my hand to her face and pressed it there. 'You good!' she cried, and ran ahead of me, and stopped and looked back and smiled, and ran ahead of me again, thus guiding me through the edge of the bush, and by a quiet way to my own house.

The truth is, Case had done the courting for me in style – told her I was mad to have her, and cared nothing for the consequence; and the poor soul, knowing that which I was still ignorant of, believed it, every word, and had her head nigh turned with vanity and gratitude. Now, of all this I had no guess; I was one of those most opposed to any nonsense about native women, having seen so many whites eaten up by their wives' relatives, and made fools of in the bargain; and I told myself I must make a stand at once, and bring her to her bearings. But she looked so quaint and pretty as she ran away and then awaited me, and the thing was done so like a child or a kind dog, that the best I could do was just to follow her whenever she went on, to listen for the fall of her bare feet, and to watch in the dusk for the shining of her body. And there was another thought came in my head. She played kitten with me now when we were alone; but in the house she had carried it the way a countess might, so proud and humble. And what with her dress – for all there was so little of it, and that native enough – what with her fine tapa and fine scents, and her red flowers and seeds, that were quite as bright as jewels, only larger – it came over me she was a kind of countess really, dressed to hear great singers at a concert, and no even mate for a poor trader like myself.

She was the first in the house; and while I was still without I saw a match flash and the lamplight kindle in the windows. The station was a wonderful fine place, coral built, with quite a wide verandah, and the main room high and wide. My chests and cases had been piled in, and made rather of a mess; and there, in the thick of the confusion, stood Uma by the table, awaiting me. Her shadow went all the way up behind her into the hollow of the iron roof; she stood against it bright, the lamplight shining on her skin. I stopped in the door, and she looked at me, not speaking, with eyes that were eager and yet daunted; then she touched herself on the bosom.

'Me – your wifie,' she said. It had never taken me like that before; but the want of her took and shook all through me, like the wind in the luff of a sail.

I could not speak if I had wanted; and if I could, I would not. I was ashamed to be so much moved about a native, ashamed of the marriage too, and the certificate she had treasured in her kilt; and I turned aside and made believe to rummage among my cases. The first thing I lighted on was a case of gin, the only one that I had brought; and, partly for the girl's sake, and partly for horror at the recollections of old Randall, I took a sudden resolve. I prised the lid off. One by one I drew the bottles with a pocket corkscrew, and sent Uma out to pour the stuff from the verandah.

She came back after the last, and looked at me puzzled like.

'No good,' said I, for I was now a little better master of my tongue. 'Man he drink, he no good.'

She agreed with this, but kept considering. 'Why you bring him?' she asked presently. 'Suppose you no want drink, you no bring him, I think.'

'That's all right,' said I. 'One time I want drink too much; now no want. You see, I no savvy I get one little wifie. Suppose I drink gin, my little wifie be 'fraid.'

To speak to her kindly was about more than I was fit for; I had made my vow I would never let on to weakness with a native, and I had nothing for it but to stop.

She stood looking gravely down at me where I sat by the open case. 'I think you good man,' she said. And suddenly she had fallen before me on the floor. 'I belong you all-e-same pig!' she cried.

2

The Ban

I came on the verandah just before the sun rose on the morrow. My house was the last on the east; there was a cape of woods and cliffs behind that hid the sunrise. To the west, a swift cold river ran down, and beyond was the green of the village, dotted with cocoa-palms and breadfruits and houses. The shutters were some of them down and some open; I saw the mosquito bars still stretched, with shadows of people new-awakened sitting up inside; and all over the green others were stalking silent, wrapped in their many-coloured sleeping clothes like Bedouins in Bible pictures. It was mortal still and solemn and chilly, and the light of the dawn on the lagoon was like the shining of a fire.

But the thing that troubled me was nearer at hand. Some dozen young men and children made a piece of a half-circle, flanking my house: the river divided them, some were on the near side, some on the far, and one on a boulder in the midst; and they all sat silent, wrapped in their sheets, and stared at me and my house as straight as pointer dogs. I thought it strange as I went out. When I had bathed and come back again, and found them all there, and two or three more along with them, I thought it stranger still. What could they see to gaze at in my house, I wondered, and went in.

But the thought of these starers stuck in my mind, and presently I came out again. The sun was now up, but it was still behind the cape of woods. Say a quarter of an hour had come and gone. The crowd was greatly increased, the far bank of the river was lined for quite a way – perhaps thirty grown folk, and of children twice as many, some standing, some squatted on the ground, and all staring at my house. I have seen a house in a South Sea village thus surrounded, but then a trader was thrashing his wife inside, and she singing out. Here was nothing – the stove was alight, the smoke going up in a Christian manner; all was shipshape and Bristol fashion. To be sure, there was a stranger come, but they had a chance to see that stranger yesterday, and took it quiet enough. What ailed them now? I leaned my arms on the rail and stared back. Devil a wink they had in them! Now and then I could see the children chatter, but they spoke so low not even the hum of their speaking came my length. The rest were like graven images: they stared at me, dumb and sorrowful, with their bright eyes; and it came upon me things would look not much different if I were on the platform of the gallows, and these good folk had come to see me hanged.

I felt I was getting daunted, and began to be afraid I looked it, which would never do. Up I stood, made believe to stretch myself, came down the verandah stair, and strolled towards the river. There went a short buzz from one to the other, like what you hear in theatres when the curtain goes up; and some of the nearest gave back the matter of a pace. I saw a girl lay one hand on a young man and make a gesture upward with the other; at the same time she said something in the native with a gasping voice. Three little boys sat beside my path, where I must pass within three feet of them. Wrapped in their sheets, with their shaved heads and bits of topknots and queer faces, they looked like figures on a chimney-piece. Awhile they sat their ground, solemn as judges. I came up hand over fist, doing my five knots, like a man that meant business; and I thought I saw a sort of a wink and gulp in the three faces. Then one jumped up (he was the farthest off) and ran for his mammy. The other two, trying to follow suit, got foul, came to ground together bawling, wriggled right out of their sheets mother-naked, and in a moment there were all three of them scampering for their lives and singing out like pigs. The natives, who would never let a joke slip, even at a burial, laughed and let up, as short as a dog's bark.

They say it scares a man to be alone. No such thing. What scares him in the dark or the high bush is that he can't make sure, and there might be an army at his elbow. What scares him worst is to be right in the midst of a crowd, and have no guess of what they're driving at. When that laugh stopped, I stopped too. The boys had not yet made their offing, they were still on the full stretch going the one way, when I had already gone about ship and was sheering off the other. Like a fool I had come out, doing my five knots; like a fool I went back again. It must have been the funniest thing to see, and what knocked me silly, this time no one laughed; only one old woman gave a kind of pious moan, the way you have heard Dissenters in their chapels at the sermon.

'I never saw such fools of Kanakas as your people here,' I said once to Uma, glancing out of the window at the starers.

'Savvy nothing,' says Uma, with a kind of disgusted air that she was good at.

And that was all the talk we had upon the matter, for I was

put out, and Uma took the thing so much as a matter of course
that I was fairly ashamed.

All day, off and on, now fewer and now more, the fools sat
about the west end of my house and across the river, waiting for
the show, whatever it was – fire to come down from heaven, I
suppose, and consume me, bones and baggage. But by evening,
like real islanders, they had wearied of the business, and gone
away, and had a dance instead in the big house of the village,
where I heard them singing and clapping hands till, maybe, ten
at night, and the next day it seemed they had forgotten I existed.
If fire had come down from heaven or the earth opened and
swallowed me, there would have been nobody to see the sport or
take the lesson, or whatever you like to call it. But I was to find
they hadn't forgot either, and kept an eye lifting for phenomena
over my way.

I was hard at it both these days getting my trade in order
and taking stock of what Vigours had left. This was a job that
made me pretty sick, and kept me from thinking on much else.
Ben had taken stock the trip before – I knew I could trust
Ben – but it was plain somebody had been making free in the
meantime. I found I was out by what might easily cover six
months' salary and profit, and I could have kicked myself
all round the village to have been such a blamed ass, sitting
boozing with that Case instead of attending to my own affairs
and taking stock.

However, there's no use crying over spilt milk. It was done
now, and couldn't be undone. All I could do was to get what
was left of it, and my new stuff (my own choice) in order, to go
round and get after the rats and cockroaches, and to fix up that
store regular Sydney style. A fine show I made of it; and the
third morning when I had lit my pipe and stood in the doorway
and looked in, and turned and looked far up the mountain and
saw the cocoa-mats waving and posted up the tons of copra,
and over the village green and saw the island dandies and

reckoned up the yards of print they wanted for their kilts and dresses, I felt as if I was in the right place to make a fortune, and go home again and start a public-house. There was I, sitting in that verandah, in as handsome a piece of scenery as you could find, a splendid sun, and a fine fresh healthy trade that stirred up a man's blood like sea-bathing; and the whole thing was clean gone from me, and I was dreaming of England, which is, after all, a nasty, cold, muddy hole, with not enough light to see to read by; and dreaming of the looks of my public-house, by a cant of a broad high road like an avenue and with the sign on a green tree.

So much for the morning, but the day passed and the devil anyone looked near me, and from all I knew of natives in other islands I thought this strange. People laughed a little at our firm and their fine stations, and at this station of Falesá in particular; all the copra in the district wouldn't pay for it (I had heard them say) in fifty years, which I supposed was an exaggeration. But when the day went, and no business came at all, I began to get down-hearted; and, about three in the afternoon, I went out for a stroll to cheer me up. On the green I saw a white man coming with a cassock on, by which and by the face of him I knew he was a priest. He was a good-natured old soul to look at, gone a little grizzled, and so dirty you could have written with him on a piece of paper.

'Good day, sir,' said I.

He answered me eagerly in native.

'Don't you speak any English?' said I.

'French,' says he.

'Well,' said I, 'I'm sorry, but I can't do anything there.'

He tried me awhile in the French, and then again in native, which he seemed to think was the best chance. I made out he was after more than passing the time of day with me, but had something to communicate, and I listened the harder. I heard the names of Adams and Case and of Randall – Randall the oftenest – and the word 'poison', or something like it, and a native word that he said very often. I went home, repeating it to myself.

'What does fussy-ocky mean?' I asked of Uma, for that was as near as I could come to it.

'Make dead,' said she.

'The devil it does!' says I. 'Did ever you hear that Case had poisoned Johnny Adams?'

'Every man he savvy that,' says Uma, scornful-like. 'Give him white sand – bad sand. He got the bottle still. Suppose he give you gin, you no take him.'

Now I had heard much the same sort of story in other islands, and the same white powder always to the front, which made me think the less of it. For all that, I went over to Randall's place to see what I could pick up, and found Case on the doorstep, cleaning a gun.

'Good shooting here?' says I.

'A1,' says he. 'The bush is full of all kinds of birds. I wish copra was as plenty,' says he – I thought, slyly – 'but there don't seem anything doing.'

I could see Black Jack in the store, serving a customer.

'That looks like business, though,' said I.

'That's the first sale we've made in three weeks,' said he.

'You don't tell me?' says I. 'Three weeks? Well, well.'

'If you don't believe me,' he cries, a little hot, 'you can go and look at the copra-house. It's half empty to this blessed hour.'

'I shouldn't be much the better for that, you see,' says I. 'For all I can tell, it might have been whole empty yesterday.'

'That's so,' says he, with a bit of a laugh.

'By the by,' I said, 'what sort of a party is that priest? Seems rather a friendly sort.'

At this Case laughed right out loud. 'Ah!' says he, 'I see what ails you now. Galuchet's been at you.' Father Galoshes was the name he went by most, but Case always gave it the French

93

quirk, which was another reason we had for thinking him above the common.

'Yes, I have seen him,' I says. 'I made out he didn't think much of your Captain Randall.'

'That he don't!' says Case. 'It was the trouble about poor Adams. The last day, when he lay dying, there was young Buncombe round. Ever met Buncombe?'

I told him no.

'He's a cure, is Buncombe!' laughs Case. 'Well, Buncombe took it in his head that, as there was no other clergyman about, bar Kanaka pastors, we ought to call in Father Galuchet, and have the old man administered and take the sacrament. It was all the same to me, you may suppose; but I said I thought Adams was the fellow to consult. He was jawing away about watered copra and a sight of foolery. "Look here," I said, "you're pretty sick. Would you like to see Galoshes?" He sat right up on his elbow. "Get the priest," says he, "get the priest; don't let me die here like a dog!" He spoke kind of fierce and eager, but sensible enough. There was nothing to say against that, so we sent and asked Galuchet if he would come. You bet he would. He jumped in his dirty linen at the thought of it. But we had reckoned without papa. He's a hard-shell Baptist, is papa; no Papists need apply. And he took and locked the door. Buncombe told him he was bigoted, and I thought he would have had a fit. "Bigoted!" he says. "Me bigoted? Have I lived to hear it from a jackanapes like you?" And he made for Buncombe, and I had to hold them apart; and there was Adams in the middle, gone luny again, and carrying on about copra like a born fool. It was good as the play, and I was about knocked out of time with laughing, when all of a sudden Adams sat up, clapped his hands to his chest, and went into the horrors. He died hard, did John Adams,' says Case, with a kind of a sudden sternness.

'And what became of the priest?' I asked.

'The priest?' says Case. 'Oh! he was hammering on the door

outside, and crying on the natives to come and beat it in, and singing out it was a soul he wished to save, and that. He was in a rare taking, was the priest. But what would you have? Johnny had slipped his cable; no more Johnny in the market; and the administration racket clean played out. Next thing, word came to Randall the priest was praying upon Johnny's grave. Papa was pretty full, and got a club, and lit out straight for the place, and there was Galoshes on his knees, and a lot of natives looking on. You wouldn't think papa cared that much about anything, unless it was liquor; but he and the priest stuck to it two hours, slanging each other in native, and every time Galoshes tried to kneel down papa went for him with the club. There never were such larks in Falesá. The end of it was that Captain Randall keeled over with some kind of a fit or stroke, and the priest got in his goods after all. But he was the angriest priest you ever heard of, and complained to the chiefs about the outrage, as he called it. That was no account, for our chiefs are Protestant here; and, anyway, he had been making trouble about the drum for morning school, and they were glad to give him a wipe. Now he swears old Randall gave Adams poison or something, and when the two meet they grin at each other like baboons.'

He told this story as natural as could be, and like a man that enjoyed the fun; though, now I come to think of it after so long, it seems rather a sickening yarn. However, Case never set up to be soft, only to be square and hearty, and a man all round; and, to tell the truth, he puzzled me entirely.

I went home and asked Uma if she were a Popey, which I had made out to be the native word for Catholics.

'E le ai!' says she. She always used the native when she meant 'no' more than usually strong, and, indeed, there's more of it. 'No good Popey,' she added.

Then I asked her about Adams and the priest, and she told me much the same yarn in her own way. So that I was left not much farther on, but inclined, upon the whole, to think the bottom of the matter was the row about the sacrament, and the poisoning only talk.

The next day was a Sunday, when there was no business to be looked for. Uma asked me in the morning if I was going to 'pray'; I told her she bet not, and she stopped home herself with no more words. I thought this seemed unlike a native, and a native woman, and a woman that had new clothes to show off; however, it suited me to the ground, and I made the less of it. The queer thing was that I came next door to going to church after all, a thing I'm little likely to forget. I had turned out for a stroll, and heard the hymn tune up. You know how it is. If you hear folk singing, it seems to draw you; and pretty soon I found myself alongside the church. It was a little long low place, coral built, rounded off at both ends like a whale-boat, a big native roof on the top of it, windows without sashes and doorways without doors. I stuck my head into one of the windows, and the sight was so new to me – for things went quite different in the islands I was acquainted with – that I stayed and looked on. The congregation sat on the floor on mats, the women on one side, the men on the other, all rigged out to kill – the women with dresses and trade hats, the men in white jackets and shirts. The hymn was over; the pastor, a big buck Kanaka, was in the pulpit, preaching for his life; and by the way he wagged his hand, and worked his voice, and made his points, and seemed to argue with the folk, I made out he was a gun at the business. Well, he looked up suddenly and caught my eye, and I give you my word he staggered in the pulpit; his eyes bulged out of his head, his hand rose and pointed at me like as if against his will, and the sermon stopped right there.

It isn't a fine thing to say for yourself, but I ran away; and if the same kind of a shock was given me, I should run away again tomorrow. To see that palavering Kanaka struck all of a heap at the mere sight of me gave me a feeling as if the bottom had dropped out of the world. I went right home, and stayed there, and said nothing. You might think I would tell Uma, but that was against my system. You might have thought I would have gone over and consulted Case; but the truth was I was ashamed to speak of such a thing, I thought everyone would blurt out laughing in my face. So I held my tongue, and thought all the more; and the more I thought, the less I liked the business.

By Monday night I got it clearly in my head I must be tabooed. A new store to stand open two days in a village and not a man or woman come to see the trade was past believing.

'Uma,' said I, 'I think I'm tabooed.'

'I think so,' said she.

I thought awhile whether I should ask her more, but it's a bad idea to set natives up with any notion of consulting them, so I went to Case. It was dark, and he was sitting alone, as he did mostly, smoking on the stairs.

'Case,' said I, 'here's a queer thing. I'm tabooed.'

'Oh, fudge!' says he; "tain't the practice in these islands.'

'That may be, or it mayn't,' said I. 'It's the practice where I was before. You can bet I know what it's like; and I tell it you for a fact, I'm tabooed.'

'Well,' said he, 'what have you been doing?'

'That's what I want to find out,' said I.

'Oh, you can't be,' said he; 'it ain't possible. However, I'll tell you what I'll do. Just to put your mind at rest, I'll go round and find out for sure. Just you waltz in and talk to papa.'

'Thank you,' I said, 'I'd rather stay right out here on the verandah. Your house is so close.'

'I'll call papa out here, then,' says he.

'My dear fellow,' I says, 'I wish you wouldn't. The fact is, I don't take to Mr Randall.'

Case laughed, took a lantern from the store, and set out into the village. He was gone perhaps a quarter of an hour, and he looked mighty serious when he came back.

'Well,' said he, clapping down the lantern on the verandah steps, 'I would never have believed it. I don't know where the impudence of these Kanakas'll go next; they seem to have lost all idea of respect for whites. What we want is a man-of-war – a German, if we could – they know how to manage Kanakas.'

'I *am* tabooed, then?' I cried.

'Something of the sort,' said he. 'It's the worst thing of the kind I've heard of yet. But I'll stand by you, Wiltshire, man to man. You come round here tomorrow about nine, and we'll have it out with the chiefs. They're afraid of me, or they used to be; but their heads are so big by now, I don't know what to think. Understand me, Wiltshire; I don't count this your quarrel,' he went on, with a great deal of resolution, 'I count it all of our quarrel, I count it the White Man's Quarrel, and I'll stand to it through thick and thin, and there's my hand on it.'

'Have you found out what's the reason?' I asked.

'Not yet,' said Case. 'But we'll fix them down tomorrow.'

Altogether I was pretty well pleased with his attitude, and almost more the next day, when we met to go before the chiefs, to see him so stern and resolved. The chiefs awaited us in one of their big oval houses, which was marked out to us from a long way off by the crowd about the eaves, a hundred strong if there was one – men, women and children. Many of the men were on their way to work and wore green wreaths, and it put me in thoughts of the 1st of May at home. This crowd opened and buzzed about the pair of us as we went in, with a sudden angry animation. Five chiefs were there; four mighty stately men, the fifth old and puckered. They sat on mats in their white kilts and jackets; they had fans in their hands, like fine ladies; and two of the younger ones wore Catholic medals, which gave me matter for reflection. Our place was set, and the mats laid for us over against these grandees, on the near side of the house; the midst was empty; the crowd, close at our backs, murmured and craned and jostled to look on, and the shadows of them tossed in front of us on the clean pebbles of the floor. I was just a hair put out by the excitement of the commons, but the quiet civil appearance of the chiefs reassured me, all the more when their spokesman began and made a long speech in a low tone of voice, sometimes waving his hand towards Case, sometimes towards me, and sometimes knocking with his knuckles on the mat. One thing was clear: there was no sign of anger in the chiefs.

'What's he been saying?' I asked, when he had done.

'Oh, just that they're glad to see you, and they understand through me you wish to make some kind of complaint, and you're to fire away, and they'll do the square thing.'

'It took a precious long time to say that,' said I.

'Oh, the rest was sawder and *bonjour* and that,' said Case. 'You know what Kanakas are.'

'Well, they don't get much *bonjour* out of me,' said I. 'You tell them who I am. I'm a white man, and a British subject, and no end of a big chief at home; and I've come here to do them good, and bring them civilisation; and no sooner have I got my trade sorted out than they go and taboo me, and no one dare come near my place! Tell them I don't mean to fly in the face of anything legal; and if what they want's a present, I'll do what's fair. I don't blame any man looking out for himself, tell them, for that's human nature; but if they think they're going to come any of their native ideas over me, they'll find themselves mistaken. And tell them plain that I demand the reason of this treatment as a white man and a British subject.'

That was my speech. I know how to deal with Kanakas: give them plain sense and fair dealing, and – I'll do them that much justice – they knuckle under every time. They haven't any real government or any real law, that's what you've got to knock into their heads; and even if they had, it would be a good joke if it was to apply to a white man. It would be a strange thing if we came all this way and couldn't do what we pleased. The mere idea has always put my monkey up, and I rapped my speech out pretty big. Then Case translated it – or made believe to, rather – and the first chief replied, and then a second, and a third, all in the same style – easy and genteel, but solemn underneath. Once a question was put to Case, and he answered it, and all hands (both chiefs and commons) laughed out aloud, and looked at me. Last of all, the puckered old fellow and the big young chief that spoke first started in to put Case through a kind of catechism. Sometimes I made out that Case was trying to fence, and they stuck to him like hounds, and the sweat ran down his face, which was no very pleasant sight to me, and at some of his answers the crowd moaned and murmured, which was a worse hearing. It's a cruel shame I knew no native, for (as I now believe) they were asking Case about my marriage, and he must have had a tough job of it to clear his feet. But leave Case alone; he had the brains to run a parliament.

'Well, is that all?' I asked, when a pause came.

'Come along,' says he, mopping his face; 'I'll tell you outside.'

'Do you mean they won't take the taboo off?' I cried.

'It's something queer,' said he. 'I'll tell you outside. Better come away.'

'I won't take it at their hands,' cried I. 'I ain't that kind of a man. You don't find me turn my back on a parcel of Kanakas.'

'You'd better,' said Case.

He looked at me with a signal in his eye; and the five chiefs looked at me civilly enough, but kind of pointed; and the people looked at me and craned and jostled. I remembered the folks that watched my house, and how the pastor had jumped in his pulpit at the bare sight of me; and the whole business seemed so out of the way that I rose and followed Case. The crowd opened again to let us through, but wider than before, the children on the skirts running and singing out, and as we two white men walked away they all stood and watched us.

'And now,' said I, 'what is all this about?'

'The truth is I can't rightly make it out myself. They have a down on you,' says Case.

'Taboo a man because they have a down on him!' I cried. 'I never heard the like.'

'It's worse than that, you see,' said Case. 'You ain't tabooed – I told you that couldn't be. The people won't go near you, Wiltshire, and there's where it is.'

'They won't go near me? What do you mean by that? Why won't they go near me?' I cried.

Case hesitated. 'Seems they're frightened,' says he, in a low voice.

I stopped dead short. 'Frightened?' I repeated. 'Are you gone crazy, Case? What are they frightened of?'

'I wish I could make out,' Case answered, shaking his head. 'Appears like one of their tomfool superstitions. That's what I don't cotton to,' he said. 'It's like the business about Vigours.'

'I'd like to know what you mean by that, and I'll trouble you to tell me,' says I.

'Well, you know Vigours lit out and left all standing,' said he. 'It was some superstition business – I never got the hang of it; but it began to look bad before the end.'

'I've heard a different story about that,' said I, 'and I had better tell you so. I heard he ran away because of you.'

'Oh! well, I suppose he was ashamed to tell the truth,' says Case; 'I guess he thought it silly. And it's a fact that I packed him off. "What would you do, old man?" says he. "Get," says I, "and not think twice about it." I was the gladdest kind of man to see him clear away. It ain't my notion to turn my back on a mate when he's in a tight place, but there was that much trouble in the village that I couldn't see where it might likely end. I was a fool to be so much about with Vigours. They cast it up to me today. Didn't you hear Maea – that's the young chief, the big one – ripping out about "Vika"? That was him they were after. They don't seem to forget it, somehow.'

'This is all very well,' said I, 'but it don't tell me what's wrong; it don't tell me what they're afraid of – what their idea is.'

'Well, I wish I knew,' said Case. 'I can't say fairer than that.'

'You might have asked, I think,' says I.

'And so I did,' says he. 'But you must have seen for yourself, unless you're blind, that the asking got the other way. I'll go as far as I dare for another white man; but when I find I'm in the scrape myself, I think first of my own bacon. The loss of me is I'm too good-natured. And I'll take the freedom of telling you you show a queer kind of gratitude to a man who's got into all this mess along of your affairs.'

'There's a thing I am thinking of,' said I. 'You were a fool to be so much about with Vigours. One comfort, you haven't been much about with me. I notice you've never been inside my house. Own up now; you had word of this before?'

'It's a fact I haven't been,' said he. 'It was an oversight, and I am sorry for it, Wiltshire. But about coming now, I'll be quite plain.'

'You mean you won't?' I asked.

'Awfully sorry, old man, but that's the size of it,' says Case.

'In short, you're afraid?' says I.

'In short, I'm afraid,' says he.

'And I'm still to be tabooed for nothing?' I asked

'I tell you you're not tabooed,' said he. 'The Kanakas won't go near you, that's all. And who's to make 'em? We traders have a lot of gall, I must say; we make these poor Kanakas take back their laws, and take up their taboos, and that, whenever it happens to suit us. But you don't mean to say you expect a law obliging people to deal in your store whether they want to or not? You don't mean to tell me you've got the gall for that? And if you had, it would be a queer thing to propose to me. I would just like to point out to you, Wiltshire, that I'm a trader myself.'

'I don't think I would talk of gall if I was you,' said I. 'Here's about what it comes to, as well as I can make out: None of the people are to trade with me, and they're all to trade with you. You're to have the copra, and I'm to go to the devil and shake myself. And I don't know any native, and you're the only man here worth mention that speaks English, and you have the gall to up and hint to me my life's in danger, and all you've got to tell me is you don't know why!'

'Well, it *is* all I have to tell you,' said he. 'I don't know – I wish I did.'

'And so you turn your back and leave me to myself! Is that the position?' says I.

'If you like to put it nasty,' says he. 'I don't put it so. I say merely, "I'm going to keep clear of you; or, if I don't, I'll get in danger for myself." '

'Well,' says I, 'you're a nice kind of a white man!'

'Oh, I understand; you're riled,' said he. 'I would be myself. I can make excuses.'

'All right,' I said, 'go and make excuses somewhere else. Here's my way, there's yours!'

With that we parted, and I went straight home, in a hot temper, and found Uma trying on a lot of trade goods like a baby.

'Here,' I said, 'you quit that foolery! Here's a pretty mess to have made, as if I wasn't bothered enough anyway! And I thought I told you to get dinner!'

And then I believe I gave her a bit of the rough side of my tongue, as she deserved. She stood up at once, like a sentry to his officer; for I must say she was always well brought up, and had a great respect for whites.

'And now,' says I, 'you belong round here, you're bound to understand this. What am I tabooed for, anyway? Or, if I ain't tabooed, what makes the folks afraid of me?'

She stood and looked at me with eyes like saucers.

'You no savvy?' she gasps at last.

'No,' said I. 'How would you expect me to? We don't have any such craziness where I come from.'

'Ese no tell you?' she asked again.

(Ese was the name the natives had for Case; it may mean foreign, or extraordinary; or it might mean a mummy-apple; but most like it was only his own name misheard and put in a Kanaka spelling.)

'Not much,' said I.

'Damn Ese!' she cried.

You might think it funny to hear this Kanaka girl come out with a big swear. No such thing. There was no swearing in her – no, nor anger; she was beyond anger, and meant the word simple and serious. She stood there straight as she said it. I cannot justly say that I ever saw a woman look like that before or after, and it struck me mum. Then she made a kind of an obeisance, but it was the proudest kind, and threw her hands out open.

'I 'shamed,' she said. 'I think you savvy. Ese he tell me you savvy, he tell me you no mind, tell me you love me too much. Taboo belong me,' she said, touching herself on the bosom, as she had done upon our wedding-night. 'Now I go 'way, taboo he go 'way too. Then you get too much copra. You like more better, I think. Tofá, alii,' says she in the native – 'Farewell, chief!'

'Hold on!' I cried. 'Don't be in such a hurry.'

She looked at me sidelong with a smile. 'You see, you get copra,' she said, the same as you might offer candies to a child.

'Uma,' said I, 'hear reason. I didn't know, and that's a fact; and Case seems to have played it pretty mean upon the pair of us. But I do know now, and I don't mind; I love you too much. You no go 'way, you no leave me, I too much sorry.'

'You no love me,' she cried, 'you talk me bad words!' And she threw herself in a corner of the floor, and began to cry.

Well, I'm no scholar, but I wasn't born yesterday, and I thought the worst of that trouble was over. However, there she lay – her back turned, her face to the wall – and shook with sobbing like a little child, so that her feet jumped with it. It's strange how it hits a man when he's in love; for there's no use mincing things; Kanaka and all, I was in love with her, or just as good. I tried to take her hand, but she would none of that. 'Uma,' I said, 'there's no sense in carrying on like this. I want you stop here, I want my little wifie, I tell you true.'

'No tell me true,' she sobbed.

'All right,' says I, 'I'll wait till you're through with this.' And I sat right down beside her on the floor, and set to smooth her hair with my hand. At first she wriggled away when I touched her; then she seemed to notice me no more; then her sobs grew gradually less, and presently stopped; and the next thing I knew, she raised her face to mime.

'You tell me true? You like me stop?' she asked.

'Uma,' I said, 'I would rather have you than all the copra in the South Seas,' which was a very big expression, and the strangest thing was that I meant it.

She threw her arms about me, sprang close up, and pressed her face to mine in the island way of kissing, so that I was all wetted with her tears, and my heart went out to her wholly. I never had anything so near me as this little brown bit of a girl. Many things went together, and all helped to turn my head. She was pretty enough to eat; it seemed she was my only friend in that queer place; I was ashamed that I had spoken rough to her: and she was a woman, and my wife, and a kind of a baby besides that I was sorry for; and the salt of her tears was in my mouth. And I forgot Case and the natives; and I forgot that I knew nothing of the story, or only remembered it to banish the remembrance; and I forgot that I was to get no copra, and so could make no livelihood; and I forgot my employers, and the strange kind of service I was doing them when I preferred my fancy to their business; and I forgot even that Uma was no true wife of mine, but just a maid beguiled, and that in a pretty shabby style. But that is to look too far on. I will come to that part of it next.

It was late before we thought of getting dinner. The stove was out, and gone stone-cold; but we fired up after a while, and cooked each a dish, helping and hindering each other, and making a play of it like children. I was so greedy of her nearness that I sat down to dinner with my lass upon my knee, made sure of her with one hand and ate with the other. Ay, and more than that. She was the worst cook I suppose God made; the things she set her hand to it would have sickened an honest horse to eat of; yet I made my meal that day on Uma's cookery, and can never call to mind to have been better pleased.

I didn't pretend to myself, and I didn't pretend to her. I saw I was clean gone; and if she was to make a fool of me, she must. And I suppose it was this that set her talking, for now she made sure that we were friends. A lot she told me, sitting in my lap and eating my dish, as I ate hers, from foolery – a lot about herself and her mother and Case, all which would be very tedious, and fill sheets if I set it down in Beach de Mar, but which I must give a hint of in plain English, and one thing about myself which had a very big effect on my concerns, as you are soon to hear.

It seems she was born in one of the Line Islands; had been only two or three years in these parts, where she had come with a white man, who was married to her mother and then died; and only the one year in Falesá. Before that they had been a good deal on the move, trekking about after the white man, who was one of those rolling stones that keep going round after a soft job. They talk about looking for gold at the end of a rainbow; but if a man wants an employment that'll last him till he dies, let him start out on the soft-job hunt. There's meat and drink in it too, and beer and skittles, for you never hear of them starving, and rarely see them sober; and as for steady sport, cock-fighting isn't in the same county with it. Anyway, this beachcomber carried the woman and her daughter all over the shop, but mostly to out-of-the-way islands, where there were no police, and where he thought, perhaps, the soft job hung out. I've my own view of this old party; but I was just as glad he had kept Uma clear of Apia and Papeete and these flash towns. At last he struck Fale-alii on this island, got some trade – the Lord knows how! – muddled it all away in the usual style, and died worth next to nothing, bar a bit of land at Falesá that he had got for a bad debt, which was what put it in the minds of the mother and daughter to come there and live. It seems Case encouraged them all he could, and helped to get their house built. He was very kind those days, and gave Uma trade, and there is no doubt he had his eye on her from the beginning. However, they had scarce settled, when up turned a young man, a native, and wanted to marry her. He was a small chief, and had some fine mats and old songs in his family, and was 'very pretty', Uma said; and, altogether, it was an extraordinary match for a penniless girl and an out-islander.

At the first word of this I got downright sick with jealousy.

'And you mean to say you would have married him?' I cried.

'Ioe, yes,' said she. 'I like too much!'

'Well!' I said. 'And suppose I had come round after?'

'I like you more better now,' said she. 'But, suppose I marry Ioane, I one good wife. I no common Kanaka. Good girl!' says she.

Well, I had to be pleased with that; but I promise you I didn't care about the business one little bit. And I liked the end of that yarn no better than the beginning. For it seems this proposal of marriage was the start of all the trouble. It seems, before that, Uma and her mother had been looked down upon, of course, for kinless folk and out-islanders, but nothing to hurt; and, even when Ioane came forward, there was less trouble at first than might have been looked for. And then, all of a sudden, about six months before my coming, Ioane backed out and left that part of the island, and from that day to this Uma and her mother had found themselves alone. None called at their house, none spoke to them on the roads. If they went to church, the other women drew their mats away and left them in a clear place by themselves. It was a regular excommunication, like what you read of in the Middle Ages; and the cause or sense of it beyond guessing. It was some *tala pepelo*, Uma said, some lie, some calumny; and all she knew of it was that the girls who had been jealous of her luck with Ioane used to twit her with his desertion, and cry out, when they met her alone in the woods, that she would never be married. 'They tell me no man he marry me. He too much 'fraid,' she said.

The only soul that came about them after this desertion was Master Case. Even he was chary of showing himself, and turned up mostly by night; and pretty soon he began to table his cards and make up to Uma. I was still sore about Ioane, and when Case turned up in the same line of business I cut up downright rough.

'Well,' I said, sneering, 'and I suppose you thought Case "very pretty" and "liked too much"?'

'Now you talk silly,' said she. 'White man, he come here, I marry him all-e-same Kanaka; very well then, he marry me all-e-same white woman. Suppose he no marry, he go 'way, woman he stop. All-e-same thief, empty hand, Tonga-heart – no can love! Now you come marry me. You big heart – you no 'shamed island-girl. That thing I love you for too much. I proud.'

I don't know that ever I felt sicker all the days of my life. I laid down my fork, and I put away 'the island-girl'; I didn't seem somehow to have any use for either, and I went and walked up and down in the house, and Uma followed me with her eyes, for she was troubled, and small wonder! But troubled was no word for it with me. I so wanted, and so feared, to make a clean breast of the sweep that I had been.

And just then there came a sound of singing out of the sea; it sprang up suddenly clear and near, as the boat turned the headland, and Uma, running to the window, cried out it was 'Misi' come upon his rounds.

I thought it was a strange thing I should be glad to have a missionary; but, if it was strange, it was still true.

'Uma,' said I, 'you stop here in this room, and don't budge a foot out of it till I come back.'

3

The Missionary

As I came out on the verandah, the mission-boat was shooting for the mouth of the river. She was a long whale-boat painted white; a bit of an awning astern; a native pastor crouched on the wedge of the poop, steering; some four-and-twenty paddles flashing and dipping, true to the boat-song; and the missionary under the awning, in his white clothes, reading in a book, and set him up! It was pretty to see and hear; there's no smarter sight in the islands than a missionary boat with a good crew and a good pipe to them; and I considered it for half a minute, with a bit of envy perhaps, and then strolled down towards the river.

From the opposite side there was another man aiming for the same place, but he ran and got there first. It was Case; doubtless his idea was to keep me apart from the missionary, who might serve me as interpreter; but my mind was upon other things. I was thinking how he had jockeyed us about the marriage, and tried his hand on Uma before; and at the sight of him rage flew into my nostrils.

'Get out of that, you low, swindling thief!' I cried.

'What's that you say?' says he.

I gave him the word again, and rammed it down with a good oath. 'And if ever I catch you within six fathoms of my house,' I cried, 'I'll clap a bullet in your measly carcase.'

'You must do as you like about your house,' said he, 'where I told you I have no thought of going; but this is a public place.'

'It's a place where I have private business,' said I. 'I have no idea of a hound like you eavesdropping, and I give you notice to clear out.'

'I don't take it, though,' says Case.

'I'll show you, then,' said I.

'We'll have to see about that,' said he.

He was quick with his hands, but he had neither the height nor the weight, being a flimsy creature alongside a man like me, and, besides, I was blazing to that height of wrath that I could have bit into a chisel. I gave him first the one and then the other, so that I could hear his head rattle and crack, and he went down straight.

'Have you had enough?' cried I. But he only looked up white and blank, and the blood spread upon his face like wine upon a napkin. 'Have you had enough?' I cried again. 'Speak up, and don't lie malingering there, or I'll take my feet to you.'

He sat up at that, and held his head – by the look of him you could see it was spinning – and the blood poured on his pyjamas.

'I've had enough for this time,' says he, and he got up staggering, and went off by the way that he had come.

The boat was close in; I saw the missionary had laid his book to one side, and I smiled to myself. 'He'll know I'm a man, anyway,' thinks I.

This was the first time, in all my years in the Pacific, I had ever exchanged two words with any missionary, let alone asked one for a favour. I didn't like the lot, no trader does; they look down upon us, and make no concealment; and, besides, they're partly Kanakaised, and suck up with natives instead of with other white men like themselves. I had on a rig of clean striped pyjamas – for, of course, I had dressed decent to go before the chiefs; but when I saw the missionary step out of this boat in the regular uniform, white duck clothes, pith helmet, white shirt and tie, and yellow boots to his feet, I could have bunged stones at him. As he came nearer, queering me pretty curious (because of the fight, I suppose), I saw he looked mortal sick, for the truth was he had a fever on and had just had a chill in the boat.

'Mr Tarleton, I believe?' says I, for I had got his name.

'And you, I suppose, are the new trader?' says he.

'I want to tell you first that I don't hold with missions,' I went on, 'and that I think you and the likes of you do a sight of harm, filling up the natives with old wives' tales and bumptiousness.'

'You are perfectly entitled to your opinions,' says he, looking a bit ugly, 'but I have no call to hear them.'

'It so happens that you've got to hear them,' I said. 'I'm no missionary, nor missionary lover; I'm no Kanaka, nor favourer of Kanakas – I'm just a trader; I'm just a common, low-down, God-damned white man and British subject, the sort you would like to wipe your boots on. I hope that's plain!'

'Yes, my man,' said he. 'It's more plain than creditable. When you are sober, you'll be sorry for this.'

He tried to pass on, but I stopped him with my hand. The Kanakas were beginning to growl. Guess they didn't like my tone, for I spoke to that man as free as I would to you.

'Now, you can't say I've deceived you,' said I, 'and I can go on. I want a service – I want two services, in fact; and, if you care to give me them, I'll perhaps take more stock in what you call your Christianity.'

He was silent for a moment. Then he smiled. 'You are rather a strange sort of man,' says he.

'I'm the sort of man God made me,' says I. 'I don't set up to be a gentleman,' I said.

'I am not quite so sure,' said he. 'And what can I do for you, Mr —?'

'Wiltshire,' I says, 'though I'm mostly called Welsher; but Wiltshire is the way it's spelt, if the people on the beach could only get their tongues about it. And what do I want? Well, I'll tell you the first thing. I'm what you call a sinner – what I call a sweep – and I want you to help me make it up to a person I've deceived.'

He turned and spoke to his crew in the native. 'And now I am at your service,' said he, 'but only for the time my crew are dining. I must be much farther down the coast before night. I was delayed at Papa-Malulu till this morning, and I have an engagement in Fale-alii tomorrow night.'

I led the way to my house in silence, and rather pleased with myself for the way I had managed the talk, for I like a man to keep his self-respect.

'I was sorry to see you fighting,' says he.

'Oh, that's part of the yarn I want to tell you,' I said. 'That's service number two. After you've heard it you'll let me know whether you're sorry or not.'

We walked right in through the store, and I was surprised to find Uma had cleared away the dinner things. This was so unlike her ways that I saw she had done it out of gratitude, and liked her the better. She and Mr Tarleton called each other by name, and he was very civil to her seemingly. But I thought little of that; they can always find civility for a Kanaka, it's us white men they lord it over. Besides, I didn't want much Tarleton just then. I was going to do my pitch.

'Uma,' said I, 'give us your marriage certificate.' She looked put out. 'Come,' said I, 'you can trust me. Hand it up.'

She had it about her person, as usual; I believe she thought it was a pass to heaven, and if she died without having it handy she would go to hell. I couldn't see where she put it the first time, I couldn't see now where she took it from; it seemed to jump into her hand like that Blavatsky business in the papers. But it's the same way with all island women, and I guess they're taught it when young.

'Now,' said I, with the certificate in my hand, 'I was married to this girl by Black Jack the negro. The certificate was wrote by Case, and it's a dandy piece of literature, I promise you. Since then I've found that there's a kind of cry in the place against this wife of mine, and so long as I keep her I cannot trade. Now,

what would any man do in my place, if he was a man?' I said.
'The first thing he would do is this, I guess.' And I took and tore
up the certificate and bunged the pieces on the floor.

'Aué!' cried Uma, and began to clap her hands; but I caught
one of them in mine.

'And the second thing that he would do,' said I, 'if he was
what I would call a man and you would call a man, Mr Tarleton,
is to bring the girl right before you or any other missionary,
and to up and say: "I was wrong married to this wife of mine,
but I think a heap of her, and now I want to be married to her
right." Fire away, Mr Tarleton. And I guess you'd better do it
in native; it'll please the old lady,' I said, giving her the proper
name of a man's wife upon the spot.

So we had in two of the crew for to witness, and were spliced
in our own house; and the parson prayed a good bit, I must say –
but not so long as some – and shook hands with the pair of us.

'Mr Wiltshire,' he says, when he had made out the lines and
packed off the witnesses, 'I have to thank you for a very lively
pleasure. I have rarely performed the marriage ceremony with
more grateful emotions.'

That was what you would call talking. He was going on,
besides, with more of it, and I was ready for as much taffy as he
had in stock, for I felt good. But Uma had been taken up with
something half through the marriage, and cut straight in.

'How your hand he get hurt?' she asked.

'You ask Case's head, old lady,' says I.

She jumped with joy, and sang out.

'You haven't made much of a Christian of this one,' says I to
Mr Tarleton.

'We didn't think her one of our worst,' says he, 'when she
was at Fale-alii; and if Uma bears malice I shall be tempted to
fancy she has good cause.'

'Well, there we are at service number two,' said I. 'I want to
tell you our yarn, and see if you can let a little daylight in.'

'Is it long?' he asked.

'Yes,' I cried; 'it's a goodish bit of a yarn!'

'Well, I'll give you all the time I can spare,' says he, looking at his watch. 'But I must tell you fairly, I haven't eaten since five this morning, and, unless you can let me have something I am not likely to eat again before seven or eight tonight.'

'By God, we'll give you dinner!' I cried.

I was a little caught up at my swearing, just when all was going straight; and so was the missionary, I suppose, but he made believe to look out of the window, and thanked us.

So we ran him up a bit of a meal. I was bound to let the old lady have a hand in it, to show off, so I deputised her to brew the tea. I don't think I ever met such tea as she turned out. But that was not the worst, for she got round with the salt-box, which she considered an extra European touch, and turned my stew into sea-water. Altogether, Mr Tarleton had a devil of a dinner of it; but he had plenty entertainment by the way, for all the while that we were cooking, and afterwards, when he was making believe to eat, I kept posting him up on Master Case and the beach of Falesá, and he putting questions that showed he was following close.

'Well,' said he at last, 'I am afraid you have a dangerous enemy. This man Case is very clever and seems really wicked. I must tell you I have had my eye on him for nearly a year, and have rather had the worst of our encounters. About the time when the last representative of your firm ran so suddenly away, I had a letter from Namu, the native pastor, begging me to come to Falesá at my earliest convenience, as his flock were all "adopting Catholic practices". I had great confidence in Namu; I fear it only shows how easily we are deceived. No one could hear him preach and not be persuaded he was a man of extra-ordinary parts. All our islanders easily acquire a kind of eloquence, and can roll out and illustrate, with a great deal of vigour and fancy, second-hand sermons; but Namu's sermons are his own, and I cannot deny that I have found them means of grace. Moreover, he has a keen curiosity in secular things, does not fear work, is clever at carpentering, and has made himself so much respected among the neighbouring pastors that we call him, in a jest which is half serious, the Bishop of the East. In short, I was proud of the man; all the more puzzled by his letter, I took an occasion to come this way. The morning before my arrival, Vigours had been sent on board the *Lion*, and Namu was perfectly at his ease, apparently ashamed of his letter, and quite unwilling to explain it. This, of course, I could not allow, and he ended by confessing that he had been much concerned to find his people using the sign of the cross, but since he had learned the explanation his mind was satisfied. For Vigours had the Evil Eye, a common thing in a country of Europe called Italy, where men were often struck dead by that kind of devil, and it appeared the sign of the cross was a charm against its power.

' "And I explain it, Misi," said Namu, "in this way: The country in Europe is a Popey country, and the devil of the Evil Eye may be a Catholic devil, or, at least, used to Catholic ways. So then I reasoned thus: if this sign of the cross were used in a Popey manner it would be sinful, but when it is used only to protect men from a devil, which is a thing harmless in itself, the sign too must be, as a bottle is neither good nor bad, harmless. For the sign is neither good nor bad. But if the bottle be full of gin, the gin is bad; and if the sign be made in idolatry bad, so is the idolatry." And, very like a native pastor, he had a text apposite about the casting out of devils.

' "And who has been telling you about the Evil Eye?" I asked.

'He admitted it was Case. Now, I am afraid you will think me very narrow, Mr Wiltshire, but I must tell you I was displeased, and cannot think a trader at all a good man to advise or have an influence upon my pastors. And, besides, there had been some flying talk in the country of old Adams and his being poisoned, to which I had paid no great heed; but it came back to me at the moment.

' "And is this Case a man of a sanctified life?" I asked.

'He admitted he was not; for, though he did not drink, he was profligate with women, and had no religion.

' "Then," said I, "I think the less you have to do with him the better."

'But it is not easy to have the last word with a man like Namu. He was ready in a moment with an illustration. "Misi," said he, "you have told me there were wise men, not pastors, not even holy, who knew many things useful to be taught – about trees, for instance, and beasts, and to print books, and about the stones that are burned to make knives of. Such men teach you in your college, and you learn from them, but take care not to learn to be unholy. Misi, Case is my college."

'I knew not what to say. Mr Vigours had evidently been driven out of Falesá by the machinations of Case and with something not very unlike the collusion of my pastor. I called to mind it was Namu who had reassured me about Adams and traced the rumour to the ill-will of the priest. And I saw I must inform myself more thoroughly from an impartial source. There is an old rascal of a chief here, Faiaso, whom I dare say you saw today at the council; he has been all his life turbulent and sly, a great fomenter of rebellions, and a thorn in the side of the mission and the island. For all that he is very shrewd, and, except in politics or about his own misdemeanours, a teller of the truth. I went to his house, told him what I had heard, and besought him to be frank. I do not think I had ever a more painful interview. Perhaps you will understand me, Mr Wiltshire, if I tell you that I am perfectly serious in these old wives' tales with which you reproached me, and as anxious to do well for these islands as you can be to please and to protect your pretty wife. And you are to remember that I thought Namu a paragon, and was proud of the man as one of the first ripe fruits of the mission. And now I was informed that he had fallen in a sort of dependence upon Case. The beginning of it was not corrupt; it began, doubtless, in fear and respect, produced by trickery and pretence; but I was shocked to find that another element had been lately added, that Namu helped himself in the store, and was believed to be deep in Case's debt. Whatever the trader said, that Namu believed with trembling. He was not alone in this; many in the village lived in a similar subjection; but Namu's case was the most influential; it was through Namu Case had wrought most evil; and with a certain following among the chiefs, and the pastor in his pocket, the man was as good as master of the village. You know something of Vigours and Adams, but perhaps you have never heard of old Underhill, Adams's predecessor. He was a quiet, mild old fellow, I remember, and we were told he had died suddenly: white men die very suddenly in Falesá. The truth, as I now heard it, made my blood run cold. It seems he was struck with a general palsy, all of him dead but one eye, which he continually winked. Word was started that the helpless old man was now a devil, and this vile fellow Case worked upon the natives' fears, which he professed to share, and pretended he durst not go into the house alone. At last a grave was dug, and the living body buried at the far end of the village. Namu, my pastor, whom I had helped to educate, offered up a prayer at the hateful scene.

'I felt myself in a very difficult position. Perhaps it was my duty to have denounced Namu and had him deposed. Perhaps I think so now, but at the time it seemed less clear. He had a great influence, it might prove greater than mine. The natives are prone to superstition; perhaps by stirring them up I might but ingrain and spread these dangerous fancies. And Namu besides, apart from this novel and accursed influence, was a good pastor, an able man and spiritually minded. Where should I look for a better? How was I to find as good? At that moment, with Namu's failure fresh in my view, the work of my life appeared a mockery; hope was dead in me. I would rather repair such tools as I had than go abroad in quest of others that must certainly prove worse; and a scandal is, at the best, a thing to be avoided when humanly possible. Right or wrong, then, I determined on a quiet course. All that night I denounced and reasoned with the erring pastor, twitted him with his ignorance and want of faith, twitted him with his wretched attitude, making clean the outside of the cup and platter, callously helping at a murder, childishly flying in excitement about a few childish, unnecessary and in-convenient gestures; and long before day I had him on his knees and bathed in the tears of what seemed a genuine repentance. On Sunday I took the pulpit in the morning, and preached from First Kings, nineteenth, on the fire, the earthquake, and the voice, distinguishing the true spiritual power, and referring with such plainness as I dared to recent events in Falesá. The effect produced was great, and it was much increased when Namu rose in his turn and confessed that he had been wanting in faith and conduct, and was convinced of sin. So far, then, all was well; but there was one unfortunate circumstance. It was nearing the time of our "May" in the island, when the native contributions to the missions are received; it fell in my duty to make a notification on the subject, and this gave my enemy his chance, by which he was not slow to profit.

'News of the whole proceedings must have been carried to Case as soon as church was over, and the same afternoon he made an occasion to meet me in the midst of the village. He came up with so much intentness and animosity that I felt it would be damaging to avoid him.

' "So," says he, in native, "here is the holy man. He has been preaching against me; but that was not in his heart. He has been preaching upon the love of God; but that was not in his heart, it was between his teeth. Will you know what was in his heart?" cries he. "I will show it you!" And, making a snatch at my head, he made believe to pluck out a dollar, and held it in the air.

'There went that rumour through the crowd with which Polynesians receive a prodigy. As for myself, I stood amazed. The thing was a common conjuring trick which I have seen performed at home a score of times; but how was I to convince the villagers of that? I wished I had learned legerdemain instead of Hebrew, that I might have paid the fellow out with his own coin. But there I was; I could not stand there silent, and the best I could find to say was weak.

' "I will trouble you not to lay hands on me again," said I.

' "I have no such thought," said he, "nor will I deprive you of your dollar. Here it is," he said, and flung it at my feet. I am told it lay where it fell three days.'

'I must say it was well played, said I.

'Oh! he is clever,' said Mr Tarleton, 'and you can now see for yourself how dangerous. He was a party to the horrid death of the paralytic; he is accused of poisoning Adams; he drove Vigours out of the place by lies that might have led to murder; and there is no question but he has now made up his mind to rid himself of you. How he means to try we have no guess; only be sure, it's something new. There is no end to his readiness and invention.'

'He gives himself a sight of trouble,' says I. 'And after all, what for?'

'Why, how many tons of copra may they make in this district?' asked the missionary.

'I dare say as much as sixty tons,' says I.

'And what is the profit to the local trader?' he asked.

'You may call it three pounds,' said I.

'Then you can reckon for yourself how much he does it for,' said Mr Tarleton. 'But the more important thing is to defeat him. It is clear he spread some report against Uma, in order to isolate and have his wicked will of her. Failing of that, and seeing a new rival come upon the scene, he used her in a different way. Now, the first point to find out is about Namu.

Uma, when people began to leave you and your mother alone, what did Namu do?'

'Stop away all-e-same,' says Uma.

'I fear the dog has returned to his vomit,' said Mr Tarleton. 'And now what am I to do for you? I will speak to Namu, I will warn him he is observed; it will be strange if he allow anything to go on amiss when he is put upon his guard. At the same time, this precaution may fail, and then you must turn elsewhere. You have two people at hand to whom you might apply. There is, first of all, the priest, who might protect you by the Catholic interest; they are a wretchedly small body, but they count two chiefs. And then there is old Faiaso. Ah! if it had been some years ago you would have needed no one else; but his influence is much reduced, it has gone into Maea's hands, and Maea, I fear, is one of Case's jackals. In fine, if the worst comes to the worst, you must send up or come yourself to Fale-alii, and though I am not due at this end of the island for a month, I will just see what can be done.'

So Mr Tarleton said farewell; and half an hour later the crew were singing and the paddles flashing in the missionary-boat.

4

Devil-Work

Near a month went by without much doing. The same night of our marriage Galoshes called round, and made himself mighty civil, and got into a habit of dropping in about dark and smoking his pipe with the family. He could talk to Uma, of course, and started to teach me native and French at the same time. He was a kind old buffer, though the dirtiest you would wish to see, and he muddled me up with foreign languages worse than the Tower of Babel.

That was one employment we had, and it made me feel less lonesome; but there was no profit in the thing, for though the priest came and sat and yarned, none of his folks could be enticed into my store; and if it hadn't been for the other occupation I struck out, there wouldn't have been a pound of copra in the house. This was the idea: Fa'avao (Uma's mother) had a score of bearing trees. Of course we could get no labour, being all as good as tabooed, but the two women and I turned to and made copra with our own hands. It was copra to make your mouth water when it was done – I never understood how much the natives cheated me till I had made that four hundred pounds with my own hand – and it weighed so light I felt inclined to take and water it myself.

When we were at the job a good many Kanakas used to put in the best of the day looking on, and once that nigger turned up. He stood back with the natives and laughed and did the big don and the funny dog, till I began to get riled.

'Here, you nigger!' says I.

'I don't address myself to you, sah,' says the nigger. 'Only speak to gen'le'um.'

'I know,' says I, 'but it happens I was addressing myself to you, Mr Black Jack. And all I want to know is just this: did you see Case's figurehead about a week ago?'

'No, sah,' says he.

'That's all right, then,' says I; 'for I'll show you the own brother to it, only black, in the inside of about two minutes.'

And I began to walk towards him, quite slow, and my hands down; only there was trouble in my eye, if anybody took the pains to look.

'You're a low, obstropulous fellow, sah,' says he.

'You bet!' says I.

By that time he thought I was about as near as convenient, and lit out so it would have done your heart good to see him travel. And that was all I saw of that precious gang until what I am about to tell you.

It was one of my chief employments these days to go pot-hunting in the woods, which I found (as Case had told me) very rich in game. I have spoken of the cape which shut up the village and my station from the east. A path went about the end of it, and led into the next bay. A strong wind blew here daily, and as the line of the barrier reef stopped at the end of the cape, a heavy surf ran on the shores of the bay. A little cliffy hill cut the valley in two parts, and stood close on the beach; and at high water the sea broke right on the face of it, so that all passage was stopped. Woody mountains hemmed the place all round; the barrier to the east was particularly steep and leafy, the lower parts of it, along the sea, falling in sheer black cliffs streaked with cinnabar; the upper part lumpy with the tops of the great trees. Some of the trees were bright green, and some red, and the sand of the beach as black as your shoes. Many birds hovered round the bay, some of them snow-white; and the flying-fox (or vampire) flew there in broad daylight, gnashing its teeth.

For a long while I came as far as this shooting, and went no farther. There was no sign of any path beyond, and the cocoa-palms in the front of the foot of the valley were the last this way. For the whole 'eye' of the island, as natives call the wind-ward end, lay desert. From Falesá round about to Papa-malulu, there was neither house, nor man, nor planted fruit-tree; and the reef being mostly absent, and the shores bluff, the sea beat direct among crags, and there was scarce a landing-place.

I should tell you that after I began to go in the woods, although no one offered to come near my store, I found people willing enough to pass the time of day with me where nobody could see them; and as I had begun to pick up native, and most of them had a word or two of English, I began to hold little odds and ends of conversation, not to much purpose to be sure, but they took off the worst of the feeling, for it's a miserable thing to be made a leper of.

It chanced one day towards the end of the month, that I was sitting in this bay in the edge of the bush, looking east, with a

Kanaka. I had given him a fill of tobacco, and we were making out to talk as best we could; indeed, he had more English than most.

I asked him if there was no road going eastward.

'One time one road,' said he. 'Now he dead.'

'Nobody he go there?' I asked.

'No good,' said he. 'Too much devil he stop there.'

'Oho!' says I, 'got-um plenty devil, that bush?'

'Man devil, woman devil; too much devil,' said my friend. 'Stop there all-e-time. Man he go there, no come back.'

I thought if this fellow was so well posted on devils and spoke of them so free, which is not common, I had better fish for a little information about myself and Uma.

'You think me one devil?' I asked.

'No think devil,' said he soothingly. 'Think all-e-same fool.'

'Uma, she devil?' I asked again.

'No, no; no devil. Devil stop bush,' said the young man.

I was looking in front of me across the bay, and I saw the hanging front of the woods pushed suddenly open, and Case, with a gun in his hand, step forth into the sunshine on the black beach. He was got up in light pyjamas, near white, his gun sparkled, he looked mighty conspicuous; and the land-crabs scuttled from all round him to their holes.

'Hello, my friend!' says I, 'you no talk all-e-same true. Ese he go, he come back.'

'Ese no all-e-same; Ese *Tiapolo*,' says my friend; and, with a 'Goodbye', slunk off among the trees.

I watched Case all round the beach, where the tide was low; and let him pass me on the homeward way to Falesá. He was in deep thought, and the birds seemed to know it, trotting quite near him on the sand, or wheeling and calling in his ears. When he passed me I could see by the working of his lips that he was talking to himself and, what pleased me mightily, he had still my trademark on his brow. I tell you the plain truth: I had a mind to give him a gunful in his ugly mug, but I thought better of it.

All this time, and all the time I was following him home, I kept repeating that native word, which I remembered by 'Polly, put the kettle on and make us all some tea', tea-a-pollo.

'Uma,' says I, when I got back, 'what does *Tiapolo* mean?'

'Devil,' says she.

'I thought *aitu* was the word for that,' I said.

'*Aitu* 'nother kind of devil,' said she; 'stop bush, eat Kanaka. Tiapolo big chief devil, stop home; all-e-same Christian devil.'

'Well then,' said I, 'I'm no further forward. How can Case be Tiapolo?'

'No all-e-same,' said she. 'Ese belong Tiapolo; Tiapolo too much like; Ese all-e-same his son. Suppose Ese he wish something, Tiapolo he make him.'

'That's mighty convenient for Ese,' says I. 'And what kind of things does he make for him?'

Well, out came a rigmarole of all sorts of stories, many of which (like the dollar he took from Mr Tarleton's head) were plain enough to me, but others I could make nothing of; and the thing that most surprised the Kanakas was what surprised me least – namely, that he would go in the desert among all the *aitus*. Some of the boldest, however, had accompanied him, and had heard him speak with the dead and give them orders, and, safe in his protection, had returned unscathed. Some said he had a church there, where he worshipped Tiapolo, and Tiapolo appeared to him; others swore that there was no sorcery at all, that he performed his miracles by the power of prayer, and the church was no church, but a prison, in which he had confined a dangerous *aitu*. Namu had been in the bush with him once, and returned glorifying God for these wonders. Altogether, I began to have a glimmer of the man's position, and the means by which he had acquired it, and, though I saw he was a tough nut to crack, I was noways cast down.

'Very well,' said I, 'I'll have a look at Master Case's place of worship myself, and we'll see about the glorifying.'

At this Uma fell in a terrible taking; if I went in the high bush I should never return; none could go there but by the protection of Tiapolo.

'I'll chance it on God's,' said I. 'I'm a good sort of a fellow, Uma, as fellows go, and I guess God'll con me through.'

She was silent for a while. 'I think,' said she, mighty solemn – and then, presently – 'Victoreea, he big chief?'

'You bet!' said I.

'He like you too much?' she asked again.

I told her, with a grin, I believed the old lady was rather partial to me.

'All right,' said she. 'Victoreea he big chief, like you too much. No can help you here in Falesá; no can do – too far off. Maea he small chief – stop here. Suppose he like you – make you all right. All-e-same God and Tiapolo. God he big chief – got too much work. Tiapolo he small chief – he like too much make-see, work very hard.'

'I'll have to hand you over to Mr Tarleton,' said I. 'Your theology's out of its bearings, Uma.'

However, we stuck to this business all the evening, and, with the stories she told me of the desert and its dangers, she came near frightening herself into a fit. I don't remember half a quarter of them, of course, for I paid little heed; but two come back to me kind of clear.

About six miles up the coast there is a sheltered cove they call Fanga-anaana' – 'the haven full of caves'. I've seen it from the sea myself, as near as I could get my boys to venture in; and it's a little strip of yellow sand. Black cliffs overhang it, full of the black mouths of caves; great trees overhang the cliffs and dangle-down lianas; and in one place, about the middle, a big brook pours over in a cascade. Well, there was a boat going by here, with six young men of Falesá, 'all very pretty', Uma said, which was the loss of them. It blew strong, there was a heavy head sea, and by the time they opened Fanga-anaana, and saw the white cascade and the shady beach, they were all tired and thirsty, and their water had run out. One proposed to land and get a drink, and, being reckless fellows, they were all of the same mind except the youngest. Lotu was his name; he was a very good young gentleman, and very wise; and he held out that they were crazy, telling them the place was given over to spirits and devils and the dead, and there were no living folk nearer than six miles the one way, and maybe twelve the other. But they laughed at his words, and, being five to one, pulled in, beached the boat, and landed. It was a wonderful pleasant place, Lotu said, and the water excellent. They walked round the beach, but could see nowhere any way to mount the cliffs, which made them easier in their mind; and at last they sat down to make a meal on the food they had brought with them. They were scarce set, when there came out of the mouth of one of the black caves six of the most beautiful ladies ever seen: they had flowers in their hair, and the most beautiful breasts, and necklaces of scarlet seeds; and began to jest with these young gentlemen, and the young gentlemen to jest back with them, all but Lotu. As for Lotu, he saw there could be no living woman in such a place, and ran, and flung himself in the bottom of the boat, and covered his face, and prayed. All the time the business lasted Lotu made one clean break of prayer, and that was all he knew of it, until his friends came back, and made him sit up, and they put to sea again out of the bay, which was now quite desert, and no word of the six ladies. But, what frightened Lotu most, not one of the five remembered anything of what had passed, but they were all like drunken men, and sang and laughed in the boat, and skylarked. The wind freshened and came squally, and the sea rose extraordinary high; it was such weather as any man in the islands would have turned his back to and fled home to Falesá; but these five were like crazy folk, and

cracked on all sail and drove their boat into the seas. Lotu went
to the bailing; none of the others thought to help him, but sang
and skylarked and carried on, and spoke singular things beyond
a man's comprehension, and laughed out loud when they said
them. So the rest of the day Lotu bailed for his life in the
bottom of the boat, and was all drenched with sweat and cold
sea-water; and none heeded him. Against all expectation, they
came safe in a dreadful tempest to Papa-malulu, where the
palms were singing out and the coconuts flying like cannonballs
about the village green; and the same night the five young
gentlemen sickened, and spoke never a reasonable word until
they died.

'And do you mean to tell me you can swallow a yarn like
that?' I asked.

She told me the thing was well known, and with handsome
young men alone it was even common; but this was the only
case where five had been slain the same day and in a company
by the love of the women-devils; and it had made a great stir in
the island, and she would be crazy if she doubted.

'Well, anyway,' says I, 'you needn't be frightened about me.
I've no use for the women-devils. You're all the women I want,
and all the devil too, old lady.'

To this she answered there were other sorts, and she had
seen one with her own eyes. She had gone one day alone to the
next bay, and, perhaps, got too near the margin of the bad
place. The boughs of the high bush overshadowed her from the
cant of the hill, but she herself was outside on a flat place, very
stony and growing full of young mummy-apples four and five
feet high. It was a dark day in the rainy season, and now there
came squalls that tore off the leaves and sent them flying, and
now it was all still as in a house. It was in one of these still times
that a whole gang of birds and flying foxes came pegging out of
the bush like creatures frightened. Presently after she heard a
rustle nearer hand, and saw, coming out of the margin of the

trees, among the mummy-apples, the appearance of a lean grey old boar. It seemed to think as it came, like a person; and all of a sudden, as she looked at it coming, she was aware it was no boar but a thing that was a man with a man's thoughts. At that she ran, and the pig after her, and as the pig ran it holla'd aloud, so that the place rang with it.

'I wish I had been there with my gun,' said I. 'I guess that pig would have holla'd so as to surprise himself.'

But she told me a gun was of no use with the like of these, which were the spirits of the dead.

Well, this kind of talk put in the evening, which was the best of it; but of course it didn't change my notion, and the next day, with my gun and a good knife, I set off upon a voyage of discovery. I made, as near as I could, for the place where I had seen Case come out; for if it was true he had some kind of establishment in the bush I reckoned I should find a path. The beginning of the desert was marked off by a wall, to call it so, for it was more of a long mound of stones. They say it reaches right across the island, but how they know it is another question, for I doubt if anyone has made the journey in a hundred years, the natives sticking chiefly to the sea and their little colonies along the coast, and that part being mortal high and steep and full of cliffs. Up to the west side of the wall, the ground has been cleared, and there are cocoa palms and mummy-apples and guavas, and lots of sensitive plants. Just across, the bush begins outright; high bush at that, trees going up like the masts of ships, and ropes of liana hanging down like a ship's rigging, and nasty orchids growing in the forks like funguses. The ground where there was no underwood looked to be a heap of boulders. I saw many green pigeons which I might have shot, only I was there with a different idea. A number of butterflies flopped up and down along the ground like dead leaves; sometimes I would hear a bird calling, sometimes the wind overhead, and always the sea along the coast.

But the queerness of the place it's more difficult to tell of, unless to one who has been alone in the high bush himself. The brightest kind of a day it is always dim down there. A man can see to the end of nothing; whichever way he looks the wood shuts up, one bough folding with another like the fingers of your hand; and whenever he listens he hears always something new – men talking, children laughing, the strokes of an axe a far way ahead of him, and sometimes a sort of a quick, stealthy scurry near at hand that makes him jump and look to his weapons. It's all very well for him to tell himself that he's alone, bar trees and birds; he can't make out to believe it; whichever way he turns the whole place seems to be alive and looking on. Don't think it was Uma's yarns that put me out; I don't value native talk a fourpenny-piece; it's a thing that's natural in the bush, and that's the end of it.

As I got near the top of the hill, for the ground of the wood goes up in this place steep as a ladder, the wind began to sound straight on, and the leaves to toss and switch open and let in the sun. This suited me better; it was the same noise all the time, and nothing to startle. Well, I had got to a place where there was an underwood of what they call wild coconut – mighty pretty with its scarlet fruit – when there came a sound of singing in the wind that I thought I had never heard the like of. It was all very fine to tell myself it was the branches; I knew better. It was all very fine to tell myself it was a bird; I knew never a bird that sang like that. It rose and swelled and died away and swelled again; and now I thought it was like someone weeping, only prettier; and now I thought it was like harps; and there was one thing I made sure of, it was a sight too sweet to be wholesome in a place like that. You may laugh if you like; but I declare I called to mind the six young ladies that came, with their scarlet necklaces, out of the cave at Fanga-anaana, and wondered if they sang like that. We laugh at the natives and their superstitions; but see how many traders take them up, splendidly educated white men, that have been bookkeepers (some of them) and clerks in the old country. It's my belief a superstition grows up in a place like the different kind of weeds; and as I stood there and listened to that wailing I twittered in my shoes.

You may call me a coward to be frightened; I thought myself brave enough to go on ahead. But I went mighty carefully, with my gun cocked, spying all about me like a hunter, fully expecting to see a handsome young woman sitting somewhere in the bush, and fully determined (if I did) to try her with a charge of duck-shot. And sure enough, I had not gone far when I met with a queer thing. The wind came on the top of the wood in a strong puff, the leaves in front of me burst open, and I saw for a second something hanging in a tree. It was gone in a wink, the puff blowing by and the leaves closing. I tell you the truth: I had made up my mind to see an *aitu*; and if the thing had looked like a pig or a woman, it wouldn't have given me the same turn. The trouble was that it seemed kind of square, and the idea of a square thing that was alive and sang knocked me sick and silly. I must have stood quite a while; and I made pretty certain it was right out of the same tree that the singing came. Then I began to come to myself a bit.

'Well,' says I, 'if this is really so, if this is a place where there are square things that sing, I'm gone up anyway. Let's have my fun for my money.'

But I thought I might as well take the off chance of a prayer being any good; so I plumped on my knees and prayed out loud; and all the time I was praying the strange sounds came out of the tree, and went up and down, and changed, for all the world like music, only you could see it wasn't human – there was nothing there that you could whistle.

As soon as I had made an end in proper style, I laid down my gun, stuck my knife between my teeth, walked right up to that tree, and began to climb. I tell you my heart was like ice. But presently, as I went up, I caught another glimpse of the thing, and that relieved me, for I thought it seemed like a box; and when I had got right up to it I near fell out of the tree with laughing.

A box it was, sure enough, and a candle-box at that, with the brand upon the side of it; and it had banjo strings stretched so as to sound when the wind blew. I believe they call the thing a Tyrolean harp, whatever that may mean.

'Well, Mr Case,' said I, 'you've frightened me once, but I defy you to frighten me again,' I says, and slipped down the tree, and set out again to find my enemy's head office, which I guessed would not be far away.

The undergrowth was thick in this part; I couldn't see before my nose, and must burst my way through by main force and ply the knife as I went, slicing the cords of the lianas and slashing down whole trees at a blow. I call them trees for the bigness, but in truth they were just big weeds, and sappy to cut through like carrot. From all this crowd and kind of vegetation, I was just thinking to myself, the place might have once been cleared, when I came on my nose over a pile of stones, and saw in a moment it was some kind of a work of man. The Lord knows when it was made or when deserted, for this part of the island has lain undisturbed since long before the whites came. A few steps beyond I hit into the path I had been always looking for. It was narrow, but well beaten, and I saw that Case had plenty of disciples. It seems, indeed, it was a piece of fashionable boldness to venture up here with the trader, and a young man scarce reckoned himself grown till he had got his breech tattooed, for one thing, and seen Case's devils for another. This is mighty like Kanakas; but, if you look at it another way, it's mighty like white folks too.

A bit along the path I was brought to a clear stand, and had to rub my eyes. There was a wall in front of me, the path passing it by a gap; it was tumbledown and plainly very old, but built of big stones very well laid; and there is no native alive today upon that island that could dream of such a piece of building. Along all the top of it was a line of queer figures, idols or scarecrows or what not. They had carved and painted faces ugly to view, their eyes and teeth were of shell, their hair and their bright clothes blew in the wind, and some of them worked with the tugging. There are islands up west where they make these kind of figures till today; but if ever they were made in this island, the practice and the very recollection of it are now long forgotten. And the singular thing was that all these bogies were as fresh as toys out of a shop.

Then it came in my mind that Case had let out to me the first day that he was a good forger of island curiosities, a thing by which so many traders turn an honest penny. And with that I saw the whole business, and how this display served the man a double purpose: first of all, to season his curiosities, and then to frighten those that came to visit him.

But I should tell you (what made the thing more curious) that all the time the Tyrolean harps were harping round me in the trees, and even while I looked, a green-and-yellow bird (that, I suppose, was building) began to tear the hair off the head of one of the figures.

A little farther on I found the best curiosity of the museum. The first I saw of it was a longish mound of earth with a twist to it. Digging off the earth with my hands, I found underneath tarpaulin stretched on boards, so that this was plainly the roof of a cellar. It stood right on the top of the hill, and the entrance was on the far side, between two rocks, like the entrance to a cave. I went as far in as the bend, and, looking round the corner, saw a shining face. It was big and ugly, like a pantomime mask, and the brightness of it waxed and dwindled, and at times it smoked.

'Oho!' says I, 'luminous paint!'

And I must say I rather admired the man's ingenuity. With a box of tools and a few mighty simple contrivances he had made out to have a devil of a temple. Any poor Kanaka brought up here in the dark, with the harps whining all round him, and shown that smoking face in the bottom of a hole, would make no kind of doubt but he had seen and heard enough devils for a lifetime. It's easy to find out what Kanakas think. Just go back to yourself any way round from ten to fifteen years old, and there's an average Kanaka. There are some pious, just as there are pious boys; and the most of them, like the boys again, are middling honest and yet think it rather larks to steal, and are easy scared and rather like to be so. I remember a boy I was at school with at home who played the Case business. He didn't know anything, that boy; he couldn't do anything; he had no luminous paint and no Tyrolean harps; he just boldly said he was a sorcerer, and frightened us out of our boots, and we loved it. And then it came in my mind how the master had once flogged that boy, and the surprise we were all in to see the sorcerer catch it and hum like anybody else. Thinks I to myself, 'I must find some way of fixing it so for Master Case.' And the next moment I had my idea.

I went back by the path, which, when once you had found it, was quite plain and easy walking; and when I stepped out on the black sands, who should I see but Master Case himself. I cocked my gun and held it handy, and we marched up and passed without a word, each keeping the tail of his eye on the other; and no sooner had we passed than we each wheeled round like fellows drilling, and stood face to face. We had each taken the same notion in his head, you see, that the other fellow might give him the load of his gun in the stern.

'You've shot nothing,' says Case.

'I'm not on the shoot today,' said I.

'Well, the devil go with you for me,' says he.

'The same to you,' says I.

But we stuck just the way we were; no fear of either of us moving.

Case laughed. 'We can't stop here all day, though,' said he.

'Don't let me detain you,' says I.

He laughed again. 'Look here, Wiltshire, do you think me a fool?' he asked.

'More of a knave, if you want to know,' says I.

'Well, do you think it would better me to shoot you here, on this open beach?' said he. 'Because I don't. Folks come fishing every day. There may be a score of them up the valley now, making copra; there might be half a dozen on the hill behind you, after pigeons; they might be watching us this minute, and I shouldn't wonder. I give you my word I don't want to shoot you. Why should I? You don't hinder me any. You haven't got one pound of copra but what you made with your own hands, like a negro slave. You're vegetating – that's what I call it – and I don't care where you vegetate, nor yet how long. Give me your word you don't mean to shoot me, and I'll give you a lead and walk away.'

'Well,' said I, 'You're frank and pleasant, ain't you? And I'll be the same. I don't mean to shoot you today. Why should I? This business is beginning; it ain't done yet, Mr Case. I've given you one turn already; I can see the marks of my knuckles on your head to this blooming hour, and I've more cooking for you. I'm not a paralee, like Underhill. My name ain't Adams, and it ain't Vigours; and I mean to show you that you've met your match.'

'This is a silly way to talk,' said he. 'This is not the talk to make me move on with.'

'All right,' said I, 'stay where you are. I ain't in any hurry, and you know it. I can put in a day on this beach and never mind. I ain't got any copra to bother with. I ain't got any luminous paint to see to.'

I was sorry I said that last, but it whipped out before I knew. I could see it took the wind out of his sails, and he stood and stared at me with his brow drawn up. Then I suppose he made up his mind he must get to the bottom of this.

'I take you at your word,' says he, and turned his back, and walked right into the devil's bush.

I let him go, of course, for I had passed my word. But I watched him as long as he was in sight, and after he was gone lit out for cover as lively as you would want to see, and went the rest of the way home under the bush, for I didn't trust him sixpence-worth. One thing I saw, I had been ass enough to give him warning, and that which I meant to do I must do at once.

You would think I had had about enough excitement for one morning, but there was another turn waiting me. As soon as I got far enough round the cape to see my house I made out there were strangers there; a little farther, and no doubt about it. There was a couple of armed sentinels squatting at my door. I could only suppose the trouble about Uma must have come to a head, and the station been seized. For aught I could think, Uma was taken up already, and these armed men were waiting to do the like with me.

However, as I came nearer, which I did at top speed, I saw there was a third native sitting on the verandah like a guest, and Uma was talking with him like a hostess. Nearer still I made out it was the big young chief, Maea, and that he was smiling away and smoking. And what was he smoking? None of your European cigarettes fit for a cat, not even the genuine big, knock-me-down native article that a fellow can really put in the time with if his pipe is broke – but a cigar, and one of my Mexicans at that, that I could swear to. At sight of this my heart started beating, and I took a wild hope in my head that the trouble was over, and Maea had come round.

Uma pointed me out to him as I came up, and he met me at the head of my own stairs like a thorough gentleman.

'Vilivili,' said he, which was the best they could make of my name, 'I pleased.'

There is no doubt when an island chief wants to be civil he can do it. I saw the way things were from the word go. There was no call for Uma to say to me: 'He no 'fraid Ese now, come bring copra.' I tell you I shook hands with that Kanaka like as if he was the best white man in Europe.

The fact was, Case and he had got after the same girl; or Maea suspected it, and concluded to make hay of the trader on the chance. He had dressed himself up, got a couple of his retainers cleaned and armed to kind of make the thing more public, and, just waiting till Case was clear of the village, came round to put the whole of his business my way. He was rich as well as powerful. I suppose that man was worth fifty thousand nuts per annum. I gave him the price of the beach and a quarter cent better, and as for credit, I would have advanced him the inside of the store and the fittings besides, I was so pleased to see him. I must say he bought like a gentleman: rice and tins and biscuits enough for a week's feast, and stuffs by the bolt. He was agreeable besides; he had plenty fun to him; and we cracked jests together, mostly through the interpreter, because he had mighty little English, and my native was still off colour. One thing I made out: he could never really have thought much harm of Uma; he could never have been really frightened, and must just have made believe from dodginess, and because he thought Case had a strong pull in the village and could help him on.

This set me thinking that both he and I were in a tightish place. What he had done was to fly in the face of the whole village, and the thing might cost him his authority. More than that, after my talk with Case on the beach, I thought it might very well cost me my life. Case had as good as said he would pot me if ever I got any copra; he would come home to find the best business in the village had changed hands; and the best thing I thought I could do was to get in first with the potting.

'See here, Uma,' says I, 'tell him I'm sorry I made him wait, but I was up looking at Case's Tiapolo store in the bush.'

'He want savvy if you no 'fraid?' translated Uma.

I laughed out. 'Not much!' says I. 'Tell him the place is a blooming toy-shop! Tell him in England we give these things to the kids to play with.'

'He want savvy if you hear devil sing?' she asked next.

'Look here,' I said, 'I can't do it now because I've got no banjo-strings in stock; but the next time the ship comes round I'll have one of these same contraptions right here in my verandah, and he can see for himself how much devil there is to it. Tell him, as soon as I can get the strings I'll make one for his piccaninnies. The name of the concern is a Tyrolean harp; and you can tell him the name means in English that nobody but damn fools give a cent for it.'

This time he was so pleased he had to try his English again. 'You talk true?' says he.

'Rather!' said I. 'Talk all-e-same Bible. Bring out a Bible here, Uma, if you've got such a thing, and I'll kiss it. Or, I'll tell you what's better still,' says I, taking a header, 'ask him if he's afraid to go up there himself by day.'

It appeared he wasn't; he could venture as far as that by day and in company.

'That's the ticket, then!' said I. 'Tell him the man's a fraud and the place foolishness, and if he'll go up there tomorrow he'll see all that's left of it. But tell him this, Uma, and mind he understands it. If he gets talking, it's bound to come to Case, and I'm a dead man! I'm playing his game, tell him, and if he says one word my blood will be at his door and be the damnation of him here and after.'

She told him, and he shook hands with me up to the hilt, and, says he: 'No talk. Go up tomorrow. You my friend?'

'No, sir,' says I, 'no such foolishness. I've come here to trade, tell him, and not to make friends. But, as to Case, I'll send that man to glory!'

So off Maea went, pretty well pleased, as I could see.

5
Nigt in the Bush

Well, I was committed now; Tiapolo had to be smashed up before next day, and my hands were pretty full, not only with preparations, but with argument. My house was like a mechanics' debating society: Uma was so made up that I shouldn't go into the bush by night, or that, if I did, I was never to come back again. You know her style of arguing: you've had a specimen about Queen Victoria and the devil; and I leave you to fancy if I was tired of it before dark.

At last I had a good idea. What was the use of casting my pearls before her? I thought; some of her own chopped hay would be likelier to do the business.

'I'll tell you what, then,' said I. 'You fish out your Bible, and I'll take that up along with me. That'll make me right.'

She swore a Bible was no use.

'That's just your Kanaka ignorance,' said I. 'Bring the Bible out.'

She brought it, and I turned to the title-page, where I thought there would likely be some English, and so there was. 'There!' said I. 'Look at that! "London: Printed for the British and Foreign Bible Society, Blackfriars", and the date, which I can't read, owing to its being in these Xs. There's no devil in hell can look near the Bible Society, Blackfriars. Why, you silly!' I said, 'how do you suppose we get along with our own *aitus* at home? All Bible Society!'

'I think you no got any,' said she. 'White man, he tell me you no got.'

'Sounds likely, don't it?' I asked. 'Why would these islands all be chock full of them and none in Europe?'

'Well, you no got breadfruit,' said she.

I could have torn my hair. 'Now look here, old lady,' said I, 'you dry up, for I'm tired of you. I'll take the Bible, which'll put me as straight as the mail, and that's the last word I've got to say.'

The night fell extraordinary dark, clouds coming up with sundown and overspreading all; not a star showed; there was only an end of a moon, and that not due before the small hours. Round the village, what with the lights and the fires in the open houses, and the torches of many fishers moving on the reef, it kept as gay as an illumination; but the sea and the mountains and woods were all clean gone. I suppose it might be eight o'clock when I took the road, laden like a donkey. First there was that Bible, a book as big as your head, which I had let myself in for by my own tomfoolery. Then there was my gun, and knife, and lantern, and patent matches, all necessary. And then there was the real plant of the affair in hand, a mortal weight of gunpowder, a pair of dynamite fishing-bombs, and two or three pieces of slow match that I had hauled out of the tin cases and spliced together the best way I could; for the match was only trade stuff, and a man would be crazy that trusted it. Altogether, you see, I had the materials of a pretty good blow-up! Expense was nothing to me; I wanted that thing done right.

As long as I was in the open, and had the lamp in my house to steer by, I did well. But when I got to the path, it fell so dark I could make no headway, walking into trees and swearing there, like a man looking for the matches in his bedroom. I knew it was risky to light up, for my lantern would be visible all the way to the point of the cape, and as no one went there after dark, it would be talked about and come to Case's ears. But what was I to do? I had either to give the business over and lose caste with Maea, or light up, take my chance, and get through the thing the smartest I was able.

As long as I was on the path I walked hard, but when I came to the black beach I had to run. For the tide was now nearly flowed; and to get through with my powder dry, between the surf and the steep hill, took all the quickness I possessed. As it was, even, the wash caught me to the knees, and I came near falling on a stone. All this time the hurry I was in, and the free air and smell of the sea, kept my spirits lively; but when I was once in the bush and began to climb the path I took it easier. The fearsomeness of the wood had been a good bit rubbed off for me by Master Case's banjo-strings and graven images, yet I thought it was a dreary walk, and guessed, when the disciples went up there, they must be badly scared. The light of the lantern, striking among all these trunks and forked branches and twisted rope-ends of lianas, made the whole place, or all that you could see of it, a kind of a puzzle of turning shadows. They came to meet you, solid and quick like giants, and then span off and vanished; they hove up over your head like clubs, and flew away into the night like birds. The floor of the bush glimmered with dead wood, the way the matchbox used to shine after you had struck a lucifer. Big, cold drops fell on me from the branches overhead like sweat. There was no wind to mention; only a little icy breath of a land-breeze that stirred nothing; and the harps were silent.

The first landfall I made was when I got through the bush of wild coconuts, and came in view of the bogies on the wall. Mighty queer they looked by the shining of the lantern, with their painted faces and shell eyes, and their clothes and their hair hanging. One after another I pulled them all up and piled them in a bundle on the cellar roof, so as they might go to glory with the rest. Then I chose a place behind one of the big stones at the entrance, buried my powder and the two shells, and arranged my match along the passage. And then I had a look at the smoking head, just for goodbye. It was doing fine.

'Cheer up,' says I. 'You're booked.'

It was my first idea to light up and be getting homeward; for the darkness and the glimmer of the dead wood and the shadows of the lantern made me lonely. But I knew where one of the harps hung; it seemed a pity it shouldn't go with the rest; and at the same time I couldn't help letting on to myself that I was mortal tired of my employment, and would like best to be at home and have the door shut. I stepped out of the cellar and argued it fore and back. There was a sound of the sea far down below me on the coast; nearer hand not a leaf stirred; I might have been the only living creature this side of Cape Horn. Well, as I stood there thinking, it seemed the bush woke and became full of little noises. Little noises they were, and nothing to hurt; a bit of a crackle, a bit of a rush; but the breath jumped right out of me and my throat went as dry as a biscuit. It wasn't Case I was afraid of, which would have been common-sense; I never thought of Case; what took me, as sharp as the colic, was the old wives' tales, the devil-women and the man-pigs. It was the toss of a penny whether I should run; but I got a purchase on myself, and stepped out, and held up the lantern (like a fool) and looked all round.

In the direction of the village and the path there was nothing to be seen; but when I turned inland it's a wonder to me I didn't drop. There, coming right up out of the desert and the bad bush – there, sure enough, was a devil-woman, just the way I had figured she would look. I saw the light shine on her bare arms and her bright eyes, and there went out of me a yell so big that I thought it was my death.

'Ah! No sing out!' says the devil-woman, in a kind of a high whisper. 'Why you talk big voice? Put out light! Ese he come.'

'My God Almighty, Uma, is that you?' says I.

'Ioe,' says she. 'I come quick. Ese here soon.'

'You come alone?' I asked. 'You no 'fraid?'

'Ah, too much 'fraid!' she whispered, clutching me. 'I think die.'

'Well,' says I, with a kind of a weak grin, 'I'm not the one to laugh at you, Mrs Wiltshire, for I'm about the worst scared man in the South Pacific myself.'

She told me in two words what brought her. I was scarce

gone, it seems, when Fa'avao came in, and the old woman had met Black Jack running as hard as he was fit from our house to Case's. Uma neither spoke nor stopped, but lit right out to come and warn me. She was so close at my heels that the lantern was her guide across the beach, and afterwards, by the glimmer of it in the trees, she got her line uphill. It was only when I had got to the top or was in the cellar that she wandered Lord knows where! and lost a sight of precious time, afraid to call out lest Case was at the heels of her, and falling in the bush, so that she was all knocked and bruised. That must have been when she got too far to the southward, and how she came to take me in the flank at last and frighten me beyond what I've got the words to tell of.

Well, anything was better than a devil-woman, but I thought her yarn serious enough. Black Jack had no call to be about my house, unless he was set there to watch; and it looked to me as if my tomfool word about the paint, and perhaps some chatter of Maea's, had got us all in a clove hitch. One thing was clear: Uma and I were here for the night; we daren't try to go home before day, and even then it would be safer to strike round up the mountain and come in by the back of the village, or we might walk into an ambuscade. It was plain, too, that the mine should be sprung immediately, or Case might be in time to stop it.

I marched into the tunnel, Uma keeping tight hold of me, opened my lantern and lit the match. The first length of it burned like a spill of paper, and I stood stupid, watching it burn, and thinking we were going aloft with Tiapolo, which was none of my views. The second took to a better rate, though faster than I cared about; and at that I got my wits again, hauled Uma clear of the passage, blew out and dropped the lantern, and the pair of us groped our way into the bush until I thought it might be safe, and lay down together by a tree.

'Old lady,' I said, 'I won't forget this night. You're a trump, and that's what's wrong with you.'

She humped herself close up to me. She had run out the way she was, with nothing on her but her kilt; and she was all wet with the dews and the sea on the black beach, and shook straight on with cold and the terror of the dark and the devils.

'Too much 'fraid,' was all she said.

The far side of Case's hill goes down near as steep as a precipice into the next valley. We were on the very edge of it, and I could see the dead wood shine and hear the sea sound far below. I didn't care about the position, which left me no retreat, but I was afraid to change. Then I saw I had made a worse mistake about the lantern, which I should have left lighted, so that I could have had a crack at Case when he stepped into the shine of it. And even if I hadn't had the wit to do that, it seemed a senseless thing to leave the good lantern to blow up with the graven images. The thing belonged to me, after all, and was worth money, and might come in handy. If I could have trusted the match, I might have run in still and rescued it. But who was going to trust the match? You know what trade is. The stuff was good enough for Kanakas to go fishing with, where they've got to look lively anyway, and the most they risk is only to have their hand blown off. But for anyone that wanted to fool around a blow-up like mine that match was rubbish.

Altogether the best I could do was to lie still, see my shotgun handy, and wait for the explosion. But it was a solemn kind of a business. The blackness of the night was like solid; the only thing you could see was the nasty bogy glimmer of the dead wood, and that showed you nothing but itself; and as for sounds, I stretched my ears till I thought I could have heard the match burn in the tunnel, and that bush was as silent as a coffin. Now and then there was a bit of a crack; but whether it was near or far, whether it was Case stubbing his toes within a few yards of me, or a tree breaking miles away, I knew no more than the babe unborn.

And then, all of a sudden, Vesuvius went off. It was a long

time coming, but when it came (though I say it that shouldn't) no man could ask to see a better. At first it was just a son of a gun of a row, and a spout of fire, and the wood lighted up so that you could see to read. And then the trouble began. Uma and I were half buried under a waggonful of earth, and glad it was no worse, for one of the rocks at the entrance of the tunnel was fired clean into the air, fell within a couple of fathoms of where we lay, bounded over the edge of the hill and went pounding down into the next valley. I saw I had rather under-calculated our distance, or over-done the dynamite and powder, which you please.

And presently I saw I had made another slip. The noise of the thing began to die off, shaking the island; the dazzle was over; and yet the night didn't come back the way I expected. For the whole wood was scattered with red coals and brands from the explosion; they were all round me on the flat; some had fallen below in the valley, and some stuck and flared in the treetops. I had no fear of fire, for these forests are too wet to kindle. But the trouble was that the place was all lit up – not very bright, but good enough to get a shot by; and the way the coals were scattered, it was just as likely Case might have the advantage as myself. I looked all round for his white face, you may be sure; but there was not a sign of him. As for Uma, the life seemed to have been knocked right out of her by the bang and blaze of it.

There was one bad point in my game. One of the blessed graven images had come down all afire, hair and clothes and body, not four yards away from me. I cast a mighty noticing glance all round; there was still no Case, and I made up my mind I must get rid of that burning stick before he came, or I should be shot there like a dog.

It was my first idea to have crawled, and then I thought speed was the main thing, and stood half up to make a rush. The same moment from somewhere between me and the sea there came a flash and a report, and a rifle bullet screeched in my ear. I swung straight round and up with my gun, but the brute had a Winchester, and before I could as much as see him his second shot knocked me over like a ninepin. I seemed to fly in the air, then came down by the run and lay half a minute, silly; and then I found my hands empty, and my gun had flown over my head as I fell. It makes a man mighty wide awake to be in the kind of box that I was in. I scarcely knew where I was hurt, or whether I was hurt or not, but turned right over on my face to crawl after my weapon. Unless you have tried to get about with a smashed leg you don't know what pain is, and I let out a howl like a bullock's.

This was the unluckiest noise that ever I made in my life. Up to then Uma had stuck to her tree like a sensible woman, knowing she would be only in the way; but as soon as she heard me sing out, she ran forward. The Winchester cracked again, and down she went.

I had sat up, leg and all, to stop her; but when I saw her tumble I clapped down again where I was, lay still, and felt the handle of my knife. I had been scurried and put out before. No more of that for me. He had knocked over my girl, I had got to fix him for it; and I lay there and gritted my teeth, and footed up the chances. My leg was broke, my gun was gone. Case had still ten shots in his Winchester. It looked a kind of hopeless business. But I never despaired nor thought upon despairing: that man had got to go.

For a goodish bit not one of us let on. Then I heard Case begin to move nearer in the bush, but mighty careful. The image had burned out; there were only a few coals left here and there, and the wood was main dark, but had a kind of a low glow in it like a fire on its last legs. It was by this that I made out Case's head looking at me over a big tuft of ferns, and at the same time the brute saw me and shouldered his Winchester. I lay quite still, and as good as looked into the barrel; it was my last chance, but I thought my heart would have come right out of its bearings. Then he fired. Lucky for me it was no shotgun, for the bullet struck within an inch of me and knocked the dirt in my eyes.

Just you try and see if you can lie quiet, and let a man take a sitting shot at you and miss you by a hair. But I did, and lucky too. A while Case stood with the Winchester at the port-arms; then he gave a little laugh to himself, and stepped round the ferns.

'Laugh!' thought I. 'If you had the wit of a louse you would be praying!'

I was all as taut as a ship's hawser or the spring of a watch, and as soon as he came within reach of me I had him by the ankle, plucked the feet right out from under him, laid him out, and was upon the top of him, broken leg and all, before he breathed. His Winchester had gone the same road as my shot-gun; it was nothing to me – I defied him now. I'm a pretty strong man anyway, but I never knew what strength was till I got hold of Case. He was knocked out of time by the rattle he came down with, and threw up his hands together, more like a frightened woman, so that I caught both of them with my left. This wakened him up, and he fastened his teeth in my forearm like a weasel. Much I cared. My leg gave me all the pain I had any use for, and I drew my knife and got it in the place.

'Now,' said I, 'I've got you; and you're gone up, and a good job too! Do you feel the point of that? That's for Underhill! And there's for Adams! And now here's for Uma, and that's going to knock your blooming soul right out of you!'

With that I gave him the cold steel for all I was worth. His body kicked under me like a spring sofa; he gave a dreadful kind of a long moan, and lay still.

'I wonder if you're dead? I hope so!' I thought, for my head was swimming. But I wasn't going to take chances; I had his own example too close before me for that; and I tried to draw the knife out to give it him again. The blood came over my hands, I remember, hot as tea; and with that I fainted clean away, and fell with my head on the man's mouth.

When I came to myself it was pitch dark; the cinders had burned out; there was nothing to be seen but the shine of the dead wood, and I couldn't remember where I was nor why I was in such pain nor what I was all wetted with. Then it came back, and the first thing I attended to was to give him the knife again a half-a-dozen times up to the handle. I believe he was dead already, but it did him no harm and did me good.

'I bet you're dead now,' I said, and then I called to Uma.

Nothing answered, and I made a move to go and grope for her, fouled my broken leg, and fainted again.

When I came to myself the second time the clouds had all cleared away, except a few that sailed there, white as cotton. The moon was up – a tropic moon. The moon at home turns a wood black, but even this old butt-end of a one showed up that forest as green as by day. The night birds – or, rather, they're a kind of early-morning bird – sang out with their long, falling notes like nightingales. And I could see the dead man, that I was still half resting on, looking right up into the sky with his open eyes, no paler than when he was alive; and a little way off Uma tumbled on her side. I got over to her the best way I was able, and when I got there she was broad awake, and crying and sobbing to herself with no more noise than an insect. It appears she was afraid to cry out loud, because of the *aitus*. Altogether she was not much hurt, but scared beyond belief; she had come to her senses a long while ago, cried out to me, heard nothing in reply, made out we were both dead, and had lain there ever since, afraid to budge a finger. The ball had ploughed up her shoulder, and she had lost a main quantity of blood; but I soon had that tied up the way it ought to be with the tail of my shirt and a scarf I had on, got her head on my sound knee and my back against a trunk, and settled down to wait for morning. Uma was good for neither use nor ornament, and could only clutch hold of me and shake and cry. I don't suppose there was ever anybody worse scared, and, to do her justice, she had had a lively night of it. As for me, I was in a good bit of pain and fever, but not so bad when I sat still; and every time I looked over to Case I could have sung and whistled. Talk about meat and drink! To see that man lying there dead as a herring filled me full.

The night birds stopped after a while; and then the light began to change, the east came orange, the whole wood began to whirr with singing like a musical box, and there was the broad day.

I didn't expect Maea for a long while yet; and, indeed, I thought there was an off-chance he might go back on the whole idea and not come at all. I was the better pleased when, about an hour after daylight, I heard sticks smashing and a lot of Kanakas laughing and singing out to keep their courage up. Uma sat up quite brisk at the first word of it; and presently we saw a party come stringing out of the path, Maea in front, and behind him a white man in a pith helmet. It was Mr Tarleton, who had turned up late last night in Falesá, having left his boat and walked the last stage with a lantern.

They buried Case upon the field of glory, right in the hole where he had kept the smoking head. I waited till the thing was done; and Mr Tarleton prayed, which I thought tomfoolery, but I'm bound to say he gave a pretty sick view of the dear departed's prospects, and seemed to have his own ideas of hell. I had it out with him afterwards, told him he had scamped his duty, and what he had ought to have done was to up like a man and tell the Kanakas plainly Case was damned, and a good riddance; but I never could get him to see it my way. Then they made me a litter of poles and carried me down to the station. Mr Tarleton set my leg, and made a regular missionary splice of it, so that I limp to this day. That done, he took down my evidence, and Uma's, and Maea's, wrote it all out fine, and had us sign it; and then he got the chiefs and marched over to Papa Randall's to seize Case's papers.

All they found was a bit of a diary, kept for a good many years, and all about the price of copra, and chickens being stolen, and that; and the books of the business and the will I told you of in the beginning, by both of which the whole thing (stock, lock and barrel) appeared to belong to the Samoa woman. It was I that bought her out at a mighty reasonable figure, for she was in a hurry to get home. As for Randall and the black, they had to tramp; got into some kind of a station on the Papa-malulu side; did very bad business, for the truth is neither of the pair was fit for it, and lived mostly on fish, which was the means of Randall's death. It seems there was a nice shoal in one day, and papa went after them with the dynamite; either the match burned too fast, or papa was full, or both, but the shell went off (in the usual way) before he threw it, and where was papa's hand? Well, there's nothing to hurt in that; the islands up north are all full of one-handed men, like the parties in the *Arabian Nights*; but either Randall was too old, or he drank too much, for the short and the long of it was that he died. Pretty soon after, the nigger was turned out of the island for stealing from white men, and went off to the west, where he found men of his own colour, in case he liked that, and the men of his own colour took and ate him at some kind of a corroborree, and I'm sure I hope he was to their fancy!

So there was I, left alone in my glory at Falesá; and when the schooner came round I filled her up, and gave her a deck-cargo half as high as the house. I must say Mr Tarleton did the right thing by us; but he took a meanish kind of a revenge.

'Now, Mr Wiltshire,' said he, 'I've put you all square with everybody here. It wasn't difficult to do, Case being gone; but I have done it, and given my pledge besides that you will deal fairly with the natives. I must ask you to keep my word.'

Well, so I did. I used to be bothered about my balances, but I reasoned it out this way: We all have queerish balances; and the natives all know it, and water their copra in a proportion so that it's fair all round; but the truth is, it did use to bother me, and, though I did well in Falesá, I was half glad when the firm moved me on to another station, where I was under no kind of a pledge and could look my balances in the face.

As for the old lady, you know her as well as I do. She's only the one fault. If you don't keep your eye lifting she would give away the roof off the station. Well, it seems it's natural in Kanakas. She's turned a powerful big woman now, and could throw a London bobby over her shoulder. But that's natural in Kanakas too, and there's no manner of doubt that she's an A1 wife.

Mr Tarleton's gone home, his trick being over. He was the best missionary I ever struck, and now, it seems, he's parsonising down Somerset way. Well, that's best for him; he'll have no Kanakas there to get luny over.

My public-house? Not a bit of it, nor ever likely. I'm stuck here, I fancy. I don't like to leave the kids, you see: and – there's no use talking – they're better here than what they would be in a white man's country, though Ben took the eldest up to Auckland, where he's being schooled with the best. But what bothers me is the girls. They're only half-castes, of course; I know that as well as you do, and there's nobody thinks less of half-castes than I do; but they're mine, and about all I've got. I can't reconcile my mind to their taking up with Kanakas, but I'd like to know where I'm to find them whites?

ARTHUR CONAN DOYLE

Sir Arthur Conan Doyle (1859–1930) was born in Edinburgh into an Irish Roman Catholic family. His father was a clerk in the Board of Works, and his uncle, Richard Doyle, was the artist who drew the well-known cover design of *Punch*. Doyle was educated at Stonyhurst and Edinburgh University, where he qualified as a doctor, practising at Southsea from 1882 to 1890. In 1882 he published *A Study in Scarlet,* an adventure story which introduced the famous character Sherlock Holmes. Doyle served as a doctor in the South African War and wrote a history of the conflict, *The Great Boer War* (1900). He was a prolific author of detective and science-fiction stories, plays, poetry and historical novels. In 1902 he was knighted. In his later years Doyle was deeply interested in psychic phenomena and wrote a *History of Spiritualism* (1926).

The Adventure of Black Peter

I have never known my friend to be in better form, both mental and physical, than in the year 1895. His increasing fame had brought with it an immense practice, and I should be guilty of an indiscretion if I were even to hint at the identity of some of the illustrious clients who crossed our humble threshold in Baker Street. Holmes, however, like all great artists, lived for his art's sake, and, save in the case of the Duke of Holdernesse, I have seldom known him claim any large reward for his inestimable services. So unworldly was he – or so capricious – that he frequently refused his help to the powerful and wealthy where the problem made no appeal to his sympathies, while he would devote weeks of most intense application to the affairs of some humble client whose case presented those strange and dramatic qualities which appealed to his imagination and challenged his ingenuity.

In this memorable year 1895 a curious and incongruous succession of cases had engaged his attention, ranging from his famous investigation of the sudden death of Cardinal Tosca – an enquiry which was carried out by him at the express desire of His Holiness the Pope – down to his arrest of Wilson, the notorious canary-trainer, which removed a plague-spot from the East End of London. Close on the heels of these two famous cases came the tragedy of Woodman's Lee, and the very obscure circumstances which surrounded the death of Captain Peter Carey. No record of the doings of Mr Sherlock Holmes would be complete which did not include some account of this very unusual affair.

During the first week of July my friend had been absent so often and so long from our lodgings that I knew he had something on hand. The fact that several rough-looking men called during that time and enquired for Captain Basil made me understand that Holmes was working somewhere under one of the numerous disguises and names with which he concealed his own formidable identity. He had at least five small refuges in different parts of London in which he was able to change his personality. He said nothing of his business to me, and it was not my habit to force a confidence. The first positive sign which he gave me of the direction which his investigation was taking was an extraordinary one. He had gone out before breakfast, and I had sat down to mine, when he strode into the room, his hat upon his head and a huge barbed-headed spear tucked like an umbrella under his arm.

'Good gracious, Holmes!' I cried. 'You don't mean to say that you have been walking about London with that thing?'

'I drove to the butcher's and back.'

'The butcher's?'

'And I return with an excellent appetite. There can be no question, my dear Watson, of the value of exercise before break-fast. But I am prepared to bet that you will not guess the form that my exercise has taken.'

'I will not attempt it.'

He chuckled as he poured out the coffee.

'If you could have looked into Allardyce's back shop you would have seen a dead pig swung from a hook in the ceiling, and a gentleman in his shirt-sleeves furiously stabbing at it with this weapon. I was that energetic person, and I have satisfied myself that by no exertion of my strength can I transfix the pig with a single blow. Perhaps you would care to try?'

'Not for worlds. But why were you doing this?'

'Because it seemed to me to have an indirect bearing upon the mystery of Woodman's Lee. Ah, Hopkins, I got your wire last night, and I have been expecting you. Come and join us.'

Our visitor was an exceedingly alert man, thirty years of age, dressed in a quiet tweed suit, but retaining the erect bearing of one who was accustomed to official uniform. I recognised him at once as Stanley Hopkins, a young police inspector for whose future Holmes had high hopes, while he in turn professed the admiration and respect of a pupil for the scientific methods of the famous amateur. Hopkins's brow was clouded, and he sat down with an air of deep dejection.

'No, thank you, sir. I breakfasted before I came round. I spent the night in town, for I came up yesterday to report.'

'And what had you to report?'

'Failure, sir; absolute failure.'

'You have made no progress?'

'None.'

'Dear me! I must have a look at the matter.'

'I wish to heavens that you would, Mr Holmes. It's my first big chance, and I am at my wit's end. For goodness' sake come down and lend me a hand.'

'Well, well, it just happens that I have already read all the available evidence, including the report of the inquest, with some care. By the way, what do you make of that tobacco-pouch found on the scene of the crime? Is there no clue there?'

Hopkins looked surprised.

'It was the man's own pouch, sir. His initials were inside it. And it was of sealskin – and he an old sealer.'

'But he had no pipe.'

'No, sir, we could find no pipe; indeed, he smoked very little. And yet he might have kept some tobacco for his friends.'

'No doubt. I only mention it because if I had been handling the case I should have been inclined to make that the starting-point of my investigation. However, my friend Dr Watson knows nothing of this matter, and I should be none the worse for hearing the sequence of events once more. Just give us some short sketch of the essentials.'

Stanley Hopkins drew a slip of paper from his pocket.

'I have a few dates here which will give you the career of the dead man, Captain Peter Carey. He was born in 1845 – fifty years of age. He was a most daring and successful seal and whale fisher. In 1883 he commanded the steam sealer *Sea Unicorn* of Dundee. He had then had several successful voyages in succession, and in the following year, 1884, he retired. After that he travelled for some years, and finally he bought a small place called Woodman's Lee, near Forest Row, in Sussex. There he has lived for six years, and there he died just a week ago today.

'There were some most singular points about the man. In ordinary life he was a strict Puritan – a silent, gloomy fellow. His household consisted of his wife, his daughter, aged twenty, and two female servants. These last were continually changing, for it was never a very cheery situation, and sometimes it became past all bearing. The man was an intermittent drunkard, and when he had the fit on him he was a perfect fiend. He has been known to drive his wife and his daughter out of doors in the middle of the night, and flog them through the park until the whole village outside the gates was aroused by their screams.

'He was summoned once for a savage assault upon the old vicar, who had called upon him to remonstrate with him upon his conduct. In short, Mr Holmes, you would go far before you found a more dangerous man than Peter Carey, and I have heard that he bore the same character when he commanded his ship. He was known in the trade as Black Peter, and the name was given him, not only on account of his swarthy features and the colour of his huge beard, but for the humours which were the terror of all around him. I need not say that he was loathed and avoided by every one of his neighbours, and that I have not heard one single word of sorrow about his terrible end.

'You must have read in the account of the inquest about the man's cabin, Mr Holmes; but perhaps your friend here has not heard of it. He had built himself a wooden outhouse – he always called it "the cabin" – a few hundred yards from his house, and it was here that he slept every night. It was a little, single-roomed hut, sixteen feet by ten. He kept the key in his pocket, made his own bed, cleaned it himself, and allowed no other foot to cross the threshold. There are small windows on each side, which were covered by curtains and never opened. One of these windows was turned towards the high road, and when the light burned in it at night the folk used to point it out to each other and wonder what Black Peter was doing in there. That's the window, Mr Holmes, which gave us one of the few bits of positive evidence that came out at the inquest.

'You remember that a stonemason, named Slater, walking from Forest Row about one o'clock in the morning – two days before the murder – stopped as he passed the grounds and looked at the square of light still shining among the trees. He swears that the shadow of a man's head turned sideways was clearly visible on the blind, and that this shadow was certainly not that of Peter Carey, whom he knew well. It was that of a bearded man, but the beard was short and bristled forwards in a way very different from that of the captain. So he says, but he had been two hours in the public-house, and it is some distance from the road to the window. Besides, this refers to the Monday, and the crime was done upon the Wednesday.

'On the Tuesday Peter Carey was in one of his blackest moods, flushed with drink and as savage as a dangerous wild beast. He roamed about the house, and the women ran for it when they heard him coming. Late in the evening he went down to his own hut. About two o'clock the following morning his daughter, who slept with her window open, heard a most fearful yell from that direction, but it was no unusual thing for him to bawl and shout when he was in drink, so no notice was taken. On rising at seven one of the maids noticed that the door of the hut was open, but so great was the terror which the man caused that it was midday before anyone would venture down to see what had become of him. Peeping into the open door they saw a sight which sent them flying with white faces into the village. Within an hour I was on the spot and had taken over the case.

'Well, I have fairly steady nerves, as you know, Mr Holmes, but I give you my word that I got a shake when I put my head into that little house. It was droning like a harmonium with the flies and bluebottles, and the floor and walls were like a slaughterhouse. He had called it a cabin, and a cabin it was sure enough, for you would have thought that you were in a ship. There was a bunk at one end, a sea-chest, maps and charts, a picture of the *Sea Unicorn*, a line of logbooks on a shelf, all exactly as one would expect to find it in a captain's room. And there in the middle of it was the man himself, his face twisted like a lost soul in torment, and his great brindled beard stuck upwards in his agony. Right through his broad breast a steel harpoon had been driven, and it had sunk deep into the wood of the wall behind him. He was pinned like a beetle on a card. Of course, he was quite dead, and had been so from the instant that he had uttered that last yell of agony.

'I know your methods, sir, and I applied them. Before I permitted anything to be moved I examined most carefully the ground outside, and also the floor of the room. There were no footmarks.'

'Meaning that you saw none?'

'I assure you, sir, that there were none.'

'My good Hopkins, I have investigated many crimes, but I have never yet seen one which was committed by a flying creature. As long as the criminal remains upon two legs so long must there be some indentation, some abrasion, some trifling displacement which can be detected by the scientific searcher. It is incredible that this blood-bespattered room contained no trace which could have aided us. I understand, however, from the inquest that there were some objects which you failed to overlook?'

The young inspector winced at my companion's ironical comments.

'I was a fool not to call you in at the time, Mr Holmes. However, that's past praying for now. Yes, there were several objects in the room which called for special attention. One was the harpoon with which the deed was committed. It had been snatched down from a rack on the wall. Two others remained there, and there was a vacant place for the third. On the stock was engraved "S.S. *Sea Unicorn*, Dundee". This seemed to establish that the crime had been done in a moment of fury, and that the murderer had seized the first weapon which came in his way. The fact that the crime was committed at two in the morning, and yet Peter Carey was fully dressed, suggested that he had an appointment with the murderer, which is borne out by the fact that a bottle of rum and two dirty glasses stood upon the table.'

'Yes,' said Holmes; 'I think that both inferences are permissible. Was there any other spirit but rum in the room?'

'Yes; there was a tantalus containing brandy and whisky on the sea-chest. It is of no importance to us, however, since the decanters were full, and it had therefore not been used.'

'For all that its presence has some significance,' said Holmes. 'However, let us hear some more about the objects which do seem to you to bear upon the case.'

'There was this tobacco-pouch upon the table.'

'What part of the table?'

'It lay in the middle. It was of coarse sealskin – the straight-haired skin, with a leather thong to bind it. Inside was "P.C." on the flap. There was half an ounce of strong ship's tobacco in it.'

'Excellent! What more?'

Stanley Hopkins drew from his pocket a drab-covered note-book. The outside was rough and worn, the leaves discoloured. On the first page were written the initials 'J.H.N.' and the date '1883'. Holmes laid it on the table and examined it in his minute way, while Hopkins and I gazed over each shoulder. On the second page were the printed letters 'C.P.R.', and then came several sheets of numbers. Another heading was Argentine, another Costa Rica and another São Paulo, each with pages of signs and figures after it.

'What do you make of these?' asked Holmes.

'They appear to be lists of Stock Exchange securities. I thought that "J.H.N." were the initials of a broker, and that "C.P.R." may have been his client.'

'Try Canadian Pacific Railway,' said Holmes.

Stanley Hopkins swore between his teeth and struck his thigh with his clenched hand.

'What a fool I have been!' he cried. 'Of course, it is as you say. Then "J.H.N." are the only initials we have to solve. I have already examined the old Stock Exchange lists, and I can find no one in 1883 either in the House or among the outside brokers whose initials correspond with these. Yet I feel that the clue is the most important one that I hold. You will admit, Mr Holmes, that there is a possibility that these initials are those of the second person who was present – in other words, of the murderer. I would also urge that the introduction into the case of a document relating to large masses of valuable securities gives us for the first time some indication of a motive for the crime.'

Sherlock Holmes's face showed that he was thoroughly taken aback by this new development.

'I must admit both your points,' said he. 'I confess that this notebook, which did not appear at the inquest, modifies any views which I may have formed. I had come to a theory of the crime in which I can find no place for this. Have you endeavoured to trace any of the securities here mentioned?'

'Enquiries are now being made at the offices, but I fear that the complete register of the stockholders of these South American concerns is in South America, and that some weeks must elapse before we can trace the shares.'

Holmes had been examining the cover of the notebook with his magnifying lens.

'Surely there is some discoloration here,' said he.

'Yes, sir, it is a bloodstain. I told you that I picked the book off the floor.'

'Was the bloodstain above or below?'

'On the side next the boards.'

'Which proves, of course, that the book was dropped after the crime was committed.'

'Exactly, Mr Holmes. I appreciated that point, and I conjectured that it was dropped by the murderer in his hurried flight. It lay near the door.'

'I suppose that none of these securities have been found among the property of the dead man?'

'No, sir.'

'Have you any reason to suspect robbery?'

'No, sir. Nothing seemed to have been touched.'

'Dear me, it is certainly a very interesting case. Then there was a knife, was there not?'

'A sheath-knife, still in its sheath. It lay at the feet of the dead man. Mrs Carey has identified it as being her husband's property.'

Holmes was lost in thought for some time.

'Well,' said he, at last, 'I suppose I shall have to come out and have a look at it.'

Stanley Hopkins gave a cry of joy.

'Thank you, sir. That will indeed be a weight off my mind.'

Holmes shook his finger at the inspector.

'It would have been an easier task a week ago,' said he. 'But even now my visit may not be entirely fruitless. Watson, if you can spare the time I should be very glad of your company. If you will call a four-wheeler, Hopkins, we shall be ready to start for Forest Row in a quarter of an hour.'

Alighting at the small wayside station, we drove for some miles through the remains of widespread woods, which were once part of that great forest which for so long held the Saxon invaders at bay – the impenetrable 'weald', for sixty years the bulwark of Britain. Vast sections of it have been cleared, for this is the seat of the first ironworks of the country, and the trees have been felled to smelt the ore. Now the richer fields of the north have absorbed the trade, and nothing save these ravaged groves and great scars in the earth show the work of the past. Here in a clearing upon the green slope of a hill stood a long, low stone house, approached by a curving drive running through the fields. Nearer the road, and surrounded on three sides by bushes, was a small outhouse, one window and the door facing in our direction. It was the scene of the murder!

Stanley Hopkins led us first to the house, where he introduced us to a haggard, grey-haired woman, the widow of the murdered man, whose gaunt and deep-lined face, with the furtive look of terror in the depths of her red-rimmed eyes, told of the years of hardship and ill-usage which she had endured. With her was her daughter, a pale, fair-haired girl, whose eyes blazed defiantly at us as she told us that she was glad that her father was dead, and that she blessed the hand which had struck him down. It was a terrible household that Black Peter Carey had made for himself, and it was with a sense of relief that we found ourselves in the sunlight again and making our way along a path which had been worn across the fields by the feet of the dead man.

The outhouse was the simplest of dwellings, wooden-walled, shingle-roofed, one window beside the door and one on the farther side. Stanley Hopkins drew the key from his pocket, and had stooped to the lock, when he paused with a look of attention and surprise upon his face.

'Someone has been tampering with it,' he said.

There could be no doubt of the fact. The woodwork was cut and the scratches showed white through the paint, as if they had been that instant done. Holmes had been examining the window.

'Someone has tried to force this also. Whoever it was failed to make his way in. He must have been a very poor burglar.'

'This is a most extraordinary thing,' said the inspector; 'I could swear that these marks were not here yesterday evening.'

'Some curious person from the village, perhaps,' I suggested.

'Very unlikely. Few of them would dare to set foot in the grounds, far less try to force their way into the cabin. What do you think of it, Mr Holmes?'

'I think that fortune is very kind to us.'

'You mean that the person will come again?'

'It is very probable. He came expecting to find the door open. He tried to get in with the blade of a very small penknife. He could not manage it. What would he do?'

'Come again next night with a more useful tool.'

'So I should say. It will be our fault if we are not here to receive him. Meanwhile, let me see the inside of the cabin.'

The traces of the tragedy had been removed, but the furniture within the little room still stood as it had been on the night of the crime. For two hours, with most intense concentration, Holmes examined every object in turn, but his face showed that his quest was not a successful one. Once only he paused in his patient investigation.

'Have you taken anything off this shelf, Hopkins?'

'No; I have moved nothing.'

'Something has been taken. There is less dust in this corner of the shelf than elsewhere. It may have been a book lying on its side. It may have been a box. Well, well, I can do nothing more. Let us walk in these beautiful woods, Watson, and give a few hours to the birds and the flowers. We shall meet you here later, Hopkins, and see if we can come to closer quarters with the gentleman who has paid this visit in the night.'

It was past eleven o'clock when we formed our little ambuscade. Hopkins was for leaving the door of the hut open, but Holmes was of the opinion that this would rouse the suspicions of the stranger. The lock was a perfectly simple one, and only a strong blade was needed to push it back. Holmes also suggested that we should wait, not inside the hut, but outside it among the bushes which grew round the farther window. In this way we should be able to watch our man if he struck a light, and see what his object was in this stealthy nocturnal visit.

It was a long and melancholy vigil, and yet brought with it something of the thrill which the hunter feels when he lies beside the water pool and waits for the coming of the thirsty beast of prey. What savage creature was it which might steal upon us out of the darkness? Was it a fierce tiger of crime, which could only be taken fighting hard with flashing fang and claw, or would it prove to be some skulking jackal, dangerous only to the weak and unguarded?

In absolute silence we crouched amongst the bushes, waiting for whatever might come. At first the steps of a few belated villagers, or the sound of voices from the village, lightened our vigil; but one by one these interruptions died away and an absolute stillness fell upon us, save for the chimes of the distant church, which told us of the progress of the night, and for the rustle and whisper of a fine rain falling amid the foliage which roofed us in.

Half-past two had chimed, and it was the darkest hour which precedes the dawn, when we all started as a low but sharp click came from the direction of the gate. Someone had entered the drive. Again there was a long silence, and I had begun to fear that it was a false alarm, when a stealthy step was heard upon the other side of the hut, and a moment later a metallic scraping and clinking. The man was trying to force the lock! This time his skill was greater or his tool was better, for there was a sudden snap and the creak of the hinges. Then a match was struck, and next instant the steady light from a candle filled the interior of the hut. Through the gauze curtain our eyes were all riveted upon the scene within.

The nocturnal visitor was a young man, frail and thin, with a black moustache which intensified the deadly pallor of his face. He could not have been much above twenty years of age. I have never seen any human being who appeared to be in such a pitiable fright, for his teeth were visibly chattering and he was shaking in every limb. He was dressed like a gentleman, in Norfolk jacket and knickerbockers, with a cloth cap upon his head. We watched him staring round with frightened eyes. Then he laid the candle-end upon the table and disappeared from our view into one of the corners. He returned with a large book, one of the logbooks which formed a line upon the shelves. Leaning on the table he rapidly turned over the leaves of this volume until he came to the entry which he sought. Then, with an angry gesture of his clenched hand, he closed the book, replaced it in the corner, and put out the light. He had hardly turned to leave the hut when Hopkins's hand was on the fellow's collar, and I heard his loud gasp of terror as he understood that he was taken. The candle was re-lit, and there was our wretched captive shivering and cowering in the grasp of the detective. He sank down upon the sea-chest, and looked helplessly from one of us to the other.

'Now, my fine fellow,' said Stanley Hopkins, 'who are you, and what do you want here?'

The man pulled himself together and faced us with an effort at self-composure.

'You are detectives, I suppose?' said he. 'You imagine I am connected with the death of Captain Peter Carey. I assure you that I am innocent.'

'We'll see about that,' said Hopkins. 'First of all, what is your name?'

'It is John Hopley Neligan.'

I saw Holmes and Hopkins exchange a quick glance.

'What are you doing here?'

'Can I speak confidentially?'

'No, certainly not.'

'Why should I tell you?'

'If you have no answer it may go badly with you at the trial.'

The young man winced.

'Well, I will tell you,' he said. 'Why should I not? And yet I hate to think of this old scandal gaining a new lease of life. Did you ever hear of Dawson and Neligan?'

I could see from Hopkins's face that he never had; but Holmes was keenly interested.

'You mean the West Country bankers,' said he. 'They failed for a million, ruined half the county families of Cornwall, and Neligan disappeared.'

'Exactly. Neligan was my father.'

At last we were getting something positive, and yet it seemed a long gap between an absconding banker and Captain Peter Carey pinned against the wall with one of his own harpoons. We all listened intently to the young man's words.

'It was my father who was really concerned. Dawson had retired. I was only ten years of age at the time, but I was old enough to feel the shame and horror of it all. It has always been said that my father stole all the securities and fled. It is not true. It was his belief that if he were given time in which to realise them all would be well and every creditor paid in full. He started in his little yacht for Norway just before the warrant was issued for his arrest. I can remember that last night when he bade farewell to my mother. He left us a list of the securities he was taking, and he swore that he would come back with his honour cleared, and that none who had trusted him would suffer. Well, no word was ever heard from him again. Both the yacht and he vanished utterly. We believed, my mother and I, that he and it, with the securities that he had taken with him, were at the bottom of the sea. We had a faithful friend, however, who is a businessman, and it was he who discovered some time ago that some of the securities which my father had with him have reappeared on the London market. You can imagine our amazement. I spent months in trying to trace them, and at last, after many doublings and difficulties, I discovered that the original seller had been Captain Peter Carey, the owner of this hut.

'Naturally, I made some enquiries about the man. I found that he had been in command of a whaler which was due to return from the Arctic seas at the very time when my father was crossing to Norway. The autumn of that year was a stormy one, and there was a long succession of southerly gales. My father's yacht may well have been blown to the north, and there met by Captain Peter Carey's ship. If that were so, what had become of my father? In any case, if I could prove from Peter Carey's evidence how these securities came on the market it would be a proof that my father had not sold them, and that he had no view to personal profit when he took them.

'I came down to Sussex with the intention of seeing the captain, but it was at this moment that his terrible death occurred. I read at the inquest a description of his cabin, in which it stated that the old logbooks of his vessel were preserved in it. It struck me that if I could see what occurred in the month of August 1883 on board the *Sea Unicorn*, I might settle the mystery of my father's fate. I tried last night to get at these logbooks, but was unable to open the door. Tonight I tried again, and succeeded; but I find that the pages which deal with that month have been torn from the book. It was at that moment I found myself a prisoner in your hands.'

'Is that all?' asked Hopkins.

'Yes, that is all.' His eyes shifted as he said it.

'You have nothing else to tell us?'

He hesitated.

'No; there is nothing.'

'You have not been here before last night?'

'No.'

'Then how do you account for *that*?' cried Hopkins, as he held up the damning notebook, with the initials of our prisoner on the first leaf and the bloodstain on the cover.

The wretched man collapsed. He sank his face in his hands and trembled all over.

'Where did you get it?' he groaned. 'I did not know. I thought I had lost it at the hotel.'

'That is enough,' said Hopkins, sternly. 'Whatever else you have to say you must say in court. You will walk down with me now to the police-station. Well, Mr Holmes, I am very much obliged to you and to your friend for coming down to help me. As it turns out your presence was unnecessary, and I would have brought the case to this successful issue without you; but none the less I am very grateful. Rooms have been reserved for you at the Brambletye Hotel, so we can all walk down to the village together.'

'Well, Watson, what do you think of it?' asked Holmes, as we travelled back next morning.

'I can see that you are not satisfied.'

'Oh, yes, my dear Watson, I am perfectly satisfied. At the same time Stanley Hopkins's methods do not commend themselves to me. I am disappointed in Stanley Hopkins. I had hoped for better things from him. One should always look for a possible alternative and provide against it. It is the first rule of criminal investigation.'

'What, then, is the alternative?'

'The line of investigation which I have myself been pursuing. It may give us nothing. I cannot tell. But at least I shall follow it to the end.'

Several letters were waiting for Holmes at Baker Street. He snatched one of them up, opened it, and burst out into a triumphant chuckle of laughter.

'Excellent, Watson. The alternative develops. Have you telegraph forms? Just write a couple of messages for me: "Sumner, Shipping Agent, Ratcliff Highway. Send three men on, to arrive ten tomorrow morning – Basil." That's my name in those parts. The other is: "Inspector Stanley Hopkins, 46 Lord Street, Brixton. Come breakfast tomorrow at nine-thirty. Important. Wire if unable to come – Sherlock Holmes." There, Watson, this infernal case has haunted me for ten days. I hereby banish it completely from my presence. Tomorrow I trust that we shall hear the last of it for ever.'

Sharp at the hour named, Inspector Stanley Hopkins appeared, and we sat down together to the excellent breakfast which Mrs Hudson had prepared. The young detective was in high spirits at his success.

'You really think that your solution must be correct?' asked Holmes.

'I could not imagine a more complete case.'

'It did not seem to me conclusive.'

'You astonish me, Mr Holmes. What more could one ask for?'

'Does your explanation cover every point?'

'Undoubtedly. I find that young Neligan arrived at the Brambletye Hotel on the very day of the crime. He came on the pretence of playing golf. His room was on the ground floor, and he could get out when he liked. That very night he went down to Woodman's Lee, saw Peter Carey at the hut, quarrelled with him, and killed him with the harpoon. Then, horrified by what he had done, he fled out of the hut, dropping the notebook which he had brought with him in order to question Peter Carey about these different securities. You may have observed that some of them were marked with ticks, and the others – the great majority – were not. Those which are ticked have been traced on the London market; but the others presumably were still in the possession of Carey, and young Neligan, according to his own account, was anxious to recover them in order to do the right thing by his father's creditors. After his flight he did not dare to approach the hut again for some time; but at last he forced himself to do so in order to obtain the information which he needed. Surely that is all simple and obvious?'

Holmes smiled and shook his head.

'It seems to me to have only one drawback, Hopkins, and that is that it is intrinsically impossible. Have you tried to drive a harpoon through a body? No? Tut, tut, my dear sir, you must really pay attention to these details. My friend Watson could tell you that I spent a whole morning in that exercise. It is no easy matter, and requires a strong and practised arm. But this blow was delivered with such violence that the head of the weapon sank deep into the wall. Do you imagine that this anaemic youth was capable of so frightful an assault? Is he the man who hobnobbed in rum and water with Black Peter in the dead of the night? Was it his profile that was seen on the blind two nights before? No, no, Hopkins; it is another and a more formidable person for whom we must seek.'

The detective's face had grown longer and longer during Holmes's speech. His hopes and his ambitions were all crumbling about him. But he would not abandon his position without a struggle.

'You can't deny that Neligan was present that night, Mr Holmes. The book will prove that. I fancy that I have evidence enough to satisfy a jury, even if you are able to pick a hole in it. Besides, Mr Holmes, I have laid my hand upon *my* man. As to this terrible person of yours, where is he?'

'I rather fancy that he is on the stair,' said Holmes, serenely. 'I think, Watson, that you would do well to put that revolver where you can reach it.' He rose, and laid a written paper upon a side-table. 'Now we are ready,' said he.

There had been some talking in gruff voices outside, and now Mrs Hudson opened the door to say that there were three men enquiring for Captain Basil.

'Show them in one by one,' said Holmes.

The first who entered was a little Ribston-pippin of a man, with ruddy cheeks and fluffy white side-whiskers. Holmes had drawn a letter from his pocket.

'What name?' he asked.

'James Lancaster.'

'I am sorry, Lancaster, but the berth is full. Here is half a sovereign for your trouble. Just step into this room and wait there for a few minutes.'

The second man was a long, dried-up creature, with lank hair and sallow cheeks. His name was Hugh Pattins. He also received his dismissal, his half-sovereign, and the order to wait.

The third applicant was a man of remarkable appearance. A fierce bulldog face was framed in a tangle of hair and beard, and two bold dark eyes gleamed behind the cover of thick, tufted, overhung eyebrows. He saluted and stood sailor-fashion, turning his cap round in his hands.

'Your name?' asked Holmes.

'Patrick Cairns.'

'Harpooner?'

'Yes, sir. Twenty-six voyages.'

'Dundee, I suppose?'

'Yes, sir.'

'And ready to start with an exploring ship?'

'Yes, sir.'

'What wages?'

'Eight pounds a month.'

'Could you start at once?'

'As soon as I get my kit.'

'Have you your papers?'

'Yes, sir.' He took a sheaf of worn and greasy forms from his pocket. Holmes glanced over them and returned them.

'You are just the man I want,' said he. 'Here's the agreement on the side-table. If you sign it the whole matter will be settled.'

The seaman lurched across the room and took up the pen.

'Shall I sign here?' he asked, stooping over the table.

Holmes leaned over his shoulder and passed both hands over his neck. 'This will do,' said he.

I heard a click of steel and a bellow like an enraged bull. The next instant Holmes and the seaman were rolling on the ground together. He was a man of such gigantic strength that, even with the handcuffs which Holmes had so deftly fastened upon his wrists, he would have very quickly overpowered my friend had Hopkins and I not rushed to his rescue. Only when I pressed the cold muzzle of the revolver to his temple did he at last understand that resistance was vain. We lashed his ankles with cord and rose breathless from the struggle.

'I must really apologise, Hopkins,' said Sherlock Holmes; 'I fear that the scrambled eggs are cold. However, you will enjoy the rest of your breakfast all the better, will you not, for the thought that you have brought your case to a triumphant conclusion.'

Stanley Hopkins was speechless with amazement.

'I don't know what to say, Mr Holmes,' he blurted out at last, with a very red face. 'It seems to me that I have been making a fool of myself from the beginning. I understand now, what I should never have forgotten, that I am the pupil and you are the master. Even now I see what you have done, but I don't know how you did it, or what it signifies.'

'Well, well,' said Holmes, good-humouredly. 'We all learn by experience, and your lesson this time is that you should never lose sight of the alternative. You were so absorbed in young Neligan that you could not spare a thought to Patrick Cairns, the true murderer of Peter Carey.'

The hoarse voice of the seaman broke in on our conversation.

'See here, mister,' said he, 'I make no complaint of being manhandled in this fashion, but I would have you call things by their right names. You say I murdered Peter Carey; I say I *killed* Peter Carey, and there's all the difference. Maybe you don't believe what I say. Maybe you think I am just slinging you a yarn.'

'Not at all,' said Holmes. 'Let us hear what you have to say.'

'It's soon told, and, by the Lord, every word of it is truth. I knew Black Peter, and when he pulled out his knife I whipped a harpoon through him sharp, for I knew that it was him or me. That's how he died. You can call it murder. Anyhow, I'd as soon die with a rope round my neck as with Black Peter's knife in my heart.'

'How came you there?' asked Holmes.

'I'll tell it you from the beginning. Just sit me up a little so as I can speak easy. It was in 1883 that it happened – August of that year. Peter Carey was master of the *Sea Unicorn*, and I was spare harpooner. We were coming out of the ice-pack on our way home, with head winds and a week's southerly gale, when we picked up a little craft that had been blown north. There was one man on her – a landsman. The crew had thought she would founder, and had made for the Norwegian coast in the dinghy. I guess they were all drowned. Well, we took him on board, this man, and he and the skipper had some long talks in the cabin. All the baggage we took off with him was one tin box. So far as I know, the man's name was never mentioned, and on the second night he disappeared as if he had never been. It was given out that he had either thrown himself overboard or fallen overboard in the heavy weather that we were having. Only one man knew what had happened to him, and that was me, for with my own eyes I saw the skipper tip up his heels and put him over the rail in the middle watch of a dark night, two days before we sighted the Shetland lights.

'Well, I kept my knowledge to myself and waited to see what would come of it. When we got back to Scotland it was easily hushed up, and nobody asked any questions. A stranger died by an accident, and it was nobody's business to enquire. Shortly after Peter Carey gave up the sea, and it was long years before I could find where he was. I guessed that he had done the deed for the sake of what was in that tin box, and that he could afford now to pay me well for keeping my mouth shut.

'I found out where he was through a sailor man that had met him in London, and down I went to squeeze him. The first night he was reasonable enough, and was ready to give me what would make me free of the sea for life. We were to fix it all two nights later. When I came I found him three parts drunk and in a vile temper. We sat down and we drank and we yarned about old times, but the more he drank the less I liked the look on his face. I spotted that harpoon upon the wall, and I thought I might need it before I was through. Then at last he broke out at me, spitting and cursing, with murder in his eyes and a great clasp-knife in his hand. He had not time to get it from the sheath before I had the harpoon through him. Heavens! what a yell he gave; and his face gets between me and my sleep! I stood there, with his blood splashing round me, and I waited for a bit; but all was quiet, so I took heart once more. I looked round, and there was the tin box on a shelf. I had as much right to it as Peter Carey, anyhow, so I took it with me and left the hut. Like a fool I left my baccy-pouch upon the table.

'Now I'll tell you the queerest part of the whole story. I had hardly got outside the hut when I heard someone coming, and I hid among the bushes. A man came slinking along, went into the hut, gave a cry as if he had seen a ghost, and legged it as hard as he could run until he was out of sight. Who he was or what he wanted is more than I can tell. For my part I walked ten miles, got a train at Tunbridge Wells, and so reached London, and no one the wiser.

'Well, when I came to examine the box I found there was no money in it, and nothing but papers that I would not dare to sell. I had lost my hold on Black Peter, and was stranded in London without a shilling. There was only my trade left. I saw these advertisements about harpooners and high wages, so I went to the shipping agents, and they sent me here. That's all I know, and I say again that if I killed Black Peter the law should give me thanks, for I saved them the price of a hempen rope.'

'A very clear statement,' said Holmes, rising and lighting his pipe. 'I think, Hopkins, that you should lose no time in conveying your prisoner to a place of safety. This room is not well adapted for a cell, and Mr Patrick Cairns occupies too large a proportion of our carpet.'

'Mr Holmes,' said Hopkins, 'I do not know how to express my gratitude. Even now I do not understand how you attained this result.'

'Simply by having the good fortune to get the right clue from the beginning. It is very possible if I had known about this notebook it might have led away my thoughts, as it did yours. But all I heard pointed in the one direction. The amazing strength, the skill in the use of the harpoon, the rum and water, the sealskin tobacco-pouch, with the coarse tobacco – all these pointed to a seaman, and one who had been a whaler. I was convinced that the initials "P.C." upon the pouch were a coincidence, and not those of Peter Carey, since he seldom smoked, and no pipe was found in his cabin. You remember that I asked whether whisky and brandy were in the cabin. You said they were. How many landsmen are there who would drink rum when they could get these other spirits? Yes, I was certain it was a seaman.'

'And how did you find him?'

'My dear sir, the problem had become a very simple one. If it were a seaman, it could only be a seaman who had been with him on the *Sea Unicorn*. So far as I could learn he had sailed in no other ship. I spent three days in wiring to Dundee, and at the end of that time I had ascertained the names of the crew of the *Sea Unicorn* in 1883. When I found Patrick Cairns among the harpooners my research was nearing its end. I argued that the man was probably in London, and that he would desire to leave the country for a time. I therefore spent some days in the East End, devised an Arctic expedition, put forth tempting terms for harpooners who would serve under Captain Basil – and behold the result!'

'Wonderful!' cried Hopkins. 'Wonderful!'

'You must obtain the release of young Neligan as soon as possible,' said Holmes. 'I confess that I think you owe him some apology. The tin box must be returned to him, but, of course, the securities which Peter Carey has sold are lost for ever. There's the cab, Hopkins, and you can remove your man. If you want me for the trial, my address and that of Watson will be somewhere in Norway – I'll send particulars later.'

ANTHONY TROLLOPE

Anthony Trollope (1815–1882) was the son of Frances Trollope
and brother of Thomas Trollope. Although a post-office official
for many years, Trollope was a prolific writer, producing a large
number of novels dealing with Victorian life. He declared that 'a
novel should give a picture of common life enlivened by humour
and sweetened by pathos', which is a fair estimation of his own
work. His best-known novels are those included in two series,
the so-called Chronicles of Barsetshire and the Parliamentary
Novels, which were overshadowed by Disraeli's popular novels
of the same type. Among his other novels are *The Claverings*
(1867) and *The Eustace Diamonds* (1873). He also wrote a
number of travel books, a study of W. M. Thackeray, and an
Autobiography (1883).

The Journey to Panama

There is perhaps no form of life in which men and women of
the present day frequently find themselves for a time existing
so unlike their customary conventional life as that experienced
on board the large ocean steamers. On the voyages so made,
separate friendships are formed and separate enmities are
endured. Certain lines of temporary politics are originated by
the energetic, and intrigues, generally innocent in their
conclusions, are carried on with the keenest spirit by those to
whom excitement is necessary; whereas the idle and torpid sink
into insignificance and general contempt – as it is their lot to
do on board ship as in other places. But the enjoyments and
activity of such a life do not display themselves till the third or
fourth day of the voyage. The men and women at first regard

each with distrust and ill-concealed dislike. They by no means anticipate the strong feelings which are to arise, and look forward to ten, fifteen or twenty days of gloom or seasickness. Seasickness disappears, as a general condition, on the evening of the second day, and the gloom about noon on the fourth. Then the men begin to think that the women are not so ugly, vulgar and insipid; and the women drop their monosyllables, discontinue the close adherence to their own niches, which they first observed, and become affable, perhaps even beyond their wont on shore. And alliances spring up among the men themselves. On their first entrance to this new world, they generally regard each other with marked aversion, each thinking that those nearest to him are low fellows, or perhaps worse; but by the fourth day, if not sooner, every man has his two or three intimate friends with whom he talks and smokes, and to whom he communicates those peculiar politics, and perhaps intrigues, of his own voyage. The female friendships are slower in their growth, for the suspicion of women is perhaps stronger than that of men; but when grown they also are stronger, and exhibit themselves sometimes in instances of feminine affection.

But the most remarkable alliances are those made between gentlemen and ladies. This is a matter of course on board ship quite as much as on shore, and it is of such an alliance that the present tale purports to tell the story. Such friendships, though they may be very dear, can seldom be very lasting. Though they may be full of sweet romance – for people become very romantic among the discomforts of a sea voyage – such romance is generally short-lived and delusive, and occasionally is dangerous.

There are several of these great ocean routes, of which, by the common consent, as it seems, of the world, England is the centre. There is the Great Eastern Line, running from Southampton across the Bay of Biscay and up the Mediterranean. It crosses the Isthmus of Suez, and branches away to

Australia, to India, to Ceylon and to China. There is the Great American Line, traversing the Atlantic to New York and Boston with the regularity of clockwork. The voyage here is so much a matter of everyday routine, that romance has become scarce upon the route. There are one or two other North American lines, perhaps open to the same objection. Then there is the line of packets to the African coast – very romantic as I am given to understand; and there is the great West Indian route, to which the present little history is attached – great, not on account of our poor West Indian Islands, which cannot at the present moment make anything great, but because it spreads itself out from thence to Mexico and Cuba, to Guiana and the republics of Grenada and Venezuela, to Central America, the Isthmus of Panama, and from thence to California, Vancouver's Island, Peru and Chile.

It may be imagined how various are the tribes which leave the shores of Great Britain by this route. There are Frenchmen for the French sugar islands, as a rule not very romantic; there are old Spaniards, Spaniards of Spain, seeking to renew their fortunes amid the ruins of their former empire; and new Spaniards – Spaniards, that is, of the American republics, who speak Spanish, but are unlike the Don both in manners and physiognomy – men and women with a touch perhaps of Indian blood, very keen after dollars, and not much given to the graces of life. There are Dutchmen too, and Danes, going out to their own islands. There are citizens of the Stars and Stripes, who find their way everywhere – and, alas! perhaps, now also citizens of the new Southern flag, with the palmetto leaf. And there are Englishmen of every shade and class, and Englishwomen also.

It is constantly the case that women are doomed to make the long voyage alone. Some are going out to join their husbands, some to find a husband, some few peradventure to leave a husband. Girls who have been educated at home in England, return to their distant homes across the Atlantic, and others follow their relatives who have gone before them as pioneers into a strange land. It must not be supposed that these females absolutely embark in solitude, putting their feet upon the deck without the aid of any friendly arm. They are generally consigned to some prudent elder, and appear as they first show themselves on the ship to belong to a party. But as often as not their real loneliness shows itself after a while. The prudent elder is not, perhaps, congenial; and by the evening of the fourth day a new friendship is created.

Not a long time since, such a friendship was formed under the circumstances which I am now about to tell. A young man – not very young, for he had turned his thirtieth year, but still a young man – left Southampton by one of the large West Indian steamboats, purposing to pass over the Isthmus of Panama, and thence up to California and Vancouver's Island. It would be too long to tell the cause which led to these distant voyagings. Suffice to say, it was not the accursed hunger after gold – *auri sacra fames* – which so took him; nor had he any purpose of permanently settling himself in those distant colonies of Great Britain. He was at the time a widower, and perhaps his home was bitter to him without the young wife whom he had early lost. As he stepped on board he was accompanied by a gentleman some fifteen years his senior, who was to be the companion of his sleeping apartment as far as St Thomas. The two had been introduced to each other, and therefore appeared as friends on board the *Serrapiqui*; but their acquaintance had commenced in Southampton, and my hero, Ralph Forrest by name, was alone in the world as he stood looking over the side of the ship at the retreating shores of Hampshire.

'I say, old fellow, we'd better see about our places,' said his new friend, slapping him on his back. Mr Matthew Morris was an old traveller, and knew how to become intimate with his temporary allies at a very short notice. A long course of travelling had knocked all bashfulness out of him, and when he had a mind to do so he could make any man his brother in half an hour, and any woman his sister in ten minutes.

'Places? what places?' said Forrest.

'A pretty fellow you are to go to California. If you don't look sharper than that you'll get little to drink and nothing to eat till you come back again. Don't you know the ship's as full as ever she can hold?'

Forrest acknowledged that she was full.

'There are places at table for about a hundred, and we have a hundred and thirty on board. As a matter of course those who don't look sharp will have to scramble. However, I've put cards on the plates and taken the seats. We had better go down and see that none of these Spanish fellows ousts us.' So Forrest descended after his friend, and found that the long tables were already nearly full of expectant dinner eaters. When he took his place a future neighbour informed him, not in the most gracious voice, that he was encroaching on a lady's seat; and when he immediately attempted to leave that which he held, Mr Matthew Morris forbade him to do so. Thus a little contest arose, which, however, happily was brought to a close without bloodshed. The lady was not present at the moment, and the grumpy gentleman agreed to secure for himself a vacant seat on the other side.

For the first three days the lady did not show herself. The grumpy gentleman, who, as Forrest afterwards understood, was the owner of stores in Bridgetown, Barbados, had other ladies with him also. First came forth his daughter, creeping down to dinner on the second day, declaring that she would be unable to eat a morsel, and prophesying that she would be forced to retire in five minutes. On this occasion, however, she agreeably surprised herself and her friends. Then came the grumpy gentleman's wife, and the grumpy gentleman's wife's brother – on whose constitution the sea seemed to have an effect quite as violent as on that of the ladies; and lastly, at breakfast on the fourth day, appeared Miss Viner, and took her place as Mr Forrest's neighbour at his right hand.

He had seen her before on deck, as she lay on one of the benches, vainly endeavouring to make herself comfortable, and had remarked to his companion that she was very unattractive and almost ugly. Dear young ladies, it is thus that men always speak of you when they first see you on board ship! She was disconsolate, sick at heart, and ill at ease in body also. She did not like the sea. She did not in the least like the grumpy gentleman, in whose hands she was placed. She did not especially like the grumpy gentleman's wife; and she altogether hated the grumpy gentleman's daughter, who was the partner of her berth. That young lady had been very sick and very selfish; and Miss Viner had been very sick also, and perhaps equally selfish. They might have been angels, and yet have hated each other under such circumstances. It was no wonder that Mr Forrest thought her ugly as she twisted herself about on the broad bench, vainly striving to be comfortable.

'She'll brighten up wonderfully before we're in the Tropics,' said Mr Morris. 'And you won't find her so bad then. It's she that is to sit next you.'

'Heaven forbid!' said Forrest. But, nevertheless, he was very civil to her when she did come down on the fourth morning. On board the West Indian packets, the world goes down to its meals. In crossing between Liverpool and the States, the world goes up to them.

Miss Viner was by no means a very young lady. She also was nearly thirty. In guessing her age on board the ship the ladies said that she was thirty-six, but the ladies were wrong. She was an Irishwoman, and when seen on shore, in her natural state, and with all her wits about her, was by no means without attraction. She was bright-eyed, with a clear dark skin, and good teeth; her hair was of a dark brown and glossy, and there was a touch of feeling and also of humour about her mouth, which would have saved her from Mr Forrest's ill-considered criticism had he first met her under more favourable circumstances.

'You'll see a good deal of her,' Mr Morris said to him, as they began to prepare themselves for luncheon by a cigar immediately after breakfast. 'She's going across the Isthmus and down to Peru.'

'How on earth do you know?'

'I pretty well know where they're all going by this time. Old Grumpy told me so. He has her in tow as far as St Thomas, but knows nothing about her. He gives her up there to the captain. You'll have a chance of making yourself very agreeable as you run across with her to the Spanish Main.'

Mr Forrest replied that he did not suppose he should know her much better than he did now; but he made no further remark as to her ugliness. She had spoken a word or two to him at table, and he had seen that her eyes were bright, and had found that her tone was sweet.

'I also am going to Panama,' he said to her, on the morning of the fifth day. The weather at that time was very fine, and the October sun as it shone on them, while hour by hour they made more towards the south, was pleasant and genial. The big ship lay almost without motion on the bosom of the Atlantic, as she was driven through the waters at the rate of twelve miles per hour. All was as pleasant now as things can be on board a ship, and Forrest had forgotten that Miss Viner had seemed so ugly to him when he first saw her. At this moment, as he spoke to her, they were running through the Azores, and he had been assisting her with his field-glass to look for orange-groves on their sloping shores, orange-groves they had not succeeded in seeing, but their failure had not disturbed their peace.

'I also am going to Panama.'

'Are you, indeed?' said she. 'Then I shall not feel so terribly alone and disconsolate. I have been looking forward with such fear to that journey on from St Thomas.'

'You shall not be disconsolate, if I can help it,' he said. 'I am not much of a traveller myself, but what I can do I will.'

'Oh, thank you!'

'It is a pity Mr Morris is not going on with you. He's at home everywhere, and knows the way across the Isthmus as well as he does down Regent Street.'

'Your friend, you mean?'

'My friend, if you call him so; and indeed I hope he is, for I like him. But I don't know more of him than I do of you. I am as much alone as you are. Perhaps more so.'

'But,' she said, 'a man never suffers in being alone.'

'Oh! does he not? Don't think me uncivil, Miss Viner, if I say that you may be mistaken in that. You feel your own shoe when it pinches, but do not realise the tight boot of your neighbour.'

'Perhaps not,' said she. And then there was a pause, during which she pretended to look again for the orange groves. 'But there are worse things, Mr Forrest, than being alone in the world. It is often a woman's lot to wish that she were let alone.' Then she left him and retreated to the side of the grumpy gentleman's wife, feeling perhaps that it might be prudent to discontinue a conversation which, seeing that Mr Forrest was quite a stranger to her, was becoming particular.

'You're getting on famously, my dear,' said the lady from Barbados.

'Pretty well, thank you, ma'am,' said Miss Viner.

'Mr Forrest seems to be making himself quite agreeable. I tell Amelia' – Amelia was the young lady to whom in their joint cabin Miss Viner could not reconcile herself – 'I tell Amelia that she is wrong not to receive attentions from gentlemen on board ship. If it is not carried too far,' and she put great emphasis on the 'too far' – 'I see no harm in it.'

'Nor I, either,' said Miss Viner.

'But then Amelia is so particular.'

'The best way is to take such things as they come,' said Miss Viner – perhaps meaning that such things never did come in the way of Amelia. 'If a lady knows what she is about she need not fear a gentleman's attentions.'

'That's just what I tell Amelia; but then, my dear, she has not had so much experience as you and I.'

Such being the amenities which passed between Miss Viner and the prudent lady who had her in charge, it was not wonderful that the former should feel ill at ease with her own 'party', as the family of the Grumpy Barbadian was generally considered to be by those on board.

'You're getting along like a house on fire with Miss Viner,' said Matthew Morris to his young friend.

'Not much fire I can assure you,' said Forrest.

'She ain't so ugly as you thought her?'

'Ugly! – no; she's not ugly. I don't think I ever said she was. But she is nothing particular as regards beauty.'

'No; she won't be lovely for the next three days to come, I dare say. By the time you reach Panama, she'll be all that is perfect in woman. I know how these things go.'

'Those sort of things don't go at all quickly with me,' said Forrest, gravely. 'Miss Viner is a very interesting young woman, and as it seems that her route and mine will be together for some time, it is well that we should be civil to each other. And the more so, seeing that the people she is with are not congenial to her.'

'No; they are not. There is no young man with them. I generally observe that on board ship no one is congenial to unmarried ladies except unmarried men. It is a recognised nautical rule. Uncommon hot, isn't it? We are beginning to feel the tropical air. I shall go and cool myself with a cigar in the fiddle.' The 'fiddle' is a certain part of the ship devoted to smoking, and thither Mr Morris betook himself. Forrest, however, did not accompany him, but going forward into the bow of the vessel, threw himself along upon the sail, and meditated on the loneliness of his life.

On board the *Serrapiqui*, the upper tier of cabins opened on to a long gallery, which ran round that part of the ship immediately over the saloon, so that from thence a pleasant inspection could be made of the viands as they were being placed on the tables. The custom on board these ships is for two bells to ring preparatory to dinner, at an internal of half an hour. At the sound of the first, ladies would go to their cabins to adjust their toilets; but as dressing for dinner is not carried to an extreme at sea, these operations are generally over before the second bell, and the lady passengers would generally assemble in the balcony for some fifteen minutes before dinner. At first they would stand here alone, but by degrees they were joined by some of the more enterprising of the men, and so at last a kind of little drawing-room was formed. The cabins of Miss Viner's party opened to one side of this gallery, and that of Mr Morris and Forrest on the other. Hitherto Forrest had been contented to remain on his own side, occasionally throwing a word across to the ladies on the other; but on this day he boldly went over as soon as he had washed his hands and took his place between Amelia and Miss Viner.

'We are dreadfully crowded here, ma'am,' said Amelia.

'Yes, my dear, we are,' said her mother. 'But what can one do?'

'There's plenty of room in the ladies' cabin,' said Miss Viner. Now if there be one place on board a ship more distasteful to ladies than another, it is the ladies' cabin. Mr Forrest stood his ground, but it may be doubted whether he would have done so had he fully understood all that Amelia had intended.

Then the last bell rang. Mr Grumpy gave his arm to Mrs Grumpy. The brother-in-law gave his arm to Amelia, and Forrest did the same to Miss Viner. She hesitated for a moment, and then took it, and by so doing transferred herself mentally and bodily from the charge of the prudent and married Mr Grumpy to that of the perhaps imprudent, and certainly unmarried Mr Forrest. She was wrong. A kind-hearted, motherly old lady from Jamaica, who had seen it all, knew that she was wrong, and wished that she could tell her so.

But there are things of this sort which kind-hearted old ladies cannot find it in their hearts to say. After all, it was only for the voyage. Perhaps Miss Viner was imprudent, but who in Peru would be the wiser? Perhaps, indeed, it was the world that was wrong, and not Miss Viner. *Honi soit qui mal y pense*, she said to herself, as she took his arm, and leaning on it, felt that she was no longer so lonely as she had been. On that day she allowed him to give her a glass of wine out of his decanter. 'Hadn't you better take mine, Miss Viner?' asked Mr Grumpy, in a loud voice, but before he could be answered, the deed had been done.

'Don't go too fast, old fellow,' Morris said to our hero that night, as they were walking the deck together before they turned in. 'One gets into a hobble in such matters before one knows where one is.'

'I don't think I have anything particular to fear,' said Forrest.

'I dare say not, only keep your eyes open. Such harridans as Mrs Grumpy allow any latitude to their tongues out in these diggings. You'll find that unpleasant tidings will be put on board the ship going down to Panama, and everybody's eye will be upon you.' So warned, Mr Forrest did put himself on his guard, and the next day and a half his intimacy with Miss Viner progressed but little. These were, probably, the dullest hours that he had on the whole voyage.

Miss Viner saw this and drew back. On the afternoon of that second day she walked a turn or two on deck with the weak brother-in-law, and when Mr Forrest came near her, she applied herself to her book. She meant no harm; but if she were not afraid of what people might say, why should he be so? So she turned her shoulder towards him at dinner, and would not drink of his cup.

'Have some of mine, Miss Viner,' said Mr Grumpy, very loudly. But on that day Miss Viner drank no wine.

The sun sets quickly as one draws near to the Tropics, and the day was already gone, and the dusk had come on, when Mr Forrest walked out upon the deck that evening a little after six. But the night was beautiful and mild, and there was a hum of many voices from the benches. He was already uncomfortable, and sore with a sense of being deserted. There was but one person on board the ship that he liked, and why should he avoid her and be avoided? He soon perceived where she was standing. The Grumpy family had a bench to themselves, and she was opposite to it, on her feet, leaning against the side of the vessel. 'Will you walk this evening, Miss Viner?' he asked.

'I think not,' she answered.

'Then I shall persevere in asking till you are sure. It will do you good, for I have not seen you walking all day.'

'Have you not? Then I will take a turn. Oh, Mr Forrest, if you knew what it was to have to live with such people as those.' And then, out of that, on that evening, there grew up between them something like the confidence of real friendship. Things were told such as none but friends do tell to one another, and warm answering words were spoken such as the sympathy of friendship produces. Alas, they were both foolish; for friendship and sympathy should have deeper roots.

She told him all her story. She was going out to Peru to be married to a man who was nearly twenty years her senior. It was a long engagement, of ten years' standing. When first made, it was made as being contingent on certain circumstances. An option of escaping from it had then been given to her, but now there was no longer an option. He was rich, and she was penniless. He had even paid her passage-money and her outfit. She had not at last given way and taken these irrevocable steps till her only means of support in England had been taken from her. She had lived the last two years with a relative who was now dead. 'And he also is my cousin – a distant cousin – you understand that.'

'And do you love him?'

'Love him! What; as you loved her whom you have lost? – as she loved you when she clung to you before she went? No; certainly not. I shall never know anything of that love.'

'And is he good?'

'He is a hard man. Men become hard when they deal in money as he has done. He was home five years since, and then I swore to myself that I would not marry him. But his letters to me are kind.'

Forrest sat silent for a minute or two, for they were up in the bow again, seated on the sail that was bound round the bowsprit, and then he answered her, 'A woman should never marry a man unless she loves him.'

'Ah,' says she, 'of course you will condemn me. That is the way in which women are always treated. They have no choice given them, and are then scolded for choosing wrongly.'

'But you might have refused him.'

'No; I could not. I cannot make you understand the whole – how it first came about that the marriage was proposed, and agreed to by me under certain conditions. Those conditions have come about, and I am now bound to him. I have taken his money and have no escape. It is easy to say that a woman should not marry without love, as easy as it is to say that a man should not starve. But there are men who starve – starve although they work hard.'

'I did not mean to judge you, Miss Viner.'

'But I judge myself, and condemn myself so often. Where should I be in half an hour from this if I were to throw myself forward into the sea? I often long to do it. Don't you feel tempted sometimes to put an end to it all?'

'The waters look cool and sweet, but I own I am afraid of the bourne beyond.'

'So am I, and that fear will keep me from it.'

'We are bound to bear our burden of sorrow. Mine, I know, is heavy enough.'

'Yours, Mr Forrest! Have you not all the pleasures of memory to fall back on, and every hope for the future? What can I remember, or what can I hope? But, however, it is near eight o'clock, and they have all been at tea this hour past. What will my Cerberus say to me? I do not mind the male mouth, if only the two feminine mouths could be stopped.' Then she rose and went back to the stern of the vessel; but as she slid into a seat, she saw that Mrs Grumpy was standing over her.

From thence to St Thomas the voyage went on in the customary manner. The sun became very powerful, and the passengers in the lower part of the ship complained loudly of having their portholes closed. The Spaniards sat gambling in the cabin all day, and the ladies prepared for the general move which was to be made at St Thomas. The alliance between Forrest and Miss Viner went on much the same as ever, and Mrs Grumpy said very ill-natured things. On one occasion she ventured to lecture Miss Viner; but that lady knew how to take her own part, and Mrs Grumpy did not get the best of it. The dangerous alliance, I have said, went on the same as ever; but it must not be supposed that either person in any way committed aught that was wrong. They sat together and talked together, each now knowing the other's circumstances; but had it not been for the prudish caution of some of the ladies there would have been nothing amiss. As it was there was not much amiss. Few of the passengers really cared whether or no Miss Viner had found an admirer. Those who were going down to Panama were mostly Spaniards, and as the great separation became nearer, people had somewhat else of which to think.

And then the separation came. They rode into that pretty

harbour of St Thomas early in the morning, and were ignorant, the most of them, that they were lying in the very worst centre of yellow fever among all those plague-spotted islands. St Thomas is very pretty as seen from the ships; and when that has been said, all has been said that can be said in its favour. There was a busy, bustling time of it then. One vessel after another was brought up alongside of the big ship that had come from England, and each took its separate freight of passengers and luggage. First started the boat that ran down the Leeward Islands to Demerara, taking with her Mr Grumpy and all his family.

'Goodbye, Miss Viner,' said Mrs Grumpy. 'I hope you'll get quite safely to the end of your voyage; but do take care.'

'I'm sure I hope everything will be right,' said Amelia, as she absolutely kissed her enemy. It is astonishing how well young women can hate each other, and yet kiss at parting.

'As to everything being right,' said Miss Viner, 'that is too much to hope. But I do not know that anything is going especially wrong – Goodbye, sir,' and then she put out her hand to Mr Grumpy. He was at the moment leaving the ship laden with umbrellas, sticks and coats, and was forced to put them down in order to free his hand.

'Well, goodbye,' he said. 'I hope you'll do, till you meet your friends at the Isthmus.'

'I hope I shall, sir,' she replied; and so they parted.

Then the Jamaica packet started.

'I dare say we shall never see each other again,' said Morris, as he shook his friend's hand heartily. 'One never does. Don't interfere with the rights of that gentleman in Peru, or he might run a knife into you.'

'I feel no inclination to injure him on that point.'

'That's well; and now goodbye.' And thus they also were parted. On the following morning the branch ship was dispatched to Mexico; and then on the afternoon of the third day that for Colon – as we Englishmen call the town on this side of the Isthmus of Panama. Into that vessel Miss Viner and Mr Forrest moved themselves and their effects; and now that the three-headed Cerberus was gone, she had no longer hesitated in allowing him to do for her all those little things which it is well that men should do for women when they are travelling. A woman without assistance under such circumstances is very forlorn, very apt to go to the wall, very ill able to assert her rights as to accommodation; and I think that few can blame Miss Viner for putting herself and her belongings under the care of the only person who was disposed to be kind to her.

Late in the evening the vessel steamed out of St Thomas's harbour, and as she went Ralph Forrest and Emily Viner were standing together at the stern of the boat looking at the retreating lights of the Danish town. If there be a place on the earth's surface odious to me, it is that little Danish isle to which so many of our young seamen are sent to die – there being no good cause whatever for such sending. But the question is one which cannot well be argued here.

'I have five more days of self and liberty left me,' said Miss Viner. 'That is my life's allowance.'

'For heaven's sake do not say words that are so horrible.'

'But am I to lie for heaven's sake, and say words that are false; or shall I be silent for heaven's sake, and say nothing during these last hours that are allowed to me for speaking? It is so. To you I can say that it is so, and why should you begrudge me the speech?'

'I would begrudge you nothing that I could do for you.'

'No, you should not. Now that my incubus has gone to Barbados, let me be free for a day or two. What chance is there, I wonder, that the ship's machinery should all go wrong, and that we should be tossed about in the seas here for the next six months? I suppose it would be very wicked to wish it?'

'We should all be starved; that's all.'

'What, with a cow on board, and a dozen live sheep, and

thousands of cocks and hens! But we are to touch at Santa Martha and Cartagena. What would happen to me if I were to run away at Santa Martha?'

'I suppose I should be bound to run with you.'

'Oh, of course. And therefore, as I would not wish to destroy you, I won't do it. But it would not hurt you much to be shipwrecked, and wait for the next packet.'

'Miss Viner,' he said after a pause – and in the meantime he had drawn nearer to her, too near to her considering all things – 'in the name of all that is good, and true, and womanly, go back to England. With your feelings, if I may judge of them by words which are spoken half in jest – '

'Mr Forrest, there is no jest.'

'With your feelings, a poorhouse in England would be better than a palace in Peru.'

'An English workhouse would be better, but an English poorhouse is not open to me. You do not know what it is to have friends – no, not friends, but people belonging to you – just so near as to make your respectability a matter of interest to them, but not so near that they should care for your happiness. Emily Viner married to Mr Gorloch in Peru is put out of the way respectably. She will cause no further trouble, and her name may be mentioned in family circles without annoyance. The fact is, Mr Forrest, that there are people who have no business to live at all.'

'I would go back to England,' he added, after another pause. 'When you talk to me with such bitterness of five more days of living liberty you scare my very soul. Return, Miss Viner, and brave the worst. He is to meet you at Panama. Remain on this side of the Isthmus, and send him word that you must return. I will be the bearer of the message.'

'And shall I walk back to England?' said Miss Viner.

'I had not quite forgotten all that,' he replied, very gently. 'There are moments when a man may venture to propose that which under ordinary circumstances would be a liberty. Money, in a small moderate way, is not greatly an object to me. As a return for my valiant defence of you against your West Indian Cerberus, you shall allow me to arrange that with the agent at Colon.'

'I do so love plain English, Mr Forrest. You are proposing, I think, to give me something about fifty guineas.'

'Well, call it so if you will,' said he, 'if you will have plain English that is what I mean.'

'So that by my journey out here, I should rob and deceive the man I do know, and also rob the man I don't know. I am afraid of that bourne beyond the waters of which we spoke but I would rather face that than act as you suggest.'

'Of the feelings between him and you, I can of course be no judge.'

'No; no; you cannot. But what a beast I am not to thank you! I do thank you. That which it would be mean in me to take, it is noble, very noble, in you to offer. It is a pleasure to me – I cannot tell why – but it is a pleasure to me to have had the offer. But think of me as a sister, and you will feel that it would not be accepted – could not be accepted, I mean, even if I could bring myself to betray that other man.'

Thus they ran across the Caribbean Sea, renewing very often such conversations as that just given. They touched at Santa Martha and Cartagena on the coast of the Spanish Main and at both places he went with her on shore. He found that she was fairly well educated, and anxious to see and to learn all that might be seen and learned in the course of her travels. On the last day, as they neared the Isthmus, she became more tranquil and quiet in the expression of her feelings than before, and spoke with less of gloom than she had done.

'After all ought I not to love him?' she said. 'He is coming all the way up from Callao merely to meet me. What man would go from London to Moscow to pick up a wife?'

'I would – and thence round the world to Moscow again – if she were the wife I wanted.'

'Yes; but a wife who has never said that she loved you! It is purely a matter of convenience. Well; I have locked my big box, and I shall give the key to him before it is ever again unlocked. He has a right to it, for he has paid for nearly all that it holds.'

'You look at things from such a mundane point of view.'

'A woman should, or she will always be getting into difficulty. Mind, I shall introduce you to him, and tell him all that you have done for me. How you braved Cerberus and the rest of it.'

'I shall certainly be glad to meet him.'

'But I shall not tell him of your offer – not yet at least. If he be good and gentle with me, I shall tell him that too after a time. I am very bad at keeping secrets – as no doubt you have perceived. We go across the Isthmus at once, do we not?'

'So the captain says.'

'Look!' – and she handed him back his own field-glass. 'I can see the men on the wooden platform. Yes; and I can see the smoke of an engine.' And then, in little more than an hour from that time, the ship had swung round on her anchor.

Colon, or Aspinwall as it should be called, is a place in itself as detestable as St Thomas. It is not so odious to an Englishman, for it is not used by Englishmen more than is necessary. We have no great depot of traffic there, which we might with advantage move elsewhere. Taken, however, on its own merits, Aspinwall is not a detestable place. Luckily, however, travellers across the Isthmus to the Pacific are never doomed to remain there long. If they arrive early in the day, the railway thence to Panama takes them on at once. If it be not so, they remain on board ship till the next morning. Of course it will be understood that the transit line chiefly affects Americans, as it is the high road from New York to California.

In less than an hour from their landing, their baggage had been examined by the custom-house officers of New Grenada, and they were on the railway cars, crossing the Isthmus. The officials in those out-of-the-way places always seem like apes imitating the doings of men. The officers at Aspinwall open and look at the trunks just as monkeys might do, having clearly no idea of any duty to be performed, nor any conception that goods of this or that class should not be allowed to pass. It is the thing in Europe to examine luggage going into a new country; and why should not they be as good as Europeans?

'I wonder whether he will be at the station?' she said, when the three hours of the journey had nearly passed. Forrest could perceive that her voice trembled as she spoke, and that she was becoming nervous.

'If he has already reached Panama, he will be there. As far as I could learn the arrival up from Peru had not been telegraphed.'

'Then I have another day – perhaps two. We cannot say how many. I wish he were there. Nothing is so intolerable as suspense.'

'And the box must be opened again.'

When they reached the station at Panama they found that the vessel from the South American coast was in the roads, but that the passengers were not yet on shore. Forrest, therefore, took Miss Viner down to the hotel, and there remained with her, sitting next to her in the common drawing-room of the house when she had come back from her own bedroom. It would be necessary that they should remain there four or five days, and Forrest had been quick in securing a room for her. He had assisted in taking up her luggage, had helped her in placing her big box, and had thus been recognised by the crowd in the hotel as her friend. Then came the tidings that the passengers were landing, and he became nervous as she was. 'I will go down and meet him,' said he, 'and tell him that you are here. I shall soon find him by his name.' And so he went out.

Everybody knows the scrambling manner in which passengers arrive at a hotel out of a big ship. First come two or three energetic, heated men, who, by dint of screeching and bullying, have gotten themselves first disposed. They always get the worst rooms at the inns, the housekeepers having a notion that the richest people, those with the most luggage, must be more tardy in their movements. Four or five of this nature passed by Forrest in the hall, but he was not tempted to ask questions of them. One, from his age, might have been Mr Gorloch, but he instantly declared himself to be Count Sapparello. Then came an elderly man alone, with a small bag in his hand. He was one of those who pride themselves on going from Pole to Pole without encumbrance, and who will be behoved to no one for the carriage of their luggage. To him, as he was alone in the street, Forrest addressed himself. 'Gorloch?' said he.

'Gorloch: are you a friend of his?'

'A friend of mine is so,' said Forrest.

'Ah, indeed; yes,' said the other. And then he hesitated. 'Sir,' he then said, 'Mr Gorloch died at Callao, just seven days before the ship sailed. You had better see Mr Cox.' And then the elderly man passed in with his little bag.

Mr Gorloch was dead. 'Dead!' said Forrest, to himself, as he leaned back against the wall of the hotel, still standing on the street pavement. 'She has come out here; and now he is gone!' And then a thousand thoughts crowded on him. Who should tell her? And how would she bear it? Would it in truth be a relief to her to find that that liberty for which she had sighed had come to her? Or now that the testing of her feelings had come to her, would she regret the loss of home and wealth, and such position as life in Peru would give her? And above all would this sudden death of one who was to have been so near to her strike her to the heart?

But what was he to do? How was he now to show his friendship? He was returning slowly in at the hotel door, where crowds of men and women were now thronging, when he was addressed by a middle-aged, good-looking gentleman, who asked him whether his name was Forrest. 'I am told,' said the gentleman, when Forrest had answered him, 'that you are a friend of Miss Viner's. Have you heard the sad tidings from Callao?' It then appeared that this gentleman had been a stranger to Mr Gorloch, but had undertaken to bring a letter up to Miss Viner. This letter was handed to Mr Forrest, and he found himself burdened with the task of breaking the news to his poor friend. Whatever he did do, he must do at once, for all those who had come up by the Pacific steamer knew the story, and it was incumbent on him that Miss Viner should not hear the tidings in a sudden manner and from a stranger's mouth.

He went up into the drawing-room, and found Miss Viner seated there in the midst of a crew of women. He went up to her, and taking her hand, asked her in a whisper whether she would come out with him for a moment.

'Where is he?' said she. 'I know that something is the matter. What is it?'

'There is such a crowd here. Step out for a moment.' And he led her away to her own room.

'Where is he?' said she. 'What is the matter? He has sent to say that he no longer wants me. Tell me; am I free from him?'

'Miss Viner, you are free.'

Though she had asked the question herself, she was astounded by the answer; but, nevertheless, no idea of the truth had yet come upon her. 'It is so,' she said. 'Well, what else? Has he written? He has bought me, as he would a beast of burden, and has, I suppose, a right to treat me as he pleases.'

'I have a letter; but, dear Miss Viner – '

'Well, tell me all – out at once. Tell me everything.'

'You are free, Miss Viner; but you will be cut to the heart when you learn the meaning of your freedom.'

'He has lost everything in trade. He is ruined.'

'Miss Viner, he is dead!'

She stood staring at him for a moment or two, as though she could not realise the information which he gave her. Then gradually she retreated to the bed, and sat upon it. 'Dead, Mr Forrest!' she said. He did not answer her, but handed her the letter, which she took and read as though it were mechanically. The letter was from Mr Gorloch's partner, and told her everything which it was necessary that she should know.

'Shall I leave you now?' he said, when he saw that she had finished reading it.

'Leave me; yes – no. But you had better leave me, and let me think about it. Alas me, that I should have so spoken of him!'

'But you have said nothing unkind.'

'Yes; much that was unkind. But spoken words cannot be recalled. Let me be alone now, but come to me soon. There is no one else here that I can speak to.'

He went out, and finding that the hotel dinner was ready, he went in and dined. Then he strolled into the town, among the hot, narrow, dilapidated streets; and then, after two hours' absence, returned to Miss Viner's room. When he knocked, she came and opened the door, and he found that the floor was strewn with clothes.

'I am preparing, you see, for my return. The vessel starts back for St Thomas the day after tomorrow.'

'You are quite right to go – to go at once. Oh, Miss Viner! Emily, now at least you must let me help you.'

He had been thinking of her most during those last two hours, and her voice had become pleasant to his ears, and her eyes very bright to his sight.

'You shall help me,' she said. 'Are you not helping me when at such a time you come to speak to me?'

'And you will let me think that I have a right to act as your protector?'

'My protector! I do know that I want such aid as that. During the days that we are here together you shall be my friend.'

'You shall not return alone. My journeys are nothing to me. Emily, I will return with you to England.'

Then she rose up from her seat and spoke to him.

'Not for the world,' she said. 'Putting out of question the folly of your forgetting your own objects, do you think it possible that I should go with you, now that he is dead? To you I have spoken of him harshly; and now that it is my duty to mourn for him, could I do so heartily if you were with me? While he lived, it seemed to me that in those last days I had a right to speak my thoughts plainly. You and I were to part and meet no more, and I regarded us both as people apart, who for a while might drop the common usages of the world. It is so no longer. Instead of going with you farther, I must ask you to forget that we were ever together.'

'Emily, I shall never forget you.'

'Let your tongue forget me. I have given you no cause to speak good of me, and you will be too kind to speak evil.'

After that she explained to him all that the letter had contained. The arrangements for her journey had all been made; money also had been sent to her; and Mr Gorloch in his will had provided for her, not liberally, seeing that he was rich, but still sufficiently.

And so they parted at Panama. She would not allow him even to cross the Isthmus with her, but pressed his hand warmly as he left her at the station.

'God bless you!' he said.

'And may God bless you, my friend!' she answered.

Thus alone she took her departure for England, and he went on his way to California.

AMELIA B. EDWARDS

Amelia Ann Blandford Edwards, the daughter of one of the Duke of Wellington's officers, was born in London in 1831. At a very early age she displayed considerable literary and artistic talent. She became a contributor to various magazines and newspapers, and besides many miscellaneous works she wrote eight novels, the most successful of which were *Debenham's Vow* (1870) and *Lord Brackenbury* (1880). In the winter of 1873–4 she visited Egypt and was profoundly impressed by the new openings for archaeological research. She learnt the hieroglyphic characters and made a considerable collection of Egyptian antiquities. In 1877 she published *A Thousand Miles Up the Nile*, with illustrations by herself, and in 1882 was largely instrumental in founding the Egypt Exploration Fund. It was at this point that she abandoned her other literary work, writing only on Egyptology. She died in Weston-super-Mare, Somerset, in 1892, bequeathing her valuable collection of Egyptian antiquities to University College, London, together with a sum to found a chair of Egyptology.

The Phantom Coach

The circumstances I am about to relate to you have truth to recommend them. They happened to myself and my recollection of them is as vivid as if they had taken place only yesterday. Twenty years, however, have gone by since that night. During those twenty years I have told the story to but one other person. I tell it now with a reluctance which I find it difficult to overcome. All I entreat, meanwhile, is that you will abstain from forcing your own conclusions upon me. I want nothing explained away. I desire no arguments. My mind on this subject is quite made up and, having the testimony of my own senses to rely upon, I prefer to abide by it.

Well! It was just twenty years ago and within a day or two of the end of the grouse season. I had been out all day with my gun and had had no sport to speak of. The wind was due east; the month, December; the place, a bleak wide moor in the far north of England. And I had lost my way. It was not a pleasant place in which to lose one's way, with the first feathery flakes of a coming snowstorm just fluttering down upon the heather and the leaden evening closing in all around. I shaded my eyes with my hand and stared anxiously into the gathering darkness, where the purple moorland melted into a range of low hills, some ten or twelve miles distant. Not the faintest smoke-wreath, not the tiniest cultivated patch or fence or sheep-track, met my eyes in any direction. There was nothing for it but to walk on and take my chance of finding what shelter I could, by the way. So I shouldered my gun again and pushed wearily forward; for I had been on foot since an hour after daybreak and had eaten nothing since breakfast.

Meanwhile, the snow began to come down with ominous steadiness and the wind fell. After this, the cold became more intense and the night came rapidly up. As for me, my prospects darkened with the darkening sky and my heart grew heavy as I thought how my young wife was already watching for me through the window of our little inn parlour and thought of all the suffering in store for her throughout this weary night. We had been married four months and, having spent our autumn in the Highlands, were now lodging in a remote little village situated just on the verge of the great English moorlands. We were very much in love and, of course, very happy. This morning, when we parted, she had implored me to return before dusk and I had promised her that I would. What would I not have given to have kept my word!

Even now, weary as I was, I felt that with a supper, an hour's rest, and a guide, I might still get back to her before midnight, if only guide and shelter could be found.

And all this time, the snow fell and the night thickened. I stopped and shouted every now and then, but my shouts seemed only to make the silence deeper. Then a vague sense of uneasiness came upon me and I began to remember stories of travellers who had walked on and on in the falling snow until, wearied out, they were fain to lie down and sleep their lives away. Would it be possible, I asked myself, to keep on thus through all the long dark night? Would there not come a time when my limbs must fail and my resolution give way? When I, too, must sleep the sleep of death. Death! I shuddered. How hard to die just now, when life lay all so bright before me! How hard for my darling, whose whole loving heart – but that thought was not to be borne! To banish it, I shouted again, louder and longer, and then listened eagerly. Was my shout answered, or did I only fancy that I heard a far-off cry? I hallooed again and again the echo followed. Then a wavering speck of light came suddenly out of the dark, shifting, disappearing, growing momentarily nearer and brighter. Running towards it at full speed, I found myself, to my great joy, face to face with an old man and a lantern.

'Thank God!' was the exclamation that burst involuntarily from my lips.

Blinking and frowning, he lifted his lantern and peered into my face.

'What for?' growled he, sulkily.

'Well – for you. I began to fear I should be lost in the snow.'

'Eh, then, folks do get cast away hereabouts fra' time to time, an' what's to hinder you from bein' cast away likewise, if the Lord's so minded?'

'If the Lord is so minded that you and I shall be lost together, friend, we must submit,' I replied; 'but I don't mean to be lost without you. How far am I now from Dwolding?'

'A gude twenty mile, more or less.'

'And the nearest village?'

'The nearest village is Wyke, an' that's twelve mile t'other side.'

'Where do you live, then?'

'Out yonder,' said he, with a vague jerk of the lantern.

'You're going home, I presume?'

'Maybe I am.'

'Then I'm going with you.'

The old man shook his head and rubbed his nose reflectively with the handle of the lantern.

'It ain't o' no use,' growled he. 'He 'ont let you in – not he.'

'We'll see about that,' I replied, briskly. 'Who is he?'

'The master.'

'Who is the master?'

'That's nowt to you,' was the unceremonious reply.

'Well, well; you lead the way and I'll engage that the master shall give me shelter and a supper tonight.'

'Eh you can try him!' muttered my reluctant guide; and, still shaking his head, he hobbled, gnome-like, away through the falling snow. A large mass loomed up presently out of the darkness, and a huge dog rushed out, barking furiously.

'Is this the house?' I asked.

'Ay, it's the house. Down, bey!' And he fumbled in his pocket for the key.

I drew up close behind him, prepared to lose no chance of entrance, and saw in the little circle of light shed by the lantern that the door was heavily studded with iron nails, like the door of a prison. In another minute he had turned the key and I had pushed past him into the house.

Once inside, I looked round with curiosity and found myself in a great raftered hall, which served, apparently, a variety of uses. One end was piled to the roof with corn, like a barn. The other was stored with flour-sacks, agricultural implements, casks and all kinds of miscellaneous lumber; while from the beams overhead hung rows of hams, flitches and bunches of dried herbs for winter use. In the centre of the floor stood some huge object gauntly dressed in a dingy wrapping-cloth, and reaching half way to the rafters. Lifting a corner of this cloth I saw, to my surprise, a telescope of very considerable size, mounted on a rude movable platform, with four small wheels. The tube was made of painted wood, bound round with bands of metal rudely fashioned; the speculum, so far as I could estimate its size in the dim light, measured at least fifteen inches in diameter. While I was yet examining the instrument and asking myself whether it was not the work of some self-taught optician, a bell rang sharply.

'That's for you,' said my guide, with a malicious grin. 'Yonder's his room.'

He pointed to a low black door at the opposite side of the hall. I crossed over, rapped somewhat loudly and went in, without waiting for an invitation. A huge, white-haired old man rose from a table covered with books and papers and confronted me sternly.

'Who are you?' said he. 'How came you here? What do you want?'

'James Murray, barrister-at-law. On foot across the moor. Meat, drink and sleep.'

He bent his bushy brows into a portentous frown.

'Mine is not a house of entertainment,' he said, haughtily. 'Jacob, how dared you admit this stranger?'

'I didn't admit him.' grumbled the old man. 'He followed me over the muir and shouldered his way in before me. I'm no match for six foot two.'

'And pray, sir, by what right have you forced an entrance into my house?'

'The same by which I should have clung to your boat, if I were drowning. The right of self-preservation.'

'Self-preservation?'

'There's an inch of snow on the ground already,' I replied, briefly; 'and it would be deep enough to cover my body before daybreak.'

He strode to the window, pulled aside a heavy black curtain and looked out.

'It is true,' he said. 'You can stay, if you choose, till morning. Jacob, serve the supper.'

With this he waved me to a seat, resumed his own and became at once absorbed in the studies from which I had disturbed him.

I placed my gun in a corner, drew a chair to the hearth and examined my quarters at leisure. Smaller and less incongruous in its arrangements than the hall, this room contained, nevertheless, much to awaken my curiosity. The floor was carpetless. The whitewashed walls were in parts scrawled over with strange diagrams and in others covered with shelves crowded with philosophical instruments, the uses of many of which were unknown to me. On one side of the fireplace, stood a bookcase filled with dingy folios; on the other, a small organ, fantastically decorated with painted carvings of medieval saints and devils. Through the half-opened door of a cupboard at the farther end of the room, I saw a long array of geological specimens, surgical preparations, crucibles, retorts and jars of chemicals; while on the mantelshelf beside me, amid a number of small objects, stood a model of the solar system, a small galvanic battery and a microscope. Every chair had its burden. Every corner was heaped high with books. The very floor was littered over with maps, casts, papers, tracings and learned lumber of all conceivable kinds.

I stared about me with an amazement increased by every fresh object upon which my eyes chanced to rest. So strange a room I had never seen; yet seemed it stranger still to find such a room in a lone farmhouse amid those wild and solitary moors! Over and over again, I looked from my host to his surroundings and from his surroundings back to my host, asking myself who and what he could be? His head was singularly fine; but it was more the head of a poet than of a philosopher. Broad in the temples, prominent over the eyes and clothed with a rough profusion of perfectly white hair, it had all the ideality and much of the ruggedness that characterises the head of Ludwig van Beethoven. There were the same deep lines about the mouth and the same stern furrows in the brow. There was the same concentration of expression. While I was yet observing him, the door opened and Jacob brought in the supper. His master then closed his book, rose and with more courtesy of manner than he had yet shown, invited me to the table.

A dish of ham and eggs, a loaf of brown bread and a bottle of admirable sherry were placed before me.

'I have but the homeliest farmhouse fare to offer you, sir,' said my entertainer. 'Your appetite, I trust, will make up for the deficiencies of our larder.'

I had already fallen upon the viands and now protested, with the enthusiasm of a starving sportsman, that I had never eaten anything so delicious.

He bowed stiffly and sat down to his own supper, which consisted, primitively, of a jug of milk and a basin of porridge. We ate in silence and, when we had done, Jacob removed the tray. I then drew my chair back to the fireside. My host, somewhat to my surprise, did the same and, turning abruptly towards me, said: 'Sir, I have lived here in strict retirement for three-and-twenty years. During that time, I have not seen as many strange faces and I have not read a single newspaper. You are the first stranger who has crossed my threshold for more than four years. Will you favour me with a few words of information respecting that outer world from which I have parted company so long?'

'Pray interrogate me,' I replied. 'I am heartily at your service.'

He bent his head in acknowledgment; leaned forward, with

his elbows resting on his knees and his chin supported in the palms of his hands; stared fixedly into the fire; and proceeded to question me.

His enquiries related chiefly to scientific matters, with the later progress of which, as applied to the practical purposes of life, he was almost wholly unacquainted. No student of science myself, I replied as well as my slight information permitted; but the task was far from easy and I was much relieved when, passing from interrogation to discussion, he began pouring forth his own conclusions upon the facts which I had been attempting to place before him. He talked and I listened spellbound. He talked till I believe he almost forgot my presence and only thought aloud. I had never heard anything like it then; I have never heard anything like it since. Familiar with all systems of all philosophies, subtle in analysis, bold in generalisation, he poured forth his thoughts in an uninterrupted stream and, still leaning forward in the same moody attitude with his eyes fixed upon the fire, wandered from topic to topic, from speculation to speculation, like an inspired dreamer. From practical science to mental philosophy; from electricity in the wire to electricity in the nerve; from Watts to Mesmer, from Mesmer to Reichenbach, from Reichenbach to Swedenborg, Spinoza, Condillac, Descartes, Berkeley, Aristotle, Plato, and the Magi and mystics of the East, were transitions which, however bewildering in their variety and scope, seemed easy and harmonious upon his lips as sequences in music. By and by – I forget now by what link of conjecture or illustration – he passed on to that field which lies beyond the boundary line of even conjectural philosophy and reaches no man knows whither. He spoke of the soul and its aspirations; of the spirit and its powers; of second sight; of prophecy; of those phenomena which, under the names of ghosts, spectres and supernatural appearances, have been denied by the sceptics and attested by the credulous of all ages.

'The world,' he said, 'grows hourly more and more sceptical

of all that lies beyond its own narrow radius; and our men of science foster the fatal tendency. They condemn as fable all that resists experiment. They reject as false all that cannot be brought to the test of the laboratory or the dissecting-room. Against what superstition have they waged so long and obstinate a war as against the belief in apparitions? And yet what superstition has maintained its hold upon the minds of men so long and so firmly? Show me any fact in physics, in history, in archaeology, which is supported by testimony so wide and so various. Attested by all races of men, in all ages and in all climates, by the soberest sages of antiquity, by the rudest savage of today, by the Christian, the Pagan, the Pantheist, the Materialist, this phenomenon is treated as a nursery tale by the philosophers of our century. Circumstantial evidence weighs with them as a feather in the balance. The comparison of causes with effects, however valuable in physical science, is put aside as worthless and unreliable. The evidence of competent witnesses, however conclusive in a court of justice, counts for nothing. He who pauses before he pronounces, is condemned as a trifler. He who believes, is a dreamer or a fool.'

He spoke with bitterness and, having said thus, relapsed for some minutes into silence. Presently he raised his head from his hands and added, with an altered voice and manner: 'I, sir, paused, investigated, believed, and was not ashamed to state my convictions to the world. I, too, was branded as a visionary, held up to ridicule by my contemporaries, and hooted from that field of science in which I had laboured with honour during all the best years of my life. These things happened just three-and-twenty years ago. Since then, I have lived as you see me living now and the world has forgotten me, as I have forgotten the world. You have my history.'

'It is a very sad one,' I murmured, scarcely knowing what to answer.

'It is a very common one,' he replied. 'I have only suffered for the truth, as many a better and wiser man has suffered before me.'

He rose, as if desirous of ending the conversation, and went over to the window.

'It has ceased snowing,' he observed, as he dropped the curtain, and came back to the fireside.

'Ceased!' I exclaimed, starting eagerly to my feet. 'Oh, if it were only possible – but no! it is hopeless. Even if I could find my way across the moor, I could not walk twenty miles tonight.'

'Walk twenty miles tonight!' repeated my host. 'What are you thinking of?'

'Of my wife,' I replied, impatiently. 'Of my young wife, who does not know that I have lost my way and who is at this moment breaking her heart with suspense and terror.'

'Where is she?'

'At Dwolding, twenty miles away.'

'At Dwolding,' he echoed, thoughtfully. 'Yes, the distance, it is true, is twenty miles; but – are you so very anxious to save the next six or eight hours?'

'So very, very anxious, that I would give ten guineas at this moment for a guide and a horse.'

'Your wish can be gratified at a less costly rate,' said he, smiling. 'The night mail from the north, which changes horses at Dwolding, passes within five miles of this spot and will be due at a certain crossroad in about an hour and a quarter. If Jacob were to go with you across the moor and put you into the old coach-road, you could find your way, I suppose, to where it joins the new one?'

'Easily – gladly.'

He smiled again, rang the bell, gave the old servant his directions and, taking a bottle of whisky and a wineglass from the cupboard in which he kept his chemicals, said: 'The snow lies deep and it will be difficult walking tonight on the moor. A glass of usquebaugh before you start?'

I would have declined the spirit, but he pressed it on me and I drank it. It went down my throat like liquid flame and almost took my breath away.

'It is strong,' he said; 'but it will help to keep out the cold. And now you have no moments to spare. Good-night!'

I thanked him for his hospitality and would have shaken hands but that he had turned away before I could finish my sentence. In another minute I had traversed the hall, Jacob had locked the outer door behind me and we were out on the wide white moor.

Although the wind had fallen, it was still bitterly cold. Not a star glimmered in the black vault overhead. Not a sound, save the rapid crunching of the snow beneath our feet, disturbed the heavy stillness of the night. Jacob, not too well pleased with his mission, shambled on before in sullen silence, his lantern in his hand and his shadow at his feet. I followed, with my gun over my shoulder, as little inclined for conversation as himself. My thoughts were full of my late host. His voice yet rang in my ears. His eloquence yet held my imagination captive. I remember to this day, with surprise, how my over-excited brain retained whole sentences and parts of sentences, troops of brilliant images and fragments of splendid reasoning, in the very words in which he had uttered them. Musing thus over what I had heard, and striving to recall a lost link here and there, I strode on at the heels of my guide, absorbed and unobservant.

Presently – at the end, as it seemed to me, of only a few minutes – he came to a sudden halt and said: 'Yon's your road. Keep the stone fence to your right hand and you can't fail of the way.'

'This, then, is the old coach-road?'

'Ay, 'tis the old coach-road.'

'And how far do I go, before I reach the crossroads?'

'Nigh upon three mile.'

I pulled out my purse, and he became more communicative. 'The road's a fair road enough,' said he, 'for foot passengers;

but 'twas over steep and narrow for the northern traffic. You'll mind where the parapet's broken away, close again the signpost. It's never been mended since the accident.'

'What accident?'

'Eh, the night mail pitched right over into the valley below – a gude fifty feet an' more – just at the worst bit o' road in the whole county.'

'Horrible! Were many lives lost?'

'All. Four were found dead and t'other two died next morning.'

'How long is it since this happened?'

'Just nine year.'

'Near the signpost, you say? I will bear it in mind. Goodnight.'

'Gude night, sir, and thankee.' Jacob pocketed his half-crown, made a faint pretence of touching his hat and trudged back by the way he had come.

I watched the light of his lantern till it quite disappeared and then turned to pursue my way alone. This was no longer matter of the slightest difficulty, for, despite the dead darkness overhead, the line of stone fence showed distinctly enough against the pale gleam of the snow. How silent it seemed now, with only my footsteps to listen to; how silent and how solitary! A strange disagreeable sense of loneliness stole over me. I walked faster. I hummed a fragment of a tune. I cast up enormous sums in my head and accumulated them at compound interest. I did my best, in short, to forget the startling speculations to which I had but just been listening and, to some extent, I succeeded.

Meanwhile the night air seemed to become colder and colder and though I walked fast I found it impossible to keep myself warm. My feet were like ice. I lost sensation in my hands and grasped my gun mechanically. I even breathed with difficulty, as though, instead of traversing a quiet north-country highway, I were scaling the uppermost heights of some gigantic Alp. This last symptom became presently so distressing, that I was forced to stop for a few minutes and lean against the stone fence. As I did so, I chanced to look back up the road and there, to my infinite relief, I saw a distant point of light, like the gleam of an approaching lantern. I at first concluded that Jacob had retraced his steps and followed me; but even as the conjecture presented itself, a second light flashed into sight – a light evidently parallel with the first, and approaching at the same rate of motion. It needed no second thought to show me that these must be the carriage-lamps of some private vehicle, though it seemed strange that any private vehicle should take a road professedly disused and dangerous.

There could be no doubt, however, of the fact, for the lamps grew larger and brighter every moment, and I even fancied I could already see the dark outline of the carriage between them. It was coming up very fast, and quite noiselessly, the snow being nearly a foot deep under the wheels.

And now the body of the vehicle became distinctly visible behind the lamps. It looked strangely lofty. A sudden suspicion flashed upon me. Was it possible that I had passed the crossroads in the dark without observing the signpost, and could this be the very coach which I had come to meet? No need to ask myself that question a second time, for here it came round the bend of the road, guard and driver, one outside passenger, and four steaming greys, all wrapped in a soft haze of light, through which the lamps blazed out, like a pair of fiery meteors.

I jumped forward, waved my hat and shouted. The mail came down at full speed, and passed me. For a moment I feared that I had not been seen or heard, but it was only for a moment. The coachman pulled up; the guard, muffled to the eyes in capes and comforters, and apparently sound asleep in the rumble, neither answered my hail nor made the slightest effort to dismount; the outside passenger did not even turn his head. I opened the door for myself, and looked in. There were but three travellers inside, so I stepped in, shut the door, slipped into the vacant corner, and congratulated myself on my good fortune.

The atmosphere of the coach seemed, if possible, colder than that of the outer air, and was pervaded by a singularly damp and disagreeable smell. I looked round at my fellow-passengers. They were, all three, men, and all silent. They did not seem to be asleep, but each leaned back in his corner of the vehicle as if absorbed in his own reflections. I attempted to open a conversation.

'How intensely cold it is tonight,' I said, addressing my opposite neighbour.

He lifted his head, looked at me, but made no reply.

'The winter,' I added, 'seems to have begun in earnest.'

Although the corner in which he sat was so dim that I could distinguish none of his features clearly, I saw that his eyes were still turned full upon me. And yet he answered never a word.

At any other time I should have felt, and perhaps expressed, some annoyance, but at the moment I felt too ill to do either. The icy coldness of the night air had struck a chill to my very marrow, and the strange smell inside the coach was affecting me with an intolerable nausea. I shivered from head to foot, and turning to my left-hand neighbour asked if he had any objection to an open window?

He neither spoke nor stirred.

I repeated the question somewhat more loudly, but with the same result. Then I lost patience, and let the sash down. As I did so the leather strap broke in my hand, and I observed that the glass was covered with a thick coat of mildew, the accumulation, apparently of years. My attention being thus drawn to the condition of the coach, I examined it more narrowly, and saw by the uncertain light of the outer lamps that it was in the last stage of dilapidation. Every part of it was not only out of repair, but in a condition of decay. The sashes splintered at a touch. The leather fittings were crusted over with mould, and literally rotting from the woodwork. The floor was almost breaking away beneath my feet. The whole machine, in short, was foul with damp, and had evidently been dragged from some outhouse, in which it had been mouldering away for years, to do another day or two of duty on the road.

I turned to the third passenger, whom I had not yet addressed, and hazarded one more remark.

'This coach,' I said, 'is in a deplorable condition. The regular mail, I suppose, is under repair?'

He moved his head slowly, and looked me in the face, without speaking a word. I shall never forget that look while I live. I turned cold at heart under it. I turn cold at heart even now when I recall it. His eyes glowed with a fiery unnatural lustre. His face was livid as the face of a corpse. His bloodless lips were drawn back as if in the agony of death, and showed the gleaming teeth between.

The words that I was about to utter died upon my lips, and a strange horror – a dreadful horror – came upon me. My sight had by this time become used to the gloom of the coach, and I could see with tolerable distinctness. I turned to my opposite neighbour. He, too, was looking at me, with the same startling pallor in his face and the same stony glitter in his eyes. I passed my hand across my brow. I turned to the passenger on the seat beside my own and saw – oh, heaven! how shall I describe what I saw? I saw that he was no living man – that none of them were living men, like myself! A pale phosphorescent light – the light of putrefaction – played upon their awful faces; upon their hair, dank with the dews of the grave; upon their clothes, earth-stained and dropping to pieces; upon their hands, which were as the hands of corpses long buried. Only their eyes, their terrible eyes, were living; and those eyes were all turned menacingly upon me!

A shriek of terror, a wild unintelligible cry for help and mercy, burst from my lips as I flung myself against the door and strove in vain to open it.

In that single instant, brief and vivid as a landscape beheld in a flash of summer lightning, I saw the moon shining down through a rift of stormy cloud – the ghastly signpost rearing its warning finger by the wayside – the broken parapet – the plunging horses – the black gulf below. Then, the coach reeled like a ship at sea. Then, came a mighty crash – a sense of crushing pain – and then, darkness.

It seemed as if years had gone by when I awoke one morning from a deep sleep and found my wife watching by my bedside. I will pass over the scene that ensued and give you, in half a dozen words, the tale she told me with tears of thanksgiving. I had fallen over a precipice, close against the junction of the old coach-road and the new, and had only been saved from certain death by lighting upon a deep snowdrift that had accumulated at the foot of the rock beneath. In this snowdrift I was discovered at daybreak by a couple of shepherds, who carried me to the nearest shelter and brought a surgeon to my aid. The surgeon found me in a state of raving delirium, with a broken arm and a compound fracture of the skull. The letters in my pocketbook showed my name and address; my wife was summoned to nurse me; and, thanks to youth and a fine constitution, I came out of danger at last. The place of my fall, I need scarcely say, was precisely that at which a frightful accident had happened to the north mail nine years before.

I never told my wife the fearful events which I have just related to you. I told the surgeon who attended me; but he treated the whole adventure as a mere dream born of the fever in my brain. We discussed the question over and over again, until we found that we could discuss it with temper no longer and then we dropped it. Others may form what conclusions they please – I *know* that twenty years ago I was the fourth inside passenger in that Phantom Coach.

GEORGE MOORE

George Augustus Moore was born on 24 February 1852 in Ballyglass, County Mayo, in Ireland. He left his homeland when he was eighteen and went to France to study painting. He came to England in 1882 to begin a writing career and published his first novel, *A Modern Lover*, in 1883, which borrowed much from French literary technique. His best work is *Esther Waters* (1894), which was a commercial success and was followed by *Evelyn Innes* (1898) and *Sister Teresa* (1901). Moore moved to Dublin in 1901, where he assisted in the planning of the Abbey Theatre (Irish National Theatre). He published an excellent collection of short stories, *The Untilled Field*, in 1903. He also produced a number of autobiographical works – *Confessions of a Young Man* (1888), *Memoirs of My Dead Life* (1906) and *Hail and Farewell* (1911). Moore returned to England in 1911 where he produced *The Brook Kerith* (1916), *Heloïse and Abelard* (1921) and *Ulick and Soracha* (1924). He died in London on 21 January 1933.

Home Sickness

He told the doctor he was due in the bar-room at eight o'clock in the morning; the bar-room was in a slum in the Bowery; and he had only been able to keep himself in health by getting up at five o'clock and going for long walks in the Central Park.

'A sea voyage is what you want,' said the doctor. 'Why not go to Ireland for two or three months? You will come back a new man.'

'I'd like to see Ireland again.'

And then he began to wonder how the people at home were

getting on. The doctor was right. He thanked him, and three weeks afterwards he landed in Cork.

As he sat in the railway carriage he recalled his native village – he could see it and its lake, and then the fields one by one, and the roads. He could see a large piece of rocky land – some three or four hundred acres of headland stretching out into the winding lake. Upon this headland the peasantry had been given permission to build their cabins by former owners of the Georgian house standing on the pleasant green hill. The present owners considered the village a disgrace, but the villagers paid high rents for their plots of ground, and all the manual labour that the Big House required came from the village: the gardeners, the stable helpers, the house- and the kitchen-maids.

He had been thirteen years in America, and when the train stopped at his station, he looked round to see if there were any changes in it. It was just the same blue limestone station-house as it was thirteen years ago. The platform and the sheds were the same, and there were five miles of road from the station to Duncannon. The sea voyage had done him good, but five miles were too far for him today; the last time he had walked the road, he had walked it in an hour and a half, carrying a heavy bundle on a stick.

He was sorry he did not feel strong enough for the walk; the evening was fine, and he would meet many people coming home from the fair, some of whom he had known in his youth, and they would tell him where he could get a clean lodging. But the carman would be able to tell him that; he called the car that was waiting at the station, and soon he was answering questions about America. But Bryden wanted to hear of those who were still living in the old country, and after hearing the stories of many people he had forgotten, he heard that Mike Scully, who had been away in a situation for many years as a coachman in the King's County, had come back and built a fine house with a concrete floor. Now there was a good loft in

Mike Scully's house, and Mike would be pleased to take in a lodger.

Bryden remembered that Mike had been in a situation at the Big House; he had intended to be a jockey, but had suddenly shot up into a fine tall man, and had had to become a coachman instead. Bryden tried to recall the face, but he could only remember a straight nose, and a somewhat dusky complexion. Mike was one of the heroes of his childhood, and his youth floated before him, and he caught glimpses of himself, something that was more than a phantom and less than a reality. Suddenly his reverie was broken: the carman pointed with his whip, and Bryden saw a tall, finely built, middle-aged man coming through the gates, and the driver said: 'There's Mike Scully.'

Mike had forgotten Bryden even more completely than Bryden had forgotten him, and many aunts and uncles were mentioned before he began to understand.

'You've grown into a fine man, James,' he said, looking at Bryden's great width of chest. 'But you are thin in the cheeks, and you're sallow in the cheeks too.'

'I haven't been very well lately – that is one of the reasons I have come back; but I want to see you all again.'

Bryden paid the carman, wished him 'God-speed', and he and Mike divided the luggage between them, Mike carrying the bag and Bryden the bundle, and they walked round the lake, for the townland was at the back of the demesne; and while they walked, James proposed to pay Mike ten shillings a week for his board and lodging.

He remembered the woods thick and well forested; now they were windworn, the drains were choked and the bridge leading across the lake inlet was falling away. Their way led between long fields where herds of cattle were grazing; the road was broken – Bryden wondered how the villagers drove their carts over it, and Mike told him that the landlord could not keep it in repair, and he would not allow it to be kept in repair out of the rates, for then it would be a public road, and he did not think there should be a public road through his property.

At the end of many fields they came to the village, and it looked a desolate place, even on this fine evening, and Bryden remarked that the country did not seem to be as much lived in as it used to be. It was at once strange and familiar to see the chickens in the kitchen; and, wishing to re-knit himself to the old habits, he begged of Mrs Scully not to drive them out, saying he did not mind them. Mike told his wife that Bryden was born in Duncannon, and when he mentioned Bryden's name she gave him her hand, after wiping it on her apron, saying he was heartily welcome, only she was afraid he would not care to sleep in a loft.

'Why wouldn't I sleep in a loft, a dry loft! You're thinking a good deal of America over here,' said he, 'but I reckon it isn't all you think it. Here you work when you like and you sit down when you like; but when you have had a touch of blood-poisoning as I had, and when you have seen young people walking with a stick, you think that there is something to be said for old Ireland.'

'Now won't you be taking a sup of milk? You'll be wanting a drink after travelling,' said Mrs Scully.

And when he had drunk the milk, Mike asked him if he would like to go inside or if he would like to go for a walk.

'Maybe it is sitting down you would like to be.'

And they went into the cabin, and started to talk about the wages a man could get in America, and the long hours of work.

And after Bryden had told Mike everything about America that he thought would interest him, he asked Mike about Ireland. But Mike did not seem to be able to tell him much that was of interest. They were all very poor – poorer, perhaps, than when he left them.

'I don't think anyone except myself has a five-pound note to his name.'

Bryden hoped he felt sufficiently sorry for Mike. But after all Mike's life and prospects mattered little to him. He had come back in search of health; and he felt better already; the milk had done him good, and the bacon and cabbage in the pot sent forth a savoury odour. The Scullys were very kind, they pressed him to make a good meal; a few weeks of country air and food, they said, would give him back the health he had lost in the Bowery; and when Bryden said he was longing for a smoke, Mike said there was no better sign than that. During his long illness he had never wanted to smoke, and he was a confirmed smoker.

It was comfortable to sit by the mild peat fire watching the smoke of their pipes drifting up the chimney, and all Bryden wanted was to be let alone; he did not want to hear of anyone's misfortunes, but about nine o'clock a number of villagers came in, and their appearance was depressing. Bryden remembered one or two of them – he used to know them very well when he was a boy; their talk was as depressing as their appearance, and he could feel no interest whatever in them. He was not moved when he heard that Higgins the stonemason was dead; he was not affected when he heard that Mary Kelly, who used to go to do the laundry at the Big House, had married; he was only interested when he heard she had gone to America. No, he had not met her there, America is a big place. Then one of the peasants asked him if he remembered Patsy Carabine, who used to do the gardening at the Big House. Yes, he remembered Patsy well. Patsy was in the poorhouse. He had not been able to do any work on account of his arm; his house had fallen in; he had given up his holding and gone into the poorhouse. All this was very sad, and to avoid hearing any further unpleasantness, Bryden began to tell them about America. And they sat round listening to him; but all the talking was on his side; he wearied of it; and looking round the group he recognised a ragged hunchback with grey hair; twenty years ago he was a young hunchback, and, turning to him, Bryden asked him if he was doing well with his five acres.

'Ah, not much. This has been a bad season. The potatoes failed; they were watery – there is no diet in them.'

These peasants were all agreed that they could make nothing out of their farms. Their regret was that they had not gone to America when they were young; and after striving to take an interest in the fact that O'Connor had lost a mare and foal worth forty pounds, Bryden began to wish himself back in the slum. And when they left the house he wondered if every evening would be like the present one. Mike piled fresh sods on the fire, and he hoped it would show enough light in the loft for Bryden to undress himself by.

The cackling of some geese in the road kept him awake, and the loneliness of the country seemed to penetrate to his bones, and to freeze the marrow in them. There was a bat in the loft – a dog howled in the distance – and then he drew the clothes over his head. Never had he been so unhappy, and the sound of Mike breathing by his wife's side in the kitchen added to his nervous terror. Then he dozed a little; and lying on his back he dreamed he was awake, and the men he had seen sitting round the fireside that evening seemed to him like spectres come out of some unknown region of morass and reedy tarn. He stretched out his hands for his clothes, determined to fly from this house, but remembering the lonely road that led to the station he fell back on his pillow. The geese still cackled, but he was too tired to be kept awake any longer. He seemed to have been asleep only a few minutes when he heard Mike calling him. Mike had come halfway up the ladder and was telling him that breakfast was ready. 'What kind of breakfast will he give me?' Bryden asked himself as he pulled on his clothes. There were tea and hot griddle cakes for breakfast, and there were fresh eggs; there was sunlight in the kitchen and he liked to hear Mike tell of the work he was going to do in the fields. Mike rented a farm of about fifteen acres, at least ten of which were grass; he grew an acre of potatoes and some corn, and some turnips for his sheep. He had a nice bit of meadow, and he took down his scythe, and as he put the whetstone in his belt Bryden noticed a second scythe, and he asked Mike if he should go down with him and help him to finish the field.

'You haven't done any mowing this many a year; I don't think you'd be of much help. You'd better go for a walk by the lake, but you may come in the afternoon if you like and help to turn the grass over.'

Bryden was afraid he would find the lake shore very lonely, but the magic of returning health is sufficient distraction for the convalescent, and the morning passed agreeably. The weather was still and sunny. He could hear the ducks in the reeds. The hours dreamed themselves away, and it became his habit to go to the lake every morning. One morning he met the landlord, and they walked together, talking of the country, of what it had been, and the ruin it was slipping into. James Bryden told him that ill health had brought him back to Ireland; and the landlord lent him his boat, and Bryden rowed about the islands, and resting upon his oars he looked at the old castles, and remembered the prehistoric raiders that the landlord had told him about. He came across the stones to which the lake dwellers had tied their boats, and these signs of ancient Ireland were pleasing to Bryden in his present mood.

As well as the great lake there was a smaller lake in the bog where the villagers cut their turf. This lake was famous for its pike, and the landlord allowed Bryden to fish there, and one evening when he was looking for a frog with which to bait his line he met Margaret Dirken driving home the cows for the milking. Margaret was the herdsman's daughter, and she lived in a cottage near the Big House; but she came up to the village whenever there was a dance, and Bryden had found himself opposite to her in the reels. But until this evening he had had little opportunity of speaking to her, and he was glad to speak to someone, for the evening was lonely, and they stood talking together.

'You're getting your health again,' she said. 'You'll soon be leaving us.'

'I'm in no hurry.'

'You're grand people over there; I hear a man is paid four dollars a day for his work.'

'And how much,' said James, 'has he to pay for his food and for his clothes?'

Her cheeks were bright and her teeth small, white and beautifully even; and a woman's soul looked at Bryden out of her soft Irish eyes. He was troubled and turned aside, and catching sight of a frog looking at him out of a tuft of grass he said: 'I have been looking for a frog to put upon my pike line.'

The frog jumped right and left, and nearly escaped in some bushes, but he caught it and returned with it in his hand.

'It is just the kind of frog a pike will like,' he said. 'Look at its great white belly and its bright yellow back.'

And without more ado he pushed the wire to which the hook was fastened through the frog's fresh body, and dragging it through the mouth he passed the hook through the hind legs and tied the line to the end of the wire.

'I think,' said Margaret, 'I must be looking after my cows; it's time I got them home.'

'Won't you come down to the lake while I set my line?'

She thought for a moment and said: 'No, I'll see you from here.'

He went down to the reedy tarn, and at his approach several snipe got up, and they flew above his head uttering sharp cries. His fishing-rod was a long hazel stick, and he threw the frog as far as he could into the lake. In doing this he roused some wild ducks; a mallard and two ducks got up, and they flew towards the larger lake. Margaret watched them; they flew in a line with an old castle; and they had not disappeared from view when Bryden came towards her, and he and she drove the cows home together that evening.

They had not met very often when she said, 'James, you had better not come here so often calling to me.'

'Don't you wish me to come?'

'Yes, I wish you to come well enough, but keeping company is not the custom of the country, and I don't want to be talked about.'

'Are you afraid the priest would speak against us from the altar?'

'He has spoken against keeping company, but it is not so much what the priest says, for there is no harm in talking.'

'But if you are going to be married there is no harm in walking out together?'

'Well, not so much, but marriages are made differently in these parts; there is not much courting here.'

And next day it was known in the village that James was going to marry Margaret Dirken.

His desire to excel the boys in dancing had aroused much gaiety in the parish, and for some time past there had been dancing in every house where there was a floor fit to dance upon; and if the cottager had no money to pay for a barrel of beer, James Bryden, who had money, sent him a barrel, so that Margaret might get her dance. She told him that they sometimes crossed over into another parish where the priest was not so averse to dancing, and James wondered. And next morning at mass he wondered at their simple fervour. Some of them held their hands above their heads as they prayed, and all this was very new and very old to James Bryden. But the obedience of these people to their priest surprised him. When he was a lad they had not been so obedient, or he had forgotten their obedience; and he listened in mixed anger and wonderment to the priest who was scolding his parishioners, speaking to them by name, saying that he had heard there was dancing going on in their homes. Worse than that, he said he had seen boys and girls loitering about the roads, and the talk that went on was of one kind – love. He said that newspapers containing love-stories were finding their way into the people's houses, stories about love, in which there was nothing elevating or ennobling. The people listened, accepting the priest's opinion without question. And their submission was pathetic. It was the submission of a primitive people clinging to religious authority, and Bryden contrasted the weakness and incompetence of the people about him with the modern restlessness and cold energy of the people he had left behind him.

One evening, as they were dancing, a knock came to the door, and the piper stopped playing, and the dancers whispered: 'Someone has told on us; it is the priest.'

And the awe-stricken villagers crowded round the cottage fire, afraid to open the door. But the priest said that if they did not open the door he would put his shoulder to it and force it open. Bryden went towards the door, saying he would allow no one to threaten him, priest or no priest, but Margaret caught his arm and told him that if he said anything to the priest, the priest would speak against them from the altar, and they would be shunned by the neighbours. It was Mike Scully who went to the door and let the priest in, and he came in saying they were dancing their souls into hell.

'I've heard of your goings on,' he said – 'of your beer-drinking and dancing. I will not have it in my parish. If you want that sort of thing you had better go to America.'

'If that is intended for me, sir, I will go back tomorrow. Margaret can follow.'

'It isn't the dancing, it's the drinking I'm opposed to,' said the priest, turning to Bryden.

'Well, no one has drunk too much, sir,' said Bryden.

'But you'll sit here drinking all night,' and the priest's eyes went towards the corner where the women had gathered, and Bryden felt that the priest looked on the women as more dangerous than the porter.

'It's after midnight,' he said, taking out his watch. By Bryden's watch it was only half-past eleven, and while they were arguing about the time Mrs Scully offered Bryden's umbrella to the priest, for in his hurry to stop the dancing the priest had gone out without his; and, as if to show Bryden that he bore him no ill-will, the priest accepted the loan of the umbrella, for he was thinking of the big marriage fee that Bryden would pay him.

'I shall be badly off for the umbrella tomorrow,' Bryden said, as soon as the priest was out of the house. He was going with his father-in-law to a fair. His father-in-law was learning him how to buy and sell cattle. And his father-in-law was saying that the country was mending, and that a man might become rich in Ireland if he only had a little capital. Bryden had the capital, and Margaret had an uncle on the other side of the lake who would leave her all he had, that would be fifty pounds, and never in the village of Duncannon had a young couple begun life with so much prospect of success as would James Bryden and Margaret Dirken.

Some time after Christmas was spoken of as the best time for the marriage; James Bryden said that he would not be able to get his money out of America before the spring. The delay seemed to vex him, and he seemed anxious to be married, until one day he received a letter from America, from a man who had served in the bar with him. This friend wrote to ask Bryden if he were coming back. The letter was no more than a passing wish to see Bryden again. Yet Bryden stood looking at it, and everyone wondered what could be in the letter. It seemed momentous, and they hardly believed him when he said it was from a friend who wanted to know if his health were better. He tried to forget the letter, and he looked at the worn fields, divided by walls of loose stones, and a great longing came upon him.

The smell of the Bowery slum had come across the Atlantic, and had found him out in this western headland; and one night he awoke from a dream in which he was hurling some drunken customer through the open doors into the darkness. He had seen his friend in his white duck jacket throwing drink from glass into glass amid the din of voices and strange accents; he had heard the clang of money as it was swept into the till, and his sense sickened for the bar-room. But how should he tell Margaret Dirken that he could not marry her? She had built her life upon this marriage. He could not tell her that he would not marry her . . . yet he must go. He felt as if he were being hunted; the thought that he must tell Margaret that he could not marry her hunted him day after day as a weasel hunts a rabbit. Again and again he went to meet her with the intention of telling her that he did not love her, that their lives were not for one another, that it had all been a mistake, and that happily he had found out it was a mistake soon enough. But Margaret, as if she guessed what he was about to speak of, threw her arms about him and begged him to say he loved her, and that they would be married at once. He agreed that he loved her, and that they would be married at once. But he had not left her many minutes before the feeling came upon him that he could not marry her – that he must go away. The smell of the bar-room hunted him down. Was it for the sake of the money that he might make there that he wished to go back? No, it was not the money. What then? His eyes fell on the bleak country, on the little fields divided by bleak walls; he remembered the pathetic ignorance of the people, and it was these things that he could not endure. It was the priest who came to forbid the dancing. Yes, it was the priest. As he stood looking at the line of the hills the bar-room called to him. He heard the politicians, and the excitement of politics was in his blood again. He must go away from this place – he must get back to the bar-room. Looking up he saw the scanty orchard, and he hated the spare road that led to the village, and he hated the little hill at the top of which the village began, and he hated more than all other places the house where he was to live with Margaret Dirken – if he married her. He could see it from where he stood – by the edge of the lake, with twenty acres of pasture land about it, for the landlord had given up part of his demesne land to them.

He caught sight of Margaret, and he called to her to come through the stile. 'I have just had a letter from America.'

'About the money?' she said.

'Yes, about the money. But I shall have to go over there.'

He stood looking at her, seeking for words; and she guessed from his embarrassment that he would say to her that he must go to America before they were married.

'Do you mean, James, you will have to go at once?'

'Yes,' he said, 'at once. But I shall come back in time to be married in August. It will only mean delaying our marriage a month.'

They walked on a little way talking; every step he took James felt that he was a step nearer the Bowery slum. And when they came to the gate Bryden said: 'I must hasten or I shall miss the train.'

'But,' she said, 'you are not going now – you are not going today?'

'Yes, this morning. It is seven miles. I shall have to hurry not to miss the train.'

And then she asked him if he would ever come back.

'Yes,' he said, 'I am coming back.'

'If you are coming back, James, why not let me go with you?'

'You could not walk fast enough. We should miss the train.'

'One moment, James. Don't make me suffer; tell me the truth. You are not coming back. Your clothes – where shall I send them?'

He hurried away, hoping he would come back. He tried to think that he liked the country he was leaving, that it would be better to have a farmhouse and live there with Margaret Dirken than to serve drinks behind a counter in the Bowery. He did not think he was telling her a lie when he said he was coming back. Her offer to forward his clothes touched his heart, and at the end of the road he stood and asked himself if he should go back to her. He would miss the train if he waited another minute, and he ran on. And he would have missed the train if he had not met a car. Once he was on the car he felt himself safe – the country was already behind him. The train and the boat at Cork were mere formulae; he was already in America.

The moment he landed he felt the thrill of home that he had not found in his native village, and he wondered how it was that the smell of the bar seemed more natural than the smell of the fields, and the roar of crowds more welcome than the silence of the lake's edge. However, he offered up a thanksgiving for his escape, and entered into negotiations for the purchase of the bar-room.

He took a wife, she bore him sons and daughters, the bar-room prospered, property came and went; he grew old, his wife died, he retired from business, and reached the age when a man begins to feel there are not many years in front of him, and that all he has had to do in life has been done. His children married, lonesomeness began to creep about him; in the evening, when he looked into the firelight, a vague, tender reverie floated up, and Margaret's soft eyes and name vivified the dusk. His wife and children passed out of mind, and it seemed to him that that memory was the only real thing he possessed, and the desire to see Margaret again grew intense. But she was an old woman, she had married, maybe she was dead. Well, he would like to be buried in the village where he was born.

There is an unchanging, silent life within every man that none knows but himself, and his unchanging, silent life was his memory of Margaret Dirken. The bar-room was forgotten and all that concerned it, and the things he saw most clearly were the green hillside, and the bog lake and the rushes about it, and the greater lake in the distance, and behind it the blue lines of wandering hills.

RICHARD MIDDLETON

Richard Barham Middleton (1882–1911), a poet born at Staines in Middlesex, was descended, as his name indicates, from the author of the *Ingoldsby Legends.* Educated at St Paul's and Merchant Taylors', he became a clerk with an insurance firm in 1901, but after six years could endure it no longer and threw up the job to try to live by his pen. Despairing of success he poisoned himself with chloroform while in Brussels. As a writer Middleton belongs really to the nineties, and he had a great admiration for Dowson and Symons. In 1912, after his death, there appeared his *Poems and Songs* (two series), *The Ghost Ship,* a collection of stories, and *The Day Before Yesterday,* containing delightful child studies after the manner of Kenneth Grahame. His *Letters to Henry Savage* was published in 1929 and *The Pantomime Man,* a collection of prose pieces, in 1933.

On the Brighton Road

Slowly the sun had climbed up the hard white downs, till it broke with little of the mysterious ritual of dawn upon a sparkling world of snow. There had been a hard frost during the night, and the birds, who hopped about here and there with scant tolerance of life, left no trace of their passage on the silver pavements. In places the sheltered caverns of the hedges broke the monotony of the whiteness that had fallen upon the coloured earth, and overhead the sky melted from orange to deep blue, from deep blue to a blue so pale that it suggested a thin paper screen rather than illimitable space. Across the level fields there came a cold, silent wind which blew a fine dust of snow from the trees, but hardly stirred the crested hedges. Once above the skyline, the sun seemed to climb more quickly, and as it rose higher it began to give out a heat that blended with the keenness of the wind.

It may have been this strange alternation of heat and cold that disturbed the tramp in his dreams, for he struggled for a moment with the snow that covered him, like a man who finds himself twisted uncomfortably in the bedclothes, and then sat up with staring, questioning eyes. 'Lord! I thought I was in bed,' he said to himself as he took in the vacant landscape, 'and all the while I was out here.' He stretched his limbs, and, rising carefully to his feet, shook the snow off his body. As he did so the wind set him shivering, and he knew that his bed had been warm.

'Come, I feel pretty fit,' he thought. 'I suppose I am lucky to wake at all in this. Or unlucky – it isn't much of a business to come back to.' He looked up and saw the downs shining against the blue, like the Alps on a picture-postcard. 'That means another forty miles or so, I suppose,' he continued grimly. 'Lord knows what I did yesterday. Walked till I was done, and now I'm only about twelve miles from Brighton. Damn the snow, damn Brighton, damn everything!' The sun crept higher and higher, and he started walking patiently along the road with his back turned to the hills.

'Am I glad or sorry that it was only sleep that took me, glad or sorry, glad or sorry?' His thoughts seemed to arrange themselves in a metrical accompaniment to the steady thud of his footsteps, and he hardly sought an answer to his question. It was good enough to walk to.

Presently, when three milestones had loitered past, he overtook a boy who was stooping to light a cigarette. He wore no overcoat, and looked unspeakably fragile against the snow, 'Are you on the road, guv'nor?' asked the boy huskily as he passed.

'I think I am,' the tramp said.

'Oh! then I'll come a bit of the way with you if you don't walk too fast. It's bit lonesome walking this time of day.'

The tramp nodded his head, and the boy started limping along by his side.

'I'm eighteen,' he said casually. 'I bet you thought I was younger.'

'Fifteen, I'd have said.'

'You'd have backed a loser. Eighteen last August, and I've been on the road six years. I ran away from home five times when I was a little 'un, and the police took me back each time. Very good to me, the police was. Now I haven't got a home to run away from.'

'Nor have I,' the tramp said calmly.

'Oh, I can see what you are,' the boy panted; 'you're a gentleman come down. It's harder for you than for me.' The tramp glanced at the limping, feeble figure and lessened his pace.

'I haven't been at it as long as you have,' he admitted.

'No, I could tell that by the way you walk. You haven't got tired yet. Perhaps you expect something at the other end?'

The tramp reflected for a moment. 'I don't know,' he said bitterly, 'I'm always expecting things.'

'You'll grow out of that;' the boy commented. 'It's warmer in London, but it's harder to come by grub. There isn't much in it really.'

'Still, there's the chance of meeting somebody there who will understand –'

'Country people are better,' the boy interrupted. 'Last night I took a lease of a barn for nothing and slept with the cows, and this morning the farmer routed me out and gave me tea and toke because I was so little. Of course, I score there; but in London, soup on the Embankment at night, and all the rest of the time coppers moving you on.'

'I dropped by the roadside last night and slept where I fell. It's a wonder I didn't die,' the tramp said. The boy looked at him sharply.

'How did you know you didn't?' he said.

'I don't see it,' the tramp said, after a pause.

'I tell you,' the boy said hoarsely, 'people like us can't get away from this sort of thing if we want to. Always hungry and thirsty and dog-tired and walking all the while. And yet if anyone offers me a nice home and work my stomach feels sick. Do I look strong? I know I'm little for my age, but I've been knocking about like this for six years, and do you think I'm not dead? I was drowned bathing at Margate, and I was killed by a gypsy with a spike; he knocked my head and yet I'm walking along here now, walking to London to walk away from it again, because I can't help it. Dead! I tell you we can't get away if we want to.'

The boy broke off in a fit of coughing, and the tramp paused while he recovered.

'You'd better borrow my coat for a bit, Tommy,' he said, 'your cough's pretty bad.'

'You go to hell!' the boy said fiercely, puffing at his cigarette; 'I'm all right. I was telling you about the road. You haven't got down to it yet, but you'll find out presently. We're all dead, all of us who're on it, and we're all tired, yet somehow we can't leave it. There's nice smells in the summer, dust and hay and the wind smack in your face on a hot day – and it's nice waking up in the wet grass on a fine morning. I don't know, I don't know – ' he lurched forward suddenly, and the tramp caught him in his arms.

'I'm sick,' the boy whispered – 'sick.'

The tramp looked up and down the road, but he could see no houses or any sign of help. Yet even as he supported the boy doubtfully in the middle of the road a motor car suddenly flashed in the middle distance, and came smoothly through the snow.

'What's the trouble?' said the driver quietly as he pulled up. 'I'm a doctor.' He looked at the boy keenly and listened to his strained breathing.

'Pneumonia,' he commented. 'I'll give him a lift to the infirmary, and you, too, if you like.'

The tramp thought of the workhouse and shook his head. 'I'd rather walk,' he said.

The boy winked faintly as they lifted him into the car. 'I'll meet you beyond Reigate,' he murmured to the tramp. 'You'll see.' And the car vanished along the white road.

All the morning the tramp splashed through the thawing snow, but at midday he begged some bread at a cottage door and crept into a lonely barn to eat it. It was warm in there, and after his meal he fell asleep among the hay. It was dark when he woke, and started trudging once more through the slushy roads.

Two miles beyond Reigate a figure, a fragile figure, slipped out of the darkness to meet him.

'On the road, guv'nor?' said a husky voice. 'Then I'll come a bit of the way with you if you don't walk too fast. It's a bit lonesome walking this time of day.'

'But the pneumonia!' cried the tramp, aghast.

'I died at Crawley this morning,' said the boy.

F. SCOTT FITZGERALD

F. Scott Fitzgerald was born in St Paul, Minnesota, in 1896. He went to Princeton University but left before graduating to join the army in 1917 when America entered World War I. He was assigned to a camp in Alabama where, at a social event, he met Zelda Sayre. *This Side of Paradise* was published in March 1920 to great critical acclaim and the couple were married a week later. Together they embarked on an extravagant celebrity lifestyle that epitomised the 'Jazz Age'. *The Beautiful and Damned*, the second novel, was published in 1922 and *The Great Gatsby* in 1925. Fitzgerald earned only modestly from his novels, living on short stories and screenwriting. His fourth novel, *Tender is the Night*, appeared in 1934, and he was midway through his last when he died in 1940.

Three Hours Between Planes

It was a wild chance but Donald was in the mood, healthy and bored, with a sense of tiresome duty done. He was now rewarding himself. Maybe.

When the plane landed he stepped out into a Midwestern summer night and headed for the isolated pueblo airport building, conventionalised as an old red 'railway depot'. He did not know whether she was alive, or, if alive, still living in this town, or what her present name was. With mounting excitement he looked through the phone book for her father, who might be dead too somewhere in these twenty years.

No. Judge Harmon Holmes – Hillside 3194.

A woman's amused voice answered his enquiry for Miss Nancy Holmes.

'Nancy is Mrs Walter Gifford now. Who is this?'

But Donald hung up without answering. He had found out what he wanted to know and had only three hours. He did not remember any Walter Gifford and there was another suspended moment while he scanned the phone book. She might have married out of town. No. Walter Gifford – Hillside 1191. Blood flowed back into his fingertips.

'Hello?'

'Hello. Is Mrs Gifford there – this is an old friend of hers.'

'This is Mrs Gifford.'

He remembered, or thought he remembered, the funny magic in the voice. 'This is Donald Plant. I haven't seen you since I was twelve years old.'

'Oh–h–h!' The note was utterly surprised, very polite, but he could distinguish in it neither joy nor certain recognition.

' – Donald!' added the voice. This time there was something more in it than struggling memory.

' . . . when did you come back to town?' Then cordially, 'Where *are* you?'

'I'm out at the airport – for just a few hours.'

'Well, come up and see me.'

'Sure you're not just going to bed?'

'Heavens, no!' she exclaimed. 'I was sitting here – having a highball by myself. Just tell your taxi man . . . '

On his way Donald analysed the conversation. His words 'at the airport' established that he had retained his position in the upper bourgeoisie. Nancy's aloneness might indicate that she had matured into an unattractive woman without friends. Her husband might be either away or in bed. And – because she was always ten years old in his dreams – the highball shocked him. But he adjusted himself with a smile – she was very close to thirty.

At the end of a curved drive he saw a dark-haired little beauty standing against the lighted door, a glass in her hand. Startled by her final materialisation, Donald got out of the cab, saying: 'Mrs Gifford?'

She turned on the porch light and stared at him, wide-eyed and tentative. A smile broke through the puzzled expression.

'Donald – it is you – we all change so. Oh, this is remarkable!'

As they walked inside, their voices jingled the words 'all these years', and Donald felt a sinking in his stomach. This derived in part from a vision of their last meeting – when she rode past him on a bicycle, cutting him dead – and in part from fear lest they have nothing to say. It was like a college reunion – but there the failure to find the past was disguised by the hurried boisterous occasion. Aghast, he realised that this might be a long and empty hour. He plunged in desperately.

'You always were a lovely person. But I'm a little shocked to find you as beautiful as you are.'

It worked. The immediate recognition of their changed state, the bold compliment, made them interesting strangers instead of fumbling childhood friends.

'Have a highball?' she asked. 'No? Please don't think I've become a secret drinker, but this was a blue night. I expected my husband but he wired he'd be two days longer. He's very nice, Donald, and very attractive. Rather your type and colouring.' She hesitated, ' – and I think he's interested in someone in New York – and I don't know.'

'After seeing you it sounds impossible,' he assured her. 'I was married for six years, and there was a time I tortured myself that way. Then one day I just put jealousy out of my life for ever. After my wife died I was very glad of that. It left a very rich memory – nothing marred or spoiled or hard to think over.'

She looked at him attentively, then sympathetically as he spoke.

'I'm very sorry,' she said. And after a proper moment, 'You've changed a lot. Turn your head. I remember father saying, "That boy has a brain."'

'You probably argued against it.'

'I was impressed. Up to then I thought everybody had a brain. That's why it sticks in my mind.'

'What else sticks in your mind?' he asked smiling.

Suddenly Nancy got up and walked quickly a little away.

'Ah, now,' she reproached him. 'That isn't fair! I suppose I was a naughty girl.'

'You were not,' he said stoutly. 'And I *will* have a drink now.'

As she poured it, her face still turned from him, he continued: 'Do you think you were the only little girl who was ever kissed?'

'Do you like the subject?' she demanded. Her momentary irritation melted and she said: 'What the hell! We *did* have fun. Like in the song.'

'On the sleigh-ride.'

'Yes – and somebody's picnic – Trudy James's. And at Frontenac that – those summers.'

It was the sleigh-ride he remembered most and kissing her cool cheeks in the straw in one corner while she laughed up at the cold white stars. The couple next to them had their backs turned and he kissed her little neck and her ears and never her lips.

'And the Macks' party where they played post office and I couldn't go because I had the mumps,' he said.

'I don't remember that.'

'Oh, you were there. And you were kissed and I was crazy with jealousy like I never have been since.'

'Funny I don't remember. Maybe I wanted to forget.'

'But why?' he asked in amusement. 'We were two perfectly innocent kids. Nancy, whenever I talked to my wife about the past, I told her you were the girl I loved almost as much as I loved her. But I think I really loved you just as much. When we moved out of town I carried you like a cannon ball in my insides.'

'Were you *that* much – stirred up?'

'My God, yes! I – ' He suddenly realised that they were standing just two feet from each other, that he was talking as if he loved her in the present, that she was looking up at him with her lips half-parted and a clouded look in her eyes.

'Go on,' she said, 'I'm ashamed to say – I like it. I didn't know you were so upset *then*. I thought it was *me* who was upset.'

'You!' he exclaimed. 'Don't you remember throwing me over at the drugstore.' He laughed. 'You stuck out your tongue at me.'

'I don't remember at all. It seemed to me you did the throwing over.' Her hand fell lightly, almost consolingly on his arm. 'I've got a photograph book upstairs I haven't looked at for years. I'll dig it out.'

Donald sat for five minutes with two thoughts – first the hopeless impossibility of reconciling what different people remembered about the same event – and secondly that in a frightening way Nancy moved him as a woman as she had moved him as a child. Half an hour had developed an emotion that he had not known since the death of his wife – that he had never hoped to know again.

Side by side on a couch they opened the book between them. Nancy looked at him, smiling and very happy.

'Oh, this is *such* fun,' she said. 'Such fun that you're so nice, that you remember me so – beautifully. Let me tell you – I wish I'd known it then! After you'd gone, I hated you.'

'What a pity,' he said gently.

'But not now,' she reassured him, and then impulsively, 'Kiss and make up . . . '

' . . . that isn't being a good wife,' she said after a minute. 'I really don't think I've kissed two men since I was married.'

He was excited – but most of all confused. Had he kissed Nancy? or a memory? or this lovely trembly stranger who looked away from him quickly and turned a page of the book?

'Wait!' he said. 'I don't think I could *see* a picture for a few seconds.'

'We won't do it again. I don't feel so very calm myself.'

Donald said one of those trivial things that cover so much ground. 'Wouldn't it be awful if we fell in love again?'

'Stop it!' She laughed, but very breathlessly. 'It's all over. It was a moment. A moment I'll have to forget.'

'Don't tell your husband.'

'Why not? Usually I tell him everything.'

'It'll hurt him. Don't ever tell a man such things.'

'All right, I won't.'

'Kiss me once more,' he said inconsistently, but Nancy had turned a page and was pointing eagerly at a picture.

'Here's you,' she cried. 'Right away!'

He looked. It was a little boy in shorts standing on a pier with a sailboat in the background.

'I remember – ' she laughed triumphantly, ' – the very day it was taken. Kitty took it and I stole it from her.'

For a moment Donald failed to recognise himself in the photo – then, bending closer – he failed utterly to recognise himself.

'That's not me,' he said.

'Oh yes. It was at Frontenac – the summer we – we used to go to the cave.'

'What cave? I was only three days in Frontenac.' Again he strained his eyes at the slightly yellowed picture. 'And that isn't me. That's Donald Bowers. We did look rather alike.'

Now she was staring at him – leaning back, seeming to lift away from him.

'But you're Donald Bowers!' she exclaimed; her voice rose a little. 'No, you're not. You're Donald *Plant*.'

'I told you on the phone.'

She was on her feet – her face faintly horrified.

'Plant! Bowers! I must be crazy. Or was it that drink? I was mixed up a little when I first saw you. Look here! What have I told you?'

He tried for a monkish calm as he turned a page of the book. 'Nothing at all,' he said. Pictures that did not include him formed and re-formed before his eyes – Frontenac – a cave – Donald Bowers – 'You threw *me* over!'

Nancy spoke from the other side of the room. 'You'll never tell this story,' she said. 'Stories have a way of getting around.'

'There isn't any story,' he hesitated. But he thought: So she was a bad little girl.

And now suddenly he was filled with wild raging jealousy of little Donald Bowers – he who had banished jealousy from his life for ever. In the five steps he took across the room he crushed out twenty years and the existence of Walter Gifford with his stride.

'Kiss me again, Nancy,' he said, sinking to one knee beside her chair, putting his hand upon her shoulder. But Nancy strained away.

'You said you had to catch a plane.'

'It's nothing. I can miss it. It's of no importance.'

'Please go,' she said in a cool voice. 'And please try to imagine how I feel.'

'But you act as if you don't remember me,' he cried, ' – as if you don't remember Donald *Plant*!'

'I do. I remember you too . . . But it was all so long ago.' Her voice grew hard again. 'The taxi number is Crestwood 8484.'

On his way to the airport Donald shook his head from side to side. He was completely himself now but he could not digest the experience. Only as the plane roared up into the dark sky and its passengers became a different entity from the corporate world below did he draw a parallel from the fact of its flight. For five blinding minutes he had lived like a madman in two worlds at once. He had been a boy of twelve and a man of thirty-two, indissolubly and helplessly commingled.

Donald had lost a good deal, too, in those hours between the planes – but since the second half of life is a long process of getting rid of things, that part of the experience probably didn't matter.

JACK LONDON

John Griffith London (1876–1916), who wrote under the name
Jack London, was born in San Francisco, the illegitimate son of an
Irish vagabond and an American girl who afterwards married
John London, a grocer. Brought up in poverty, he worked at all
sorts of odd jobs, but read omnivorously. About the age of
nineteen he attended Oakland High School for a short time and
then had a year at the University of California. But an ordered
existence was impossible for him. The open sea and the open
road were his passions, and at one time he was arrested as a
vagrant. In 1897 he took part in the Klondike gold rush; he got
no gold, but from his experiences he afterwards wrote *The Call of
the Wild* (1903), which sold nearly a million and a half copies. In
1904 he was a special correspondent in the Russo-Japanese War,
and in 1907 he set off with his wife on a world cruise; after
visiting Honolulu, they abandoned the voyage in Australia, and
he wrote of it in *The Cruise of the Snark* (1911). In 1912 he sailed
round the Horn. At this time he was reckoned the best paid and
most popular writer in America, but drink and extravagance caused
his work to deteriorate, and he finally committed suicide. He is
best remembered for such stories as *The God of his Fathers*
(1901), *The Sea Wolf* (1904), *White Fang* (1905), *Before Adam*
(1906), *Smoke Bellew* (1912), *John Barleycorn* (1913), *The Star
Rover* (1914) and *Jerry of the Islands* (1917).

The Seed of McCoy

The *Pyrenees*, her iron sides pressed low in the water by her
cargo of wheat, rolled sluggishly and made it easy for the man
who was climbing aboard from out a tiny outrigger canoe. As

his eyes came level with the rail, so that he could see inboard, it seemed to him that he saw a dim, almost indiscernible haze. It was more like an illusion, like a blurring film that had spread abruptly over his eyes. He felt an inclination to brush it away, and the same instant he thought that he was growing old and that it was time to send to San Francisco for a pair of spectacles.

As he came over the rail he cast a glance aloft at the tall masts, and, next, at the pumps. They were not working. There seemed nothing the matter with the big ship, and he wondered why she had hoisted the signal of distress. He thought of his happy islanders, and hoped it was not disease. Perhaps the ship was short of water or provisions. He shook hands with the captain whose gaunt face and care-worn eyes made no secret of the trouble, whatever it was. At the same moment the newcomer was aware of a faint, indefinable smell. It seemed like that of burnt bread, but different.

He glanced curiously about him. Twenty feet away a weary-faced sailor was calking the deck. As his eyes lingered on the man, he saw suddenly arise from under his hands a faint spiral of haze that curled and twisted and was gone. By now he had reached the deck. His bare feet were pervaded by a dull warmth that quickly penetrated the thick calluses. He knew now the nature of the ship's distress. His eyes roved swiftly forward, where the full crew of weary-faced sailors regarded him eagerly. The glance from his liquid brown eyes swept over them like a benediction, soothing them, wrapping them about as in the mantle of a great peace. 'How long has she been afire, captain?' he asked in a voice so gentle and unperturbed that it was as the cooing of a dove.

At first the captain felt the peace and content of it stealing in upon him; then the consciousness of all that he had gone through and was going through smote him, and he was resentful. By what right did this ragged beachcomber, in dungaree trousers and a cotton shirt, suggest such a thing as peace and content to him and his overwrought, exhausted soul? The captain did not reason this; it was the unconscious process of emotion that caused his resentment.

'Fifteen days,' he answered shortly. 'Who are you?'

'My name is McCoy,' came the answer in tones that breathed tenderness and compassion.

'I mean, are you the pilot?'

McCoy passed the benediction of his gaze over the tall, heavy-shouldered man with the haggard, unshaven face who had joined the captain.

'I am as much a pilot as anybody,' was McCoy's answer. 'We are all pilots here, captain, and I know every inch of these waters.'

But the captain was impatient.

'What I want is some of the authorities. I want to talk with them, and blame quick.'

'Then I'll do just as well.'

Again that insidious suggestion of peace, and his ship a raging furnace beneath his feet! The captain's eyebrows lifted impatiently and nervously, and his fist clenched as if he were about to strike a blow with it.

'Who in hell are you?' he demanded.

'I am the chief magistrate,' was the reply in a voice that was still the softest and gentlest imaginable.

The tall, heavy-shouldered man broke out in a harsh laugh that was partly amusement, but mostly hysterical. Both he and the captain regarded McCoy with incredulity and amazement. That this barefooted beachcomber should possess such high-sounding dignity was inconceivable. His cotton shirt, unbuttoned, exposed a grizzled chest and the fact that there was no undershirt beneath.

A worn straw hat failed to hide the ragged grey hair. Halfway down his chest descended an untrimmed patriarchal beard. In any slop shop, two shillings would have outfitted him complete as he stood before them.

'Any relation to the McCoy of the *Bounty*?' the captain asked.

'He was my great-grandfather.'

'Oh,' the captain said, then bethought himself. 'My name is Davenport, and this is my first mate, Mr Konig.'

They shook hands.

'And now to business.' The captain spoke quickly, the urgency of a great haste pressing his speech. 'We've been on fire for over two weeks. She's ready to break all hell loose any moment. That's why I held for Pitcairn. I want to beach her, or scuttle her, and save the hull.'

'Then you made a mistake, captain,' said McCoy. 'You should have slacked away for Mangareva. There's a beautiful beach there, in a lagoon where the water is like a mill pond.'

'But we're here, ain't we?' the first mate demanded. 'That's the point. We're here, and we've got to do something.'

McCoy shook his head kindly.

'You can do nothing here. There is no beach. There isn't even anchorage.'

'Gammon!' said the mate. 'Gammon!' he repeated loudly, as the captain signalled him to be more soft spoken. 'You can't tell me that sort of stuff. Where d'ye keep your own boats, hey – your schooner, or cutter, or whatever you have? Hey? Answer me that.'

McCoy smiled as gently as he spoke. His smile was a caress, an embrace that surrounded the tired mate and sought to draw him into the quietude and rest of McCoy's tranquil soul.

'We have no schooner or cutter,' he replied. 'And we carry our canoes to the top of the cliff.'

'You've got to show me,' snorted the mate. 'How d'ye get around to the other islands, heh? Tell me that.'

'We don't get around. As governor of Pitcairn, I sometimes go. When I was younger, I was away a great deal – sometimes on the trading schooners, but mostly on the missionary brig. But she's gone now, and we depend on passing vessels. Sometimes we have had as high as six calls in one year. At other times, a year, and even longer, has gone by without one passing ship. Yours is the first in seven months.'

'And you mean to tell me – ' the mate began.

But Captain Davenport interfered.

'Enough of this. We're losing time. What is to be done, Mr McCoy?'

The old man turned his brown eyes, sweet as a woman's, shoreward, and both captain and mate followed his gaze around from the lonely rock of Pitcairn to the crew clustering forward and waiting anxiously for the announcement of a decision. McCoy did not hurry. He thought smoothly and slowly, step by step, with the certitude of a mind that was never vexed or outraged by life.

'The wind is light now,' he said finally. 'There is a heavy current setting to the westward.'

'That's what made us fetch to leeward,' the captain interrupted, desiring to vindicate his seamanship.

'Yes, that is what fetched you to leeward,' McCoy went on. 'Well, you can't work up against this current today. And if you did, there is no beach. Your ship will be a total loss.'

He paused, and captain and mate looked despair at each other.

'But I will tell you what you can do. The breeze will freshen tonight around midnight – see those tails of clouds and that thickness to windward, beyond the point there? That's where she'll come from, out of the southeast, hard. It is three hundred miles to Mangareva. Square away for it. There is a beautiful bed for your ship there.'

The mate shook his head.

'Come into the cabin, and we'll look at the chart,' said the captain.

McCoy found a stifling, poisonous atmosphere in the pent cabin. Stray waftures of invisible gases bit his eyes and made them sting. The deck was hotter, almost unbearably hot to his bare feet. The sweat poured out of his body. He looked almost with apprehension about him. This malignant, internal heat was astounding. It was a marvel that the cabin did not burst into flames. He had the feeling he was in a huge bake oven where the heat might at any moment increase tremendously and shrivel him up like a blade of grass.

As he lifted one foot and rubbed the hot sole against the leg of his trousers, the mate laughed in a savage, snarling fashion.

'The anteroom of hell,' he said. 'Hell herself is right down there under your feet.'

'It's hot!' McCoy cried involuntarily, mopping his face with a bandana handkerchief.

'Here's Mangareva,' the captain said, bending over the table and pointing to a black speck in the midst of the white blankness of the chart. 'And here, in between, is another island. Why not run for that?'

McCoy did not look at the chart.

'That's Crescent Island,' he answered. 'It is uninhabited, and it is only two or three feet above water. Lagoon, but no entrance. No, Mangareva is the nearest place for your purpose.'

'Mangareva it is, then,' said Captain Davenport, interrupting the mate's growling objection. 'Call the crew aft, Mr Konig.'

The sailors obeyed, shuffling wearily along the deck and painfully endeavouring to make haste. Exhaustion was evident in every movement. The cook came out of his galley to hear, and the cabin boy hung about near him.

When Captain Davenport had explained the situation and announced his intention of running for Mangareva, an uproar broke out. Against a background of throaty rumbling arose inarticulate cries of rage, with here and there a distinct curse, or word, or phrase. A shrill Cockney voice soared and dominated for a moment, crying: 'Gawd! After bein' in 'ell for fifteen days – an' now e wants us to sail this floatin' 'ell to sea again?'

The captain could not control them, but McCoy's gentle

presence seemed to rebuke and calm them, and the muttering and cursing died away, until the full crew, save here and there an anxious face directed at the captain, yearned dumbly towards the green clad peaks and beetling coast of Pitcairn.

Soft as a spring zephyr was the voice of McCoy: 'Captain, I thought I heard some of them say they were starving.'

'Ay,' was the answer, 'and so we are. I've had a sea biscuit and a spoonful of salmon in the last two days. We're on whack. You see, when we discovered the fire, we battened down immediately to suffocate the fire. And then we found how little food there was in the pantry. But it was too late. We didn't dare break out the lazarette. Hungry? I'm just as hungry as they are.'

He spoke to the men again, and again the throaty rumbling and cursing arose, their faces convulsed and animal-like with rage. The second and third mates had joined the captain, standing behind him at the break of the poop. Their faces were set and expressionless; they seemed bored, more than anything else, by this mutiny of the crew. Captain Davenport glanced questioningly at his first mate, and that person merely shrugged his shoulders in token of his helplessness.

'You see,' the captain said to McCoy, 'you can't compel sailors to leave the safe land and go to sea on a burning vessel. She has been their floating coffin for over two weeks now. They are worked out, and starved out, and they've had enough of her. We'll beat up for Pitcairn.'

But the wind was light, the *Pyrenees*'s bottom was foul, and she could not beat up against the strong westerly current. At the end of two hours she had lost three miles. The sailors worked eagerly, as if by main strength they could compel the *Pyrenees* against the adverse elements. But steadily, port tack and starboard tack, she sagged off to the westward. The captain paced restlessly up and down, pausing occasionally to survey the vagrant smoke wisps and to trace them back to the portions of the deck from which they sprang. The carpenter was engaged constantly in attempting to locate such places, and, when he succeeded, in calking them tighter and tighter.

'Well, what do you think?' the captain finally asked McCoy, who was watching the carpenter with all a child's interest and curiosity in his eyes.

McCoy looked shoreward, where the land was disappearing in the thickening haze.

'I think it would be better to square away for Mangareva. With that breeze that is coming, you'll be there tomorrow evening.'

'But what if the fire breaks out? It is liable to do it any moment.'

'Have your boats ready in the falls. The same breeze will carry your boats to Mangareva if the ship burns out from under.'

Captain Davenport debated for a moment, and then McCoy heard the question he had not wanted to hear, but which he knew was surely coming.

'I have no chart of Mangareva. On the general chart it is only a fly speck. I would not know where to look for the entrance into the lagoon. Will you come along and pilot her in for me?'

McCoy's serenity was unbroken.

'Yes, captain,' he said, with the same quiet unconcern with which he would have accepted an invitation to dinner; 'I'll go with you to Mangareva.'

Again the crew was called aft, and the captain spoke to them from the break of the poop.

'We've tried to work her up, but you see how we've lost ground. She's setting off in a two-knot current. This gentleman is the Honourable McCoy, Chief Magistrate and Governor of Pitcairn Island. He will come along with us to Mangareva. So you see the situation is not so dangerous. He would not make such an offer if he thought he was going to lose his life. Besides, whatever risk there is, if he of his own free will come on board and take it, we can do no less. What do you say for Mangareva?'

This time there was no uproar. McCoy's presence, the surety and calm that seemed to radiate from him, had had its effect. They conferred with one another in low voices. There was little urging. They were virtually unanimous, and they shoved the Cockney out as their spokesman. That worthy was overwhelmed with consciousness of the heroism of himself and his mates, and with flashing eyes he cried: 'By Gawd! If 'e will, we will!'

The crew mumbled its assent and started forward.

'One moment, captain,' McCoy said, as the other was turning to give orders to the mate. 'I must go ashore first.'

Mr Konig was thunderstruck, staring at McCoy as if he were a madman.

'Go ashore!' the captain cried. 'What for? It will take you three hours to get there in your canoe.'

McCoy measured the distance of the land away, and nodded.

'Yes, it is six now. I won't get ashore till nine. The people cannot be assembled earlier than ten. As the breeze freshens up tonight, you can begin to work up against it, and pick me up at daylight tomorrow morning.'

'In the name of reason and common sense,' the captain burst forth, 'what do you want to assemble the people for? Don't you realise that my ship is burning beneath me?'

McCoy was as placid as a summer sea, and the other's anger produced not the slightest ripple upon it.

'Yes, captain,' he cooed in his dove-like voice. 'I do realise that your ship is burning. That is why I am going with you to Mangareva. But I must get permission to go with you. It is our custom. It is an important matter when the governor leaves the island. The people's interests are at stake, and so they have the right to vote their permission or refusal. But they will give it, I know that.'

'Are you sure?'

'Quite sure.'

'Then if you know they will give it, why bother with getting it? Think of the delay – a whole night.'

'It is our custom,' was the imperturbable reply. 'Also, I am the governor, and I must make arrangements for the conduct of the island during my absence.'

'But it is only a twenty-four-hour run to Mangareva,' the captain objected. 'Suppose it took you six times that long to return to windward; that would bring you back by the end of a week.'

McCoy smiled his large, benevolent smile.

'Very few vessels come to Pitcairn, and when they do, they are usually from San Francisco or from around the Horn. I shall be fortunate if I get back in six months. I may be away a year, and I may have to go to San Francisco in order to find a vessel that will bring me back. My father once left Pitcairn to be gone three months, and two years passed before he could get back. Then, too, you are short of food. If you have to take to the boats, and the weather comes up bad, you may be days in reaching land. I can bring off two canoe loads of food in the morning. Dried bananas will be best. As the breeze freshens, you beat up against it. The nearer you are, the bigger loads I can bring off. Goodbye.'

He held out his hand. The captain shook it, and was reluctant to let go. He seemed to cling to it as a drowning sailor clings to a lifebuoy.

'How do I know you will come back in the morning?' he asked.

'Yes, that's it!' cried the mate. 'How do we know but what he's skinning out to save his own hide?'

McCoy did not speak. He looked at them sweetly and benignantly, and it seemed to them that they received a message from his tremendous certitude of soul.

The captain released his hand, and, with a last sweeping

glance that embraced the crew in its benediction, McCoy went over the rail and descended into his canoe.

The wind freshened, and the *Pyrenees*, despite the foulness of her bottom, won half a dozen miles away from the westerly current. At daylight, with Pitcairn three miles to windward, Captain Davenport made out two canoes coming off to him. Again McCoy clambered up the side and dropped over the rail to the hot deck. He was followed by many packages of dried bananas, each package wrapped in dry leaves.

'Now, captain,' he said, 'swing the yards and drive for dear life. You see, I am no navigator,' he explained a few minutes later, as he stood by the captain aft, the latter with gaze wandering from aloft to overside as he estimated the *Pyrenees*'s speed. 'You must fetch her to Mangareva. When you have picked up the land, then I will pilot her in. What do you think she is making?'

'Eleven,' Captain Davenport answered, with a final glance at the water rushing past.

'Eleven. Let me see, if she keeps up that gait, we'll sight Mangareva between eight and nine o'clock tomorrow morning. I'll have her on the beach by ten or by eleven at latest. And then your troubles will all be over.'

It almost seemed to the captain that the blissful moment had already arrived, such was the persuasive convincingness of McCoy.

Captain Davenport had been under the fearful strain of navigating his burning ship for over two weeks, and he was beginning to feel that he had had enough.

A heavier flaw of wind struck the back of his neck and whistled by his ears. He measured the weight of it, and looked quickly overside.

'The wind is making all the time,' he announced. 'The old girl's doing nearer twelve than eleven right now. If this keeps up, we'll be shortening down tonight.'

All day the *Pyrenees*, carrying her load of living fire, tore across the foaming sea. By nightfall, royals and topgallant sails were in, and she flew on into the darkness, with great, crested seas roaring after her. The auspicious wind had had its effect, and fore and aft a visible brightening was apparent. In the second dog-watch some careless soul started a song, and by eight bells the whole crew was singing.

Captain Davenport had his blankets brought up and spread on top the house.

'I've forgotten what sleep is,' he explained to McCoy. 'I'm all in. But give me a call at any time you think necessary.'

At three in the morning he was aroused by a gentle tugging at his arm. He sat up quickly, bracing himself against the skylight, stupid yet from his heavy sleep. The wind was thrumming its war song in the rigging, and a wild sea was buffeting the *Pyrenees*. Amidships she was wallowing first one rail under and then the other, flooding the waist more often than not. McCoy was shouting something he could not hear. He reached out, clutched the other by the shoulder, and drew him close so that his own ear was close to the other's lips.

'It's three o'clock,' came McCoy's voice, still retaining its dovelike quality, but curiously muffled, as if from a long way off. 'We've run two hundred and fifty. Crescent Island is only thirty miles away, somewhere there dead ahead. There's no lights on it. If we keep running, we'll pile up, and lose ourselves as well as the ship.'

'What d'ye think – heave to?'

'Yes; heave to till daylight. It will only put us back four hours.'

So the *Pyrenees*, with her cargo of fire, was hove to, biting the teeth of the gale and fighting and smashing the pounding seas. She was a shell, filled with a conflagration, and on the outside of the shell, clinging precariously, the little motes of men, by pull and haul, helped her in the battle.

'It is most unusual, this gale,' McCoy told the captain, in the lee of the cabin. 'By rights there should be no gale at this time of the year. But everything about the weather has been unusual. There has been a stoppage of the trades, and now it's howling right out of the trade quarter.' He waved his hand into the darkness, as if his vision could dimly penetrate for hundreds of miles. 'It is off to the westward. There is something big making off there somewhere – a hurricane or something. We're lucky to be so far to the eastward. But this is only a little blow,' he added. 'It can't last. I can tell you that much.'

By daylight the gale had eased down to normal. But daylight revealed a new danger. It had come on thick. The sea was covered by a fog, or rather by a pearly mist that was fog-like in density, in so far as it obstructed vision, but that was no more than a film on the sea, for the sun shot it through and filled it with a glowing radiance.

The deck of the *Pyrenees* was making more smoke than on the preceding day, and the cheerfulness of officers and crew had vanished. In the lee of the galley the cabin boy could be heard whimpering. It was his first voyage, and the fear of death was at his heart. The captain wandered about like a lost soul, nervously chewing his moustache, scowling, unable to make up his mind what to do.

'What do you think?' he asked, pausing by the side of McCoy, who was making a breakfast off fried bananas and a mug of water.

McCoy finished the last banana, drained the mug, and looked slowly around. In his eyes was a smile of tenderness as he said: 'Well, captain, we might as well drive as burn. Your decks are not going to hold out for ever. They are hotter this morning. You haven't a pair of shoes I can wear? It is getting uncomfortable for my bare feet.'

The *Pyrenees* shipped two heavy seas as she was swung off and put once more before it, and the first mate expressed a desire to have all that water down in the hold, if only it could be introduced without taking off the hatches. McCoy ducked his head into the binnacle and watched the course set.

'I'd hold her up some more, captain,' he said. 'She's been making drift when hove to.'

'I've set it to a point higher already,' was the answer. 'Isn't that enough?'

'I'd make it two points, captain. This bit of a blow kicked that westerly current ahead faster than you imagine.'

Captain Davenport compromised on a point and a half, and then went aloft, accompanied by McCoy and the first mate, to keep a lookout for land. Sail had been made, so that the *Pyrenees* was doing ten knots. The following sea was dying down rapidly. There was no break in the pearly fog, and by ten o'clock Captain Davenport was growing nervous. All hands were at their stations, ready, at the first warning of land ahead, to spring like fiends to the task of bringing the *Pyrenees* up on the wind. That land ahead, a surf-washed outer reef, would be perilously close when it revealed itself in such a fog.

Another hour passed. The three watchers aloft stared intently into the pearly radiance. 'What if we miss Mangareva?' Captain Davenport asked abruptly.

McCoy, without shifting his gaze, answered softly: 'Why, let her drive, captain. That is all we can do. All the Paumotus are before us. We can drive for a thousand miles through reefs and atolls. We are bound to fetch up somewhere.'

'Then drive it is.' Captain Davenport evidenced his intention of descending to the deck. 'We've missed Mangareva. God knows where the next land is. I wish I'd held her up that other half-point,' he confessed a moment later. 'This cursed current plays the devil with a navigator.'

'The old navigators called the Paumotus the Dangerous Archipelago,' McCoy said, when they had regained the poop. 'This very current was partly responsible for that name.'

'I was talking with a sailor chap in Sydney, once,' said

Mr Konig. 'He'd been trading in the Paumotus. He told me insurance was eighteen per cent. Is that right?'

McCoy smiled and nodded.

'Except that they don't insure,' he explained. 'The owners write off twenty per cent of the cost of their schooners each year.'

'My God!' Captain Davenport groaned. 'That makes the life of a schooner only five years!' He shook his head sadly, murmuring, 'Bad waters! Bad waters!'

Again they went into the cabin to consult the big general chart; but the poisonous vapours drove them coughing and gasping on deck.

'Here is Moerenhout Island,' Captain Davenport pointed it out on the chart, which he had spread on the house. 'It can't be more than a hundred miles to leeward.'

'A hundred and ten.' McCoy shook his head doubtfully. 'It might be done, but it is very difficult. I might beach her, and then again I might put her on the reef. A bad place, a very bad place.'

'We'll take the chance,' was Captain Davenport's decision, as he set about working out the course.

Sail was shortened early in the afternoon, to avoid running past in the night; and in the second dog-watch the crew manifested its regained cheerfulness. Land was so very near, and their troubles would be over in the morning.

But morning broke clear, with a blazing tropic sun. The southeast trade had swung around to the eastward, and was driving the *Pyrenees* through the water at an eight-knot clip. Captain Davenport worked up his dead reckoning, allowing generously for drift, and announced Moerenhout Island to be not more than ten miles off. The *Pyrenees* sailed the ten miles; she sailed ten miles more; and the lookouts at the three mastheads saw naught but the naked, sun-washed sea.

'But the land is there, I tell you,' Captain Davenport shouted to them from the poop.

McCoy smiled soothingly, but the captain glared about him like a madman, fetched his sextant, and took a chronometer sight.

'I knew I was right,' he almost shouted, when he had worked up the observation. 'Twenty-one, fifty-five, south; one-thirty-six, two, west. There you are. We're eight miles to windward yet. What did you make it out, Mr Konig?'

The first mate glanced at his own figures, and said in a low voice: 'Twenty-one, fifty-five all right; but my longitude's one-thirty-six, forty-eight. That puts us considerably to leeward – '

But Captain Davenport ignored his figures with so contemptuous a silence as to make Mr Konig grit his teeth and curse savagely under his breath.

'Keep her off,' the captain ordered the man at the wheel. 'Three points – steady there, as she goes!'

Then he returned to his figures and worked them over. The sweat poured from his face. He chewed his moustache, his lips, and his pencil, staring at the figures as a man might at a ghost. Suddenly, with a fierce, muscular outburst, he crumpled the scribbled paper in his fist and crushed it under foot. Mr Konig grinned vindictively and turned away, while Captain Davenport leaned against the cabin and for half an hour spoke no word, contenting himself with gazing to leeward with an expression of musing hopelessness on his face.

'Mr McCoy,' he broke silence abruptly. 'The chart indicates a group of islands, but not how many, off there to the north'ard, or nor'-nor'westward, about forty miles – the Acteon Islands. What about them?'

'There are four, all low,' McCoy answered. 'First to the southeast is Matuerui – no people, no entrance to the lagoon. Then comes Tenarunga. There used to be about a dozen people there, but they may be all gone now. Anyway, there is no entrance for a ship – only a boat entrance, with a fathom of water. Vehauga and Teua-raro are the other two. No entrances, no people, very low. There is no bed for the *Pyrenees* in that group. She would be a total wreck.'

'Listen to that!' Captain Davenport was frantic. 'No people! No entrances! What in the devil are islands good for?'

'Well, then,' he barked suddenly, like an excited terrier, 'the chart gives a whole mess of islands off to the nor'west. What about them? What one has an entrance where I can lay my ship?'

McCoy calmly considered. He did not refer to the chart. All these islands, reefs, shoals, lagoons, entrances and distances were marked on the chart of his memory. He knew them as the city dweller knows his buildings, streets and alleys.

'Papakena and Vanavana are off there to the westward, or west-nor'westward a hundred miles and a bit more,' he said. 'One is uninhabited, and I heard that the people on the other had gone off to Cadmus Island. Anyway, neither lagoon has an entrance. Ahunui is another hundred miles on to the nor'west. No entrance, no people.'

'Well, forty miles beyond them are two islands?' Captain Davenport queried, raising his head from the chart.

McCoy shook his head.

'Paros and Manuhungi – no entrances, no people. Nengo-Nengo is forty miles beyond them, in turn, and it has no people and no entrance. But there is Hao Island. It is just the place. The lagoon is thirty miles long and five miles wide. There are plenty of people. You can usually find water. And any ship in the world can go through the entrance.'

He ceased and gazed solicitously at Captain Davenport, who, bending over the chart with a pair of dividers in hand, had just emitted a low groan.

'Is there any lagoon with an entrance anywhere nearer than Hao Island?' he asked.

'No, captain; that is the nearest.'

'Well, it's three hundred and forty miles.' Captain Davenport was speaking very slowly, with decision. 'I won't risk the responsibility of all these lives. I'll wreck her on the Acteons. And she's a good ship, too,' he added regretfully, after altering the course, this time making more allowance than ever for the westerly current.

An hour later the sky was overcast. The southeast trade still held, but the ocean was a checkerboard of squalls.

'We'll be there by one o'clock,' Captain Davenport announced confidently. 'By two o'clock at the outside. McCoy, you put her ashore on the one where the people are.'

The sun did not appear again, nor, at one o'clock, was any land to be seen. Captain Davenport looked astern at the *Pyrenees*'s canting wake.

'Good Lord!' he cried. 'An easterly current? Look at that!'

Mr Konig was incredulous. McCoy was noncommittal, though he said that in the Paumotus there was no reason why it should not be an easterly current. A few minutes later a squall robbed the *Pyrenees* temporarily of all her wind, and she was left rolling heavily in the trough.

'Where's that deep lead? Over with it, you there!' Captain Davenport held the lead line and watched it sag off to the northeast. 'There, look at that! Take hold of it for yourself.'

McCoy and the mate tried it, and felt the line thrumming and vibrating savagely to the grip of the tidal stream.

'A four-knot current,' said Mr Konig.

'An easterly current instead of a westerly,' said Captain Davenport, glaring accusingly at McCoy, as if to cast the blame for it upon him.

'That is one of the reasons, captain, for insurance being eighteen per cent in these waters,' McCoy answered cheerfully. 'You can never tell. The currents are always changing. There was a man who wrote books, I forget his name, in the yacht *Casco*. He missed Takaroa by thirty miles and fetched Tikei, all because of the shifting currents. You are up to windward now, and you'd better keep off a few points.'

'But how much has this current set me?' the captain demanded irately. 'How am I to know how much to keep off?'

'I don't know, captain,' McCoy said with great gentleness.

The wind returned, and the *Pyrenees*, her deck smoking and shimmering in the bright grey light, ran off dead to leeward. Then she worked back, port tack and starboard tack, criss-crossing her track, combing the sea for the Acteon Islands, which the masthead lookouts failed to sight.

Captain Davenport was beside himself. His rage took the form of sullen silence, and he spent the afternoon in pacing the poop or leaning against the weather shrouds. At nightfall, without even consulting McCoy, he squared away and headed into the northwest. Mr Konig, surreptitiously consulting chart and binnacle, and McCoy, openly and innocently consulting the binnacle, knew that they were running for Hao Island. By midnight the squalls ceased, and the stars came out. Captain Davenport was cheered by the promise of a clear day.

'I'll get an observation in the morning,' he told McCoy, 'though what my latitude is, is a puzzler. But I'll use the Sumner method, and settle that. Do you know the Sumner line?'

And thereupon he explained it in detail to McCoy.

The day proved clear, the trade blew steadily out of the east, and the *Pyrenees* just as steadily logged her nine knots. Both the captain and mate worked out the position on a Sumner line, and agreed, and at noon agreed again, and verified the morning sights by the noon sights.

'Another twenty-four hours and we'll be there,' Captain Davenport assured McCoy. 'It's a miracle the way the old girl's decks hold out. But they can't last. They can't last. Look at them smoke, more and more every day. Yet it was a tight deck to begin with, fresh-calked in Frisco. I was surprised when the fire first broke out and we battened down. Look at that!'

He broke off to gaze with dropped jaw at a spiral of smoke

that coiled and twisted in the lee of the mizzenmast twenty feet above the deck.

'Now, how did that get there?' he demanded indignantly.

Beneath it there was no smoke. Crawling up from the deck, sheltered from the wind by the mast, by some freak it took form and visibility at that height. It writhed away from the mast, and for a moment overhung the captain like some threatening portent. The next moment the wind whisked it away, and the captain's jaw returned to place.

'As I was saying, when we first battened down, I was surprised. It was a tight deck, yet it leaked smoke like a sieve. And we've calked and calked ever since. There must be tremendous pressure underneath to drive so much smoke through.'

That afternoon the sky became overcast again, and squally, drizzly weather set in. The wind shifted back and forth between southeast and northeast, and at midnight the *Pyrenees* was caught aback by a sharp squall from the southwest, from which point the wind continued to blow intermittently.

'We won't make Hao until ten or eleven,' Captain Davenport complained at seven in the morning, when the fleeting promise of the sun had been erased by hazy cloud masses in the eastern sky. And the next moment he was plaintively demanding, 'And what are the currents doing?'

Lookouts at the mastheads could report no land, and the day passed in drizzling calms and violent squalls. By nightfall a heavy sea began to make from the west. The barometer had fallen to 29.50. There was no wind, and still the ominous sea continued to increase. Soon the *Pyrenees* was rolling madly in the huge waves that marched in an unending procession from out of the darkness of the west. Sail was shortened as fast as both watches could work, and, when the tired crew had finished, its grumbling and complaining voices, peculiarly animal-like and menacing, could be heard in the darkness. Once the starboard watch was called aft to lash down and make secure, and the men openly advertised their sullenness and unwillingness. Every slow movement was a protest and a threat. The atmosphere was moist and sticky like mucilage, and in the absence of wind all hands seemed to pant and gasp for air. The sweat stood out on faces and bare arms, and Captain Davenport for one, his face more gaunt and care-worn than ever, and his eyes troubled and staring, was oppressed by a feeling of impending calamity.

'It's off to the westward,' McCoy said encouragingly. 'At worst, we'll be only on the edge of it.'

But Captain Davenport refused to be comforted, and by the light of a lantern read up the chapter in his *Epitome* that related to the strategy of shipmasters in cyclonic storms. From somewhere amidships the silence was broken by a low whimpering from the cabin boy.

'Oh, shut up!' Captain Davenport yelled suddenly and with such force as to startle every man on board and to frighten the offender into a wild wail of terror.

'Mr Konig,' the captain said in a voice that trembled with rage and nerves, 'will you kindly step for'ard and stop that brat's mouth with a deck mop?'

But it was McCoy who went forward, and in a few minutes had the boy comforted and asleep.

Shortly before daybreak the first breath of air began to move from out the southeast, increasing swiftly to a stiff and stiffer breeze. All hands were on deck waiting for what might be behind it. 'We're all right now, captain,' said McCoy, standing close to his shoulder. 'The hurricane is to the west'ard, and we are south of it. This breeze is the in-suck. It won't blow any harder. You can begin to put sail on her.'

'But what's the good? Where shall I sail? This is the second day without observations, and we should have sighted Hao Island yesterday morning. Which way does it bear – north, south, east, or what? Tell me that, and I'll make sail in a jiffy.'

'I am no navigator, captain,' McCoy said in his mild way.

'I used to think I was one,' was the retort, 'before I got into these Paumotus.'

At midday the cry of 'Breakers ahead!' was heard from the lookout. The *Pyrenees* was kept off, and sail after sail was loosed and sheeted home. The *Pyrenees* was sliding through the water and fighting a current that threatened to set her down upon the breakers. Officers and men were working like mad, cook and cabin boy, Captain Davenport himself and McCoy all lending a hand.

It was a close shave. It was a low shoal, a bleak and perilous place over which the seas broke unceasingly, where no man could live, and on which not even sea birds could rest. The *Pyrenees* was swept within a hundred yards of it before the wind carried her clear, and at this moment the panting crew, its work done, burst out in a torrent of curses upon the head of McCoy – of McCoy who had come on board, and proposed the run to Mangareva, and lured them all away from the safety of Pitcairn Island to certain destruction in this baffling and terrible stretch of sea. But McCoy's tranquil soul was undisturbed. He smiled at them with simple and gracious benevolence, and, somehow, the exalted goodness of him seemed to penetrate to their dark and sombre souls, shaming them, and from very shame stilling the curses vibrating in their throats.

'Bad waters! Bad waters!' Captain Davenport was murmuring as his ship forged clear; but he broke off abruptly to gaze at the shoal which should have been dead astern, but which was already on the *Pyrenees*'s weather-quarter and working up rapidly to windward.

He sat down and buried his face in his hands. And the first mate saw, and McCoy saw, and the crew saw, what he had seen. South of the shoal an easterly current had set them down upon it; north of the shoal an equally swift westerly current had clutched the ship and was sweeping her away.

'I've heard of these Paumotus before,' the captain groaned,

lifting his blanched face from his hands. 'Captain Moyendale told me about them after losing his ship on them. And I laughed at him behind his back. God forgive me, I laughed at him. What shoal is that?' he broke off, to ask McCoy.

'I don't know, captain.'

'Why don't you know?'

'Because I never saw it before, and because I have never heard of it. I do know that it is not charted. These waters have never been thoroughly surveyed.'

'Then you don't know where we are?'

'No more than you do,' McCoy said gently.

At four in the afternoon coconut trees were sighted, apparently growing out of the water. A little later the low land of an atoll was raised above the sea.

'I know where we are now, captain.' McCoy lowered the glasses from his eyes. 'That's Resolution Island. We are forty miles beyond Hao Island, and the wind is in our teeth.'

'Get ready to beach her then. Where's the entrance?'

'There's only a canoe passage. But now that we know where we are, we can run for Barclay de Tolley. It is only one hundred and twenty miles from here, due nor'-nor'west. With this breeze we can be there by nine o'clock tomorrow morning.'

Captain Davenport consulted the chart and debated with himself.

'If we wreck her here,' McCoy added, 'we'd have to make the run to Barclay de Tolley in the boats just the same.'

The captain gave his orders, and once more the *Pyrenees* swung off for another run across the inhospitable sea.

And the middle of the next afternoon saw despair and mutiny on her smoking deck. The current had accelerated, the wind had slackened, and the *Pyrenees* had sagged off to the west. The lookout sighted Barclay de Tolley to the eastward, barely visible from the masthead, and vainly and for hours the *Pyrenees* tried to beat up to it. Ever, like a mirage, the coconut trees hovered on the horizon, visible only from the masthead. From the deck they were hidden by the bulge of the world.

Again Captain Davenport consulted McCoy and the chart. Makemo lay seventy-five miles to the southwest. Its lagoon was thirty miles long, and its entrance was excellent. When Captain Davenport gave his orders, the crew refused duty. They announced that they had had enough of hellfire under their feet. There was the land. What if the ship could not make it? They could make it in the boats. Let her burn, then. Their lives amounted to something to them. They had served faithfully the ship, now they were going to serve themselves.

They sprang to the boats, brushing the second and third mates out of the way, and proceeded to swing the boats out and to prepare to lower away. Captain Davenport and the first mate, revolvers in hand, were advancing to the break of the poop, when McCoy, who had climbed on top of the cabin, began to speak.

He spoke to the sailors, and at the first sound of his dovelike, cooing voice they paused to hear. He extended to them his own ineffable serenity and peace. His soft voice and simple thoughts flowed out to them in a magic stream, soothing them against their wills. Long forgotten things came back to them, and some remembered lullaby songs of childhood and the content and rest of the mother's arm at the end of the day. There was no more trouble, no more danger, no more irk, in all the world. Everything was as it should be, and it was only a matter of course that they should turn their backs upon the land and put to sea once more with hellfire hot beneath their feet.

McCoy spoke simply; but it was not what he spoke. It was his personality that spoke more eloquently than any word he could utter. It was an alchemy of soul occultly subtle and profoundly deep – a mysterious emanation of the spirit, seductive, sweetly humble and terribly imperious. It was illumination in the dark crypts of their souls, a compulsion of purity and gentleness vastly greater than that which resided in the shining, death-spitting revolvers of the officers.

The men wavered reluctantly where they stood, and those who had loosed the turns made them fast again. Then one, and then another, and then all of them, began to sidle awkwardly away.

McCoy's face was beaming with childlike pleasure as he descended from the top of the cabin. There was no trouble. For that matter there had been no trouble averted. There never had been any trouble, for there was no place for such in the blissful world in which he lived.

'You hypnotised 'em,' Mr Konig grinned at him, speaking in a low voice.

'Those boys are good,' was the answer. 'Their hearts are good. They have had a hard time, and they have worked hard, and they will work hard to the end.'

Mr Konig had not time to reply. His voice was ringing out orders, the sailors were springing to obey, and the *Pyrenees* was paying slowly off from the wind until her bow should point in the direction of Makemo.

The wind was very light, and after sundown almost ceased. It was insufferably warm, and fore and aft men sought vainly to sleep. The deck was too hot to lie upon, and poisonous vapours, oozing through the seams, crept like evil spirits over the ship, stealing into the nostrils and windpipes of the unwary and causing fits of sneezing and coughing. The stars blinked lazily in the dim vault overhead; and the full moon, rising in the east, touched with its light the myriads of wisps and threads and spidery films of smoke that intertwined and writhed and twisted along the deck, over the rails and up the masts and shrouds.

'Tell me,' Captain Davenport said, rubbing his smarting eyes, 'what happened with that *Bounty* crowd after they reached Pitcairn? The account I read said they burnt the *Bounty*, and that they were not discovered until many years later. But what happened in the meantime? I've always been curious to know.

They were men with their necks in the rope. There were some native men, too. And then there were women. That made it look like trouble right from the jump.'

'There was trouble,' McCoy answered. 'They were bad men. They quarrelled about the women right away. One of the mutineers, Williams, lost his wife. All the women were Tahitian women. His wife fell from the cliffs when hunting sea birds. Then he took the wife of one of the native men away from him. All the native men were made very angry by this, and they killed off nearly all the mutineers. Then the mutineers that escaped killed off all the native men. The women helped. And the natives killed each other. Everybody killed everybody. They were terrible men.

'Timiti was killed by two other natives while they were combing his hair in friendship. The white men had sent them to do it. Then the white men killed them. The wife of Tullaloo killed him in a cave because she wanted a white man for husband. They were very wicked. God had hidden His face from them. At the end of two years all the native men were murdered, and all the white men except four. They were Young, John Adams, McCoy, who was my great-grandfather, and Quintal. He was a very bad man, too. Once, just because his wife did not catch enough fish for him, he bit off her ear.'

'They were a bad lot!' Mr Konig exclaimed.

'Yes, they were very bad,' McCoy agreed and went on serenely cooing of the blood and lust of his iniquitous ancestry. 'My great-grandfather escaped murder in order to die by his own hand. He made a still and manufactured alcohol from the roots of the ti-plant. Quintal was his chum, and they got drunk together all the time. At last McCoy got delirium tremens, tied a rock to his neck and jumped into the sea.

'Quintal's wife, the one whose ear he bit off, also got killed by falling from the cliffs. Then Quintal went to Young and demanded his wife, and went to Adams and demanded his wife.

Adams and Young were afraid of Quintal. They knew he would kill them. So they killed him, the two of them together, with a hatchet. Then Young died. And that was about all the trouble they had.'

'I should say so,' Captain Davenport snorted. 'There was nobody left to kill.'

'You see, God had hidden His face,' McCoy said.

By morning no more than a faint air was blowing from the eastward, and, unable to make appreciable southing by it, Captain Davenport hauled up full-and-by on the port track. He was afraid of that terrible westerly current which had cheated him out of so many ports of refuge. All day the calm continued, and all night, while the sailors, on a short ration of dried banana, were grumbling. Also, they were growing weak and complaining of stomach pains caused by the straight banana diet. All day the current swept the *Pyrenees* to the westward, while there was no wind to bear her south. In the middle of the first dogwatch, coconut trees were sighted due south, their tufted heads rising above the water and marking the low-lying atoll beneath.

'That is Taenga Island,' McCoy said. 'We need a breeze tonight, or else we'll miss Makemo.'

'What's become of the southeast trade?' the captain demanded. 'Why don't it blow? What's the matter?'

'It is the evaporation from the big lagoons – there are so many of them,' McCoy explained. 'The evaporation upsets the whole system of trades. It even causes the wind to back up and blow gales from the southwest. This is the Dangerous Archipelago, captain.'

Captain Davenport faced the old man, opened his mouth, and was about to curse, but paused and refrained. McCoy's presence was a rebuke to the blasphemies that stirred in his brain and trembled in his larynx. McCoy's influence had been growing during the many days they had been together. Captain

Davenport was an autocrat of the sea, fearing no man, never bridling his tongue, and now he found himself unable to curse in the presence of this old man with the feminine brown eyes and the voice of a dove. When he realised this, Captain Davenport experienced a distinct shock. This old man was merely the seed of McCoy, of McCoy of the *Bounty* , the mutineer fleeing from the hemp that waited him in England, the McCoy who was a power for evil in the early days of blood and lust and violent death on Pitcairn Island.

Captain Davenport was not religious, yet in that moment he felt a mad impulse to cast himself at the other's feet – and to say he knew not what. It was an emotion that so deeply stirred him, rather than a coherent thought, and he was aware in some vague way of his own unworthiness and smallness in the presence of this other man who possessed the simplicity of a child and the gentleness of a woman.

Of course he could not so humble himself before the eyes of his officers and men. And yet the anger that had prompted the blasphemy still raged in him. He suddenly smote the cabin with his clenched hand and cried: 'Look here, old man, I won't be beaten. These Paumotus have cheated and tricked me and made a fool of me. I refuse to be beaten. I am going to drive this ship, and drive and drive and drive clear through the Paumotus to China until I find a bed for her. If every man deserts, I'll stay by her. I'll show the Paumotus. They can't fool me. She's a good girl, and I'll stick by her as long as there's a plank to stand on. You hear me?'

'And I'll stay with you, captain,' McCoy said.

During the night, light, baffling airs blew out of the south, and the frantic captain, with his cargo of fire, watched and measured his westward drift and went off by himself at times to curse softly so that McCoy should not hear.

Daylight showed more palms growing out of the water to the south.

'That's the leeward point of Makemo,' McCoy said. 'Katiu is only a few miles to the west. We may make that.'

But the current, sucking between the two islands, swept them to the northwest, and at one in the afternoon they saw the palms of Katiu rise above the sea and sink back into the sea again.

A few minutes later, just as the captain had discovered that a new current from the northeast had gripped the *Pyrenees*, the masthead lookouts raised coconut palms in the northwest.

'It is Raraka,' said McCoy. 'We won't make it without wind. The current is drawing us down to the southwest. But we must watch out. A few miles farther on a current flows north and turns in a circle to the northwest. This will sweep us away from Fakarava, and Fakarava is the place for the *Pyrenees* to find her bed.'

'They can sweep all they da – all they please,' Captain Davenport remarked with heat. 'We'll find a bed for her somewhere just the same.'

But the situation on the *Pyrenees* was reaching a culmination. The deck was so hot that it seemed an increase of a few degrees would cause it to burst into flames. In many places even the heavy-soled shoes of the men were no protection, and they were compelled to step lively to avoid scorching their feet. The smoke had increased and grown more acrid. Every man on board was suffering from inflamed eyes, and they coughed and strangled like a crew of tuberculosis patients. In the afternoon the boats were swung out and equipped. The last several packages of dried bananas were stored in them, as well as the instruments of the officers. Captain Davenport even put the chronometer into the longboat, fearing the blowing up of the deck at any moment.

All night this apprehension weighed heavily on all, and in the first morning light, with hollow eyes and ghastly faces, they stared at one another as if in surprise that the *Pyrenees* still held together and that they still were alive.

Walking rapidly at times, and even occasionally breaking into an undignified hop-skip-and-run, Captain Davenport inspected his ship's deck.

'It is a matter of hours now, if not of minutes,' he announced on his return to the poop.

The cry of land came down from the masthead. From the deck the land was invisible, and McCoy went aloft, while the captain took advantage of the opportunity to curse some of the bitterness out of his heart. But the cursing was suddenly stopped by a dark line on the water which he sighted to the northeast. It was not a squall, but a regular breeze – the disrupted trade wind, eight points out of its direction but resuming business once more.

'Hold her up, captain,' McCoy said as soon as he reached the poop. 'That's the easterly point of Fakarava, and we'll go in through the passage full-tilt, the wind abeam, and every sail drawing.'

At the end of an hour, the coconut trees and the low-lying land were visible from the deck. The feeling that the end of the *Pyrenees*'s resistance was imminent weighed heavily on everybody. Captain Davenport had the three boats lowered and dropped short astern, a man in each to keep them apart. The *Pyrenees* closely skirted the shore, the surf-whitened atoll a bare two cable lengths away.

And a minute later the land parted, exposing a narrow passage and the lagoon beyond, a great mirror, thirty miles in length and a third as broad.

'Now, captain.'

For the last time the yards of the *Pyrenees* swung around as she obeyed the wheel and headed into the passage. The turns had scarcely been made, and nothing had been coiled down, when the men and mates swept back to the poop in panic terror. Nothing had happened, yet they averred that something was going to happen. They could not tell why. They merely knew that it was about to happen. McCoy started forward to take up his position on the bow in order to con the vessel in; but the captain gripped his arm and whirled him around.

'Do it from here,' he said. 'That deck's not safe. What's the matter?' he demanded the next instant. 'We're standing still.'

McCoy smiled.

'You are bucking a seven-knot current, captain,' he said. 'That is the way the full ebb runs out of this passage.'

At the end of another hour the *Pyrenees* had scarcely gained her length, but the wind freshened and she began to forge ahead.

'Better get into the boats, some of you,' Captain Davenport commanded.

His voice was still ringing, and the men were just beginning to move in obedience, when the amidship deck of the *Pyrenees*, in a mass of flame and smoke, was flung upward into the sails and rigging, part of it remaining there and the rest falling into the sea. The wind being abeam was what had saved the men crowded aft. They made a blind rush to gain the boats, but McCoy's voice, carrying its convincing message of vast calm and endless time, stopped them.

'Take it easy,' he was saying. 'Everything is all right. Pass that boy down somebody, please.'

The man at the wheel had forsaken it in a funk, and Captain Davenport had leaped and caught the spokes in time to prevent the ship from yawing in the current and going ashore.

'Better take charge of the boats,' he said to Mr Konig. 'Tow one of them short, right under the quarter . . . When I go over, it'll be on the jump.'

Mr Konig hesitated, then went over the rail and lowered himself into the boat.

'Keep her off half a point, captain.'

Captain Davenport gave a start. He had thought he had the ship to himself.

'Ay, ay; half a point it is,' he answered.

Amidships the *Pyrenees* was an open flaming furnace, out of which poured an immense volume of smoke which rose high above the masts and completely hid the forward part of the ship. McCoy, in the shelter of the mizzen-shrouds, continued his difficult task of conning the ship through the intricate channel. The fire was working aft along the deck from the seat of explosion, while the soaring tower of canvas on the mainmast went up and vanished in a sheet of flame. Forward, though they could not see them, they knew that the head-sails were still drawing.

'If only she don't burn all her canvas off before she makes inside,' the captain groaned.

'She'll make it,' McCoy assured him with supreme confidence. 'There is plenty of time. She is bound to make it. And once inside, we'll put her before it; that will keep the smoke away from us and hold back the fire from working aft.'

A tongue of flame sprang up the mizzen, reached hungrily for the lowest tier of canvas, missed it and vanished. From aloft a burning shred of rope stuff fell square on the back of Captain Davenport's neck. He acted with the celerity of one stung by a bee as he reached up and brushed the offending fire from his skin.

'How is she heading, captain?'

'Nor'west by west.'

'Keep her west-nor-west.'

Captain Davenport put the wheel up and steadied her.

'West by north, captain.'

'West by north she is.'

'And now west.'

Slowly, point by point, as she entered the lagoon, the *Pyrenees* described the circle that put her before the wind; and point by point, with all the calm certitude of a thousand years of time to spare, McCoy chanted the changing course.

'Another point, captain.'

'A point it is.'

Captain Davenport whirled several spokes over, suddenly reversing and coming back one to check her.

'Steady.'

'Steady she is – right on it.'

Despite the fact that the wind was now astern, the heat was so intense that Captain Davenport was compelled to steal sidelong glances into the binnacle, letting go the wheel now with one hand, now with the other, to rub or shield his blistering cheeks.

McCoy's beard was crinkling and shrivelling and the smell of it, strong in the other's nostrils, compelled him to look towards McCoy with sudden solicitude. Captain Davenport was letting go the spokes alternately with his hands in order to rub their blistering backs against his trousers. Every sail on the mizzen-mast vanished in a rush of flame, compelling the two men to crouch and shield their faces.

'Now,' said McCoy, stealing a glance ahead at the low shore, 'four points up, captain, and let her drive.'

Shreds and patches of burning rope and canvas were falling about them and upon them. The tarry smoke from a smouldering piece of rope at the captain's feet set him off into a violent coughing fit, during which he still clung to the spokes.

The *Pyrenees* struck, her bow lifted and she ground ahead gently to a stop. A shower of burning fragments, dislodged by the shock, fell about them. The ship moved ahead again and struck a second time. She crushed the fragile coral under her keel, drove on, and struck a third time.

'Hard over,' said McCoy. 'Hard over?' he questioned gently, a minute later.

'She won't answer,' was the reply.

'All right. She is swinging around.' McCoy peered over the side. 'Soft, white sand. Couldn't ask better. A beautiful bed.'

As the *Pyrenees* swung around her stern away from the wind, a fearful blast of smoke and flame poured aft. Captain Davenport deserted the wheel in blistering agony. He reached the painter of the boat that lay under the quarter, then looked for McCoy, who was standing aside to let him go down.

'You first,' the captain cried, gripping him by the shoulder and almost throwing him over the rail. But the flame and smoke were too terrible, and he followed hard after McCoy, both men wriggling on the rope and sliding down into the boat together. A sailor in the bow, without waiting for orders, slashed the painter through with his sheath knife. The oars, poised in readiness, bit into the water, and the boat shot away.

'A beautiful bed, captain,' McCoy murmured, looking back.

'Ay, a beautiful bed, and all thanks to you,' was the answer.

The three boats pulled away for the white beach of pounded coral, beyond which, on the edge of a coconut grove, could be seen a half-dozen grass houses and a score or more of excited natives, gazing wide-eyed at the conflagration that had come to land.

The boats grounded and they stepped out on the white beach.

'And now,' said McCoy, 'I must see about getting back to Pitcairn.'

CHARLES WARREN STODDARD

Charles Warren Stoddard (1843–1909) began his literary career in the 1860s as one of the San Francisco group of writers that included Brett Harte, Mark Twain and Ambrose Bierce. In 1870, after two visits to Hawaii, where he fell in love with island life, he sailed on a French naval transport to Tahiti. His experiences of several months there, in penniless vagabondage, provided the material for 'A Prodigal in Tahiti', one of the stories in his best-known book, *South-Sea Idyls* (1873). Twenty years after accepting 'A Prodigal in Tahiti' for the *Atlantic Monthly,* where it first appeared, William Dean Howells wrote to Stoddard, saying, 'I think, now, that there are few such delicious bits of literature in the language.' Howells included it in his anthology. *The Great Modern American Short Stories* (1920).

A Prodigal in Tahiti

Let this confession be topped with a vignette done in broad, shadowless lines, and few of them – something like this: A little, flyblown room, smelling of garlic; I cooling my elbows on the oily slab of a table (breakfast for one), and looking through a window at a glaring, whitewashed fence high enough to shut out the universe from my point of sight. Yet it hid not all, since it brought into relief a panting cock (with one leg in a string), which had so strained to compress itself into a doubtful inch of shade that its suspended claw clutched the air in real agony.

Having dazzled my eyes with this prospect, I turned gratefully to the vanities of life that may be had for two francs in Tahiti. *Vide* bill of fare: One fried egg, like the eye of some gigantic

Albino; potatoes hollowed out bombshell fashion, primed with liver-sausage, very ingenious and palatable; the naked corpse of a fowl that cared not to live longer, from appearances, yet looked not happy in death.

Item: Wonder if there *is* a more ghastly spectacle than a chicken cooked in the French style, its knees drawn up on its breast like an Indian mummy, while its blue-black, parboiled, and melancholy visage tearfully surveys its own unshrouded remains. After a brief season of meditation, I said, and I trust I meant it, 'I thank the Lord for all these blessings.' Then I gave the corpse of the chicken Christian burial under a fold of the window curtain, disposed of the fried eye of the Albino, and transformed myself into a mortar for the time being, taking potato-bombshells according to my calibre.

There was claret all the while and plenty of butterless roll, a shaving of cheese, a banana, black coffee and cognac; when I turned again to dazzle myself with the white fence, I saw with infinite pity – a sentiment perhaps not unmixed with a suspicion of cognac or some other temporary humanising element – that the poor cock had wilted, and lay flat in the sun like a last year's duster. That was too much for me. I wheeled towards the door where gleamed the bay with its lovely ridges of light; canoes drifting over it drew the eye after them irresistibly; I heard the ship-calkers on the beach making their monotonous clatter, and the drone of the bareheaded fruit-sellers squatted in rows chatting indolently, with their eyes half shut. I could think of nothing but bees humming over their own sweet wares.

About this time a young fellow at the next table, who had scarcely a mouthful of English at his command, implored me to take beer with him; implying that we might, if desirable, become as tight as two bricks. I declined, much to his admiration, he regarding my refusal as a clear case of moral courage, whereas it arose simply and solely from my utter inability to see his treat and go him one better.

An adult in Tahiti has an eating hour allotted to him twice a day, at 10 a.m. and 5 p.m. My time being up, I returned to the store in an indifferent frame of mind, and upon entering the presence of my employer, who had arrived a moment before me, I was immediately covered with the deep humiliation of servitude, and withdrew to an obscure corner, while Monsieur and some naval guests took absinthe unblushingly, which was, of course, proper enough in them. Call it by what name you will, you cannot sweeten servility to my taste. Then why was I there and in bondage? The spirit of adventure that keeps life in us, yet comes near to worrying it out of us now and then, lured me with my handful of dollars to the Garden of the Pacific. 'You can easily get work,' said someone who had been there and didn't want it. If work I must, why not better there than here, thought I; and the less money I take with me the surer am I to seek that which might not attract me under other circumstances. A few letters which proved almost valueless; an abiding trust in Providence, afterwards somewhat shaken I am sorry to state, which convinces me that I can no longer hope to travel as a shorn lamb; considerable confidence in the good feeling of my fellow men, together with the few dollars above referred to – comprised my all when I set foot on the leaf-strewn and shady beach of Papeete.

Before the day was over I saw my case was almost hopeless; I was one too many in a very meagre congregation of foreigners. In a week I was desperate, with poverty and disgrace brooding like evil spirits on either hand. Every ten minutes someone suggested something which was almost immediately suppressed by the next man I met, to whom I applied for further information. Teach, said one: there wasn't a pupil to be had in the dominion. Clerkships were out of the question likewise. I might keep a store, if I could get anything to put in it; or go farther, as someone suggested, if I had money enough to get there. I thought it wiser to endure the ills I had than fly to others that I knew not of. In this state I perambulated the green lanes of Papeete, conscious that I was drawing down tons of immaterial sympathy from hearts of various nationalities, beating to the music of regular salaries in hard cash, and the inevitable ringing of their daily dinner-bell; and I continued to perambulate under the same depressing avalanches for a fortnight or more – a warning to the generation of the inexperienced that persists in sowing itself broadcast upon the edges of the earth, and learns too late how hard a thing it is to take root under the circumstances.

One gloomy day I was seized in the marketplace and led before a French gentleman who offered me a bed and board for such manual compensation as I might be able to give him in his office during the usual business hours, namely, from daybreak to sometime in the afternoon, unless it rained, when business was suspended and I was dropped until fair weather should set that little world wagging again.

I was invited to enter into the bosom of his family, in fact, to be *one* of them, and no single man could ask to be more; to sit at his table and hope for better days, in which diversion he proposed to join me with all his soul.

With an emotion of gratitude and a pang at being thus early a subject of charity, I began business in Papeete, and learned within the hour how sharper than most sharps it is to know only your own mother-tongue when you're away from home.

Nightly I walked two hot and dusty miles through groves of bread-fruit and colonnades of palms to my new master's. I skirted, with loitering steps, a placid sea whose crystalline depths sheltered leagues and leagues of sun-painted corals, where a myriad fish, dyed like the rainbow, sported unceasingly. Springs gushed from the mountain, singing their song of joy; the winds sang in the dark locks of the sycamore, while the palm-boughs clashed like cymbals in rhythmical accompaniment; glad children chanted their choruses, and I alone couldn't sing, nor hum, nor whistle, because it doesn't pay to work for your board, and settle for little necessities out of your own pocket, in any latitude that I ever heard of.

We lived in a grove of ten thousand cocoa-palms crowning a hill-slope to the west. How all-sufficient it sounds as I write it now, but how little I cared then, for many reasons! My cottage had prior tenants, who disputed possession with me – winged tenants who sought admission at every cranny and frequently obtained it in spite of me; these were not angels, but hens. My cottage had been a granary until it got too poor a receptacle for grains, and a better shelter left it open to the barn-fowls until I arrived. They hated me, these hungry chickens; they used to sit in rows on the window-sill and stare me out of countenance. A wide bedstead, corded with thongs, did its best to furnish my apartment. A narrow, a very narrow and thin ship's mattress, that had been a bed of torture for many a sea-sick soul before it descended to me; a flat pillow like a pancake; a condemned horse-blanket contributed by a good-natured Kanack who raked it from a heap of refuse in the yard, together with two sacks of rice, the despair of those hens in the window, were all I could boast of. With this inventory I strove (by particular request) to be one of those who were comfortable enough in the château adjoining. Summoned peremptorily to dinner, I entered a little latticed saloon connected with the château by a covered walk, discovered Monsieur seated at table and already served with soup and claret; the remainder of the company helped themselves as they best could; and I saw plainly enough that the family bosom was so crowded already, that I might seek in vain to wedge myself into any corner of it, at least until some vacancy occurred.

After dinner, sat on a sack of rice in my room while it grew dark and Monsieur received calls; wandered down to the beach at the foot of the hill and lay a long time on a bed of leaves, while the tide was out and the crabs clattered along shore and were very sociable. Natives began to kindle their evening fires of coconut husks; smoke, sweet as incense, climbed up to the plumes of the palm-trees and was lost among the stars. Morsels of fish and bread-fruit were offered me by the untutored savage, who welcomed me to his frugal meal and desired that I should at least taste before he broke his fast. Canoes shot out from dense, shadowy points, fishers standing in the bows with a poised spear in one hand; a blazing palm-branch held aloft in the other shed a warm glow of light over their superb nakedness. Bathed by the sea, in a fresh, cool spring, and returned to my little coop, which was illuminated by the glare of fifty floating beacons; looking back from the door I could see the dark outlines of the torch-bearers and hear their signal calls above the low growl of the reef a half-mile farther out from shore. It was a blessing to lie awake in my little room and watch the flicker of those fires; to think how Tahiti must look on a cloudless night from some heavenly altitude – the ocean still as death, the procession of fishermen sweeping from point to point within the reef, till the island, flooded with starlight and torchlight, lies like a green sea-garden in a girdle of flame.

A shrill bell called me from my bed at dawn. I was not unwilling to rise, for half the night I lay like a saint on the tough thongs, having turned over in sleep, thereby missing the mattress entirely. Made my toilet at a spring on the way into town; saw a glorious sunrise that was as good as breakfast, and found the whole earth and sea and all that in them is singing again while I listened and gave thanks for that privilege. At ten a.m. I went to breakfast in the small restaurant where I have sketched myself at the top of this chronicle, and whither we may return and begin over again if it please you.

I was about to remark that probably most melancholy and homesickness may be cured or alleviated by a wholesome meal of victuals; but I think I won't, for, on referring to my note-book, I find that within an hour after my return to the store I was as heart-sick as ever, and wasn't afraid to say so. It is scarcely to be wondered at: the sky was dark; aboard a schooner some sailors were making that doleful whine peculiar to them, as they hauled in to shore and tied up to a tree in a sifting rain; then everything was ominously still as though something disagreeable were about to happen; thereupon I doubled myself over the counter like a half-shut jack-knife, and burying my face in my hands said to myself, 'O, to be alone with Nature! her silence is religion and her sounds sweet music.' After which the rain blew over, and I was sent with a hand-cart and one underfed Kanack to a wharf half a mile away to drag back several loads of potatoes. We two hungry creatures struggled heroically to do our duty. Starting with a multitude of sacks it was quite impossible to proceed with, we grew weaker the farther we went, so that the load had to be reduced from time to time, and I believe the amount of potatoes deposited by the way considerably exceeded the amount we subsequently arrived at the store with. Finding life a burden, and seeing the legs of the young fellow in harness with me bend under him in his frantic efforts to get our cart out of a rut without emptying it entirely, I resolved to hire a substitute at my own expense, and save my remaining strength for a new line of business. Thus I was enabled to sit on the wharf the rest of the afternoon and enjoy myself devising new means of subsistence and watching the natives swim.

Someone before me found a modicum of sweets in his cup of bitterness, and in a complacent hour set the good against the evil in single entry, summing up the same to his advantage. I concluded to do it myself, and did it thus:

EVIL	GOOD
I find myself in a foreign land with no one to love and none to love me.	But I may do as I please in consequence, and it is nobody's business save my own.

I am working for my board and lodging (no extras), and find it very unprofitable.	But I may quit as soon as I feel like it, and shall have no occasion to dun my employer for back salary so long as I stop with him.
My clothes are in rags. I shall soon be without a stitch to my back.	But the weather is mild and the fig-tree flourisheth. Moreover many a good savage has gone naked before me.
I get hungry before breakfast and feel faint after dinner. What are two meals a day to a man of my appetite?	But fasting is saintly. Day by day I grow more spiritual, and shall shortly be a fit subject for translation to that better world which is doubtless the envy of all those who have lost it by over-eating and drinking.

Nothing can exceed the satisfaction with which I read and re-read this philosophical summary, but I had relapses every few minutes so long as I lived in Tahiti. I remember one Sunday morning, a day I had all to myself, when I cried out of the depths and felt better after it. It was a real Sunday. The fowls confessed it by the indifference with which they picked up a grain of rice now and then as though they weren't hungry. The family were moving about in an unnatural way; some people are never themselves on the Lord's Day. The canoes lay asleep off upon the water, evidently conscious of the long hours of rest they were sure of having. To sum it all, it seemed as though the cover had been taken off from the earth, and the angels were sitting in big circles looking at us. Our clock had run down, and I found myself half an hour too early at mass. Some diminutive native children talked together with infinite gesticulation, like little old men. At every lag in the conversation, two or three of them would steal away to the fence that surrounded the church and begin diligently counting the pickets thereof. They were evidently amazed at what they considered a singular coincidence, namely, that the number of pickets, beginning at the front gate and counting to the right, tallied exactly with those to the left; while they were making repeated efforts to get at the heart of this mystery, the priest rode up on horseback, dismounted in our midst, and we all followed him into chapel to mass.

A young Frenchman offered me holy-water on the tips of his fingers, and I immediately decided to confide in him to an unlimited extent if he gave me the opportunity. It was a serious disappointment when I found later that we didn't know six words in any common tongue. Concluded to be independent, and walked off by myself. Got very lonesome immediately. Tried to be meditative, philosophical, botanical, conchological, and in less than an hour gave it up – homesick again, by Jove!

Strolled to the beach and sat a long time on a bit of wreck partly imbedded in the sand; consoled by the surpassing radiance of sunset, wondered how I could ever have repined, but proceeded to do it again as soon as it grew dark. Some natives drew near, greeting me kindly. They were evidently lovers; talked in low tones, deeply interested in the most trivial things, such as a leaf falling into the sea at our feet and floating stem up, like a bowsprit; he probably made some poetic allusion to it, may have proposed braving the seas with her in a shallop as fairylike, for both fell a-dreaming and were silent for some time, he worshipping her with fascinated eyes, while she, woman-like, pretended to be all unconscious of his admiration.

Silently we sat looking over the sea at Moorea, just visible in the light of the young moon, like a spirit brooding upon the waters, till I broke the spell by saying, 'Good-night,' which was repeated in a chorus as I withdrew to my coop and found my feathered guests had beaten in the temporary barricade erected in the broken window, entered and made themselves at home during my absence – a fact that scarcely endeared the spot to me. Next morning I was unusually merry; couldn't tell why, but tried to sing as I made my toilet at the spring; laughed nearly all the way into town, saying my prayers, and blessing God, when I came suddenly upon a horseshoe in the middle of the road. Took it as an omen and a keepsake; horseshoes aren't shed everywhere nor for everybody. I thought it the prophecy of a change, and at once cancelled my engagement with my employer without having set foot into his house farther than the dining-room, or made any apparent impression upon the adamantine bosom of his family.

After formally expressing my gratitude to Monsieur for his renewed offers of hospitality, I turned myself into the street, and was once more adrift in the world. For the space of three minutes I was wild with joy at the thought of my perfect liberty. Then I grew nervous, began to feel unhappy, nay, even guilty, as though I had thrown up a good thing. Concluded it was rash of me to leave a situation where I got two meals and a mattress, with the privilege of washing at my own expense. Am not sure that it wasn't unwise, for I had no dinner that afternoon; and having no bed either, I crept into the verandah of a house to let, and dozed till daybreak.

There was but one thing to live for now, namely, to see as much of Tahiti as possible, and at my earliest convenience to return like the prodigal son to that father who would doubtless feel like killing something appropriate as soon as he saw me coming. I said as much to a couple of Frenchmen, brothers, who are living a dream-life over yonder, and whose wildest species of dissipation for the last seven years has been to rise at intervals from their settees in the arbour, go deliberately to the farther end of the garden and eat several mangoes in cold blood.

To comprehend Tahiti, a man must lose himself in forests whose resinous boughs are knotted with ribbons of sea-grass; there, overcome by the music of sibilant waters sifting through the antlers of the coral, he is supposed to sink upon drifts of orange-blossoms only to be resuscitated by the spray of an approaching shower crashing through the green solitudes like an army with chariots – so those brothers said, with a mango poised in each hand; and they added that I should have an official document addressed to the best blood in the kingdom, namely the Forty Chiefs of Tahiti, who would undoubtedly entertain me with true barbarian hospitality, better the world knows not. There was a delay for some reason; I, rather impatient, and scarcely hoping to receive so graceful a compliment from headquarters, trudged on alone with a light purse and an infinitesimal bundle of necessities, caring nothing for the weather nor the number of miles cleared per day, since I laid no plans save the one to see as much as I might with the best grace possible, keeping an eye on the road for horseshoes. Through leagues of verdure I wandered, feasting my five senses and finding life a holiday at last. There were numberless streams to be crossed, where I loafed for hours on the bridges, satisfying myself with sunshine. Not a savage in the land was freer than I. No man could say to me, 'Why stand ye here idle?' for I could continue to stand as long as I liked and as idly as it pleased me in spite of him! There were bridgeless streams to be forded; but the Tahitian is a nomad continually wandering from one edge of his fruitful world to the other; moreover, he is the soul of peace towards men of goodwill: I was invariably picked up by some barebacked Hercules, who volunteered to take me over the water on his brawny brown shoulders, and could have easily taken two like me. It was good to be up there while he strode through the swift current, for I felt that he was perfectly able to carry me to the ends of the earth without stopping, and that sense of reliance helped to reassure my faith in humanity.

As I wandered, from most native houses came the invitation to enter and eat. Night after night I found my bed in the corner of some dwelling whither I had been led by the master of it with unaffected grace. It wasn't simply showing me to a spare room, but rather unrolling the best mat and turning everything to my account so long as it pleased me to tarry. Sometimes the sea talked in its sleep not a rod from the house; frequently the mosquitoes accepted me as a delicacy and did their best to dispose of me. Once I awoke with a headache, the air was so dense with the odour of orange-blossoms.

There was frequently a strip of blue bay that ebbed and flowed languidly, and had to be lunched with; or a very deep and melodious spring, asking for an interview, and, I may add, it always got it. I remember one miniature castle built in the midst of a grassy Venice by the shore. Its moats, shining with goldfish, were spanned with slender bridges, toy fences of bamboo enclosed the rarer clumps of foliage; and there was such an air of tranquillity pervading it that I thought I must belong there. Something seemed to say, 'Come in.' I went in, but left very soon; the place was so fairylike, I felt as though I were liable to step through it and come out on some other side, and I wasn't anxious for such a change.

I ate, when I got hungry, a very good sort of a meal, consisting usually of a tiny piglet cooked in the native fashion, swathed in succulent leaves and laid between hot stones till ready for eating; bread-fruit, like mashed potato, but a great deal better; orange-tea and cocoa-milk – surely enough for two or three francs. Took a sleep whenever sleep came along, resting always where the clouds or a shadow from the mountain covered me so as to keep me cool and comfortable. Natives passed me with salutations. A white man now and then went by barely nodding, or more frequently eyeing me with suspicion, and giving me as much of his dust as he found convenient. In the wider fellowship of nature, I forswore all blood relations, and blushed for those representatives of my own colour as I footed it right royally. Therefore, I was enabled to scorn the fellow who scorned me while he flashed the steel hoofs of his charger in my face and dashed on to the village we were both approaching with the dusk.

What a spot it was! A long lane as green as a spring meadow, lying between wall-like masses of foliage whose deep arcades were frescoed with blossoms and festooned with vines. It seemed a pathway leading to infinity, for the blood-red bars of sunset glared at its farther end as though Providence had placed them there to keep out the unregenerated. Not a house visible all this time, nor a human, though I was in the heart of the hamlet. Passing up the turf-cushioned road, I beheld, on either hand, through a screen of leaves, a log spanning a rivulet that was softly singing its monody; at the end of each log the summer-house of some Tahitian, who sat in his door smoking complacently. It was a picture of still-life with a suggestion of possible motion; a village to put into a greenhouse, water, and keep fresh for ever. Let me picture it once more – one mossy street between two babbling brooks, and every house thereof set each in its own moated wilderness. This was Papeali.

Like rows of cages full of chirping birds those bamboo hats were distributed up and down the street. As I walked I knew something would cause me to turn at the right time and find a new friend ready to receive me, for it always does. So I walked slowly, and without hesitation or impatience, until I turned and met him coming out of his cage, crossing the rill by his log and holding out his hand to me in welcome. Back we went together, and I ate and slept there as though it had been arranged a thousand years ago; perhaps it was! There was a racket up at the farther end of the lane, by the chief's house; songs and nose-flutings upon the night air; moreover, a bonfire, and doubtless much nectar – too much, as usual, for I heard such cheers as the soul gives when it is careless of consequences, and caught a glimpse of the joys of barbarism such as even we poor Christians cannot wholly withstand, but turning our backs think we are safe enough. Commend me to him who has known temptation and not shunned it, but actually withstood it!

It was the dance, as ever it is the dance where all the aspirations of the soul find expression in the body; those bodies that are incarnate souls, or those souls that are spiritualised bodies, inseparable, whatever they are, for the time being. The fire glowed fervently; bananas hung out their tattered banners like decorations; palms rustled their silver plumes aloft in the moonlight; the sea panted on its sandy bed in heavy sleep; the night-blooming cereus opened its waxen chambers and gave forth its treasured sweets. Circle after circle of swart savage faces were turned upon the flame-lit arena where the dancers posed for a moment with their light drapery gathered about them and held carelessly in one hand. The music again sounded a reiteration of chords caught from the birds' treble and the wind's bass; full and resounding syllables, richly poetical, telling of orgies and of the mysteries of the forbidden revels in the charmed valleys of the gods, hearing which it were impossible not to be wrought to madness; and the dancers thereat went mad, dancing with infinite gesticulation, dancing to whirlwinds of applause till the undulation of their bodies was serpentine, and at last in frenzy they shrieked with joy, threw off their garments, and were naked as the moon. So much for a vision that kept me awake till morning, when I plodded on in the damp grass and tried to forget it, but couldn't exactly, and never have to this hour. Went on and on over more bridges spanning still-flowing streams of silver, past springs that lay like great crystals framed in moss under dripping, fern-clad cliffs that the sun never reaches. Came at last to a shining, whitewashed fort, on an eminence that commands the isthmus connecting the two hemispheres of Tahiti, where down I dropped into a narrow valley full of wind and discord and a kind of dreary neglect that made me sick for any other place. More refreshment for the wayfarer, but to be paid for by the dish, and therefore limited. Was obliged to hate a noisy fellow with too much bushy black beard and a freckled nose, and to like another who eyed me kindly over his absinthe, having first mixed a glass for me. A native asked me where I was going; being unable to give any satisfactory answer, he conducted me to his canoe, about a mile distant, where he cut a sapling for a mast, another for a gaff, twisted, in a few moments, a cord of its fibrous bark, rigged a sail of his sleeping-blanket, and we were shortly wafted onward before a light breeze between the reef and shore.

Three of us with a bull-pup in the bows dozed under the afternoon sun. He of the paddle awoke now and then to shift sail, beat the sea impetuously for a few seconds, and fell asleep again. Voices roused me occasionally, greetings from colonies of indolent Kanacks on shore, whose business it was to sit there till they got hungry, laughing weariness to scorn.

Close upon our larboard-bow lay one of the islands that had bewitched me as I passed the shore but a few days previous; under us the measureless gardens of the sea unmasked a myriad imperishable blossoms, centuries old some of them, but as fair and fresh as though born within the hour. All that afternoon we drifted between sea and shore, and beached at sunset in a new land. Footsore and weary, I approached a stable from which thrice a week stages were despatched to Papeete.

A modern pilgrim finds his scrip cumbersome if he has any, and deems it more profitable to pay his coachman than his cobbler.

I climbed to my seat by the jolly French driver, who was continually chatting with three merry nuns sitting just back of us, returning to the convent in Papeete after a vacation retreat among the hills. How they enjoyed the ride, as three children might! and were quite wild with delight at meeting a corpulent *père*, who smiled amiably from his saddle and offered to show them the interior of the pretty chapel at Faaa (only three a's in that word) – the very one I grew melancholy in when I was a man of business.

So they hurled themselves madly from the high seat, one after the other, scorning to touch anything so contaminating as a man's hand, though it looked suicidal, as the driver and I agreed while the three were at prayers by the altar. Whipping up over the road townward, I could almost recognise my own footprints left since the time I used to take the dust in my face three mornings a week from the wheels of that very vehicle as I footed it in to business. Passing the spring, my toilet of other days, drawing to the edge of the town, we stopped being jolly, and were as proper as befitted travellers. We looked over the wall of the convent garden as we drove up to the gate, and saw the mother-superior hurrying down to us with a cumbersome chair for the relief of the nuns, but before she reached us they had cast themselves to earth again in the face of destiny, and there was kissing, crying and commotion as they withdrew under the gateway like so many doves seeking shelter. When the gate closed after them, I heard them all cooing at once, but the world knows nothing further.

Where would I be dropped? asked the driver. In the middle of the street, please you, and take half my little whole for your ride, sir! He took it, dropped me where we stood, and drove away, I pretending to be very much at my ease. God help me and all poor hypocrites!

I sought a place of shelter, or rather retirement, for the air is balm in that country. There was an old house in the middle of a grassy lawn in a by-street; two of its rooms were furnished with a few papers and books, and certain gentlemen who contribute to its support lounge in when they have leisure for reading or a chat. I grew to know the place familiarly. I stole a night's lodging on its verandah in the shadow of a passion-vine; but, for fear of embarrassing some early student in pursuit of knowledge, I passed the second night on the floor of the dilapidated cook-house, where the ants covered me. I endured the tortures of one who bares his body to an unceasing shower of sparks; but I survived.

There was, in this very cook-house, a sink six feet in length and as wide as a coffin; the third night I lay like a galvanised corpse with his lid off till a rat sought to devour me, when I took to the streets and walked till morning. By this time the president of the club, whose acquaintance I had the honour of, tendered me the free use of any portion of the premises that might not be otherwise engaged. With a gleam of hope I began my explorations. Up a narrow and winding stair I found a spacious loft. It was like a mammoth tent, a solitary centre-pole its only ornament. Creeping into it on all-fours, I found a fragment of matting, a dry crust and an empty soda bottle – footprints on the sands of time.

'Poor soul!' I gasped, 'where did *you* come from? What *did* you come for? Whither, oh whither, have you flown?'

I might have added, How did you manage to get there? But the present was so important a consideration, I had no heart to look beyond it. The next ten nights I passed in the silent and airy apartment of my anonymous predecessor. Ten nights I crossed the unswept floor that threatened at every step to precipitate me into the reading-room below. With a faint heart and hollow stomach I threw myself upon my elbow and strove to sleep. I lay till my heart stopped beating, my joints were wooden, and my four limbs corky beyond all hope of reanimation. There the mosquito revelled, and it was a promising place for centipedes.

At either end of the building an open window admitted the tip of a banana-leaf; up their green ribs the sprightly mouse careered. I broke the backbones of these banana-leaves, though they were the joy of my soul and would have adorned the choicest conservatory in the land. Day was equally unprofitable to me. My best friends said, 'Why not return to California?'

Everyone I met invited me to leave the country at my earliest convenience. The American consul secured me a passage, to be settled for at home, and my career in that latitude was evidently at an end. In my superfluous confidence in humanity, I had announced myself as a correspondent for the press. It was quite necessary that I should give some plausible reason for making my appearance in Tahiti friendless and poor. Therefore, I said plainly, 'I am a correspondent, friendless and poor,' believing that anyone would see truth in the face of it, with half an eye. 'Prove it,' said one who knew more of the world than I. Then flashed upon me the alarming fact that I couldn't prove it, having nothing whatever in my possession referring to it in the slightest degree. It was a fatal mistake that might easily have been avoided, but was too well established to be rectified.

In my chagrin I looked to the good old bishop for consolation. Approaching the Mission House through sunlit cloisters of palms, I was greeted most tenderly. I would have gladly taken any amount of holy orders for the privilege of ending my troublous days in the sweet seclusion of the Mission House.

As it was, I received a blessing, an autograph and a 'God speed' to some other part of creation. Added to this I learned how the address to the Forty Chiefs of Tahiti on behalf of the foreign traveller, my poor self, had been dispatched to me by a special courier, who found me not; and doubtless the *fêtes* I heard of and was for ever missing marked the march of that messenger, my proxy, in his triumphal progress. In my innocent degradation it was still necessary to nourish the inner man.

There is a market in Papeete where, under one broad roof, threescore hucksters of both sexes congregate long before daylight, and while a few candles illumine their wares, patiently await custom. A half-dozen coolies with an eye to business serve hot coffee and chocolate at a dime per cup to any who choose to ask for it. By seven a.m. the market is so nearly sold out that only the more plentiful fruits of the country are to be obtained at any price. A prodigal cannot long survive on husks, unless he have coffee to wash them down. I took my cup of it, with two spoonfuls of sugar and ants dipped out of a cigar-box, and a crust of bread into the bargain, sitting on a bench in the market-place, with a coolie and a Kanack on either hand.

It was not the coffee nor the sugared ants that I gave my dime for, but rather the privilege of sitting in the midst of men and women who were willing to accept me as a friend and helpmate without questioning my ancestry, and any one of whom would go me halves in the most disinterested manner. Then there was sure to be some superb fellow close at hand, with a sensuous lip curled under his nostril, a glimpse of which gave me a dime's worth of satisfaction and more too. Having secreted a French roll, five cents, all hot, under my coat, and gathered the bananas that would fall in the yard so seasonably, I made my day as brief and comfortable as possible by filling up with water from time to time.

The man who has passed a grimy chop-house, wherein a frowzy fellow sat at his cheap spread, without envying the frowzy fellow his cheap spread, cannot truly sympathise with me.

The man who has not felt a great hollow in his stomach which he found necessary to fill at the first fountain he came to, or go over on his beam-ends for lack of ballast, cannot fall upon my neck and call me brother.

At daybreak I haunted those street fountains, waiting my turn while French cooks filled almost fathomless kegs, and coolies filled potbellied jars, and Kanacks filled their hollow bamboos that seemed fully a quarter of a mile in length. There I meekly made my toilet, took my first course of breakfast, rinsed out my handkerchiefs and stockings, and went my way. The whole performance was embarrassing, because I was a novice, and a dozen people watched me in curious silence. I had also a boot with a suction in the toe; there is dust in

Papeete; while I walked that boot loaded and discharged itself in a manner that amazed and amused a small mob of little natives who followed me in my free exhibition, advertising my shooting-boot gratuitously.

I was altogether shabby in my outward appearance, and cannot honestly upbraid any resident of the town for his neglect of me. I know that I suffered the agony of shame and the pangs of hunger; but they were nothing to the utter loneliness I felt as I wandered about with my heart on my sleeve, and never a bite from so much as a daw.

Did you ever question the possibility of a man's temporary transformation under certain mental, moral or physical conditions? There are seasons when he certainly isn't what he was, yet may be more and better than he has been, if you give him time enough.

I began to think I had either suffered this transformation or been maliciously misinformed as to my personality. Was I truly what I represented myself to be, or had I been a living deception all my days? No longer able to identify myself as anyone in particular, it occurred to me that it would be well to address a few lines to the gentleman I had been in the habit of calling 'father', asking for some particulars concerning his absent son. I immediately drew up this document ready for mailing:

> Mosquito Hall
> Centipede Avenue, Papeete

Dear Sir – A nondescript awaits identification at this office. Answers to the names at the foot of this page, believes himself to be your son, to have been your son or to be about to be something equally near and dear to you. He can repeat several chapters of the New Testament at the shortest notice; recites most of the Catechism and Commandments; thinks he would recognise two sisters and three brothers at sight, and know his mother with his eyes shut.

He likewise confesses to the usual strawberry-mark in fast colours. If you will kindly send by return mail a few dollars, he will clothe, feed and water himself, and return immediately to those arms which, if his memory does not belie him, have more than once sheltered his unworthy frame. I have, dear sir, the fortune to be the article above described.

The six months which would elapse before I could hope for an answer would probably have found me past all recognition, so I ceased crying to the compassionate bowels of Tom, Dick and Harry, waiting with haggard patience the departure of the vessel that was to bear me home with a palpable C.O.D. tacked on to me. Those last hours were brightened by the delicate attentions of a few good souls who learned, too late, the shocking state of my case. Thanks to them, I slept well thereafter in a real bed, and was sure of dinners that wouldn't rattle in me like a withered kernel in an old nutshell.

I had but to walk to the beach, wave my lily hand, heavily tanned about that time, when lo! a boat was immediately despatched from the plump little corvette *Cheveret*, where the tricolour waved triumphantly from sunrise to sunset, all the year round.

Such capital French dinners as I had there, such offers of bed and board and boundless sympathy as were made me by those dear fellows who wore the gold lace and had a piratical-looking cabin all to themselves, were enough to wring a heart that had been nearly wrung out in its battle with life on Tahiti.

No longer I walked the streets as one smitten with the plague, or revolved in envious circles about the marketplace, where I could have got my fill for a half-dollar, but had neither the one nor the other. No longer I went at daybreak to swell the procession at the waterspout, or sat on the shore the picture of despair, waiting sunrise, finding it my sole happiness to watch a canoe-load of children drifting out upon the bay, singing like a railful of larks; nor walked solitarily through the night up and down the narrow streets wherein the gendarmes had learned to pass me unnoticed, with my hat under my arm and my heart in my throat. Those delicious moons always seduced me from my natural sleep, and I sauntered through the cocoa-groves whose boughs glistened like row after row of crystals, whose shadows were as mosaics wrought in blocks of silver.

I used to nod at the low, whitewashed 'calabooses' fairly steaming in the sun, wherein Herman Melville got some chapters of *Omoo*.

Over and over again I tracked the ground of that delicious story, saying to the bread-fruit trees that had sheltered him, 'Shelter me also, and whoever shall follow after, so long as your branches quiver in the wind!'

O reader of *Omoo*, think of 'Motoo-Otoo', actually looking warlike in these sad days, with a row of new cannons around its edge, and pyramids of balls as big as coconuts covering its shady centre.

Walking alone on those splendid nights I used to hear a dry, ominous coughing in the huts of the natives. I felt as though I were treading upon the brinks of half-dug graves, and I longed to bring a respite to the doomed race.

One windy afternoon we cut our stern hawser in a fair wind and sailed out of the harbour; I felt a sense of relief, and moralised for five minutes without stopping. Then I turned away from all listeners, and saw those glorious green peaks growing dim in the distance; the clouds embraced them in their profound secrecy; like a lovely mirage Tahiti floated upon the bosom of the sea. Between sea and sky was swallowed up vale, garden and waterfall; point after point crowded with palms; peak above peak in that eternal crown of beauty; and with them the nation of warriors and lovers falling like the leaf, but, unlike it, with no followers in the new season.

FRANK T. BULLEN

Left an orphan in early boyhood, Frank T. Bullen (1857–1915), after several years of dodging about London as a ragged street Arab 'with wits sharpened by the constant fight for food', went to sea when he was thirteen, sailing to all parts of the world. In 1875, stranded and penniless in New Bedford, Massachusetts, he signed on an American whaling ship bound for a voyage to the Pacific Ocean. Years later, after he had left the sea for a clerk's job in London, he told the story of that voyage in *The Cruise of the Cachalot* (1899), his first book, which ranks next to Melville's *Moby Dick* among the classic narratives of whaling. The extract that follows, in effect a self-contained short story, relates an exciting adventure that befell Bullen and some of his shipmates in one of the ship's whaleboats while they were exploring the coast of Vau-Vau, an island in the Tongan Group.

The Whale in the Cave

However, just when the delightful days were beginning to pall upon us, a real adventure befell us, which, had we been attending strictly to business, we should not have encountered. For a week previous we had been cruising constantly without ever seeing a spout, except those belonging to whales out at sea, whither we knew it was folly to follow them. We tried all sorts of games to while away the time, which certainly did hang heavy, the most popular of which was for the whole crew of the boat to strip, and, getting overboard, be towed along at the ends of short warps, while I sailed her. It was quite mythological – a sort of rude reproduction of Neptune and his attendant Tritons. At last, one afternoon as we were listlessly lolling (half asleep,

298

except the look-out man) across the thwarts, we suddenly came upon a gorge between two cliffs that we must have passed before several times unnoticed. At a certain angle it opened, disclosing a wide sheet of water, extending a long distance ahead. I put the helm up, and we ran through the passage, finding it about a boat's length in width and several fathoms deep, though overhead the cliffs nearly came together in places. Within, the scene was very beautiful, but not more so than many similar ones we had previously witnessed. Still, as the place was new to us, our languor was temporarily dispelled, and we paddled along, taking in every feature of the shores with keen eyes that let nothing escape. After we had gone on in this placid manner for maybe an hour, we suddenly came to a stupendous cliff – that is, for those parts – rising almost sheer from the water for about a thousand feet. Of itself it would not have arrested our attention, but at its base was a semicircular opening, like the mouth of a small tunnel. This looked alluring, so I headed the boat for it, passing through a deep channel between two reefs which led straight to the opening. There was ample room for us to enter, as we had lowered the mast; but just as we were passing through, a heave of the unnoticed swell lifted us unpleasantly near the crown of this natural arch. Beneath us, at a great depth, the bottom could be dimly discerned, the water being of the richest blue conceivable, which the sun, striking down through, resolved into some most marvellous colour-schemes in the path of its rays. A delicious sense of coolness, after the fierce heat outside, saluted us as we entered a vast hall, whose roof rose to a minimum height of forty feet, but in places could not be seen at all. A sort of diffused light, weak, but sufficient to reveal the general contour of the place, existed, let in, I supposed, through some unseen crevices in the roof or walls. At first, of course, to our eyes fresh from the fierce glare outside, the place seemed wrapped in impenetrable gloom, and we dared not stir lest we should run into some hidden danger. Before many minutes, however, the gloom lightened as our pupils enlarged, so that, although the light was faint, we could find our way about with ease. We spoke in low tones, for the echoes were so numerous and resonant that even a whisper gave back from those massy walls in a series of recurring hisses, as if a colony of snakes had been disturbed.

We paddled on into the interior of this vast cave, finding everywhere the walls rising sheer from the silent, dark waters, with not a ledge or a crevice where one might gain foothold. Indeed, in some places there was a considerable overhang from above, as if a great dome whose top was invisible sprang from some level below the water. We pushed ahead until the tiny semicircle of light through which we had entered was only faintly visible; and then, finding there was nothing to be seen except what we were already witnessing, unless we cared to go on into the thick darkness, which extended apparently into the bowels of the mountain, we turned and started to go back. Do what we would, we could not venture to break the solemn hush that surrounded us as if we were shut within the dome of some vast cathedral in the twilight. So we paddled noiselessly along for the exit, till suddenly an awful, inexplicable roar set all our hearts thumping fit to break our bosoms. Really, the sensation was most painful, especially as we had not the faintest idea whence the noise came or what had produced it. Again it filled that immense cave with its thunderous reverberations; but this time all the sting was taken out of it, as we caught sight of its author. A goodly bull-humpback had found his way in after us, and the sound of his spout, exaggerated a thousand times in the confinement of that mighty cavern, had frightened us all so that we nearly lost our breath. So far, so good; but, unlike the old negro, though we were 'doin' blame well', we did not 'let blame well alone'. The next spout that intruder gave, he was right alongside of us. This was too much for the semi-savage instincts of my gallant harpooner, and before I had time to shout a caution he had plunged his weapon deep into old Blowhard's broad back.

I should like to describe what followed, but, in the first place, I hardly know; and, in the next, even had I been cool and collected, my recollections would sound like the ravings of a fevered dream. For of all the hideous uproars conceivable, that was, I should think, about the worst. The big mammal seemed to have gone frantic with the pain of his wound, the surprise of the attack and the hampering confinement in which he found himself. His tremendous struggles caused such a commotion that our position could only be compared to that of men shooting Niagara in a cylinder at night. How we kept afloat, I do not know. Someone had the gumption to cut the line, so that by the radiation of the disturbance we presently found ourselves close to the wall, and trying to hold the boat into it with our fingertips. Would he never be quiet? we thought, as the thrashing, banging and splashing still went on with unfailing vigour. At last, in, I suppose, one supreme effort to escape, he leaped clear of the water like a salmon. There was a perceptible hush, during which we shrank together like unfledged chickens on a frosty night; then, in a never-to-be-forgotten crash that ought to have brought down the massy roof, that mountainous carcase fell. The consequent violent upheaval of the water should have smashed the boat against the rocky walls, but that final catastrophe was mercifully spared us. I suppose the rebound was sufficient to keep us a safe distance off.

A perfect silence succeeded, during which we sat speechless, awaiting a resumption of the clamour. At last Abner broke the heavy silence by saying, 'I doan' see the do'way any mo' at all, sir.' He was right. The tide had risen, and that half-moon of light had disappeared, so that we were now prisoners for many hours, it not being at all probable that we should be able to find our way out during the night ebb. Well, we were not exactly children, to be afraid of the dark, although there is considerable difference between the velvety darkness of a dungeon and the clear, fresh night of the open air. Still, as long as that beggar of a whale would only keep quiet or leave the premises, we should be fairly comfortable. We waited and waited until an hour had passed, and then came to the conclusion that our friend was either dead or gone out, as he gave no sign of his presence.

That being settled, we anchored the boat, and lit pipes, preparatory to passing as comfortable a night as might be under the circumstances, the only thing troubling me being the anxiety of the skipper on our behalf. Presently the blackness beneath was lit up by a wide band of phosphoric light, shed in the wake of no ordinary-sized fish, probably an immense shark. Another and another followed in rapid succession, until the depths beneath were all ablaze with brilliant foot-wide ribands of green glare, dazzling to the eye and bewildering to the brain. Occasionally, a gentle splash or ripple alongside, or a smart tap on the bottom of the boat, warned us how thick the concourse was that had gathered below. Until that weariness which no terror is proof against set in, sleep was impossible, nor could we keep our anxious gaze from that glowing inferno beneath, where one would have thought all the population of Tartarus were holding high revel. Mercifully, at last we sank into a fitful slumber, though fully aware of the great danger of our position. One upward rush of any of those ravening monsters, happening to strike the frail shell of our boat, and a few fleeting seconds would have sufficed for our obliteration as if we had never been.

But the terrible night passed away, and once more we saw the tender, iridescent light stream into that abode of dread. As the day strengthened, we were able to see what was going on below, and a grim vision it presented. The water was literally alive with sharks of enormous size, tearing with never ceasing energy at the huge carcase of the whale lying on the bottom, who had met his fate in a singular but not unheard-of way. At that last titanic effort of his he had rushed downward with such terrific force that, striking his head on the bottom, he had broken his neck. I felt very grieved that we had lost the chance of securing him; but it was perfectly certain that before we could get help to raise him, all that would be left of his skeleton would be quite valueless to us. So with such patience as we could command we waited near the entrance until the receding ebb made it possible for us to emerge once more into the blessed light of day. I was horrified at the haggard, care-worn appearance of my crew, who had all, excepting the two Kanakas, aged perceptibly during that night of torment. But we lost no time in getting back to the ship, where I fully expected a severe wigging for the scrape my luckless curiosity had led me into. The captain, however, was very kind, expressing his pleasure at seeing us all safe back again, although he warned me solemnly against similar investigations in future. A hearty meal and a good rest did wonders in removing the severe effects of our adventure, so that by next morning we were all fit and ready for the day's work again.

AMBROSE BIERCE

Born in 1842, Ambrose Gwinnett Bierce was the author of supernatural stories that have secured his place in both the weird
tradition and in the wider world of American letters. He is also
noted for his tales of the Civil War, which drew on his own
experience as a Union cartographer and officer. His first job in
journalism was as editor for the *San Francisco News-Letter* and
California Advertiser (1868–72). In time, Bierce established himself
as a kind of literary dictator of the West Coast and was so
respected and feared as a critic that his judgement could 'make or
break' an aspiring author's reputation. Well known by his mere
initials, A. G. B., he was called by his enemies and detractors
'Almighty God Bierce'. He was also nicknamed 'Bitter Bierce' and
his nihilistic motto was, 'Nothing matters.' Bierce is best
remembered for his cynical but humorous *Devil's Dictionary*. In
1913, at the age of seventy-one, Bierce disappeared into
revolution-torn Mexico to fight alongside the bandit Pancho Villa.
Although a popular theory is that Bierce argued with Villa over
military strategy and was subsequently shot, he probably perished
in the battle of Ojinaga on 11 January 1914.

A Tough Tussle

One night in the autumn of 1861 a man sat alone in the heart of
a forest in western Virginia. The region was one of the wildest
on the continent – the Cheat Mountain country. There was no
lack of people close at hand, however; within a mile of where
the man sat was the now silent camp of a whole Federal brigade.
Somewhere about – it might be still nearer – was a force of the
enemy, the numbers unknown. It was this uncertainty as to its

numbers and position that accounted for the man's presence in that lonely spot; he was a young officer of a Federal infantry regiment and his business there was to guard his sleeping comrades in the camp against a surprise. He was in command of a detachment of men constituting a picket-guard. These men he had stationed just at nightfall in an irregular line, determined by the nature of the ground, several hundred yards in front of where he now sat. The line ran through the forest, among the rocks and laurel thickets, the men fifteen or twenty paces apart, all in concealment and under injunction of strict silence and unremitting vigilance. In four hours, if nothing occurred, they would be relieved by a fresh detachment from the reserve now resting in care of its captain some distance away to the left and rear. Before stationing his men the young officer of whom we are writing had pointed out to his two sergeants the spot at which he would be found if it should be necessary to consult him, or if his presence at the front line should be required.

It was a quiet enough spot – the fork of an old wood road, on the two branches of which, prolonging themselves deviously forward in the dim moonlight, the sergeants were themselves stationed, a few paces in rear of the line. If driven sharply back by a sudden onset of the enemy – and pickets are not expected to make a stand after firing – the men would come into the converging roads and naturally following them to their point of intersection could be rallied and 'formed'. In his small way the author of these dispositions was something of a strategist; if Napoleon had planned as intelligently at Waterloo he would have won that memorable battle and been overthrown later.

Second-Lieutenant Brainerd Byring was a brave and efficient officer, young and comparatively inexperienced as he was in the business of killing his fellow men. He had enlisted in the very first days of the war as a private, with no military knowledge whatever, had been made first-sergeant of his company on account of his education and engaging manner, and had been lucky enough to lose his captain to a Confederate bullet; in the resulting promotions he had gained a commission. He had been in several engagements, such as they were – at Philippi, Rich Mountain, Carrick's Ford and Green-Brier – and had borne himself with such gallantry as not to attract the attention of his superior officers. The exhilaration of battle was agreeable to him, but the sight of the dead, with their clay faces, blank eyes and stiff bodies, which when not unnaturally shrunken were unnaturally swollen, had always intolerably affected him. He felt towards them a kind of reasonless antipathy that was something more than the physical and spiritual repugnance common to us all. Doubtless this feeling was due to his unusually acute sensibilities – his keen sense of the beautiful, which these hideous things outraged. Whatever may have been the cause, he could not look upon a dead body without a loathing which had in it an element of resentment. What others have respected as the dignity of death had to him no existence – was altogether unthinkable. Death was a thing to be hated. It was not picturesque, it had no tender and solemn side – a dismal thing, hideous in all its manifestations and suggestions. Lieutenant Byring was a braver man than anybody knew, for nobody knew his horror of that which he was ever ready to incur.

Having posted his men, instructed his sergeants and retired to his station, he seated himself on a log, and with senses all alert began his vigil. For greater ease he loosened his sword-belt and taking his heavy revolver from his holster laid it on the log beside him. He felt very comfortable, though he hardly gave the fact a thought, so intently did he listen for any sound from the front which might have a menacing significance – a shout, a shot, or the footfall of one of his sergeants coming to apprise him of something worth knowing. From the vast, invisible ocean of moonlight overhead fell, here and there, a slender, broken stream that seemed to splash against the intercepting branches and trickle to earth, forming small white pools among the clumps of laurel. But these leaks were few and served only to accentuate the blackness of his environment, which his imagination found it easy to people with all manner of unfamiliar shapes, menacing, uncanny or merely grotesque.

He to whom the portentous conspiracy of night and solitude and silence in the heart of a great forest is not an unknown experience needs not to be told what another world it all is – how even the most commonplace and familiar objects take on another character. The trees group themselves differently; they draw closer together, as if in fear. The very silence has another quality than the silence of the day. And it is full of half-heard whispers – whispers that startle – ghosts of sounds long dead. There are living sounds, too, such as are never heard under other conditions: notes of strange night-birds, the cries of small animals in sudden encounters with stealthy foes or in their dreams, a rustling in the dead leaves – it may be the leap of a wood-rat, it may be the footfall of a panther. What caused the breaking of that twig? – what the low, alarmed twittering in that bushful of birds? There are sounds without a name, forms without substance, translations in space of objects which have not been seen to move, movements wherein nothing is observed to change its place. Ah, children of the sunlight and the gaslight, how little you know of the world in which you live!

Surrounded at a little distance by armed and watchful friends, Byring felt utterly alone. Yielding himself to the solemn and mysterious spirit of the time and place, he had forgotten the nature of his connection with the visible and audible aspects and phases of the night. The forest was boundless; men and the habitations of men did not exist. The universe was one primeval mystery of darkness, without form and void, himself the sole, dumb questioner of its eternal secret. Absorbed in thoughts born of this mood, he suffered the time to slip away unnoted. Meantime the infrequent patches of white light lying amongst the tree-trunks had undergone changes of size, form and place.

In one of them nearby, just at the roadside, his eye fell upon an object that he had not previously observed. It was almost before his face as he sat; he could have sworn that it had not before been there. It was partly covered in shadow, but he could see that it was a human figure. Instinctively he adjusted the clasp of his sword-belt and laid hold of his pistol – again he was in a world of war, by occupation an assassin.

The figure did not move. Rising, pistol in hand, he approached. The figure lay upon its back, its upper part in shadow, but standing above it and looking down upon the face, he saw that it was a dead body. He shuddered and turned from it with a feeling of sickness and disgust, resumed his seat upon the log and forgetting military prudence struck a match and lit a cigar. In the sudden blackness that followed the extinction of the flame he felt a sense of relief; he could no longer see the object of his aversion. Nevertheless, he kept his eyes in that direction until it appeared again with growing distinctness. It seemed to have moved a trifle nearer.

'Damn the thing!' he muttered. 'What does it want?'

It did not appear to be in need of anything but a soul.

Byring turned away his eyes and began humming a tune, but he broke off in the middle of a bar and looked at the dead body. Its presence annoyed him, though he could hardly have had a quieter neighbour. He was conscious, too, of a vague, indefinable feeling that was new to him. It was not fear, but rather a sense of the supernatural – in which he did not at all believe.

'I have inherited it,' he said to himself. 'I suppose it will require a thousand ages – perhaps ten thousand – for humanity to outgrow this feeling. Where and when did it originate? Away back, probably, in what is called the cradle of the human race – the plains of Central Asia. What we inherit as a superstition our barbarous ancestors must have held as a reasonable conviction. Doubtless they believed themselves justified by facts whose nature we cannot even conjecture in thinking a dead body a malign thing endowed with some strange power of mischief, with perhaps a will and a purpose to exert it. Possibly they had some awful form of religion of which that was one of the chief doctrines, sedulously taught by their priesthood, as ours teach the immortality of the soul. As the Aryans moved slowly on, to and through the Caucasus passes, and spread over Europe, new conditions of life must have resulted in the formulation of new religions. The old belief in the malevolence of the dead body was lost from the creeds and even perished from tradition, but it left its heritage of terror, which is transmitted from generation to generation – is as much a part of us as are our blood and bones.'

In following out his thought he had forgotten that which suggested it; but now his eye fell again upon the corpse. The shadow had now altogether uncovered it. He saw the sharp profile, the chin in the air, the whole face, ghastly white in the moonlight. The clothing was grey, the uniform of a Confederate soldier. The coat and waistcoat, unbuttoned, had fallen away on each side, exposing the white shirt. The chest seemed unnaturally prominent, but the abdomen had sunk in, leaving a sharp projection at the line of the lower ribs. The arms were extended, the left knee was thrust upward. The whole posture impressed Byring as having been studied with a view to the horrible.

'Bah!' he exclaimed; 'he was an actor – he knows how to be dead.'

He drew away his eyes, directing them resolutely along one of the roads leading to the front, and resumed his philosophising where he had left off.

'It may be that our Central Asian ancestors had not the custom of burial. In that case it is easy to understand their fear of the dead, who really were a menace and an evil. They bred pestilences. Children were taught to avoid the places where they lay, and to run away if by inadvertence they came near a corpse. I think, indeed, I'd better go away from this chap.'

He half rose to do so, then remembered that he had told his men in front and the officer in the rear who was to relieve him that he could at any time be found at that spot. It was a matter of pride, too. If he abandoned his post he feared they would think he feared the corpse. He was no coward and he was unwilling to incur anybody's ridicule. So he again seated himself, and to prove his courage looked boldly at the body. The right arm – the one farthest from him – was now in shadow. He could hardly see the hand which, he had before observed, lay at the root of a clump of laurel. There had been no change, a fact which gave him a certain comfort, he could not have said why. He did not at once remove his eyes; that which we do not wish to see has a strange fascination, sometimes irresistible. Of the woman who covers her eyes with her hands and looks between the fingers let it be said that the wits have dealt with her not altogether justly.

Byring suddenly became conscious of a pain in his right hand. He withdrew his eyes from his enemy and looked at it. He was grasping the hilt of his drawn sword so tightly that it hurt him. He observed, too, that he was leaning forward in a strained attitude – crouching like a gladiator ready to spring at the throat of an antagonist. His teeth were clenched and he was breathing hard. This matter was soon set right, and as his muscles relaxed and he drew a long breath he felt keenly enough the ludicrousness of the incident. It affected him to laughter. Heavens! what sound was that? What mindless devil was uttering an unholy glee in mockery of human merriment? He sprang to his feet and looked about him, not recognising his own laugh.

He could no longer conceal from himself the horrible fact of his cowardice; he was thoroughly frightened! He would have run from the spot, but his legs refused their office; they gave way beneath him and he sat again upon the log, violently trembling. His face was wet, his whole body bathed in a chill perspiration. He could not even cry out. Distinctly he heard behind him a stealthy tread, as of some wild animal, and dared not look over his shoulder. Had the soulless living joined forces with the soulless dead? – was it an animal? Ah, if he could but be assured of that! But by no effort of will could he now unfix his gaze from the face of the dead man.

I repeat that Lieutenant Byring was a brave and intelligent man. But what would you have? Shall a man cope, single-handed, with so monstrous an alliance as that of night and solitude and silence and the dead, while an incalculable host of his own ancestors shriek into the ear of his spirit their coward counsel, sing their doleful death-songs in his heart, and disarm his very blood of all its iron? The odds are too great – courage was not made for so rough use as that.

One sole conviction now had the man in possession: that the body had moved. It lay nearer to the edge of its plot of light – there could be no doubt of it. It had also moved its arms, for, look, they are both in the shadow! A breath of cold air struck Byring full in the face; the boughs of trees above him stirred and moaned. A strongly defined shadow passed across the face of the dead, left it luminous, passed back upon it and left it half obscured. The horrible thing was visibly moving! At that moment a single shot rang out upon the picket-line – a lonelier and louder, though more distant, shot than ever had been heard by mortal ear! It broke the spell of that enchanted man; it slew the silence and the solitude, dispersed the hindering host from Central Asia and released his modern manhood. With a cry like that of some great bird pouncing upon its prey he sprang forward, hot-hearted for action!

Shot after shot now came from the front. There were shoutings and confusion, hoof-beats and desultory cheers. Away to the rear, in the sleeping camp, were a singing of bugles and grumble of drums. Pushing through the thickets on either side the roads came the Federal pickets, in full retreat, firing backwards at random as they ran. A straggling group that had followed back one of the roads, as instructed, suddenly sprang away into the bushes as half a hundred horsemen thundered by them, striking wildly with their sabres as they passed. At headlong speed these mounted madmen shot past the spot where Byring had sat, and vanished round an angle of the road, shouting and firing their pistols. A moment later there was a roar of musketry, followed by dropping shots – they had encountered the reserve-guard in line; and back they came in dire confusion, with here and there an empty saddle and many a maddened horse, bullet-stung, snorting and plunging with pain. It was all over – 'an affair of outposts'.

The line was re-established with fresh men, the roll called, the stragglers were reformed. The Federal commander, with a part of his staff, imperfectly clad, appeared upon the scene, asked a few questions, looked exceedingly wise and retired. After standing at arms for an hour the brigade in camp 'swore a prayer or two' and went to bed.

Early the next morning a fatigue-party, commanded by a captain and accompanied by a surgeon, searched the ground for dead and wounded. At the fork of the road, a little to one side, they found two bodies lying close together – that of a Federal officer and that of a Confederate private. The officer had died of a sword-thrust through the heart, but not, apparently, until he had inflicted upon his enemy no fewer than five dreadful wounds. The dead officer lay on his face in a pool of blood, the weapon still in his heart. They turned him on his back and the surgeon removed it.

'Gad!' said the captain – 'It is Byring!' – adding, with a glance at the other, 'They had a tough tussle.'

The surgeon was examining the sword. It was that of a line officer of Federal infantry – exactly like the one worn by the captain. It was, in fact, Byring's own. The only other weapon discovered was an undischarged revolver in the dead officer's belt.

The surgeon laid down the sword and approached the other body. It was frightfully gashed and stabbed, but there was no blood. He took hold of the left foot and tried to straighten the leg. In the effort the body was displaced. The dead do not wish to be moved – it protested with a faint, sickening odour. Where it had lain were a few maggots, manifesting an imbecile activity.

The surgeon looked at the captain. The captain looked at the surgeon.

GUY DE MAUPASSANT

Guy de Maupassant (1850–93) was born probably at the Château de Miromesnil, Dieppe, in north-west France. He studied at Rouen, and spent his life in Normandy. After serving as a soldier and a government clerk, he took to writing, encouraged by Flaubert, a friend of his mother's, and joined the Naturalist group led by Zola. His stories range from the short tale to the full-length novel. His first success 'Boule de Suife' (1880) led to his being in great demand by newspapers. There followed about three hundred stories and several novels, including the supposedly autobiographical *Bel-Ami* (1885). His stories describe madness and fear with a horrifying accuracy which foreshadows the insanity which beset Maupassant in 1892 when he was committed to an asylum in Paris.

On the Journey

I

The railway carriage was full as we left Cannes. We were chatting, for everybody was acquainted. As we passed Tarascon someone remarked: 'Here's the place where they assassinate people.'

And we began to talk of the mysterious and untraceable murderer, who for the last two years had taken, from time to time, the life of a traveller. Everyone made his guess, everyone gave his opinion; the women shudderingly gazed at the dark night through the carriage windows, fearing suddenly to see a man's head at the door. We all began telling frightful stories of terrible encounters, meetings with madmen in an express train, of hours passed opposite a suspicious individual.

Each man knew an anecdote to his credit, each one had

intimidated, overpowered and throttled some evildoer in most surprising circumstances, with an admirable presence of mind and audacity.

A physician, who spent every winter in the south, desired, in his turn, to tell an adventure: 'I,' said he, 'never have had the luck to test my courage in an affair of this kind; but I knew a woman, now dead, one of my patients, to whom the most singular thing in the world happened, and also the most mysterious and pathetic.

'She was a Russian, the Comtesse Marie Baranow, a very great lady of exquisite beauty. You know how beautiful Russian women are, or at least how beautiful they seem to us, with their fine noses, their delicate mouths, their eyes of an indescribable colour, a blue-grey, and their cold, rather hard grace! They have something about them, mischievous and seductive, haughty and sweet, tender and severe, altogether charming to a Frenchman. At the bottom, it is, perhaps, the difference of race and of type which makes me see so much in them.

'Her physician had seen for many years that she was threatened with a disease of the lungs, and had tried to persuade her to come to the South of France; but she obstinately refused to leave St Petersburg. Finally, last autumn, deeming her lost, the doctor warned her husband, who directed his wife to start at once for Menton.

'She took the train, alone in her carriage, her servants occupying another compartment. She sat by the door, a little sad, seeing the fields and villages pass, feeling very lonely, very desolate in life, without children, almost without relatives, with a husband whose love was dead and who cast her thus to the end of the world without coming with her, as one sends a sick footman to hospital.

'At each station her servant Ivan came to see if his mistress wanted anything. He was an old servant, blindly devoted, ready to execute any order she might give him.

'Night fell, and the train rolled along at full speed. She could not sleep, being wearied and nervous.

'Suddenly the thought struck her to count the money which her husband had given her at the last minute, in French gold. She opened her little bag and emptied the shining flood of metal on her lap.

'But all at once a breath of cold air struck her face. Surprised, she raised her head. The door had just opened. The Comtesse Marie, in terror, hastily threw a shawl over the money spread upon her lap, and waited. Some seconds passed, then a man in evening dress appeared, bareheaded, wounded in the hand, and panting. He closed the door, sat down, looked at his neighbour with gleaming eyes, and then wrapped a handkerchief around his wrist, which was bleeding.

'The young woman felt herself fainting with fear. This man, surely, had seen her counting her money and had come to rob and kill her.

'He kept gazing at her, breathless, his features convulsed, doubtless ready to spring upon her.

'He suddenly said: "Madame, don't be afraid!"

'She made no response, being incapable of opening her mouth, hearing her heart-beats and a buzzing in her ears.

'He continued: "I am not a criminal, madame."

'She continued to be silent, but by a sudden movement which she made, her knees meeting, the gold coins began to run to the floor as water runs from a spout.

'The man, surprised, looked at this stream of metal and at once stooped to pick it up.

'Terrified, she rose, casting her whole fortune on the floor, and ran to the door to leap out on to the track.

'But he understood what she was going to do, and springing forward, seized her in his arms, seated her by force, and held her by the wrists.

' "Listen to me, madame," said he, "I am not a criminal; the

316

proof of it is that I am going to gather up this gold and return it to you. But I am a lost man, a dead man, if you do not assist me to pass the frontier. I cannot tell you more. In an hour we shall be at the last Russian station; in an hour and twenty minutes we shall cross the boundary of the Empire. If you do not help me I am lost. And yet I have neither killed anyone, nor robbed, nor done anything contrary to honour. This I swear to you. I cannot tell you more."

'And kneeling down he picked up the gold, even hunting under the seats for the last coins, which had rolled to a distance. Then, when the little leather bag was full again, he gave it to his neighbour without saying a word, and returned to seat himself in the other corner of the compartment. Neither of them moved. She kept motionless and silent, still faint from terror, but gradually growing quieter. As for him, he made no gesture, no motion, but remained sitting erect, his eyes staring in front of him, very pale, as if he were dead. From time to time she threw a quick look at him, and as quickly turned her glance away. He appeared to be about thirty years of age, and was very handsome, with the air of a gentleman.

'The train ran through the darkness, giving at intervals its shrill signals, now slowing up in its progress, and again starting off at full speed. But suddenly its progress slackened, and after several sharp whistles it came to a full stop.

'Ivan appeared at the door for his orders.

'The Comtesse Marie, her voice trembling, gave one last look at her companion; then she said to her servant, in a quick tone: "Ivan, you will return to the Comte; I do not need you any longer."

'The man, bewildered, opened his eyes wide. He stammered: "But, my lady – "

'She replied: "No, you will not come with me; I have changed my mind. I wish you to stay in Russia. Here is some money for your return home. Give me your cap and cloak."

'The old servant, frightened, took off his cap and cloak, obeying without question, accustomed to the sudden whims and caprices of his masters. And he went away, with tears in his eyes.

'The train started again, rushing towards the frontier.

'Then the Comtesse Marie said to her neighbour: "These things are for you, monsieur – you are Ivan, my servant. I make only one condition to what I am doing: that is, that you shall not speak a word to me, neither to thank me, nor for anything whatsoever."

'The unknown bowed without uttering a syllable.

'Soon the train stopped again, and officers in uniform visited the train.

'The Comtesse handed them her papers and, pointing to the man seated at the end of the compartment, said: "That is my servant Ivan, whose passport is here."

'The train started again.

'During the night they sat opposite each other, both silent.

'When morning came, as they stopped at a German station, the unknown man got out; then, standing at the door, he said: "Pardon me, madame, for breaking my promise, but as I have deprived you of a servant, it is proper that I should replace him. Have you need of anything?"

'She replied coldly: "Go and find my maid."

'He went to summon her. Then he disappeared.

'When she alighted at some station for luncheon she saw him at a distance looking at her. They reached Menton.'

2

The doctor was silent for a second, and then resumed: 'One day, while I was receiving patients in my office, a tall young man entered.

'He said to me: "Doctor, I have come to ask you news of the Comtesse Marie Baranow. I am a friend of her husband, although she does not know me."

'I answered: "She is lost. She will never return to Russia."

'And suddenly this man began to sob, then he rose and went out, staggering like a drunken man.

'I told the Comtesse that evening that a stranger had come to make enquiries about her health. She seemed moved, and told me the story which I have just related to you. She added: "That man, whom I do not know at all, follows me now like my shadow. I meet him every time I go out. He looks at me in a strange way, but he has never spoken to me!"

'She pondered a moment, then added: "Come, I'll wager that he is under the window now."

'She left her reclining-chair, went to the window and drew back the curtain, and actually showed me the man who had come to see me, seated on a bench at the edge of the side wall with his eyes raised towards the house. He perceived us, rose, and went away without once turning around.

'Then I understood a sad and surprising thing, the silent love of these two beings, who were not acquainted with each other.

'He loved her with the devotion of a rescued animal, grateful and devoted to the death. He came every day to ask me, "How is she?" understanding that I had guessed his feelings. And he wept frightfully when he saw her pass, weaker and paler every day.

'She said to me: "I have never spoken but once to that singular man, and yet it seems as if I had known him for twenty years."

'And when they met she returned his bow with a serious and charming smile. I felt that – although she was given up, and knew herself lost – she was happy to be loved thus, with this respect and constancy, with this exaggerated poetry, with this devotion, ready for anything.

'Nevertheless, faithful to her super-excited obstinacy, she absolutely refused to learn his name, to speak to him. She said: "No, no, that would spoil this strange friendship. We must remain strangers to each other."

'As for him, he was certainly a kind of Don Quixote, for he did nothing to bring himself closer to her. He intended to keep to the end the absurd promise never to speak to her which he had made in the railway carriage.

'Often, during her long hours of weakness, she rose from her reclining-chair and partly opened the curtain to see whether he were there, beneath the window. When she had seen him, always motionless upon his bench, she went back and lay down with a smile upon her lips.

'She died one day about ten o'clock. As I was leaving the hotel he came up to me with a distracted face; he had already heard the news.

' "I should like to see her, for one second, in your presence," said he.

'I took him by the arm and went back into the house.

'When he was beside the couch of the dead woman he seized her hand and kissed it long and tenderly and then fled away like a madman.'

The doctor again was silent, then continued: 'This is certainly the strangest railway adventure that I know. It must also be said that men sometimes do the maddest things.'

A woman murmured, half aloud: 'Those two people were not so crazy as you think. They were – they were –'

But she could not continue, she was crying so. As we changed the conversation to calm her, we never knew what she had wished to say.